WAR GAMES

Sheridan Anne
WAR GAMES

Cover Design: Artscandare
Editing: Fox Fiction Editing
Formatting: Sheridan Anne

For those who are currently curled up in bed listening to the chainsaw beside you otherwise known as your snoring husband.

I know you've been fantasizing about smothering him with your pillow, but you and I both know you'll miss him come morning.

On a completely unrelated topic . . . If you ever need an alibi, I'm your girl!

CONTENT WARNING

WAR GAMES is a Dark Serial Killer/Assassin Romance and is not suitable for readers under eighteen years of age. Your mental health is important to me, so please carefully consider these triggers in determining if this book is right for you.

WAR GAMES CONTAINS:

Possible cannibalism
Serial Killers
Assassins
Contract killers
Arson
Graphic murder
Graphic violence
Graphic sex scene
Mercy killings
Stalking/hunting
Attempted waterboard
An almost sexual drowning
If you catch me, you fuck me
Slight kink exploration
Breath play
Discussion of child exploitation
Discussion of baby snatching
Child assassins/spies

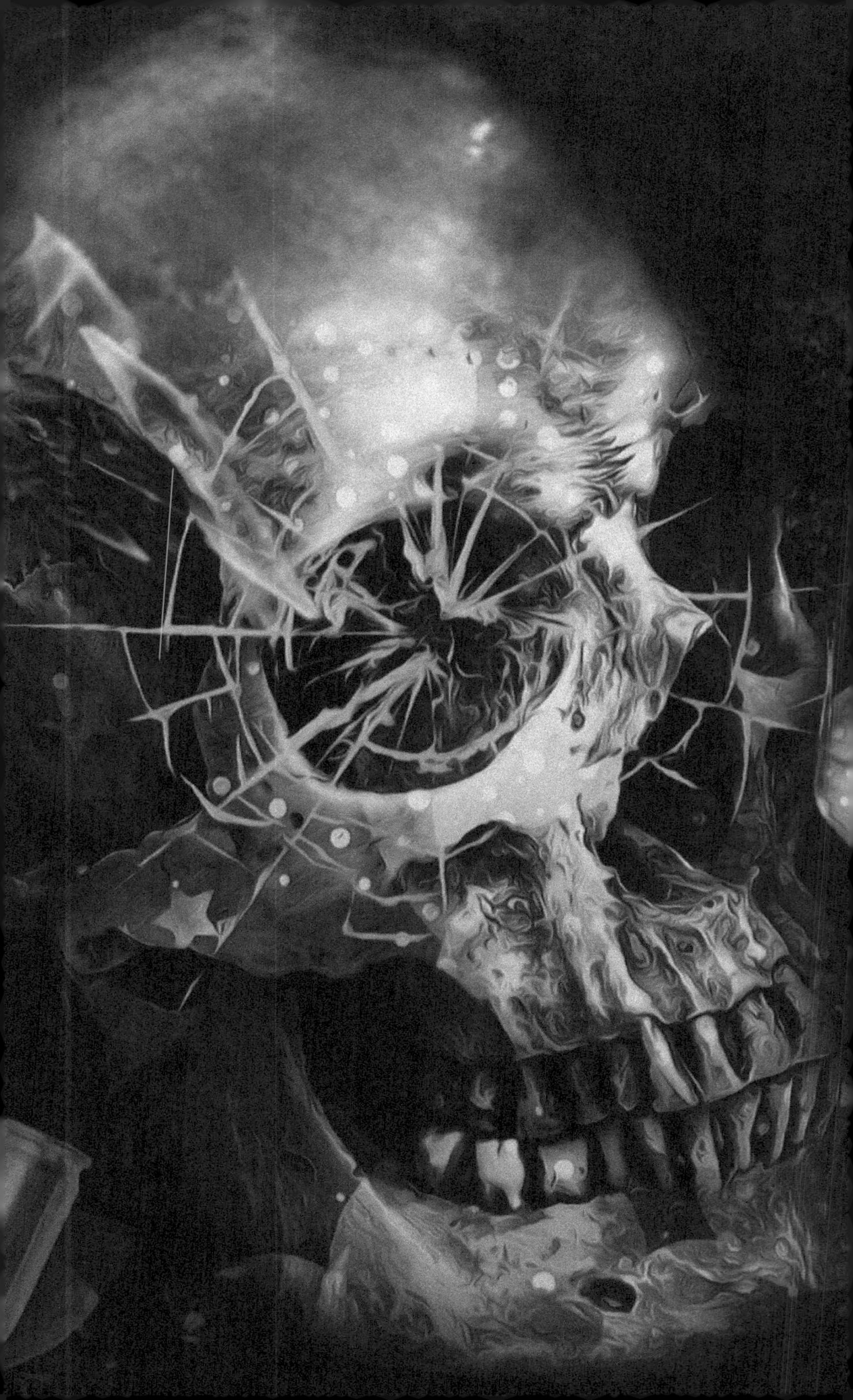

1

SIREN

oly fucking shit, my asshole!

Tears form in my eyes as I tackle the toddler-sized shapewear into place. What the fuck was I thinking? It promised me a snatched waist, but all I've gotten is trauma. I mean, shit! Why is it so hard to breathe in this thing?

The back of the thong is getting an up-close tour of my intestines while every step I take feels like a chainsaw violently ripping me in half. This is too much. The model in the ad definitely didn't look like she was getting the life sucked out of her, and she sure as hell didn't have red scratches up and down her thighs from her nails as she clawed the bastard up her body.

This is so much more than just false advertising; it's a death sentence in the form of shapewear.

The fabric bunches at my waist as I frantically try to yank it up my body, but it's so damn tight, I can practically feel my lungs screaming for freedom. The fabric rolls over itself, making it even tighter and I madly try to find the armholes, having to use my nails to dig under the shapewear and stretch it out.

"Oh, God. Oh God. Oh God. This is what death feels like."

Finding the armholes, I yank the bodysuit up only for the fabric to get caught beneath my tits, and holy fuck, I've never regretted anything so bad in my whole life.

Pinching the fabric as tight as I can in both hands, I pull it out and over my tits before finally releasing it and crying out as it compresses back around me with a tight smack.

"Holy fucking shit."

Am I supposed to be working up such a sweat?

I fall back against the door of my closet while white-knuckling the shelf in a desperate bid to keep myself upright. I try to catch my breath, positive if I were to fall, I'd never be able to get up again. But what really terrifies me is the thought of trying to get myself out of this thing. Surely it's not possible. The bodysuit and I are now destined to spend the rest of our lives together. I hope it approves of trashy TV and takeout because that's all it has to look forward to from here on out.

Bracing myself against the door, I wait a few agonizing moments for my organs to adjust to their new home before finally being able to take a decent breath. I fix myself in front of my full-length mirror and shove my hands down the front of the bodysuit, doing what I can to adjust my tits until they look just right. Damn it. Why do I have to like the way it looks so much?

Beauty is pain, right? Who needs to breathe when you can look this photoshopped? I'll put up with my ass being violated by a piece of string any day if this is how snatched I look.

Turning left and right, I check myself out, drooling over my newfound curves. I should have bought one of these years ago. Though, years ago, I probably didn't need it. What can I say? I've developed a deep love for cocktails, and if I have to sacrifice my once-toned waist to keep up the addiction, I'll happily make the sacrifice.

My phone rings across my bedroom, and I hurry out of my closet to quickly scoop it off the end of my bed. There's no caller ID, but I already know exactly who it is. There's only one person I would ever trust to have my number, and that's Mila—the best hacker and friend across the globe.

"Talk dirty to me."

"Why do you sound so worked up?" she asks with the slightest Russian accent, something she hasn't been able to shake since moving to the US as a young girl. And *by moving* I mean being abandoned here by her horrible parents and left to fend for herself. Which she did a remarkable job of, by the way. So remarkable, that it's what we first bonded over. Nothing quite like childhood trauma to bring two friends together.

We're both screwed up, one of us significantly more than the other, but we wouldn't have it any other way. Mila's daddy issues seem like a vacation in comparison to mine, and that's saying a lot. I was orphaned as a little girl after watching my father murder my mother and then come after me. He shot me twice in the stomach, and after watching me bleed out, assuming I was done for, he turned the gun on himself. If it weren't for nosey neighbors calling the police, I would have been dead a long time ago, and sometimes I can't help but wonder if it would have been better that way.

After weeks in the hospital, I was discarded into the foster system. My new life meant starting over every few months, jumping from abusive home to abusive home until I was finally forgotten about. I ended up as a runaway living in an abandoned office building, but that is where I first met Mila.

We were barely sixteen, and she was already on her way to becoming an evil mastermind computer hacker, and I loved that about her. She could hack into any system across the globe, no matter the level of security. Mila always found a way in, but she played it smart and kept to herself, not like me at all. I always had a gift for finding trouble.

What can I say? Those childhood years really did a number on me. But now at twenty-four, I would argue that I'm one of the best contract killers in the world, and that's not just my ego talking. Mila and I make an excellent team, and being each other's family, we've never allowed the other to fall.

"What are you talking about?" I ask, flopping onto the edge of my bed, my new bodysuit making it impossible to get comfortable.

"You're breathing heavy," Mila says before sucking in a horrified gasp. "Are you doing cardio?"

Before she allows me the chance to respond, I hear the familiar sound of her fingers moving across the keyboard. I let out a sigh, knowing without a doubt that she's hacking into either my home security or my laptop camera, and within seconds, she will have a perfect view into my bedroom.

Then, just as expected, Mila's laugh booms through the phone. "Holy shit. It's the bodysuit, isn't it?"

I roll my eyes and try to pull myself to my feet to show it off as a stupid grin stretches across my face. "Yeah," I admit, turning to better face my laptop when a green light appears at the top of my screen, letting me know my camera has been turned on. "What do you think? It was a challenge getting into it, and I'm pretty sure you're gonna have to get off your ass and come cut me out of this thing, but I can't lie. I'm obsessed."

"You look like a snack."

"Oh stop! You're gonna make me blush."

Mila scoffs, knowing it takes a shitload more than a simple compliment to make me blush. But before she gets a chance to hurl some ridiculous insult at me, she sucks in a gasp. "Holy shit. Check your email."

"Huh? Why?" My brows furrow as I move toward my laptop. "Wait," I say, staring directly into the little camera. "Are you in my emails again?"

"Just hurry up and check," she says, clearing her throat and reading the subject line aloud. "Welcome to the Twenty-Third Annual War Games."

My eyes widen as I dive the rest of the way toward my laptop, the bone-crushing bodysuit no longer able to hold me back. "Holy fucking shit! Are you serious?" I rush out, my fingers not able to move across the keys fast enough.

My heart races a million miles an hour. The idea of actually getting to participate in the games blows my mind. It's been an ultimate dream since before I can remember. A real chance to actually prove myself, to prove I'm the best at what I do. Sure, there might be a risk or two involved, and death is highly likely, but if you're not risking something, then is it really worth fighting for? Plus, there may or may not be a ten-million-dollar prize.

My emails finally come up on my screen, and I quickly navigate to the newest one. There are no sender details, but I didn't expect there to be. War Games was founded by an organization that predominantly uses the dark web to run their "business," and it's only because of Mila and her insane hacking skills that we discovered any kind of information about them. There's nothing special to know, just some dude living in his mother's basement pulling strings, but it's the people he's able to bring into these games that excites me.

Opening the email, I quickly scan over the subject line just as Mila had.

Welcome to the Twenty-Third Annual War Games.

A chill sails down my spine. I've been waiting to be recognized for what I'm capable of, and being invited to participate is the greatest honor, but to actually win the games? Well, shit. I've been dreaming about that for years.

The anticipation is too much, so I open the email and scan every last word.

Please join us for a month of pure madness.

Dawning on the town of Blue Springs, Montana, the 23rd Annual Serial Killer War Games will commence.
You, along with nineteen other elite killers at the top of their career, will descend on Blue Springs, Montana to battle it out for the ultimate prize.
Only one will remain and be awarded the most esteemed title—Winner of the 23rd Annual Serial Killer War Games. The winner will collect ten million dollars in cash and the ultimate prize of officially being named the best in the business! You have seventy-two hours to respond to this invitation before your place in the games is forfeited.

*<u>*Click here to review the terms and conditions of the games*</u>*
*<u>*Click here to accept or deny this invitation*</u>*

"Holy fucking shit!"

A wide grin rips across my face, and I immediately click the link to take me to the acceptance page, more than ready to dive headfirst into this.

My mouse hovers over the button to accept the invitation when my laptop remotely shuts down. "Woah, hold up, cowgirl," Mila rushes out. "What the hell do you think you're doing?"

"What do you mean? I'm accepting the invitation."

"Like hell you are," she throws back at me. "Are you literally insane? I know you've had this big fantasy about winning the games for the past few years and have scoured your emails every day of your damn life waiting for your personalized invitation, but you can't be serious. Were you planning to think about this before you just hit accept?"

"What's gotten into you today? What's there to think about? I've been wanting to do this since before I can remember."

"Oh my God. Do you have any regard for your own life?" Mila scolds.

I shrug my shoulders. We both know the answer to that, and to be completely honest, it's a sore point between us. I do what I do, not only because I enjoy it and I'm good at it, but because I have nothing to lose. Mila is my only family. I don't have brothers or sisters, nieces or nephews, and after my father attempted to kill me and I was put into foster care, my only remaining grandparents refused to take me and left me to suffer at the hands of terrible foster parents.

I don't exactly know what's waiting for me on the other side, but the one thing I do know is that it's got to be better than this.

I don't fear death.

I mean, sure. I fear the possibility of it happening in an excruciating way, of some crazed psychopath doing his worst and sending me to the other side with horror in my heart, but I don't fear what comes after that . . . assuming something comes after that, of course.

Mila is all about rainbows, flowers, and unicorns. She's my complete opposite, but we level each other out.

"You really don't want me to do this?"

"Well, of course I don't want you to do it," she says. "But I know how much you've always wanted to, so I'm not going to stand in your way. I just think you should at least sleep on it first before you rush in. Maybe check out what Blue Springs has to offer and see if we can figure out who else has been invited to compete. Don't get me wrong, I know you'll kill it. You're the best of the best, and I have faith that you'll come out of this ten million dollars richer, but these other nineteen contenders weren't selected for nothing. They're just as good. Not to mention, they wouldn't be afraid of death either."

Letting out a sigh, I flop back onto my bed, hating that she has a very real, very valid point.

These games aren't for the weak of heart. They're brutal, violent, and bloody.

There will be a mix of twenty serial killers and assassins, each of them equally as skilled. These will be killers who have made headlines, killers who have made a name for themselves, and who provoke the most fear in the general population. These are people who are just as messed up as I am. Some of them have trained as spies, and their weapons are an extension of their bodies.

This isn't something anybody should just dive headfirst into without at least considering the repercussions.

Could I be brutally murdered? Yes.

Could my whole world end in Blue Springs, Montana? Yes.

But would I have the time of my life and come out ten million dollars richer? Also yes.

As the invitation stated, War Games runs for a month, and during that time, twenty killers are bound to this one location. They must battle it out over the month. Hunt, track, and stalk before finally making their kills. Each contender will be pushed to their limits, they'll be tricked, trapped, and slaughtered like caged animals. I couldn't be more excited.

Each contender will play using their alias, keeping their true identity concealed. Mine is Siren, a name Mila gave me back when we had just met and she realized just how messed up I was. I like to lure bad men into traps, just like the way a siren of the sea lures sailors to their deaths. The name has stuck ever since, and my real name has become someone I don't even know.

Once you've made your kill, you're awarded the identification of your prey. If your prey already has kills under their belt, you also claim ownership over them. The goal is to be the last one standing by the end of the month, claiming all nineteen identifications. If more than one contender stands by the games' end, nobody wins, and you're all eliminated . . . not just from the games, but permanently.

What could possibly go wrong?

It's hunt or be hunted. Literally the real-life Hunger Games for serial killers.

At the end of the games, all the gathered identifications, along with evidence tying each of them to their many crimes, are handed to the FBI. It's a sick way of kicking you when you're down—the price you pay for not being good enough. Personally, I think it's the best incentive to ensure you don't die. Not that it would really matter, considering you'd be dead. But if you've worked all your life to ensure you fly under the radar and conceal yourself, it's a kick right in the vag to have all your secrets spilled the moment you're gone.

"Alright," I finally say, hoisting myself off the bed and wandering back into my closet. "How much time do you need to figure out who the other contenders are?" I ask, reaching up to the top of my closet and pulling my suitcase down.

"Can you give me a day? Twenty-four hours, at least?"

"I suppose," I mutter, tossing my open suitcase onto my bed and whipping back around to my closet.

"Wait," Mila says. "What are you . . . Are you packing?"

My full hands pause over the suitcase. "Uhhhhhh . . . no."

Shit.

I drop the pile of clothes and turn around to find more.

"Don't even try to lie to me," she scolds before I hear her fingers on her keyboard, hacking back into my home security system. "Holy fucking shit, Siren. You are!"

"Damn it. Okay, fine. I am. But I swear, I'm not going to accept the invitation until after you've done your research. In the meantime, I don't see the harm in packing just a little. It never hurts to be prepared."

I can practically feel the disapproval wafting off my best friend, but the moment I grab the shelving of my closet and push back the secret door to display my hidden weapons room—otherwise known as my happy place—all thoughts of disapproval disintegrate.

I'm going to the War Games, and without a doubt, it's going to be the best thirty days of my life.

2

REAPER

Passing the sign that reads *Welcome to Blue Springs, Montana*, I reach for the dial of my police scanner and tune it until I find the local Blue Springs Police Department. It's been a long drive from the Big Apple, but it should be worth my time.

I hope.

Whoever is behind War Games has reached out to me six years running, and each year I've happily declined. I don't need this shit in my life. I don't need the title of being the *War Games Champion* to prove that I'm good at what I do. I know I'm the best, and that's not my ego talking.

I don't know what possessed me to accept this year's invitation. This isn't my scene. I suppose I'm getting bored and need something to light a spark under my ass, a real challenge to keep me on my toes. So when the invitation dropped into my inbox, I found myself quickly accepting.

Blue Springs is a tourist town away from the hustle and bustle of city life and the perfect location for War Games. I have to give it to the organizers; they know how to pick a great destination. Blue Springs is a small town with picturesque scenery. We're talking impressive mountains, a magnificent lake, an expansive cave system, and that's all before I've even considered what the town itself has to offer.

There's an industrial area I'll be sure to utilize. After all, if I'm going to make the most of this trip, I might as well have a little fun with it. Fuck knows I need a little fun in my life. There are the usual places like movie theaters, a mall, parks, and budget hotels, but as I drive through the town, these places aren't calling to me.

I'm five minutes out from the warehouse where we'll make the first point of contact for the games, and as I drive, I listen to the local sheriff's department. I'm not surprised to find they're already on top of the bullshit that's about to come down on their peaceful town, but it also becomes comically clear that they're not going to be an issue. They think we're still days out from the commencement of the games.

They know we're coming, but what little resources they have aren't enough to even attempt to hold us back. There's a grand total of six cops in Blue Springs, and sure, I can guarantee they'll call in backup over the next few days when bodies begin showing up, but by the time they find any sort of evidence, the games will be long gone.

For the most part, the games have strict rules.

We're here to play, not torment the town of Blue Springs, and while there have been slip-ups in the past, we're not to mess with the people. They didn't sign up for this shit, and for the most part, we'll leave the town just as sparkly as it was when we first arrived. Minus a few slight inconveniences, of course.

After finding the industrial area, I pull my car into a dark alley, far away from the meeting spot, not wanting my car to be tagged or become familiar to any of the other contenders. After cutting the engine, I slip out into the night, silently making my way through the quiet streets, keeping to the shadows.

I hear footsteps in the streets of other contenders making their way toward the warehouse, too confident with their own skills to conceal themselves. It's people like that who'll be the first eliminated. Not by me though. People who make themselves easy targets don't interest me. I like the ones who make me work for the kill. I like the challenge of tracking a ghost, of drawing them out, blindsiding them, and the Twenty-Third Annual Serial Killer War Games promises just that. Though, I'll have to be patient. The prey I'm after won't be easy to find. They will bide their time in this twisted game.

Moving through the industrial area, I slip between old buildings, cutting through the back of rundown properties until finally launching myself over one final fence and coming to a stop in the side alley next to the warehouse.

There are a few cars parked down the street, each of them attempting to be discreet as though they're not about to step out of their cars and walk directly into the warehouse and out themselves as one of the contenders.

Despite the games not officially starting until after our induction meeting, I'm on high alert and can sense the people around me. Any of these fuckers could strike at a moment's notice, especially when ten million dollars is on the line. And while there certainly are strict rules, there are definitely a few that the bastard organizers would turn a blind eye to.

Personally, I don't care for the money.

I've been a contract killer for well over fifteen years. I charge what I want, and the assholes sick enough to hire me are willing to pay whatever it takes to get the job done. I have more money than I know what to do with, stashed in multiple accounts across the globe. I couldn't even guess how much there is, but there's more than enough to ensure I never have to work again. The only issue with retiring is that I enjoy working.

This next month though, this isn't work. This is play.

Glancing down at my watch, I take in the time. It's 11:59 p.m. One minute to go.

Contenders approach the warehouse from all directions, skeptically eyeing each other as they mentally make plans of attack. They're all looking for the weakest link.

It's already clear to me who the contract killers are opposed to the serial killers. There's a different sense of stealth between them. The assassins have training. They stick to the shadows and watch the other contenders like prey, while the serial killers walk straight through the moonlight, their egos too big for their own good. They'll be the first to go. In fact, over the past twenty-two years, I don't think a serial killer has ever won these games. It's always been a contract killer.

They start making their way into the warehouse and not having enough visibility, I slip over the top of the fence and drop to the ground, putting me right by the warehouse. Then, without skipping a beat, I move right into the building, bring my elbow up in a shallow arc, and shatter the side window.

Reaching in, I feel around for the window latch until my fingers brush over the cool metal lock. I quickly unlatch it before finally sliding the window open. Not wasting any time, I pull myself up and through the window before coming down inside what appears to be an abandoned office space.

An old desk sits covered in dust, and the shelves have been torn down and discarded haphazardly across the small office. I move around it, making my way to the internal door, and without a moment of hesitation, I reach for the handle and let myself out into the main floor of the old warehouse.

Most of the windows have been boarded up, and there's a distinct ammonia smell in the air that suggests someone has been cooking something up in here. I wouldn't blame them. It's the perfect location. Away from the busy streets, no surveillance, and it has more than enough space for the perfect setup. Either way, I don't really give a fuck.

Sensing the people around me, I make the first move, stepping out of the shadows and revealing myself. Then, one by one, the other nineteen contenders do the same until we've formed a large circle in the center of the warehouse.

This part of the initiation process is simple. Reveal yourself.

We must form a circle, and once the final contender has arrived, the clock will start. We'll stand for forty-five minutes, allowing everyone the chance to learn the faces of the other men and women they'll be responsible for hunting. During this time, they must learn as many details as they can because it's the only chance they'll have to learn who they're up against. Then, at some point during those forty-five minutes, we must reveal our aliases.

Once the clock stops, the games have officially begun and nobody will be safe. It's life or death, no holding back. It's imperative that we use our time wisely, read the competition, get inside their heads, and figure out who the fuck they are. Otherwise, you'll be the first one knocked out of the games.

In a flash of blinding light, an overhead spotlight is remotely turned on, and as the shadows are expelled from the warehouse, the faces of the killers around me become real.

There's a large clock in the center of the circle counting down the final forty-five minutes before the games commence, and I immediately begin committing their faces to memory.

My first quick scan tells me there are thirteen men and seven women, only my gaze stops on one woman . . . or *girl,* and I'm too shocked to continue my initial assessment. This blue-eyed girl with dark hair is only a child. She's no older than twelve or thirteen. There's a darkness in her eyes that tells me she's seen far more than any child should witness. However, in contrast to the youthfulness of her features, it's almost off-putting.

What the fuck is this kid thinking walking into a game like this? Does she not understand that these men and women around her won't hesitate to brutally end her life? I have a moral compass and draw the line at hurting children, but the assholes around me sure as fuck don't.

She's too young to have the experience required to win these games, and without a doubt, if it came down to me or her at the very end, I would have no choice but to sacrifice myself in order to see her survive. I couldn't live with myself afterward if I did what had to be done to win.

Fuck.

This certainly changes things.

Feeling an agonizing pain forming deep in the pit of my stomach, I tear my gaze away from the girl and try to focus on the other contenders in the competition. But seeing the way the other killers keep looking at the girl as an easy target makes my hands ball into fists.

I didn't sign up for babysitting, but something tells me that's exactly what this next month is going to look like.

Anger pulses through my veins. These games aren't something you simply sign up for. You're selected, which means some asshole in his mother's basement tracked her down on the dark web, figured out how to get in contact with her, and then thought it would be entertaining to see what would come from offering her an invitation.

Fucking bastard.

Don't get me wrong, I understand being good at what you do and wanting to prove yourself, but what the fuck is even happening here?

Could she not have waited a few years before accepting to participate in bullshit like this? She has her whole fucking life ahead of her.

I try to shake the thought from my head, knowing damn well that I'm here to do a job. I can't focus on this kid's health and well-being while I'm supposed to memorize the faces of the men and women I have to kill.

Fifteen minutes in, the man standing directly opposite me in the circle takes a slight step forward. There's a nervousness in his eyes that I understand all too well, but he holds his head high as he gives up the required information. "The name's Stone."

My brow arches as he steps back into position. The name seems familiar to me, though most of them will. I do what I can to keep up to date with all of this shit, needing to know what other monsters lurk through city streets, who poses a threat to me, and who needs to be handled for their own good. If this is the same Stone I'm thinking of, then he won't be a problem, and I'd assume he'd be targeted early on in these games.

There's at least a full thirty seconds of silence before the next contender steps forward—a woman standing to my left. "Silver," she says, her eyes bouncing around the circle as if daring someone to try something.

Her hands ball into tight fists, ready for any threat that might come her way, but before she steps back into formation, another woman with blazing red hair steps forward, a filthy smirk on her face as she pierces Silver with a laser-sharp stare. "Gasoline."

Silver's stare widens with surprise before pure rage darkens her gaze, making it more than obvious there's history between the two, which is probably the worst scenario in this situation. Every other asshole in this room now knows they'll be so focused on taking out one another that their guards will be down, which is where you make mistakes. And once you slip even a little, you're as good as dead.

The next contender steps forward. "The Executioner."

Then, like a wave, the rest follow.

"The Boneyard Slayer," a big, burly man says, his eyes dancing around the room. A cockiness in his tone suggests that he is someone I'll need to keep a close eye on.

"Blade."

"Grim."

I barely make note of these two. They're weak. They'll be gone by the end of the night.

Next up, another woman. "Crimson Rain."

This one might have potential. Her walls are up, and she's not allowing anyone to get a good read on her. I like that. It could work in her favor, but the nervousness in her eyes might be her downfall. I'll have to keep an eye on this one.

"Slasher."

"Raven."

"The Boston Maneater."

This one brings me pause, my stomach churning with unease. The Boston Maneater? He can't be serious. The majority of us have received our aliases from law enforcement or the media, and they're generally somewhat related to our crimes. Once the name has been whispered across the media, you're stuck with it for life. I just hope there's been a misunderstanding here because right now, I'm picturing this guy hovering over his kill, gnawing on a bone like a dog.

Every face around the circle mimics my disgust, and clearly sensing our indifference, The Boston Maneater goes to say something, his hand inching up as his mouth opens, probably preparing some kind of defense, but he quickly hesitates. Here and now isn't the time to get into it.

We're well past halfway when movement to my right causes my gaze to shift. A petite woman with dark hair and blazing green eyes steps forward, and her confidence makes me uneasy. "I'm Siren," she says without even a note of nervousness. Her tone suggests she's here to have the best time of her life.

Siren, huh? I know that name.

She's one hell of a threat, maybe my biggest one yet, but she's got nothing on me. She's a contract killer, and she's more than efficient at her job. Some say she's the best in the field, but that's because most think I'm more of a legend or ghost story rather than a real man.

Siren's gaze shifts around the circle, meeting the eye of every killer in the room, and when those green eyes come to mine, electricity burns through me. This woman isn't just someone I need to be cautious of; she's trouble, but I've never been so intrigued.

Perhaps these games just got interesting after all.

Sensing my lingering stare, Siren watches me as she steps back into formation, her gaze narrowed as if trying to figure out who I am and why I haven't looked away like everyone else. She's trying to get a read on me, but she won't be able to. I'm a closed book, unlike most of the assholes around me.

The kid steps forward next, and I can't help but notice how quickly she has the undivided attention of the room. "Shadow," she states in a tone that sends a chill down my spine, which is something that has never happened before.

The girl looks around the room as if this is some bullshit test at school that she's far too advanced for, and I can't help but wonder exactly how she got here. This level of confidence only comes with experience, which leaves me wondering how the fuck she ended up that way.

Did somebody do this to her? Because no innocent child willingly goes down a path like this without a shitload of trauma.

Apart from hearing everyone's aliases, the warehouse has been silent since the moment I entered, but after hearing Shadow's name come out of her mouth, the silence suddenly feels heavier. Eerie almost.

There's a good two minutes before the next contender steps forward. "343," he says, prompting a quizzical look in the eyes of everybody in the room. This dude looks like he barely passed high-school gym class, surely he's here by mistake. Or maybe he's a tech guy. Either way, he isn't somebody I need to focus on.

Next up is a guy who looks like he's lived every day of his life on a beach with a surfboard permanently attached to either himself or the roof of a hippie van. "Sharkbait," he says before quickly stepping back again.

Fifteen down, five to go.

My gaze sails over the remaining contenders—four men and one woman—each of them hesitating, wanting to be last to put their name forward, but the clock is ticking, and there are only seven minutes remaining, and fuck knows that last name given will be mine.

Six minutes.

Five.

All eyes bounce around the room, waiting to see who will cave first. After all, a name not given during our initial meeting is an automatic dismissal from the games, and it goes without saying that an automatic dismissal is paid for with your life.

Four.

Three.

"Fuck," the woman says with a cringe before finally stepping forward. "Eagle."

I watch her closely as she steps back into formation, quickly determining that she won't be a threat.

Two minutes.

One of the men begins to fidget, his gaze flicking between the rest of us and the clock, his hand pulsing at his side. It's so discreet that I'd dare say some of the people around me wouldn't even notice it, but I do. I notice everything.

His lips pull into a tight line before finally relenting and stepping forward, clearly wanting to be in the game to win, but he's not dumb enough to risk it all for the simple task of giving up his name. "The Midnight Killer," he says, his lips twisting with frustration before finally stepping back into formation.

He's not bad and has certainly made quite a name for himself across North America. He's a serial killer and lacks the kind of training required to win these games. He'll put up a good fight though.

The clock keeps ticking, and at exactly one minute left, the next contender steps forward. "They call me Graves," he grunts, but despite his cocky expression, he's just like The Midnight Killer. They lack conviction. Graves won't be a threat, this last one though . . . I don't know.

It's down to me and one other and he stares at me as though he could somehow make me break, but I won't. I don't ever break. It's not written in my DNA.

Thirty seconds.

His demeanor begins to crack.

Twenty.

"Fuck."

The asshole steps forward, and something warns me that apart from the beautiful Siren to my right, this asshole will be a heavy hitter during these games. "The Texan Reaper."

No fucking way.

A grin threatens to pull at the corners of my lips. I've more than heard of this guy. When he first came on the scene, he claimed to be me. However as his work was sloppy and unoriginal, they quickly realized he was a different guy and ended up with the name The Texan Reaper. At first, I was flattered that I had an admirer, but now I'm just pissed. Ride someone else's coattails.

I keep my eye on The Texan Reaper, counting down the clock in my head, letting it ten more seconds pass by.

Eight. Six. Four.

Two.

I step forward, holding his gaze, and finally say the name I know everybody in this room is dying to figure out.

My voice commands the undivided attention and respect of those lesser killers around me because, right now, they're not just meeting another contender, they're meeting their worst fucking nightmare.

"Reaper."

3

SIREN

Ahh fuck.

I was expecting a lot to come from this bullshit midnight meeting, but standing in an abandoned warehouse with none other than the original Reaper was not it. Judging by the audible gasps that sail through the warehouse, I'm not alone.

Reaper is . . . undefinable.

He's a ghost. A legend. Someone I had convinced myself doesn't actually exist. Yet, here he is, in the flesh, standing less than twenty feet away. I can barely believe it, and honestly, this changes things. Since the moment I received the invitation to these games, I haven't felt a shred of fear. Until right now.

Reaper isn't just some contract killer like the majority of men and women in this warehouse. He's beyond that. He's the one they call when a ghost needs to be eliminated, or when warlords who have been off the grid for thirty years need to be extinguished. He's better than the best, and if I had known he would be participating in this month-long trial, I would have run the other way and never looked back.

I'm fucked. Beyond fucked. Hell, the second Reaper accepted his invitation, we were all considered dead. Everything that happens now until the end of the games is considered nothing but pure entertainment—a way for Reaper to let off a little steam and try out a few new techniques, maybe brush up on some of his skills.

I wasn't expecting him, but what I also wasn't expecting was to be so unbelievably attracted to him. He's gorgeous in the most lethal kind of way. Tall, at least six foot four with dark unruly hair and even darker eyes that seem to suck the souls out of the people in the room simply by staring at them. It's dark in the warehouse, but despite that, I can clearly make out the warmth in his olive complexion, an indicator that he spends a lot of time out in the hot sun, and the way his muscles bulge under his black shirt, tells me that he more than just cares for his body.

He seems like a soldier in the way he holds himself, like he's had some kind of formal training, but nothing on what little I know about this man would possibly suggest that, and it leaves me curious. But not as curious as the tattoos winding up his arms and peeking above the neckline of his shirt leave me.

The fear in the eyes of the other contestants matches the horror and regret in mine, but there's not a second to dwell on it before the big countdown clock in the middle reaches zero. A loud buzzer sounds through the abandoned warehouse, the noise bouncing off the walls and creating an eerie echo that rumbles through my chest. Then, before Reaper receives another millisecond to memorize my face, I take off like lightning.

The men and women in the warehouse scatter like cockroaches, some sprinting to the front of the building while others head for the back. A handful of contenders slink deeper into the building, hiding out in old office spaces, but me? I go up. I always go up.

Diving deeper into the building, I find an emergency exit door and peek through the old plexiglass window to find a stairwell hidden behind.

Bingo. There's nothing I like more than a good, solid rooftop with an even better vantage point.

The door is old, and I have to jimmy the old lock out of place before yanking it open. Then, to keep my ass out of hot water, I slam it closed behind me and do what I can to jam it. As I work on the back of the door, my gaze shifts up to the plexiglass window, checking the cockroaches' locations. By now, the majority of them are out of sight, except one.

Reaper.

He hasn't moved an inch from the center of the warehouse as he watches the chaos disperse around him, and despite the warehouse being filled with serial killers and assassins, there's only one true predator here tonight.

What's the point of running? We might as well line up like toy soldiers and let Reaper take us out one by one. Get it over and done with instead of allowing him thirty days to play with us. But where's the fun in that? A man like Reaper would only accept an invite to War Games if he was bored.

I get back to jamming the door when a chill sails down my spine, and as I glance back up, I find Reaper's lethal stare locked on me. He doesn't move, not even the slightest twitch of a muscle and it's the eeriest thing I've ever seen. Nobody has the ability to be that still. He's like a statue in the night.

A lump forms in my throat, and I hastily try to swallow it down, hating just how uneasy he makes me. But more than that, why do I have this overwhelming need to drop to my knees and beg him not to kill me in the form of a BJ?

I wonder how a man like Reaper comes. He strikes me as the silent, brooding type. I can imagine it so clearly. The only hint he's about to come undone is the slightest narrowing of his terrifying eyes. You wouldn't want to accidentally lose your flow and edge him. You might end up with your throat slit. But then, what if he's not like that at all? What if he's the type to wrap his hand around a woman's hair and force himself deeper into her throat while whispering what a good little slut she is?

Fuck. Now I'm wet.

What the hell is wrong with me? I've always been attracted to the reddest flags. It's literally the first few seconds of War Games, and I'm daydreaming about Reaper's dirty talk instead of focusing on getting the fuck out of here. But shit. To make a man like Reaper come apart inside my mouth would be the highlight of my life.

Screw winning the games. That's never going to happen now. It's time to adapt and give myself a more achievable goal. Who knows, perhaps Reaper might give me a merciful ending if I can give him something in return. That's my only hope at this point, but that doesn't mean I shouldn't still try to enjoy these next thirty days. If I even have thirty days left.

I came here to shed blood, and until Reaper decides it's time for me to meet my end, that's exactly what I intend to do. After all, I'm just a girl with a simple dream.

Doing what I can to ignore Reaper's penetrating stare, I finish jamming the lock of the old metal door. Then after quickly meeting his haunting stare through the window one last time, I turn on my heel and sprint up the stairs, confident that if he wanted to kill me tonight, he'd have somehow already done it.

I take the stairs two at a time, pushing myself as fast as I can go before reaching the top and breaking through the next door that leads out to the roof. The wind howls the moment I open the external door, blowing my long dark hair back behind me in a woosh of cold air. I don't let it faze me as I make a break for the edge of the building, concealing myself in the best vantage space the roof has to offer, not daring to turn my back on the door as I duck down behind an old air conditioning vent.

I keep my eyes open, watching the scene unfold in front of the warehouse while making sure no one is able to get the drop on me up here. I'm close enough to the neighboring property that if anyone decides to look for me, I can jump to the next roof or race down the fire escape. I arrived here an hour before anyone else and cased the property before checking the surrounding ones. I know every possible escape route, and from here, there are at least three ways out that would keep me concealed in the shadows.

The sound of a motorcycle roars through the night before taking off down the deserted street, and all I can do is shake my head. Only a fool would come to War Games with a vehicle that could give away his location in milliseconds. There are a few other cars in the backstreets, each of them a little more discreet, and as they race out of here, I cast my attention on the chaos below.

There are at least ten people. Some are hiding in the shadows, waiting for their chance to secure the first identifications of the games, while others don't have the patience to wait them out.

Without streetlights, it's dark out, but I have just enough moonlight to make out the faces of the men and women below. Grim and Blade are the two that steal my attention first. Neither of them came off as a threat to me during our initial meeting, and judging by the way they both couldn't stand still, I'm not surprised to see them being the first to jump into the madness. Patience is a virtue, and letting your ego get the best of you isn't going to work in your favor.

Blade is a scrawny guy, and I'm not surprised when he pulls a long blade from a holster inside his jacket. After all, most of us were appointed our aliases for a reason, and this right here is clearly Blade's MO. On the other hand, Grim is simply a brute. He's big and angry like the dumb jocks in high school who were always rejected by the girls. I wouldn't be surprised if this dude was taking steroids. No amount of gym time could naturally get anybody this big.

Fear flashes in Blade's eyes, and he lunges toward Grim, making contact with the big bastard's forearm, but the adrenaline hits Grim like a shot of tequila, and he continues toward Blade, not even realizing how detrimental that decision is.

Grim captures Blade's hand in his overly big one and squeezes. The familiar sound of crushing bone fills the silent street, quickly followed by an agonized scream.

Grim yanks Blade into him, spinning him in the process so that Blade's scrawny back is pressed against his beefy chest. He brings up Blade's hand until the tip of his own knife rests against the base of his throat.

"No. No. No. No," Blade roars, his eyes wide with terror, but before he can get another protest out, Grim plunges the sharp knife right through his delicate skin until the tip of the blade protrudes from the back of his neck, instantly severing his spine.

Grim releases Blade, and his body falls lifelessly to the ground, the knife clattering on the cold concrete beside him. Grim smirks down at his kill before finally sparing a glance at the deep cut running up the length of his forearm. He looks at it for just a moment before starting to sway on his feet, which is when another player enters the chat.

Stone.

He's been watching from the shadows just like a few other contenders, but with Grim losing blood so quickly, he couldn't resist claiming the kill, which would give him possession of Blade's death as well.

Stone rushes in behind Grim before he even knows he's there and grips the front of his chin. Stone violently twists, and with a sickening crack, Grim's lifeless body falls beside Blade's.

It's almost poetic. I've always believed that karma is a bitch, and this right here is more than proof of that.

Stone hastily glances around, making sure the coast is clear, and while I admire his balls to jump in and claim the kill, he's foolish for believing there's no one else around. Right now, he's a sitting duck, and he doesn't have a single clue.

Deciding he's in the clear, he dives into Grim's pocket, fumbling as he pulls out his wallet to search for his ID. Then, finding what he's looking for, he begins searching for Blade's, only a noise across the wide entrance of the warehouse has both mine and Stone's gazes glancing that way.

A hollow groan ripples through the night, and I search the darkness before watching with a keen eye as the guy who I think called himself Graves gets the shit beat out of him by Crimson Rain, a petite woman with deep burgundy hair. She goes in on him over and over, pointed brass knuckles secured around her fingers and stabbing into his skin with every devastating blow. Only these punches aren't just about winning the game, it's personal, and I can't help but wonder what the connection is there.

Graves groans, his skin quickly being torn to shreds, all while Stone discreetly tries to slink back into the shadows. Only his foolishness knows no bounds, and when he keeps backing up, he puts himself right into The Boston Maneater's arms. All I can do is shake my head.

I suppose this particular cannibal is getting a good meal tonight.

In a flash, a blade catches against the moonlight, and I watch without surprise as it slices across the front of Stone's throat. The move instantly takes him out of the competition and decorates the concrete in a wave of splattering blood. The Boston Maneater has secured the first three kills of the game. It was a bold move, but a good one, and I don't doubt that I would have done the same in his situation.

The splattering of Stone's blood distracts Crimson Rain from her brutal attack for a fraction of a second, but it's all Graves needs to gain the upper hand, despite the way blood drenches his clothes. He shoves into her, knocking her off balance, and sends her sprawling to the ground with a loud thud.

The anger in his eyes is off-putting, something I've rarely witnessed, but among killers like this, it's not unusual. Once they get the taste for blood, there's no telling what they might do.

Crimson Rain scrambles to her feet to retreat, but he stalks her like a starved man, not allowing her to gain any traction. She has no choice but to fight. She kicks at his legs, trying to trip him up as she frantically searches for something to use as a weapon. I won't lie, it's certainly entertaining and gives me a good idea of who these people really are. These two, in particular, there's something here. Maybe this isn't their first run-in, and judging by the way she was laying into him with those pointed brass knuckles, I can only assume he broke her heart in one hell of a spectacular way.

As he continues stalking her, another figure jumps out from the side alley next to the old warehouse. I recognize him immediately. Slasher. The name has stuck with me for years after the asshole wandered his sorry ass onto my turf and started causing the type of chaos that was drawing too much attention. I was left with no other choice but to send a stern warning, and it truly is miraculous that he somehow recovered enough to gain full use of both of his kneecaps. I can't lie, I was surprised to see him standing around that circle in the warehouse, but not as surprised as he was to see me. That kill would have been sweet, but something tells me I'm not going to get the honor. I should have killed him when I had the chance.

Slasher sprints toward Graves, a dagger clutched tightly in one hand, but as another body begins carelessly slinking through the center of the mayhem, all I can do is gawk.

Fucking Reaper.

He takes leisurely stride after leisurely stride as though he doesn't even notice the bullshit around him, but that's not possible. He simply doesn't care. It's as though he knows they can't touch him, not even if the three of them worked together to bring him down. Then, as if he has all the time in the world, he pauses and turns toward Graves and Crimson Rain, watching the way Slasher races toward them.

Slasher's momentum falters under Reaper's scrutiny, and his weak-ass knees literally crumble beneath him, taking him heavily to the ground. This fumble gives Graves the opening he needs. Abandoning his advantage on Crimson Rain, he lunges for Slasher first, deciding he's the bigger threat, but he refuses to take his eyes off Reaper.

Graves takes him out quickly and efficiently with a boot directly to the back of the spine, snapping his neck with ease. He's still cautiously watching Reaper, but I don't think Reaper is even a little bit interested in getting involved. He just stopped to casually watch the show, and it also doesn't go unnoticed that the moment Reaper stepped out into the spotlight, every other bystander mysteriously vanished.

The distraction gives Crimson Rain the precious seconds she needs to get back to her feet, and instead of fleeing as any other sane person would, she lunges for Graves again, her pointed cat-ear brass knuckles plunging deep into the side of his neck.

He cries out in agony, and while it's a devastating blow, it's not a fatal one. If he can escape this, he'll give himself a second chance in these games. Assuming Crimson Rain doesn't finish him off first.

Graves whips around toward her and lunges at her, barely noticing the way half of his skin is torn into ribbons. He grabs her head and slams it against the wall of the warehouse, and I have to lean further over the edge of the roof to see the performance properly, but as I do, I feel that same chill in my bones and I tear my gaze away from the dueling couple to the ghost in the middle of the street. His haunting stare is locked on me again.

He's the only one who's been even remotely capable of spotting me on the roof. Though to be fair, he saw me make a break for the stairs, and like earlier, his stare is just as chilling. I swallow hard, my palms instantly starting to sweat, and I don't dare look away when I hear the sound of a body hitting the ground. Not even when Graves escapes with both Crimson Rain's and Slasher's identifications.

It's just me and Reaper, and the five other bodies left scattered on the concrete. I can only assume The Boston Maneater took off earlier with the coveted identifications of Stone, Grim, and Blade, and he probably took himself a finger to gnaw on. Officially, the one and only cannibal competing is currently in the lead with Graves coming in a close second, but with Reaper on the loose, I doubt either of them will hold those positions for long.

The seconds seem to last a lifetime, and all I can hear is my heartbeat pulsing in my ears. This could be it. The moment I die. Even with all this distance between us, all he'd have to do is blink and I'd be as good as dead.

I hold my breath, waiting for the sweet torture of death to rain down over me, and yet all the fucker does is wink.

Huh?

A wink?

What the hell does that mean?

My heart races even faster, and when he shifts his body weight, my back stiffens, watching as the slightest smirk pulls at the corner of his full lips.

Oh God. Oh God. Oh God. I'm a dead woman. I didn't even get to make him come yet.

Is he going to shoot me? Throw a knife through the night sky and plunge it into my chest? Take me out with nothing more than fear alone? Holy fucking hell. Why do I suddenly have the overwhelming need to shit?

This isn't okay!

My hands shake, and I brace them against the ledge of the roof, preparing to push myself to my feet if I have to make a break for it. I don't dare fool myself into believing that he didn't notice the shift in my weight. He knew my plan even before I did.

My heart races impossibly fast, and just when I think I'm about to go into cardiac arrest, Reaper turns on his heel and walks away, gingerly putting one foot in front of the other, so casually strolling right down the center of the deserted street.

4

SIREN

What in the ever-loving fuck just happened up on that rooftop?

All I could do was stare after him as he disappeared into the night, and even then, I couldn't bring myself to get up and leave. I've been a callous killer for the better part of a decade, and despite all the ridiculous situations I've found myself in, I've never been as terrified as I was on top of that warehouse. If I wasn't worried about being hunted during my sleep, I'd take a Xanax or five to chill me the fuck out.

It took me twenty minutes after Reaper left before I was able to find the nerve to march my ass off the roof and slip back through the side streets to my car. He left me shaken, and that's not a feeling I'm used to.

Driving through the empty streets of Blue Springs, I bring up Mila's number and call her over the car's Bluetooth system, listening as the first ring only gets halfway through before she quickly answers. "What the hell took you so long?" my best friend demands, her voice filling my car. "I've been waiting forever to hear what the fuck went down in that warehouse. I tried to hack my way into their footage, but they put up too many firewalls. I couldn't get through to save my life."

"Shit. You don't know then?"

"Know what?" she panics.

I let out a heavy breath, having no idea where to even start with the bullshit otherwise known as my night. "I maybe shouldn't have jumped the gun. You were right to want to do all your research first."

"What do you mean? What happened?"

"It's not *what*, but *who*."

"Huh?"

"Reaper."

"Reaper?" Mila questions, confusion thick in her tone. "You mean The Texan Reaper?"

"No," I start. "Well . . . Yes. He's here, but he won't be a problem. I mean the real Reaper. The OG Reaper. The one I assumed was a figment of my imagination."

"No," she says, and I can practically picture the way she's shaking her head with furrowed brows. "No. That's not right. He's not actually real. I've looked into this guy a million times. He literally doesn't exist. They're just stories made up by the media. A scapegoat the cops fabricated to pin their unsolved high-profile cases on."

"I know all that, but everyone is wrong. I looked him dead in the eyes, and he's . . . terrifying. I could practically hear the second every last person in that warehouse went into heart failure. He's as real as they get, but what I can't work out is why he's here. Why now? I'm sure he's probably been invited to attend War Games a million times, so why is this year different? Is he just looking for a way to pass the time or does he get off on the hunt like the rest of them? Could it be for the prize money?"

"I don't know what to tell you," Mila whispers, the heartbreak clear in her tone, realizing exactly what I did the moment I saw Reaper. My chances of winning this thing just dwindled all the way down to zero. "There's no way to back out?"

"No," I tell her. "But I wouldn't anyway. I don't back down. Ever. I just have to be better. I have to find a way to win because dying here in Montana is not an option."

"Okay, so I'll do a little digging and see what I can pull up. There's gotta be something we can use to get an edge on him. If we can at least figure out his preferred weapons or style, then you can figure out a plan to get the upper hand."

I can't keep the scoff from sailing out of my mouth. "With all the false stories and kills that have been pinned on him, it'd be impossible to tell what's real and what's not. It'll be like looking for a needle in a haystack."

"I know," she breathes. "But just like you don't like backing down, neither do I. If anyone can find this bastard, it's me. Besides, I can't have you spending all your time on this when you need to focus on the other eighteen contenders."

"Thirteen," I tell her. "Five went down outside the warehouse."

"No shit," she laughs. "You guys don't fuck around."

"They were the weak ones with egos," I say, flying down the road toward the Blue Springs holiday resort that I've decided to stay at. Not that they're aware of that, of course. "They were weeded out, and now we're left with the real competition."

"Okay. Anyone you want me to specifically look into?"

"Yeah, actually," I say, my brows furrowing as I think over the faces I memorized tonight. "There's two in particular who seemed too alike. Their facial structures were almost identical. It's like they're cousins or something. Maybe brothers. I'm not sure, but I think it's worth looking into because if they're working as a team, then I'll have to adjust my approach."

"Names?"

"The Texan Reaper and The Boneyard Slayer."

"The Boneyard Slayer?" she laughs. "What kind of ridiculous name is that? Is he some kind of caveman who kills people with the bones of his other victims?"

"Who knows, but if someone is going to find information on this guy, it's you. Though, with a name like that, something tells me digging up information won't be too hard."

"Sounds about right," she murmurs, her voice going quiet as though she's momentarily distracted, probably writing the names down. "Anyone else?"

"Ummm," I pause for a moment, going over the names. "There's this chick, Gasoline. She looked a little rough, and if her name is anything to go by, my guess is she's an arsonist. I doubt she'll be much of a problem. She seemed to know this other woman, Silver. So I'm hoping they'll take each other out so I won't have to worry about them."

"That hardly seems fun," she says, just as I pull into the holiday resort and come to a stop outside the main gate. I type the code Mila created for me into the keypad and watch with an odd satisfaction as the gate begins to open. Mila never misses.

"Tell me about it," I say, slowly easing onto the gas again. "There was one thing I found really odd, and honestly, I really don't know how to feel about it."

"What's that?"

"One of the contenders. She said her name is Shadow, and I know looks can be really deceiving these days, but I could have sworn she was only a child."

"The fuck? What do you mean? Like sixteen, seventeen years old?"

"No. Like twelve or thirteen."

"No. There's no way," Mila says, her tone shifting with unease as I drive through the resort, searching for my private villa. "I know the guy who organizes this shit is a complete bastard with absolutely no morals, but surely he's not putting children into this."

"That's what I would have thought until I was standing opposite this kid, and I don't know. There was something about the way she was watching the contenders around her. She wasn't scared or even trying to work out who her biggest competition was. She was just . . . curious. It was like she had already worked each of us out before we'd even stated our aliases, even Reaper."

Mila's fingers click across her keyboard, and I shake my head, already knowing that she's not about to find anything on this girl. She's too young, and with a common name like Shadow, it would be impossible to filter through the millions of hits.

Reaching my private villa, I pull my car into the small driveway and cut the engine before jamming my phone under my ear. Mila groans and sighs, getting more and more frustrated at not being able to find a scrap of information on this young girl.

"She's practically a ghost."

"With a name like Shadow, are you really surprised?" I ask, grabbing my bags from the back of my car before striding up the short path toward the front door. "She's probably got some kind of Black Widow story and is a trained assassin for some secret government agency."

Mila barks out a laugh. "Really?"

"Hey! It could happen."

I can practically hear her rolling her eyes through the phone. "Secret government agency or not, I'll keep searching and see if I can come up with anything. Either way, the War Games are no place for a child. You need to keep an eye out for her. They'll target her assuming she's inexperienced, and I know she's technically your competition, but you and I both know you'll never be able to live with yourself if something happens to that kid. You need to protect her."

"If I can somehow track her down, that's exactly what I'll do, but something tells me she's not as inexperienced as most would assume. There's something in her eyes. She's seen shit no child should ever have to see. I think she's more of a threat than anybody could expect. Except for Reaper, of course."

"Just keep an eye out for her . . . *or on her*," she says as I reach the front door and have to adjust the bags in my hands to be able to type in the passcode—the same one I entered at the front gate.

The door opens, and I break into the small villa. Even with the lights out and nothing but the soft moonlight streaming through the window, I can already tell it's more than enough for what I need. And I don't mean because it boasts a state-of-the-art kitchen with brand-new flooring, and every luxury amenity a woman could need. And by amenities, I mean the prime location of the front door, the back one, and the countless windows in every room that offer me an easy escape route from anywhere inside. The structure itself is sturdy enough to protect me from gunfire, and the open layout of the kitchen and living areas makes it almost impossible for anyone to get the drop on me.

"It's perfect, right?" Mila says, always so proud of herself.

I quickly glance back, scanning the darkness outside and double and triple checking that no one has followed me here before locking the door behind me. "It's as though you know me or something."

She laughs again, and a stupid smile pulls at the corner of my lips. I'm not usually the smiling type, but there's something about Mila that always makes me smile. She's gifted that way, and I wouldn't change a thing about her.

Making my way deeper into the villa, I drop my bags into the small bedroom while quickly glancing around the room, and just like the rest of the villa, I can't possibly fault it. I'll be able to sleep peacefully in here. And from the looks of the bed, comfortably as well.

"So, that's it?" Mila asks. "No other bombs to drop on me about your night?"

I can't help but laugh. "I mean, there might be one . . . or possibly two more bombs you don't know about yet."

She sucks in an audible breath. "You better not be holding out on me."

"Wait," I say. "Three. There are three bombs."

"Siren!"

I laugh to myself as I take the phone from my ear, put it on speakerphone, and drop it to the bed so that I can rummage through my bags for my favorite silk pajamas. "Well," I start. "343 . . ."

Mila sucks in an audible gasp. "The Tech Guy?" she demands. "He's one of the contestants?"

A stupid grin rips across my face. Mila has been crushing on this guy for years. Though considering she's never seen his face, I can only assume it's his skills she's attracted to. "He sure is," I tell her. "But I don't understand how he thinks he could possibly have a chance at winning this thing. I mean, sure. He'll have a better chance of tracking the contenders than most, but he's actually pretty scrawny. He doesn't strike me as the type to be able to hold his own when it comes down to it."

"Shit," she says with a heavy sigh. "You're going to have to kill him."

"Yeah . . . sorry. Unless somebody else beats me to him, of course."

"Damn. I was really hoping that behind the screen, he'd be this really awesome guy with a killer smile, and then one day, we'd accidentally run into each other at an internet café and fall madly in love."

"Sorry, Mills. There's no killer smile when it comes to 343. He's more of the *lives in his mother's basement* type. You dodged a bullet there, but never fear, if it's love at first sight you're looking for, then I can put a list together."

"Hell no. The only color you like is red. I don't need you setting me up with some guy who's going to gut me like a fish in my sleep."

"Oh come on. I set you up with a serial killer one time. It's not like I knew the guy was intending to turn you into a human pincushion. How could I have possibly known? He was hot and sweet and looked like he more than knew what he was doing in the bedroom. It was an honest accident."

"The answer is still no."

"Fine," I huff. "But speaking of red flags. Reaper really has that dark and deadly thing going for him, and I really wouldn't mind—"

"No," Mila demands, cutting me off. "You're not fucking Reaper."

"But—"

"No. Are you insane?"

I shrug my shoulders. "I mean . . ."

"Yeah, stupid question," Mila mutters. "But seriously. He's your biggest competition during these games, and your solution to figuring out how to get an edge on him is to what? Shake your ass in hopes of luring him in? Hope that if you screw him well enough he might take pity on you and give you a merciful death? What could you possibly gain from that?"

"Trust me. You didn't see the way he was looking at me. He's lethal. Every inch of his body is perfectly carved, and every movement he made was so precise. He doesn't leave room for mistakes, and I've never been so attracted to something in my life. I just . . . I'm not crazy, okay? I know getting close to him would be stupid, but can't a girl dream? Do you have any idea how well a man like that would fuck? It would be earth-shattering."

"I don't doubt that, but no amount of incredible sex is worth losing your life over."

"Uhhh . . . Well—"

"No, Siren. The answer is no. You're coming home to me at the end of the month. No question about it. Your only goal while you're there is to win these games, and that's not going to happen by fucking Reaper."

"What if I didn't fuck him? I could just go down on him instead. How lethal could he be with his cock down my throat? Actually, do you think he's pierced? He doesn't strike me as the pierced kind, but men like Reaper have the ability to surprise me in ways I never could have imagined."

"I swear—"

"Okay, okay. I'll only dream about giving the world's best BJ instead of actually giving it. But let the record state that I'm not happy about it. And Mila, after I end this man's life, I'm taking a look under the hood, and if it turns out that he's pierced with a veiny monster cock, you and I are going to have words."

"Whatever you say, princess."

I let out a huff, never having been more disappointed in my life, but she makes a very good point. In the interest of saving my life, my only goal should be to take Reaper down, learn his weaknesses, and exploit them. It'll be the biggest challenge of my life, but if I can somehow pull this off, I'll become a legend among my peers. I'll be unstoppable and known as the best of the best until my dying days. But if I can't pull this off, if I'm stupid enough to allow Reaper to get close enough to end my life, I'll just be another number, another victim, another loser who couldn't pull off the impossible.

After getting dressed into my pajamas, I grab one of my other bags and haul it onto the bed, pulling out the array of security devices I'll need to protect my home for the next thirty days. "So, you wanna hear bomb number three or not?"

"Well duh," she says as I scoop up the motion sensors and security cameras and make my way back out to the kitchen.

"You remember Raven, right?"

Mila sucks in a breath, and with just that slight sound, I can already hear her excitement. "No fucking way! The bitch who tried pinning four of her kills on you a few years back?"

"The one and only."

"Oh shit! I've been waiting for this moment."

"You and me both," I say as I grab a chair from behind the small island counter and drag it across the room, finding the best positions to set up the surveillance cameras. "I'm going to be pissed if someone beats me to her, but at least I'll always have the satisfaction of seeing her face when I stepped forward in that circle and she realized exactly who I was."

"Damn it. I'm so annoyed I couldn't get a live feed into that warehouse. It would have been so good."

"Oh, it was," I say, wishing I was allowed to bring some sort of surveillance into that warehouse, but I'm a stickler for the rules . . . kind of.

Mila and I chat as I make my way around the villa, getting everything set up. Twenty minutes later, I'm sitting at the kitchen counter with my laptop, looking over the system I just set up and checking it for blind spots.

"What do you think?" I ask Mila as she looks over the live feed.

"Couldn't have done it better myself," she says as I listen to the familiar sound of her fingers flying across her keyboard. "There. I've linked it to your phone as well. So as long as you have a decent signal, you should be able to bring it up anywhere."

"Perfect," I say, grabbing my phone and refreshing the screen to see the system staring right back at me. "I couldn't have done any of this without you, Mills."

"Iammorethanawareofthat," she says in a yawn, her words jumbling together. "Just do me a favor and don't die, because if you do, I'm going to be really fucking pissed, okay?"

"Promise, I won't die."

"Don't make promises you can't keep."

"Okay, fine. I promise that I will try my hardest not to die."

"Good. In that case, I'm out. I'll talk to your bitch ass tomorrow," she tells me. "Try to get some sleep, then in the morning, we can start hunting these assholes."

Excitement drums through my veins as the idea of really getting to start the hunt truly sinks in. I feel as though I've been waiting a lifetime for this, and now that it's finally here, I can barely keep myself contained. "It's like music to my ears," I tell my best friend. "You try and get some sleep too, okay? Because we both know that you're going to lie down in your bed and close your eyes for all of three seconds before reaching for your phone again. Reaper and 343 can wait until tomorrow. They aren't coming for me tonight."

Mila scoffs, and I hear the smile in her tone. "Yeah, yeah," she says. "I'm hanging up now."

A laugh bubbles up my throat, and before I can say another word, my best friend is gone, leaving me alone to figure out my game plan for the next thirty days. Only problem with a competition like this is that my game plan needs to constantly evolve. This game can change by the minute, and though I need to be prepared, I don't need to be prepared until tomorrow.

For now, all that matters is closing my eyes and dreaming about all the fun I won't be having with Reaper.

5

SIREN

It's officially night two of War Games, and I've never been so ready to cause havoc. I fly through the moonlit streets, handling my car like the complete wreck that I am. I can't lie, while I'm more than happy to scream from the rooftops that I'm the best career killer out there—apart from Reaper, of course—I'm not too egotistical to not acknowledge my weaknesses. And driving just happens to be at the very top of that list.

I fucking suck. There's no other way to put it. Mila and I taught ourselves how to drive, and while we're more than capable of making it from point A to point B unscathed, it's never pretty. The state of my car is embarrassing, but it's fine. When it starts looking like it's been involved in a head-on collision with a freight train, I simply dump it and steal another. It's a great little routine I have.

My laptop slides across the leather passenger seat with every reckless corner I take, fighting for its life as I clutch a burrito in my free hand. I quickly glance toward the screen as it teeters on the seat's edge, following the pinned location of The Boston Maneater as he makes his way through the industrial park of Blue Springs.

This shit is too easy.

Despite my stern demand that Mila actually get some sleep, she stayed up until the early hours of this morning researching Reaper, and neither of us was surprised to find that she came up blank. So while she crashed, I tried my hand at the basic hacking skills she's taught me over the years, and after three hours and four coffees, I found The Boston Maneater.

He has a name that draws attention so finding information about him online wasn't hard. All his kills have been in a thirty-mile radius of Boston, Massachusetts, and after seeing his face last night, I'd put him in his late thirties. From there, it was simple. All I had to do was hack into every high school system in Boston and search the graduating classes from 2005 to 2008 until I found his face. And yeah, it was easy, but fuck, it took forever.

I was about ready to give up when I found him. And not only that, but I found his real identity. Nicholas Barrington.

A quick search showed that he was born and raised in Boston. He never really went anywhere or saw anything. He had an unremarkable childhood, and although he was a strange kid, there was nothing to raise alarms. Not until his mother was killed in a freak accident during his early teens. It all went downhill after that. His father became an abusive drunk and upon getting himself a brand-new step-mommy, he was kicked out to fend for himself.

I almost feel sorry for him. I know what it's like to live on the streets as a teen and have to figure life out for yourself, but I don't feel sorry enough not to kill him.

Figuring out his identity was one thing, but actually pinning a location on him was another. Once I had his name, the rest quickly fell into my lap. Now, to be fair, Mila would have found him in all of three seconds, but me? It took just a little longer, though the second I found his Facebook account, it was over for him. Even more so when the idiot decided to log on and check his notifications using a public Wi-Fi connection.

I had his location in the blink of an eye, and before I could convince myself to let someone else take out the trash, I was already throwing a bag of weapons in the car and backing out of my spot. Then, after almost taking out one of the resort's famous pines, I found myself heading right back toward the industrial park.

To be completely honest, it's not very creative, and for that alone, he deserves to be eliminated from the games. But getting to be the one who delivers his fate makes me feel all kinds of soft and gooey inside. I won't lie, getting to make my first kill of the games excites me like never before. I've been waiting for this moment for years, but taking out a cannibal? It's like music to my ears.

As I navigate the deserted backstreets of Blue Springs, I give myself a stomachache from eating my breakfast burrito too quickly. I pull onto the road that runs directly behind the warehouse where The Boston Maneater has decided to temporarily call home.

Bringing my car to a stop in a neighboring building, I cut the engine and climb out before checking my reflection in the car's window. I'm not one who usually likes to dress the part. I like comfort, but these games are a special occasion, so I've put in all the effort. Tight black jeans that hug my ass just right with black combat boots. I've matched it with a black leather-bound corset crop, custom-made with hidden incisions that are perfect for my blades.

Straps decorate my thighs with my guns holstered in various positions, but I doubt they'll be used. I prefer knives, so you can guarantee that anywhere you look on my body, you'll find a wide array of them. Boots, jeans, crop, hair. You name it, I have a knife there somewhere.

My hair has been pulled up into a high pony with my long, dark strands plaited right down to the end, giving me the perfect whip, and while I can't do shit with it, I'm all about the aesthetics today. Which is precisely why I opted for a perfect black lip and a cat's-eye liner to complete the look.

I feel better than I ever have, and as I reach back into the car to grab my bag of weapons, I can't help but glance over the laptop screen, confirming that The Boston Maneater is exactly where he should be.

A stupid grin pulls across my lips. This is going to be as easy as taking candy from a baby.

With my weapons all strapped in place, I go to leave when I spot my favorite ring just casually chilling out in my center console, begging to be taken out for a good night. I can't possibly resist. She's just so pretty.

Grabbing the brass ring, I slide it onto my middle finger and twist it just a fraction so that the sharp cat's ears are sitting right in the center of my finger. This ring is very similar to the brass knuckles Crimson Rain wore last night. The only difference is that mine is much smaller, and it's way too pretty to get bloody. I've never used it, but I've also never been on a job without it. It's my lucky charm, and while some people don't feel completely dressed without a shirt and pants, I don't feel completely dressed without this ring.

With my ring in place, I decide that I've spent more than enough time fucking around and lock up the car before quickly scanning the old warehouse. There's no one here, not even a stray cat. I knew that the second I drove in, but I watch my surroundings anyway as I stick to the shadows, not willing to put my life at risk for some loser who likes to gnaw on human flesh. I sure hope he's had his fill tonight because it's the last meal he'll ever have.

His small warehouse hideout is in my direct line of sight as I make my move. It's a dilapidated heap of shit compared to the building I parked behind, and judging by the graffiti on the boarded windows and the beer bottles littered around the parking lot, it's fair to say it has seen its share of late nights.

My guess is that it's been abandoned for maybe ten to fifteen years. The coloring on the outside has faded with time while some of the metal sheets making up its walls are missing. Anybody could get in and out. It offers no protection, no safety.

What the fuck was he thinking coming here?

I'm almost disappointed with how easy this is going to be. I won't even need to lure him out, set a trap, or go hunting. There's no chase here, simply a chance to practice my skills.

Ugh. I can't believe I wasted a good outfit for this. I should have known better than to allow myself to get so worked up and excited. Hell, his name is The Boston Maneater for fuck's sake. I should have known this was going to leave me unsatisfied. Not even in death could a man like that satisfy a woman.

Now a man like Reaper? Damn. Killing him will be everything. Dare I suggest it will be better than sex? The adrenaline of the chase, of hunting him and subduing him will be the best foreplay I've ever had. And those dark, lethal eyes when he realizes I've got him right where I want him. Only he's going to make me work for it. He's going to test me in every way possible, push me to my limits, push me until I break, and it's going to be incredible.

Silently making my way into the small warehouse, I can't help but grin. There's a huge fan at the back, almost as tall as the building with its blades slowly rotating and constantly distorting the moonlight that shines through the building. Maybe The Boston Maneater has a little creativity after all.

It's like the set of a horror movie in here, and as I appreciate my surroundings, I hear the familiar sound of footsteps across the cold concrete ground.

Bingo.

Sinking deeper into the shadows of the building, I crouch down low, watching as The Boston Maneater cuts across the warehouse. He looks as though he's preparing to go hunting. The only issue is that his movements lack motivation, and it becomes clear that his version of hunting is to go in blind and hope he happens to find someone.

Fucking rookie.

Why are assholes like this even invited to these games? It's supposed to be the best of the best, yet here's a guy who likes to stir his coffee with someone's big toe. Just the thought of it has me ready to wring his neck. He deserves to die simply for being incompetent.

The Boston Maneater begins filling his pockets with weapons and shoves a gun down the waistband of his torn jeans, and all I can do is shake my head. This idiot is embarrassing himself, but before he gets a chance to load up with too many weapons, I decide it's finally time to make my move. After all, the sooner I get this over and done with, the sooner I get back to my holiday resort and enjoy my month-long vacation.

With The Boston Knee Nibbler more than distracted, I rise out of the shadows and slowly stride into the center of the warehouse. I watch him with every step he takes, completely unaware of his surroundings. His back doesn't stiffen once. He doesn't even flinch at the soft padding of my footsteps on the concrete. He's either too confident and thinks he's luring me into some bullshit trap, or he's just stupid.

I'm going with what's behind door number two. The guy is a fucking moron.

With the ginormous fan at my back, my shadow stretches out

across the full length of the warehouse, the slow, spinning blades distorting my shape. It's fucking beautiful. Poetic almost. And as The Boston Guts Gobbler shoves another cheap knife into his pocket, I withdraw one of mine from the incision of my corset crop.

"I really do wish I could stand here all night and watch you fill your pockets with useless weapons, but you're starting to bore me."

The Boston Testicle Taster freezes, his body stiffening like a rock as the gun in his hand drops to the hard concrete. He whips around, his eyes wide like saucers as he takes me in. "How did you get in here?" he demands.

My brows furrow. "Ummm . . . You mean how did I get into the warehouse that's practically missing all of its sheet metal? Are you serious right now? There are more holes in this building than there are walls."

He simply just stares back at me, his lips twisting into a scowl. "You made a mistake coming here, girl," he says, quickly recovering from his shock of seeing me in the middle of his holey warehouse as he begins to stalk me, taking one large stride after the other. "Let me be very clear. I'm going to kill you now."

I simply stare back at him. "Do you really eat people?"

He falters for just a second, the question throwing him off. "I . . . What? No," he yells, quickly getting angry. "I don't do that."

"I don't know," I muse. "You don't get a name like The Boston Maneater for nothing. I mean I know all you serial killers have weird and wonderful little quirks. But eating your victims? That's just taking it a little too far, don't you think?"

His jaw clenches, and as the fan continues to spin behind me and he gets closer, my shadow begins to flicker across his face.

"Tell me, oh wise ankle biter," I continue. "Is there a difference in taste between a man and a woman? I take it a woman is a little more . . . tender."

His face turns red, his hands balling into fists at his sides, and when he reaches for one of his many knives, a deep thrill pulses through me. "I DON'T FUCKING EAT PEOPLE!" He roars so loudly that even in the dark, holey warehouse, I see the spittle flying from his mouth, and then in a flash, he breaks into a sprint toward me.

His knife is clutched tightly, ready to decapitate me, but I simply watch him, timing his every step, and just when he gets close enough, I whip my body around, my foot coming out in a beautiful spinning kick that meets his temple with the force of an eighteen-wheeler.

His momentum keeps him moving forward, and I simply take a step to the side, watching him fall right to the ground. The harsh crack of his nose breaking against the concrete gives me goosebumps.

I suck in a breath through my teeth. I hadn't really intended for him to break his nose, but sometimes these things are unavoidable. It's not as though I can foresee the outcome of every ridiculous situation I get myself into, but I won't lie, I'm not mad about it.

My little love tap to the temple wasn't quite enough to knock him out completely, and as he groans in agony, I shove my foot into his shoulder and roll him onto his back. A pang of disappointment hits me when I see his own damn knife plunged through his chest. "Ahhh shit, Mr. Liver Lover, that's unfortunate. I was so looking forward to the two of us spending some good quality time together."

"You're a"—gasp—"bitch."

I simply smile, and as I step toward him, his eyes widen in fear.

"It seems you've gotten yourself into a little bit of a pickle," I tell him, crouching beside him and looking over the mess he's made as blood gushes from his broken nose. I reach forward, wrapping my hand around the hilt of the knife that's currently plunged six inches into his chest. "Here's the situation," I explain. "This blade is currently keeping you from bleeding out, it's also keeping your right lung from collapsing, but unfortunately for you, I don't really care very much. I'm going to pull it out, and you're going to slowly die right here on the ground. It's probably going to be very painful."

"But . . . No," he breathes. "I don't want to die. I—"

"Shhhhhhh," I say, gripping the hilt tighter and tearing it free from his chest.

The Boston Maneater cries out in agony, and just as I expected, he quickly begins to bleed out, and from the sound of his gurgling, I can only assume his right lung is also beginning to fill with blood. "Now," I say, meeting his graying stare. "I'm assuming your ID is in your pocket?"

He doesn't respond, but at this point, I don't really expect him to. Instead, I just offer a sugary sweet smile, and as he grows sweaty and tries to cough up the blood in his collapsed lung, I fish his wallet out of his pocket, spilling out the rest of his weapons in the process.

I sit down next to him, giving myself enough space so that I don't get any of his blood on my outfit, and rifle through his wallet, grinning as I find not only his ID, but those of the three kills he claimed last night.

Stone. Grim. And Blade.

I officially possess four IDs, and at this stage of the competition, I'm currently in the lead.

The Boston Maneater slowly begins to die beside me, and I let out a breath, having hoped it would happen just a little bit quicker. I can't leave until I know he's well and truly gone because if he survives and makes it to the end without me knowing, both of us would be eliminated because of a technicality.

"So," I say, twiddling my thumbs. "I won't lie, the whole cannibalism thing is really gross. I don't know what you were thinking when you signed up for these games. Surely you knew you would be a target based on principle."

The guy groans, his face turning an odd shade of gray. "I'm not"—cough—"a cannibal."

"No one else is here," I say. "You can just admit it. So you have the taste for human thighs. Personally, I'm a fan of chicken breast, but I can get down with a good thigh."

"Not . . . a cannibal," he grits through his teeth, the blood beginning to seep closer to me on the concrete. "You know how this goes. That story . . . was planted by some tech asshole." He stops to cough and blood spurts from his lungs. "Once you get a name, it sticks. I've never been able to escape it."

"No shit, huh? You really don't like to slurp on human sausages?"

"The fuck is wrong with you?"

All I can do is laugh as I lean back onto my palms and inch my legs to the right to avoid the growing puddle of blood. "Look, this is taking a really long time. Would you mind hurrying along the process? All I've eaten today is a breakfast burrito on the way here, and I could really go for a good steak and veg. Actually, scrap the veg. I want fries."

He sputters, starting to drown in his own blood, and as I go to get to my feet, I realize the limb licker and I aren't the only ones here. A figure stands at the opening of the warehouse, his tall, imposing body taking up the majority of the doorway as he simply watches me.

In the dark, I can't make out a single feature of his face. He's nothing but an imposing shadow, waiting for me to fuck up. My heart races with pure fear, which is how I know that this man is Reaper.

He stares back at me, those lethal eyes capable of the most wicked crimes.

This is it, just like last night. It's just me and him. The ball is in his court, and I'm backed into a corner. I can try to run, but there's nowhere I can go that he won't find me. It's best to surrender right here and now, save myself the agony of trying to run.

I catch my breath and hold it, incapable of anything else but staring right back.

The whole world fades around me. I haven't even got a clue if the man at my feet is dead or alive, and I suddenly couldn't give a flying shit. All that matters is Reaper. Only he doesn't do a damn thing. He just stares at me.

This is a test. A warning.

Something tells me he's not here for The Boston Maneater. He's here for me. He's trying to prove just how easily he can get to me, just how quickly he can find me. And damn it, the message is received loud and clear.

I'm out of my element. Out of my league.

My heart races like never before. If I'm going to try and survive this, I need to figure out a game plan. I need to get my head screwed on straight, and I need to find my zen. I don't stand a chance while I'm panicking. He'll end me with nothing more than a flick of his fingers, and I'll go down like a sack of shit because I'm too busy fretting.

I need a clear mind.

I need a fucking plan, and right now, all I've got are the weapons strapped to my body.

My hand slowly reaches for the blade sheathed in my corset and just as my fingers curl around the custom-made hilt, preparing to defend myself when his brutal attack comes, everything stops.

The shadow disappears, fading into the night like a ghost, leaving me questioning if I imagined the whole thing. My heart doesn't dare stop racing. There's no way I could have imagined that. And for whatever reason, Reaper just allowed me to escape with my life.

He's playing with me. Getting a kick out of the way I fear him, and there's no denying just how easily he senses that fear. He feeds on it the same way that I do, and just like that, I have a full understanding of his game plan.

He's going to wait me out. He's going to let the rest of us battle it out as he stands back enjoying the show, watching as the rest of us crumble under his scrutiny, and just when we think we might have a fighting chance, he'll end those of us left like the incompetent killers we are.

A chill sails down my spine, and I realize that no matter how hard I try, how much I fight, how much research and weapons I have to defend myself against this beast, I will never win. It's not possible.

And with that thought, I simply turn on my heel and escape out the back of the warehouse, the same way I came in, knowing that whatever happens here in this sleepy town, my life as I once knew it is well and truly over.

6

REAPER

The fuck is wrong with me? I had the perfect opportunity to take Siren out of the competition, and all I could do was stand there like a fucking idiot while she took The Boston Maneater's life. Well, to be honest, his own incompetence is what resulted in the loss of his life, Siren was just there to help the process along. Yet, what little of her skills I was able to witness was enough to prove that she's in a league of her own.

Mostly.

I don't know what it is about her, but she intrigues me, and I don't think I'm ready to end her life just yet. There was a beauty about her kill which I don't often see. It was captivating and calm. So often kills are messy and done without precision, and despite The Boston Maneater's rage as he raced toward her, she kept her cool and handled herself with grace, and she did so without leaving a shred of her DNA behind. Not even a single fingerprint. And she looked fucking gorgeous while she was at it.

I've seen plenty of women playing the assassin part and dressing up in leather for Halloween. I usually find it appalling. But with Siren, knowing she could back up the look with real skills only increased my intrigue.

I want to see her again. I want to know how she reacts in different situations, and I want to know how to break her. I don't believe I'll toy with her though. There's no need. It would be disrespectful toward her skills, a slap in the face almost. Siren is better than that. *She deserves better than that.*

It's not often another contract killer finds themselves deserving of my respect, but Siren somehow has it. Though there's no denying she fears me. I could smell it in the air the second she realized I was there, and while I tend to get off on the fear others hold for me, it was different with her. I didn't like it. I don't want her to fear me, though she should because when it comes down to it, I will have no choice but to end her life, and I can guarantee that I will enjoy every last second of it.

She's going to make me work for it, going to put me through my paces, and I can't fucking wait. My cock hardens at just the thought of the fun we're going to share, and as I drive out of the industrial area, tailing Siren from a distance, I reach for the front of my pants. Freeing my cock, I grasp it with one hand as the other holds on to the steering wheel, following every turn that Siren takes.

My fist works up and down my cock, gliding over my velvety skin and roaming over my tip as I picture all the fun I'll have with Siren. She's fucking beautiful. Drop dead gorgeous. And playing with her is going to be the most fun I've ever had. But more than that, I want to hear how she screams, how she feels when I spread those creamy thighs and fuck her tight little cunt. I bet she's fucking wild between the sheets, but I don't doubt for one second that she's the type to take control. Only with me, she won't. She'll have no choice but to give it up for me, to submit to me, because no matter the situation, I will never relinquish control.

I want to taste her, make her lose control, and only when she's about to explode, I want to bend her over and claim her ass. Fuck. It'll be magical. Maybe I should hold out on ending her life. The two of us could use these next twenty-nine days to our advantage, spending every last minute fucking like wild animals as the rest of the contenders take each other out.

My hips jolt at the thought, and I clench my jaw as pleasure pulses through my veins.

"Fuck."

My fingers stretch down, cupping my balls and giving them just a moment of relief before curling around my length once again. It's too much. Too good, but with her . . . it'll be incredible. I picture the warmth that will come when I sink into her, the way her cunt would squeeze me as my eyes instantly roll. I clench myself tighter, desperate for a release.

My fist works faster as I quickly push myself to the edge, mindlessly taking another corner as Siren leads me on a wild goose chase, wanting to play it smart. She's taking every precaution after seeing me tonight, not wanting to lead me right back to her temporary home, but she will fail.

My hips push up as I fuck my hand, precum pooling at my tip as my desperation becomes too much. I need to sink into her.

It's too much. This isn't what I came here for. I can't afford to be distracted by this woman, and yet, I can't bring myself to drive away. I need this like I've never needed anything else, and I feel the exact moment I become obsessed with the idea of making her lose control, the idea of tasting her as she comes on my tongue.

This woman will belong to me.

The thought of how the next twenty-nine days will play out launches me over the edge, and as my tight fist works me up and down, my balls tighten with desperation, pushing me until I can't possibly hold on a second longer. My release comes shooting out of me, hot spurts of cum pooling into my palm as I groan with satisfaction.

I suck in a breath through my clenched jaw, riding out my release while knowing that nothing will compare to how it will be with Siren. How our bodies will fit together. How a light sheen of sweat will coat her skin as she works me to completion. How she'll cater to every last desire I have. I knew these games were going to be interesting, but I never could have anticipated this.

As I drive through the streets of Blue Springs, watching Siren's tail lights disappear around a corner, I reach for a napkin in my center console to clean myself up. I can't say I anticipated this either. Madly jerking off while stalking a woman back to her home wasn't on my bingo card for War Games, and yet here we are.

I follow Siren for another hour, grinning to myself as she takes every detour imaginable to make sure no one is following her. She's smart. She knows I wouldn't have just left the warehouse without tailing her, but when she pulls into the Blue Springs holiday resort, it becomes clear that she thinks she lost me. Her ignorance is almost endearing.

Bringing my car to a stop in an old bakery parking lot, almost a block away from the entrance of the resort, I abandon my car and go on foot. I reach the back fence of the resort in no time and launch myself over to the other side, dropping down into the manicured grass.

I have to give it to Siren, she's chosen a nice location to spend the duration of the War Games. No one would have guessed a holiday resort. I can't fault her, if she wants to spend the next twenty-nine days lounging by the heated pool with bar service and relaxing in the sun, then who am I to judge? Most of the other contenders I was able to sniff out last night are staying in hourly hotels or squatting in abandoned homes, apart from The Boston Maneater, who clearly favored sleeping in old rundown warehouses. Though I'm sure as the games go on and the contenders begin to get desperate, their hotel rooms and homes will be traded out for something a little less . . . obvious. They'll have to get creative if they plan on hiding from me.

Making my way through the resort, I search every villa until I stumble upon her dented Range Rover parked on a curb. The car is beautiful, satin wrapped, all the extras, but after following her for hours, it's no secret why it looks like it's been through hell. She can't drive. At all.

I shake my head. This woman needs to find a healthy respect for vehicles.

Keeping my distance, I make a quick assessment of the villa. There are four motion sensors surrounding the small building with an additional six surveillance cameras. She's not taking any chances, and while she hasn't left a single blind spot, getting in and out won't be an issue for me.

Lights flicker on inside, and I quickly look up the resort website before finding the images of their villas and making an educated guess on the layout of the property. She's in the bedroom, probably stripping out of her tight black jeans and kicking off her combat boots before picking out something skimpy to sleep in. Then she'll take her hair out, letting it fall in thick strands down her back . . . and fuck. I'm hard again.

The fuck is wrong with me?

I stand outside her villa for well over an hour, trying to familiarize myself with her routine, and when the lights turn out, I have a decision to make. I can either go in, fuck her, and then end her life . . . or I can walk away. Only one of those choices appeals to me, so tell me why the fuck I'm turning on my heel and stalking away?

My time will come with Siren, but I've never been one to rush into shit like this. I need to learn more about her, figure out who she is and what drives her. I need to know her moves, how she strikes, and what her limits are. There's a reason she's known as one of the best in the business, and I won't make a move until I figure out exactly who I'm dealing with.

After making my way back to my car, I drive through the deserted streets of Blue Springs, and it quickly becomes apparent that after eight at night, the town's people tuck themselves into bed and don't emerge until business hours the following day. I'm sure Friday and Saturday nights will differ, but whether there are witnesses or not, it doesn't change a thing for me. I'll still be capable of doing everything I need to do during these games.

Pulling to a stop outside one of the only hotels in town, I pocket my keys before making my way inside, keeping my head down as I pass by one of the only cameras that actually work in the building. It isn't exactly the most logical type of accommodation for a competition like War Games. It doesn't boast easy escapes and there are more staff than actual guests, but for tonight, it will do. Though at some point, I need to find somewhere a little more . . . homey. Somewhere I don't have to be quite so discreet.

Don't get me wrong, I enjoy the benefits of room service with a whole staff at my beck and call, but I also prefer the privacy a real home can offer. Besides, it won't be long before the hotel maids start ignoring the *Do Not Disturb* sign hanging on my door, and once that happens, people are going to start dropping like flies. I can't risk people snooping through my room because the large array of weapons hidden beneath the bed will only bring questions I'm not willing to answer.

Making my way through the hotel lobby, I pass the bar and cast my gaze over the adjoining room. A few people linger in the bar, but for the most part, it's dead. It's late and I'm sure the bar staff are counting down the minutes until they get to close. I could really use a drink, but truth be told, I think I need a cold shower more. Siren has left me wound up, and I don't fucking like it.

I live by a code. It's me, myself, and I. Women aren't a problem for me. I take what I want and leave. I have no family. No friends. Nobody to miss me. But for the first time in my life, I can't seem to let go of the idea that I should keep Siren around. I've never cared to spare someone's life before, and yet I've now walked away from her twice. That's not in my nature, and it's starting to fuck with my head. Perhaps it's all just sexual, and after I take her, whatever is forcing me to have a moral compass will finally disappear.

Frustration burns through me, and as I continue past the hotel bar, someone at a private table catches my eye, pulling me up short.

Graves.

What are the fucking chances? Last I checked, he was staying in a rundown motel, and yet, here he is just waiting to be caught.

A grin pulls at the corner of my lips. This is going to be too fucking easy.

As if sensing my stare, Graves lifts his gaze, his brows furrowed until he spots me at the entrance. His back stiffens, and I watch the color drain from his face. He discreetly stands, not wanting to draw attention before walking further into the bar and slipping out the side exit, taking him deeper into the hotel and further away from any type of surveillance or witnesses.

Decisions. Decisions.

I could go after him, or I could walk away and let him be someone else's problem.

Shit.

While I know tonight's theme seems to be *missed opportunity*, I can't seem to let this one go, and unlike Siren, I don't have the overwhelming need to fuck this guy. I watched him murder both Slasher and Crimson Rain last night, and while I have absolutely no issues with how he went after Slasher, the way he so brutally beat Crimson Rain didn't sit well with me. Don't get me wrong, my morals would never be applauded, but when going after a woman, there's a right way and a wrong way to do it, and Graves sure as fuck didn't get that memo. He deserves to be brutally murdered, and I'm more than happy to give him exactly what he asked for.

Making the decision to go for it, I cut through the bar and slip out the same side exit that Graves just took, and despite knowing he would have broken into a sprint the second he left the bar, I take my time. There's no need to rush. I'm a hunter by nature. Whether it takes a few seconds or all night, I'll find him, and when I do, he better hope he's made peace with his maker.

After escaping through the side exit of the bar, I step out into a different portion of the hotel lobby just in time to watch the elevator door close.

Fucking moron. How obvious could one person be?

Making my way toward the elevator, I keep my gaze locked on the numbers, telling me exactly where the elevator is stopping and when I see it pause at level three, I push through the door beside the elevator shaft, taking me up the stairs.

Now, would I have preferred to have an array of weapons with me for this? Sure. But are they necessary for me to get the job done? Fuck no. I've always prided myself on being a resourceful man, so I'm sure I'll figure it out when the time comes.

Reaching level three, I push out into the main hallway and pause, listening to the sounds around me. There's not a soul in sight, but Graves doesn't strike me as a smart man, and just on cue, I hear a high-pitched woman's scream tearing through the hallway.

Bingo.

Not a moment later, the woman is launched into the hallway with such force she stumbles right across the small walkway and slams into the door directly opposite her room before crumbling to the ground. I turn on my heel and begin stalking toward her, but she's on her feet and sprinting toward me in her desperate flee to escape Graves.

"Which room?" I demand as she booms toward me, keeping my head down to avoid her seeing my face.

"309."

The woman doesn't stop to see what I'm going to do, just keeps running until she reaches the stairs, which means I only have a few minutes before the front desk calls the cops. But I won't need a few minutes. I'll only need seconds.

Making my way down to 309, a sense of elation pulses through my veins. Don't get me wrong, I kill men every day, finding the hardest targets on the planet and taking them out, and while it's exhilarating, the chase is different. This right here is purely for fun, and I find myself giddy with excitement, just like I used to when I was a teenager making my first kill.

Reaching the door Graves just tossed the woman out of, I settle to the left and knock. "Housekeeping," I call out in a cheery tone.

Naturally, there's no response, and all I can do is grin, barely able to contain the thrill pulsing through me. I knock again, this time a little slower. "Turndown service? Fresh towels?"

"You don't want to fuck with me," Graves roars.

"Uhhh . . . yeah. Actually, I think I do," I tell him, enjoying the banter. After all, I don't often get to indulge in these situations. "Why don't you be a gem and open up the door? I promise, I'll make it quick. You'll barely feel a thing."

BANG! BANG!

The bullets whiz past my face at speeds my eyes can't possibly try to track before plunging into the wall on the opposite side of the hallway. "Well, shit," I laugh, glancing back at the door Graves shamefully hides behind. "I thought we were going to be friends."

I quickly assess the door and the two massive holes staring back at me, and with their positioning, the holes might have compromised the integrity of the door just enough for me to be able to kick my way through it.

Figuring that I've got nothing to lose, I make my move, quickly stepping in front of the door and slamming my boot into the fractured wood. The door flies off its hinges, the majority of it splintering into tiny pieces while I race forward, not allowing my momentum to slow even a fraction.

Graves stands at the opposite side of the room, his gun locked and loaded before him. Only he wasn't prepared for me to burst through, and his response time is far too slow.

He pulls the trigger twice more, trying to track my movements across the room as I run toward him. *BANG! BANG!* I sidestep, anticipating his shots and avoiding the bullets like a ghost in the night, and I don't stop until my body slams into his, my big hand wrapping around his throat.

I disarm him in a flash, the gun quickly becoming mine. His eyes are wide, staring at me as though he can't comprehend how I managed to get inside the room.

I slam him against the wall, the damage to his neck and face from Crimson Rain's sharp brass knuckles staring back at me. He's a fucking mess. He deserves to die just so that the rest of us don't need to look at him a second longer. If you think about it, I'm doing him a favor by ending his miserable life.

There won't be long before the woman who occupies this room makes it down to the lobby and calls for help, so I do what I can to make this quick. "It's a real shame, you know," I start. "If you had simply opened the door like I asked, we could have done this in a much more humane way."

He stutters but can't get a single word out. Instead, he wets his pants like a scared child. All I can do is shake my head in disgust. "Are you serious? You're a fucking serial killer, man. Get it together."

"I . . . I . . . I—"

"Hushhhhh," I say, lifting a sole finger to my lips as I look over the small stab wound Crimson Rain left in his neck last night. "She really did a number on you. It's a shame she missed the artery."

"She was a fucking bitch. She deserved everything she got."

"Come on, now. We don't speak ill of the dead. But I'm curious. If she deserved everything she got, then pray tell, what is it you deserve?"

"Let me go," he begs. "We can work together. I'll hunt them down, give you the credit."

A sharp laugh booms through my chest. "In what world would I possibly require your help? You are at the bottom of the food chain. You almost let a woman get the drop on you barely three seconds after the games commenced. You and I are not on the same level."

Using my free hand, I reach for his neck injury, pushing my fingers into the small stab wounds and widening the holes as he roars in agony.

"Now, if you don't mind, I'd very much like to get out of here," I inform him. "There's a cold shower calling my name." He barely gets another cry out when I sink my two fingers deeper into the wound, taking a firm hold of his skin, then with everything I've got, I tear my hand away, ripping his skin clean off his neck and breaking right through the artery that Crimson Rain missed last night.

Graves drops to the floor, blood spurting across the room, and as the bright red bodily fluid splatters over the front of my leather jacket, disappointment floods me. "Are you fucking kidding me?" I mutter, looking at Graves with an accusatory glare as though the asshole could somehow control the rapid splatter of blood coming from his torn artery. "Do you have any idea how fucking expensive this jacket is?"

Graves clutches his throat as his blood spills over his fingers and soaks into the carpet beneath my feet. His skin quickly loses color, and I let out a heavy sigh before stealing the white duvet off the bed. After laying it down on the ground, I position Graves over it, and then before he's even finished dying, I take his identification card and roll him up in the thick blanket.

Hauling him over my shoulder, I stride out through the shattered door and back into the hallway before casually strolling down to the elevator, feeling the exact moment his body gives out and the fucker finally dies. After hitting the button, it arrives within seconds and I smile to myself as the soft ding sounds through the hallway.

I make my way onto the elevator and press the button for level six while listening to the soft drip, drip, drip, of blood soaking through the blanket and splattering on the elevator floor. The door opens on the sixth floor, and I stride out into the hallway before smiling to myself as I find the hotel's housekeeping cart abandoned in the hallway.

The maid is nowhere to be seen, and as I stride past the cleaning cart, I dump Graves' body right into it, the once white blanket now the brightest shade of red. I don't skip a beat as I continue down the hall to room 611, and after swiping my access card, I enter my room, grab my shit, and get the fuck out of there.

Despite the lack of cameras and the effort made to keep my face hidden from both staff and other guests, it's too fucking risky. In the next ten minutes, the hotel will be locked down with police tape stretching from one end to the other and when that happens, I need to be anywhere but here.

Making my way back to the elevator, I pass the cleaning cart and chuckle to myself. That really was fun. I should allow myself to indulge a little more often. Reaching the elevator, I hit the call button, and when it arrives back to my floor, I step inside. As the doors close, a loud shriek tears down the hall. I guess the maid just returned to her cart, and I can't fault myself. It was marvelous timing.

Getting my ass out of here, I dive into my car and take off, putting as much distance between me and the hotel as possible. I suppose finding myself a proper home for the duration of the games is going to come a little sooner than anticipated.

As I drive through the streets, my phone buzzes in my pocket, and I pull it out to find a notification from War Games. It's exactly midnight, and they've sent out their first update.

Opening the message, I quickly scan over it.

Congratulations on making it through the first twenty-four hours of War Games.
The death toll currently stands at seven.

Those who have been eliminated are -
- Blade
- Grim
- Stone
- Slasher
- Crimson Rain
- The Boston Maneater
- Graves

So I take it Siren and I were the only ones to make kills today, which also begs the question, how the fuck do these bastards already know that Graves is dead? It happened less than six minutes ago. Either way, I suppose I don't really care.

All that matters is finding somewhere to call home, stripping out of my blood-soaked clothes, and finally taking that cold shower.

7

SIREN

Achild's laugh breaks through the silence of the resort pool area, and I glance up just in time to watch as the kid flies down the mega slide and drops into the pool, sending a wave of water cascading over me and my laptop.

"Ahhh shit," I mutter as the kid's mother rushes after him while giving me an awkward apologetic wave.

"What's wrong?" Mila says directly in my ear as I lounge by the pool in a skimpy bikini, working on my tan. Only now that there are other people using the pool, I suddenly feel a little awkward showing quite this much skin.

"Nothing," I say, trying to wipe the water off the screen before it fucks up the laptop. "Just realizing that pools and technology don't mix well."

Mila scoffs. "Only just figuring that out now?"

I roll my eyes, and once I'm confident that my laptop isn't about to shit itself, I lean back in my sun lounger and get back to work. Only, not much work is really getting done. I've been coming up blank all morning. Not that I'm surprised. I've been trying to find information on the kid, Shadow, and so far, I haven't been able to find even a hint that she exists. She's a ghost, and while I have no intention of making her a target, I've been plagued with curiosity.

What the fuck is a child doing in a competition like this? But more so, how the hell did she become a killer worthy of gaining the attention of War Games? Something must have happened to her. Don't get me wrong, anyone in my line of business has a shitload of trauma, but it takes years to develop your skills, years to learn how to become invisible, and I doubt a child at her age would have been capable of achieving that on her own. Somebody made her the way she is, and I want to know who.

Letting out a heavy sigh, I avert my gaze from the screen and to the child playing happily in the pool. "Have you got anything?" I ask Mila.

"I've been tracking 343," she tells me. "I've got him in a basement under an old record store, and judging by what's on his screen right now, he's tracking The Midnight Killer."

My interest is piqued, but something doesn't feel right about it. "How did 343 find him?"

"That's what I'm trying to figure out," she muses as I hear

her fingers moving like lightning across her keyboard. "Oh. How disappointing. It seems like another dumbass who doesn't know anything about keeping themselves concealed in public. He was caught on a surveillance camera in a store parking lot and 343 tracked his movements from there. The idiot practically drew a map with how often he's getting caught with facial recognition."

"That almost seems too easy," I murmur. "Do you think it's a trap? Maybe he's trying to draw 343 out."

"Perhaps," she says. "Or he's simply too cocky to assume he could get caught."

"It's possible. I mean, most serial killers aren't the brightest crayons in the box. It's the assassins you have to watch your back around."

"Very true. But no matter which way you look at it, if 343 goes after The Midnight Killer, that puts both of them in the same place at the same time. And even if The Midnight Killer expects to find 343, neither of them will be expecting you. Two birds, one stone."

Shit. I like the way she thinks.

"Okay. Keep tracking them," I say, closing my laptop and getting up from the sun lounger. I grab my towel and wrap it around me before scooping up my phone and stepping into my slides. "Let me know if there's any movement. I need to go get ready for a night out."

I can picture Mila rolling her eyes so perfectly. "Okay, but if you don't use that black lipstick again, I'm going to come down there and kill you myself. I think it's your new signature look."

I laugh and roll my eyes. "I think you might be right," I tell her. "Maybe I should go get a little cat-ear headband to match my ring."

"Don't even think about it. You're taking it from sexy assassin to bad Halloween costume, and if that's the route you wanna go, then unfortunately, I'm going to have to sever ties with you. How am I supposed to be taken seriously as the go-to underground computer hacker when my partner in crime looks like she's going to her first high school party?"

"Okay, okay," I laugh. "No cat ears. Message received."

"Good. Now leave me alone. I wanna figure out The Midnight Killer's plan before 343 does so you can get there before both of them and have the best vantage point."

Mila doesn't bother with a goodbye, just ends the call and leaves me to walk peacefully back to my little villa, and as I do, I glance over my security system, making sure no one has come for me in the few hours I've been gone. Though my motion sensors would have alerted me if they had.

It's day five of the competition, and since the night I took out The Boston Maneater, no one else has been eliminated, apart from Graves, of course. But I still haven't been able to figure out who took him out. Either way, it's one less contender I have to worry about.

There are thirteen of us left in the game, but after tonight, we'll be down to eleven. Whether 343 and The Midnight Killer take themselves out, or if I have to do it myself. All I know is that I won't be leaving without two more ID cards.

Reaching my villa, I do a quick sweep of the area, making sure I'm well and truly alone, despite already having confirmation from my security system. I've been lucky here. No one has found me yet, and on top of that, while I'm not eliminating losers from the competition, I get to spend my time relaxing by the pool and working on my tan.

With the coast clear, I make my way back inside my villa and get ready for a night filled with fun. I'm sure it'll still be hours before I have to leave, but I prefer to always be ready, even if it means having to spend the next few hours with weapons strapped to my chest.

I beeline straight for my room before diving through the array of clothes I brought with me, and I can't help but reach for the same black jeans and combat boots I wore the other night. What can I say? I like to be comfortable, but more than that, I like how these jeans fit my ass, and any girl knows that when something works, you don't make changes. Why fix something that isn't broken, right?

As for my top, this is where things get difficult. I must have brought every single top I own, and yes, every last piece of clothing inside my bag is black. But when you're supposed to be sticking to the shadows and keeping out of sight, black clothing is a necessity. I go simple with a racerback tank, and the moment I'm fully dressed, I turn my attention to my hair and makeup, going for my signature look with my hair up in a high pony and the long strands plaited down to my ass. Then, just for Mila's sake, I paint my lips black before focusing on my eyes.

After forty-five minutes, I'm completely ready, and I spend the next few hours checking over my weapons before getting back to trying to find anything I can on the ghost otherwise known as Shadow.

I'm not surprised when I come up blank, but just before I can get frustrated at myself, a call comes through from Mila, and I quickly accept it.

"What have you got for me?" I say, already closing my laptop and grabbing everything I need.

"You were right. The Midnight Killer left a trail online to lure out 343, and it's working like a charm. He's going to lead him into the old burned-down gym on Tucker Boulevard. There's a new gym on the right. You'll pass that one up, and the old one will be on the left-hand side. You can't miss it."

"Got it."

"He always strikes at midnight, hence his ridiculous name, so be ready for that," she tells me. "But also, if everyone knew my tactics during a game like this, I'd be looking to change things up, so keep that in mind too. He'll be doing whatever he can to look for an edge. Same for 343, but at least they're looking for each other and not you. Let them do the dirty work and then swoop in and steal your prize at the end."

"You scare me sometimes, you know that right?"

Mila scoffs. "Says the best contract killer in the country."

"Second best," I remind her, glancing out the window before making my move to my car.

"As far as I'm concerned, Reaper is still a figment of everyone's imagination. Just because you saw him a few times, doesn't make it real. It was just your mind playing tricks on you. I refuse to believe he actually exists."

"Ahhhh, gotta love a delusional best friend."

"Shut up," she laughs. "Just get your ass moving, otherwise, they'll beat you there."

"Already leaving," I say just as the engine kicks over.

"Alright. Let me know how it goes."

I arrive at the gym within fifteen minutes and park in a side alley next to the neighboring complex. Mila wasn't lying when she said the old gym had burned down. The place is practically a shell. Well, that's a little bit of an exaggeration. Four charred walls still stand, and that's all that counts.

Breaking into the old gym consists of nothing more than stepping over yellow police tape that looks as though it's been here for years. The new gym across the road has been there long enough for the signage to start fading, so I can only assume the old gym burned down years ago and the city either didn't have the funds to level it, or they simply didn't care to.

I'm not so obvious as to stride right through the charred remains of what once was the front door, so I find a missing section of wall to make my grand entrance. Though, considering there isn't another soul in sight, there's really nothing grand about it.

I make my way inside and scope out the gym. It's not the best location for a kill, but I can definitely see why The Midnight Killer wanted to lure 343 here. It's dark with no surveillance, and the building, despite not having much to it anymore, still boasts the metal framework. It's got potential, and to be completely honest, I can't figure out why the owner has left it abandoned all these years. There's so much that could be done with it. It just needs a little love first.

It's clear that teens have often used the space as their weekend hang out area. What little walls still remain are covered in graffiti while a space has been cleared in the center that's now filled with mismatched deck chairs and loungers. Not to mention the empty beer bottles and a broken bong discarded on the ground.

I'm hidden well within the old gym when I hear the familiar sound of someone's feet crunching through the charred remains. My gaze follows the sound, expecting to see The Midnight Killer, arriving early to set his trap, only when a scrawny tech guy cuts through the gym, my brows arch. Perhaps he knew he was being lured into a trap after all.

The Midnight Killer is a big guy. It's clear he spends a lot of his time in places just like this, though I'm expecting the gyms he frequents aren't exactly in this condition. 343 on the other hand, is his polar opposite. He's scrawny and looks as though he's never ventured further than his mother's basement. I can only assume that guys like 343 spent their whole childhood running away from men like The Midnight Killer, and I hope that if 343 is able to make the kill, it gives him at least a little joy. Though that joy won't last long since I have to take him out afterward.

It's roughly fifteen minutes until midnight, and I can assume that The Midnight Killer will be arriving soon, and with what little time he has, 343 begins setting up the area, clearly unaware of his audience.

He begins moving weights around the room, putting them in easily accessible places as he tries to anticipate how this is going to go. He'll have one shot to take out The Midnight Killer before he overpowers him, so whatever he does, he's got to make it count.

He hangs ropes over the exposed metal beams and positions the stray deck chairs and loungers in ways that make any line of escape difficult. 343 clearly knows what he's doing. He's obviously very smart, which is how I assume he's been able to get this far without getting caught. It's probably also safe to assume his usual victims are men just like The Midnight Killer—men who have lived solely for the purpose of making guys like 343 miserable.

Once 343 has the gym exactly how he wants it, he fixes a few portable surveillance cameras on top of old machinery, and I hold my breath as he positions one far too close for comfort. But he's clearly not as smart as he thinks he is as he turns the camera away from me and walks over to one of the benches. He sits down, makes sure all the cameras are working and connected to his phone, and then walks straight back out of the gym.

Fucking idiot.

I take the few minutes alone to pull out my phone and give Mila a quick update.

Siren – 343 put up cameras in the gym. Can you get in?
Mila – Give me two minutes.

I wait for what feels like an eternity before I feel my phone softly vibrating in my back pocket. My finger brushes over the small earpiece in my right ear, and a second later, Mila's voice comes through the line. "I'm in," she tells me. "You good?"

"Mmhmm."

She knows I can't respond. After all, she's got my exact location at all times. She knows I'm right in the middle of the gym, doing what I can not to get sprung, so she doesn't push me for any more of a response than that.

"343 is in the back. I assume he's in what used to be a storage room. It's too small to be a bathroom."

I nod, despite Mila not being able to see me. "And The Midnight Killer?" I murmur, keeping my voice as low as possible.

"343 set up a few cameras outside. A black charger is pulling into the parking lot of the new gym. Could be him."

"What's he look like?"

She pauses, waiting as the guy finishes parking his car before finally getting out. "Big guy. Looks like he's on roids. Dressed in all black. Could be your guy," she says. "Hold up. We have a winner. He's crossing the road."

A grin pulls at the corners of my lips, excitement pulsing through my veins.

"Fuck me," Mila scoffs. "He's not even trying to be discreet about it. I think this guy's ego is too big for his own head. There's something about the way he walks. He's too confident."

"Yeah, well he's about to walk straight into a trap."

"Oop. He's got a gun. Watch your back," she tells me just as I hear 343 creeping back toward the main floor of the charred gym. "He's almost there. Walking through the main entrance in three . . . two . . . one."

A figure appears right at the door, striding into the gym as though he hasn't got a care in the world. A twisted grin rests on his lips, and as

I take my phone from my back pocket and spare a quick glance at the time, I'm not surprised to find it's exactly midnight.

It's almost poetic. Actually, I change my mind. It's more lame than poetic. It's predictable, and in this line of business, predictability is what gets you killed.

The Midnight Killer strides around the old gym, taking it all in as though he hadn't bothered to scope it out before making this the location of his hit. Big mistake if you ask me. He's done nothing more than a simple Google search, and because of that, he'll lose his life tonight.

He searches the gym for another minute before lowering himself into one of the mismatched deck chairs, facing the main entrance. Mistake number two. As a general rule, no one is stupid enough to walk straight through the front door—except this guy of course. He should be watching his back, not the door.

"Is this guy for real?" Mila scoffs in my ear, the judgment thick in her slight Russian accent.

343 appears from the back, slowly creeping closer, only as he gets the perfect visual of The Midnight Killer, he pauses to assess, taking in his position in relation to every last possible exit. Whatever conclusion he comes to, he seems to be happy to finally make his move, silently creeping toward him.

He reaches for the rope dangling from the metal beam in the exposed ceiling, clutching it tightly in his palm before fixing his stare on The Midnight Killer. He stops directly behind him, tying a noose in the rope, and as the opposite end of the rope shifts with the movement,

The Midnight Killer's head whips around. Only it's too late.

The noose is hooked over his head, and before he gets a chance to move one of those beefy muscles, 343 shoves one of the heavy weights he'd so carefully placed around the charred gym, and like lightning, the noose tightens around his neck and sends him flying to the ceiling, his neck snapping almost instantly.

"What in the ever-loving fuck just happened?" Mila murmurs, just as confused as I am.

I watch in amazement. I wasn't quite sure what I was expecting to happen, but it sure as hell wasn't that. Then, as 343 sets his sights on the dangling limp man hanging from the ceiling, I lean out from my hiding spot, trying to figure out how the hell he got up there. It takes me a moment to work it out in the dark, but it looks like he made a pulley system out of the rope, the weights, and the metal beam.

I have to give it to him. It was genius, and now The Midnight Killer is completely at his mercy. I suppose that's what happens when kids actually pay attention at school instead of spending their days trying to get laid.

343 sits back in the deck chair that The Midnight Killer so violently flew from and simply waits, his work for the night done and dusted.

It was impressive. I've got to give credit where credit is due. I wouldn't have thought of it.

The Midnight Killer is gone in seconds, and once his body goes completely still, 343 finally pulls himself from the deck chair and begins climbing up the gym equipment. He reaches toward the body, digging through the guy's pocket, probably searching for his identification, and

I figure, what better time to announce myself than now?

"Alright, Mila," I murmur, keeping my voice as low as possible. "If you don't want to see your hero go down, then I suggest it's time to look away."

"Go get him, girl." The line goes quiet, but it doesn't go dead, and I don't doubt that Mila is chilling in the background, always watching my back.

Stepping out from where I've been hidden for almost forty-five minutes, I step toward 343, my gaze cast up toward the ceiling as I watch him struggle to balance while fishing through The Midnight Killer's wallet.

I clap my hands together, giving him a round of applause. "Wow, that was quite the show," I say, only my presence in the charred gym surprises him a little too much and the idiot loses his balance. He falls back with a loud cry, and I watch in horror as he crashes to the ground, the center of his spine slamming down on a discarded dumbbell and sending a sickening crack through the gym.

His body shifts, somehow releasing the opposite end of the rope that was keeping The Midnight Killer suspended in the air. As The Midnight Killer's body slams back to the ground, the rope catches in the back of my hair, knotting itself and sending me flying right up to the ceiling.

"Holy fucking—woah! FUCK!" I cry out, suddenly dangling from my hair as I clutch onto my scalp, hoping like fuck this isn't how I die. Not like this. I'm better than this.

A second of silence passes as I try to assess the situation.

The Midnight Killer is dead. 343 is paralyzed on the ground. And I am hanging from my hair.

How the fuck did we get here?

"Siren?" Mila asks in my ear. "Please tell me I'm not seeing you hanging by your hair when you're supposed to be making a quick kill and getting your ass out of there?"

Well, shit. That's embarrassing. "I'll be fine, Mills. Just give me a minute to figure out how the hell I'm supposed to get out of this."

"Okay. Don't do anything stupid," she says. "Oh wait. You already did!"

"Bye, Mills."

"Don't die on me, moron," she says, and with that, the call goes dead, leaving me in peace to get myself out of this mess.

My gaze shifts over 343, not quite stupid enough to ask for help, but as he stares up at me in shock, I can't help but smile. "So . . . that's not how I imagined any of that going down."

"Who—Who the fuck are you?" 343 grunts in pain.

"Your worst fucking nightmare," I say in a stupid tone. I've always wanted to say that, but the right opportunity has never popped up. I laugh to myself, and seeing that he's clearly not amused, I roll my eyes and give a straight answer. "I'm Siren. Do you really not recognize me from the initial circle meeting?"

"It's dark in here. Give me a break."

"No can do," I say, feeling my hair pulling my scalp. Having no other choice, I hold on to my braid and pull myself up just an inch, trying to relieve the ache. "Listen, there's no simple way to free myself, is there?"

"Nope. You're just about as fucked as I am."

I scoff. Nobody is as fucked as he is right now. I'll figure a way out of this—one that doesn't include scalping myself—and when I do, I'll happily walk away without anybody ever having known what the hell went down here tonight. There's no denying it. This is the most humiliating moment of my career so far. What's even more frustrating is that there are at least six knives on me right now, and I can't reach for a single one of them without scalping myself.

Fuck me in the ass and call me Frank. How is this my life right now?

"So, this guy was your first kill for the games?" I ask, wanting to make small talk despite already knowing the answer.

"Yeah, and it would have been flawless if you hadn't interrupted."

"I mean, technically you made the kill. It's not like you can't claim it just because I happened to be here to watch the whole thing."

He rolls his eyes. "I suppose. What about you? Made any kills?"

"The Boston Maneater," I confirm. "He already had three others under his belt, so I guess I can claim them as well. And not to be rude or anything, but I will also have to kill you once I get my ass down from here, so I suppose I can also claim you and The Midnight Killer."

"Fuck. If I could move my arms right now, I'd put a bullet right between your eyes."

"I know," I say with a heavy sigh, disappointed in myself for allowing this to happen. I need to be better than this. I shouldn't be making mistakes at this point in my career.

"You really took out The Boston Maneater?" he questions with a chuckle. "I was hoping to get to him first. He's had it out for me ever since I planted the evidence that he was a cannibal."

"No shit," I laugh, noticing how the color is starting to drain from his skin. "That was you? The guy certainly had a complex about that."

"Yeah, I know. It was great."

"Listen," I say, glancing up at the beam above my head and wondering if I'll be able to somehow swing myself high enough to hook my legs around it and take the pressure off my scalp. "I don't think you're going to make it out of here tonight."

343 nods. "Yeah, I'm starting to see that."

I give him a tight smile, feeling bad for the guy. I enjoy killing people, sure. But 343 falling and breaking his spine was nothing more than an accident. He's slowly dying on the ground, and I can't even put him out of his misery. It's not a great way to go. If everything had gone smoothly, I would have made it quick. But this? I don't know. It pulls at the heartstrings.

Needing to focus on me and not the dying man on the ground, I clutch tighter onto my hair and try to climb up it, but it becomes ridiculously clear that I need to start logging more hours in the gym. I'm already starting to work up a sweat.

I try again, getting just an inch closer to the beam, trying to swing my legs up over my head to reach the beam but I'm simply too far away. My arms are starting to get sore, and it won't be long until the last of my strength diminishes.

My hair is strong, and with it plaited, I doubt it will break, but an accidental scalping is a real issue I don't exactly want to experience.

As I dangle from the ceiling, I realize that 343 was right. I am just as fucked as he is.

8

REAPER

My brows furrow as I watch Siren dangling from her hair at the top of the old gym, making small talk with 343, who's as good as dead on the ground. I watched the whole thing, been here since the second Siren pulled up, and yet, I still can't seem to wrap my head around how the fuck we got here. What I do know is that Siren is too far ahead in her career to be making stupid fucking mistakes like this.

I'm disappointed. I expected more out of her. Is she really as good as I thought she was, or has she been flying by on sheer luck?

She's in quite the predicament. There are weapons all over her body. She could easily reach for one of the many knives strapped to her thigh and cut her hair. But in order to do that, she would have to release the hold on her hair and risk scalping herself the second her body weight dropped. It's not exactly a position I'd ever want to find myself in, nor would I be foolish enough to get myself in that position in the first place.

As for The Midnight Killer, I had high hopes for him during these games. I thought he'd be one to make me work for the kill in the final days, but to have watched a scrawny tech guy like 343 take him out is an embarrassment. Though if I'm honest, my hopes for The Midnight Killer began to dwindle the second he made the decision to leave breadcrumbs all over the internet. He should have laid low and let the weak ones battle it out first. Instead, he took a risk and this time, it didn't pay off.

I've got to give it to 343, he played the game well. He's smart. He's aware of his strengths and weaknesses and knows how to use those weaknesses as strengths. It's impressive, and if he hadn't just paralyzed himself on a dumbbell, he had the potential to go far in this competition. That is until I inevitably took him out.

"So," Siren asks, clearly having given up on trying to free herself. "What's 343 mean anyway?"

Her gaze shifts down to the dying man, and the compassion in her eyes tells me she's not just making small talk with him because she's bored and awkward, it's because she doesn't want him to die while feeling alone.

He scoffs. "343. It's the amount of letters in The Tech Guy."

"That's it?" Siren questions in disgust. "That's the big secret of your name? I've been trying to work that out for years."

"What do you want from me? I wanted a cool name with a bit of mystery. The Tech Guy is so . . . "

"Boring? Unoriginal? Lacking?"

"Exactly."

The slightest noise sounds from my left, and my gaze whips around to find the young girl I'd seen on the very first night—Shadow. Only there's no way she could have gotten there without me seeing her, which could only mean that she was here before me. But that's not possible. I followed Siren here right from the resort. There was no one else around. I watched as Siren checked her surroundings and made sure she wasn't being watched or followed. Clearly she didn't see me, but I didn't expect her to. I've learned to be invisible. Shadow though, there's no way she could have been there too. I don't miss shit like this.

And yet, clearly I did, because this kid has been here longer than me, and it's taken until now for me to have realized. I've been here for fifty-three minutes exactly, barely three feet away from Shadow.

What the fuck is wrong with me? Am I losing my edge?

No, that's not possible. I'm too good, which could only mean that Shadow is better. But how? She's just a kid. I've spent years perfecting my skills. I'm thirty-four and made my first kill nearly twenty years ago and ever since then, I have worked my ass off to make sure I was the best. And yet, here's this kid, maybe thirteen or fourteen years old, and she's capable of evading me.

The curiosity eats me alive. I need to learn more about this girl, figure out how she is the way she is, who made her like this, and what kind of bullshit she's been through to ensure this level of competence.

My stare lingers on her when she lets out a sigh and turns to face me. "That was disappointing," she says, pushing herself off the charred wall and striding toward me. Only as a general rule, nobody ever comes toward me, especially without even a hint of fear in her eyes. She walks right by me, stepping over discarded weights and burned rubble. She takes a few steps past me before turning back and meeting my stare. "I had high hopes for Siren. Looks like it'll just be you and me battling it out at the end. Hope you can stomach the idea of going up against me. Not many can."

Shadow turns and walks away into the night, and I stare after her a moment, trying to figure out what the fuck just went down, but when she disappears around the corner, I find myself going after her.

I hurry, wanting to catch up to her, only as I turn the same corner she just went around, I find the area completely bare. Not a soul in sight.

Where the fuck did she go? She truly is a shadow, nothing more than a ghost in the night, and I don't doubt this kid is going to be the end of me.

Frustration burns through me. Nobody has ever bested me before, and it makes me uneasy, but if anybody is going to kill me, I'd prefer it be some kid over some poorly trained serial killer who learned everything he knows from watching true crime documentaries.

Returning to the gym to make sure Siren doesn't scalp herself, I settle myself exactly where I was before, only this time, my presence doesn't go unnoticed by Siren. Feeling the weight of her terrified stare locked on me, I glance up and meet her gaze, and while she's fearful, there's also something else there. Curiosity? Intrigue? Mortification? The only question is, do I save her or kill her?

Fuck.

Save her? Who the fuck do I think I am? I've never willingly saved anyone in my life, and now I'm looking at this woman as though I suddenly developed a moral compass.

What the hell is going on with me? First Shadow evades me, and now I'm willing to save someone who's only going to try and take my life later. Maybe I'm getting soft.

I need to walk away. I need to forget about this woman and find something else to occupy my thoughts. Then, letting out a sigh, I do just that, turning on my heel and leaving just the way I came, only a soft plea fills the emptiness.

"Please."

Siren's voice is like a shot straight through the chest, pulling me up short.

"Reaper, please," she begs, her tone almost inaudible. "You know I'm better than this. I've been dreaming about War Games for years. I can't let it end like this. Give me a chance."

I close my eyes, knowing I should let this go. Knowing I should walk away and forget about the woman who's left me rock hard every fucking night for the past five nights. So why the fuck can't I seem to put one foot in front of the other?

Siren is terrified of me, and asking me to return to help her would have taken a shitload of guts, so perhaps I need to locate my balls and show the same kind of strength. If she can step out of her comfort zone, then why the fuck shouldn't I?

Swallowing past the unease, I turn and lock my gaze on Siren's once again and watch as a strange mix of relief and fear flash through her eyes. She didn't expect me to turn back or to show a scrap of compassion, and honestly, the idea is fucking with me too.

I make my way deeper into the charred gym, my eyes never straying from hers as I unsheathe a blade from the holster on my belt. Siren's eyes widen, fearing the worst, but as I release the knife with a flick of my wrist and watch it sink deep into 343's throat, she begins to relax.

"I suppose you're going to want to take credit for that kill," Siren mutters.

To be honest, I couldn't give a shit about the credit. They're all going to be mine by the end of the games anyway. Assuming Shadow doesn't get the drop on me. But then, I don't see how this is supposed to end. I won't kill a child, no matter how good she is, so there's no other option but for me to die.

I make my way toward her in silence, pulling a new knife from my hip.

"Ahh fuck. You are going to kill me, aren't you? I knew I shouldn't have said anything."

My gaze settles on the rope as I try to figure out the best way to get her down. It's obvious I'll have to cut her hair. She watches me in return, her gaze narrowed as though trying to read me, and when I lift my arm, readying to throw the knife, those deadly green eyes of hers spring wide with horror. "Oh hell no. If you even think about cutting my hair, I'll gut you like a fish where you stand."

I pause at that, dropping my gaze back to hers. She's in the middle of being rescued from her stupid, foolish mistake, and she wants to threaten me? She's in no position to make threats, but I still find her threat endearing. Even on the verge of death, she doesn't let up on her attitude.

I think I like this girl.

Adjusting my hold on the knife, I let it fly through the air, severing the rope right above the knot in her hair, and like a heavy sack of shit, Siren drops to the ground with an ear-piercing scream.

"Fuck," she grunts as her ass hits the floor, and I have no doubt that will leave a nasty bruise. She gets to her feet, rubbing her ass while fixing me with a filthy stare. "Really? Out of all the ways you could have gotten me down, that's the one you chose?"

"I think the words you're looking for are thank you," I tell her, watching as she shrinks away, not having expected me to actually respond.

Her body stiffens, and she takes a reluctant step back while doing everything in her power to look unbothered by my presence.

Surprise, she's failing.

"Thank you," she says, the words sounding like poison on her tongue as she pulls her long plait over her shoulder. She gets busy doing what she can to release the remaining rope from her long strands while I stand here, unsure what to do.

"So, umm . . ." she starts awkwardly, her gaze flicking to the lifeless bodies of 343 and The Midnight Killer. "Are you going to take their IDs?"

I scoff. "You can keep them warm for me, Little Siren, but don't worry, I'll be back for them real soon." And with that, I turn on my heel and walk away.

9

SIREN

What in the ever-loving fuck just happened? I don't even know what to feel about it. Embarrassment that Reaper just witnessed the lowest point of my career or relief that he was there to save my stupid ass. Either way, I'm now left even more confused than I was before.

This is the third time he's shown up like that. Well, I suppose the first time while on the roof doesn't exactly count. He was already there and watched me make a break for the roof, but then he stayed and made a point that he was untouchable. The other two times—tonight and with The Boston Maneater—were different. He specifically made a point to be there. With The Boston Maneater, I could have easily shrugged it off as a coincidence, but twice in a row? There's no coincidence here. He's been tracking me, and he's been doing it flawlessly.

Every step I have taken has been done with caution, except for one slight mistake with a rope, but that's beside the point. I have been careful. Everywhere I go, I've made sure that I'm not being followed. I take extra precautions, watch my back at every step. There's no way he should be able to track me, but he keeps showing up.

Why me, though? Am I his biggest target? His biggest threat? Or does he simply just enjoy watching the show? Either way, I want answers, and I want them now.

Leaving the IDs of The Midnight Killer and 343 behind, I make a break for it, racing out of the burned-down gym and tracking every step that Reaper has taken. I know I shouldn't. Every fiber of my body is telling me to run in the opposite direction. But what can I say? I'm a sucker for punishment. If he was going to kill me, he would have done it when I was dangling by my hair, and for whatever reason, he didn't. Now I need to figure out why.

My gaze scans the night. He's nowhere to be seen, but I forge ahead anyway, sticking to the shadows and tracking him the way I would a target. It's not rocket science. There's a bright side of the road, lit up by the new gym and on the opposite side, there's dark alleys covered in shadows.

I'll take my chances with the dark side of the road.

Putting one foot in front of the other, I make my way down the path, keeping myself discreet as I pass building after building, checking the alleys before moving on. He's a ghost, so I have to think like one.

My head hurts from the almost scalping, and at some point, I'm going to have to take a few painkillers and lay down for the foreseeable future, maybe book a scalp massage, but until then, I'm determined to find this asshole.

Passing a twenty-four-hour laundromat, a chill sails down my spine, and that's enough to know I'm in the right spot. Reaper is the only one who's ever been capable of drawing such a reaction out of my body, and with that, I stop at the very next alley, turning to face the darkness.

I don't see a thing, but the chill in my bones doesn't fade, and as I scan the darkness, I know without a doubt he's here somewhere. But like I said, he's a ghost, and I need to start thinking like one.

Continuing forward, I head down the dark alley, taking it slow as I scan my surroundings. He's been tracking me since the second War Games started, and I've been blind to it, but that stops now.

I pass by the back entrance of the laundromat before sailing on past old, discarded boxes that have been chewed by mice and a large dumpster that hasn't seen warm water and soap for years. The smell that comes with it is disgusting, and just as I pass far enough to take a breath without wanting to gag, a hand shoots toward me, gripping my throat before slamming me against the brick wall of the laundromat.

"Why the fuck are you following me?" Reaper growls, his imposing body hovering over mine and making my knees shake with fear.

Holy fucking shit.

He's terrifying, but it's not so much his large body that has me shaking in my boots, it's the emptiness of his dark eyes. There's just something so intriguing about them. I knew he was attractive the second I saw him. He's deathly attractive, the most breathtaking human I've ever seen, but up close like this, he's simply . . . everything.

There's the slightest hint of his tattoos peeking out from the neckline of his shirt, and just like the last time I saw them, it leaves me desperate to see more. Desperate to find out what art decorates his strong body. But as I stand closer than I've ever been, I notice something new about him—a scar. It starts at the top of his brow and slices straight through to the center of his cheekbone, leaving me intrigued and needing to know exactly what happened to him.

I wonder what he would do if I were to reach up and touch it, to brush my fingers across the angry scarring on his face. Would I lose my life or just my fingers? Or perhaps I wouldn't lose anything at all. The one thing I know for sure is that being intrigued about a man like this could only mean trouble for me.

His fingers tighten on my throat, but not enough to block my airway, and I can't lie, if I weren't about to shit my pants with fear, this would absolutely turn me on. His fingers are large, and I can feel the underlying strength within them. He could snap my neck if he wanted to, and yet all that matters is how warm his skin is against mine.

What the fuck is wrong with me? I need to get my shit together before this man leaves me as nothing more than a forgotten body in an old alleyway.

Swallowing past the fear, I shove his chest, and he backs up, shock flickering in those lifeless eyes as though he hadn't expected me to be so bold. Though I suppose that doesn't happen often for him. People crumble under his stare, run in the opposite direction, never seek him out, and they sure as fuck never fight back.

"Why did you do it?" I demand. "Why spare me?"

He stares at me as though he can't get a read on me, and honestly, I don't blame him. I can't seem to get a read on me either. "Would you have preferred that I didn't?" he asks, recovering from his earlier shock and creeping back in, his fingers testing their limits on my throat.

I clench my jaw, certain he doesn't intend to kill me, at least not tonight. "You don't think I'm worth your time, do you?" I question as an ugliness begins to take hold of my chest. After all, I haven't worked as hard as I have just to be pushed aside and looked over when it actually matters.

Those lifeless eyes hold mine with such scrutiny it's hard to hold his stare. "Oh, how easily your ego is bruised, Little Siren."

I fix him with a heavy stare, letting him know I'm not backing down until I get the answers I'm looking for, and when he lets out a heavy sigh and loosens his hold on my neck, a shiver sails down my spine, only this one isn't like the chills I got earlier. This is different.

His eyes become softer, suddenly no longer lifeless, but filled with a deep excitement that makes my heart race, and I don't doubt he feels it with the heavy beat of my pulse thrumming against his fingers at the base of my throat. "Killing you would be the greatest reward I've ever achieved, Kienna James."

I suck in a gasp, my back stiffening as he uses my real name—a name that not even I have used since I was fourteen years old.

His fingers loosen further, and as he holds my stare, his hand grows heavy, sinking lower and dropping to my chest. "I have watched you closely these past few days. You have intrigued me. Your moves are divine, and when you take a life, it's like a precise dance, an absolute masterpiece. To take your life would be nothing less than an honor. When I kill you, which I will, sweet Siren, I expect it will be a kill worthy of shouting from a rooftop."

I lift my chin, and it doesn't go unnoticed how his body presses in closer, his hard edges right up against my soft ones. "I see," I whisper, his lips only a breath away from mine as the sexual tension in the air almost cripples me. "You're all about the chase? You like a woman who'll make you work for it."

His hand drops lower, grasping my waist and squeezing tight, and he presses me harder against the brick wall. "I like a woman who gets on her knees and begs for it."

Well, fuck. For him, I'll beg until my throat is raw, not that I'm about to let him know that.

My hand slips up the front of his black shirt, brushing across the hard ridges of his abs before roaming higher to his wide chest. My fingers splay over his warm skin, and as my knees grow weaker with a deep need, I can't help but fantasize about how good it could be between us. "You really think I'm about to give it up for you?" I ask, letting my fingers explore his strong chest.

His lips drop to the base of my throat, roaming over my skin the same way my fingers roam over his. "I don't see why not," he murmurs against my neck. "You'll be dead in the next twenty-five days, so I don't see why you shouldn't enjoy what little time you have left."

A sharp scoff tears out of my throat, his callous words like a bucket of ice water being tipped over my head. I shove him back, freeing my hand from the confines of his tight shirt as I hold his heated stare. "You're a little too confident for a dead man."

"Don't be foolish, Little Siren," he says, a hint of amusement in his deep tone. "You and I both know you won't get the drop on me."

"Is that so?" I ask, stepping away from him, taking note of how easily he allows me to go.

Reaper's only response is to nod, and I can't help the smile that cuts across my face. This is the best foreplay I've ever had. "We'll see about that," I tell him. "Oh, and next time you call me by my real name, I will put a bullet through your brain."

He nods again. "Noted."

"Good."

Walking away, I make my way back up the alley. Only I stop once I reach the top and glance back at him one more time, hating how fucking wet he made me. I'm going to have to get my ass home and deal with this before I explode.

He's watching me leave, and as I capture his dark gaze one last time, a wicked grin stretches across my face. "For the record, when you get me all worked up and wet like this again, you better have the fucking balls to follow through."

Reaper takes a step as if to come and show me just how well he can follow through, but before he gets a chance to show me just how good it could be, I'm gone.

After all, it's best to always keep them wanting, right? Because at least that way, when he sees me next, he's going to be thinking a little less about killing me and more about fucking me raw. And that right there is a plan I can more than get down with.

Making my way back to the old gym, I take my time, knowing that Reaper won't be coming after me again tonight. I'm sure he crossed many of his own boundaries by saving me, talking to me, and touching me tonight, just as I've crossed many of my own.

Seducing the enemy? Allowing him to get that close? Not exactly my finest hour. He could have killed me at any moment, but I felt safe with him. I believed that he didn't want to hurt me, and when I pushed him back, letting him know he was getting too close, he gave me the space I needed. Don't get me wrong, I fully believe that when the time comes, he'll end me just as he's promised, but until then, I don't think he means me any harm. If anything, I think he's curious about me, and as long as he remains curious, then I'll live to see another day.

Though if I allow myself to be as foolish as I was tonight, then perhaps that whole living to see another day thing won't actually be the case. I fucked up, made a colossal mistake, and if it weren't for Reaper's decision to show kindness, I would already be dead. But getting caught up in that rope wasn't the only mistake I made. I wasn't careful. I allowed myself to be tracked.

I've gotten too comfortable. Careless. I need to do better.

The Midnight Killer came into this old gym thinking he had the upper hand. He was luring 343 into a trap, but instead, all he managed to do was send himself to an early grave. On the other hand, 343 managed to get himself killed simply by not being aware of his surroundings. I won't be that foolish again.

After retrieving both The Midnight Killer's and 343's IDs, I add them to my small pile. I officially have six, but to be completely honest, I don't feel great about it. I killed The Boston Maneater fair and square, and I was happy to take claim over the previous kills he'd collected. As for 343 and The Midnight Killer, I can't help but feel that these belong to Reaper. I may have helped 343 fall and break his back, but Reaper was the one who finished him.

They're not mine to claim, and while I don't doubt that he'll return at some point to collect them, I feel wrong having them at all. Despite being a contract killer—and one of the most wanted persons across the globe—I like to consider myself somewhat of a rule follower. I play fair, and while I'm happy to hold onto the IDs just to ensure no one else gets their grubby hands on them, I don't consider them mine.

Now, as for the two knives Reaper so happily parted with in this charred gym, I'm more than happy to claim them as my own. They can be a souvenir, something to remind me of what comes from foolishness. Though, just like the IDs, I'm sure Reaper will come looking for these too. Unfortunately for him, if he wants them back, he will have to pry them out of his own damn chest.

I pull the first one straight out of 343's throat, and despite the blood staining the blade, it's clear that this isn't some run-of-the-mill knife. This is custom-made, the hilt created to fit perfectly in the palm of his hand, and judging by the craftsmanship and the etched design of the Grim Reaper on the blade, I can only assume this didn't come cheap.

After wiping the blood off the blade, I sheath it into one of my holsters before searching the gym for the other blade. And because nothing worth having is easy, it's hanging from the metal beam in the ceiling.

"Shit."

I consider leaving it behind, but a knife like this, covered in his fingerprints, is practically a calling card, and for whatever reason, I feel like I need to protect Reaper. After all, he threw this blade with the intention of saving my life, and for that, I owe him. The only issue is figuring out how the fuck to get up there.

Being the brightest crayon in the box, the best idea I can come up with is to simply launch shit at it until it dislodges from the metal beam, and with the confidence of a drunk sorority girl on the dance floor, I start hauling weights through the air.

My confidence quickly begins to run out when my arm starts getting sore, but I persist until a five-pound dumbbell finally slams into the blade, setting the bastard free. Only it doesn't just drop to the ground, the momentum from the hit has it whipping through the charred gym, and I fly to the ground, doing what I can to protect my head until the blade finally clatters to the ground.

I quickly find it covered in soot, and after wiping it off, I sheath it next to its match before finally getting my ass moving. Then, as I start up my black Range Rover and peel out onto the main road, I press Mila's name on my phone and wait for her to answer the call and bitch me out.

"The fuck was that?" Mila demands not a moment later. "If you were trying to get yourself killed, you should have just told me. I could have easily done it for you."

A stupid grin stretches across my face, and I relax back into the driver's seat, getting comfortable for the trip back to my villa. "I'm okay, Mills," I tell her. "There's barely a scratch on me. Besides, have you ever been hung from your hair and almost scalped? It was quite the adventure."

10

REAPER

Frustration burns through me.

Ever since my run-in with Siren, I've been in a perpetual state of hardness. No matter what I do, I can't seem to get my mind off her. I can't stop thinking about the way she smelled or how her body felt pressed up against mine. I can't force my mind not to picture the way she challenged me or erase the sweet hint of her arousal in the air.

She was wet for me, and I was fucking ruined.

Not a single person I've ever met in my lifetime has ever had the balls to step up to me like that. They know who and what I am the second their terrified stares meet mine, and as a general rule, they run in the opposite direction. Yet despite her fear, she raised that fucking chin of hers, met my eye, and stood her ground. It was the sexiest thing I've ever seen.

Sure, I could have ended it there, walked away and madly jerked off until I put it all behind me. Only when she walked out of that alley and had the audacity to suggest I didn't have the balls to man up and fuck her, I was ruined. But there's no doubt about it now, the next time I see her, I will give her exactly what she wants.

The whole time her body was pressed against mine, all I wanted was to bend her over and hear her scream for me, but what can I say? I was a gentleman. I didn't even threaten to kill her. Well, I mean, I didn't threaten that straight away. I waited. I was enjoying myself too much, and to be honest, enjoying myself with a target isn't something I often get to do.

I've said it before, and I'm sure I'll say it again, Siren intrigues me, and I suddenly find myself a little less interested in War Games, and completely focused on her. It's a real shame that I will eventually have to kill her, but I don't see why we can't spend the next twenty-five days making every second count.

I need to hear her scream for me. Taste her. Feel her. Watch how she rides my cock, and despite not having touched her yet, I can already tell that with her, it will be incredible. Siren isn't the type to hold back. She'll wind me up until I can't possibly take it anymore, and only then will she ride me harder.

I can't fucking wait, but what the hell am I supposed to do about this fucking erection until then? Like I said, I'm in a perpetual state of hardness. The second I think I've dealt with it, it comes right back, ready to cause me hell, and the only thing that's going to put me at ease is sinking into her tight little cunt.

Until then, my only hope is the next best thing—taking someone's life.

Striding through the city center, I track down the brothers—The Boneyard Slayer and The Texan Reaper. I hadn't intended on stumbling across them tonight. My plans had mostly included hiding out by Siren's villa and making sure she didn't do anything stupid enough to get herself eliminated from the games before I settled my score with her. But now that the brothers have reared their ugly heads, I can't possibly resist figuring out what—or who—has drawn them out.

For the past week, they've kept their heads down, laid low and waited for everyone else to do the brunt of the work. They don't strike me as the type to be capable of tracking and hunting in the way a trained assassin would. They're more like opportunists, picking their victims by whoever seems to be the closest when the mood strikes. When it comes to brains, these two have none. Which could only mean another contender is close by.

I watch them meticulously. Tracking their every step while keeping concealed. I don't have the intention to take them out tonight. It's too soon in the games to make such a big move. I need to lure them into a false sense of security, and just when they think they've got this shit in the bag, I'll be happy to remind them of their positions—six feet under.

The brothers stand on either side of the road, and I watch from above, situated on the roof. The Texan Reaper is leaning against a storefront, cigarette in hand, as he tries to appear inconspicuous. He watches his brother from the corner of his eye before flicking his gaze back to a takeout store, intently watching the door.

His brother takes up residence in a bus shelter, leaning back on the bench with his foot propped on his knee. He scrolls through his phone, his attention anywhere but the store that houses his current victim, making it clear which of the brothers is in charge.

The Boneyard Slayer is nothing but muscle for his brother's benefit, and from the look of it, he probably took a few too many hits to the head as a kid. However, it begs the question, who the fuck is currently purchasing takeout?

A few minutes pass before the door opens and a scrawny surfer-looking guy steps out with his food in hand, and I let out a sigh. Sharkbait. I didn't have high hopes for this guy, and quite frankly, this is going to be a simple, quick kill.

From what little information I've been able to find, the guy received his name from killing his victims and dumping their bodies into shark-infested waters in an attempt to destroy the evidence. Naturally, it didn't work. Only an idiot would think that was a flawless plan. I mean, sure, I've left bodies to be eaten before. There's nothing better than natural selection playing out right before your eyes, but if you're going to take calculated risks, you need to make sure they'll pay off. Areas with an over-population of hungry foxes or wolves is generally a foolproof plan, and you better make sure it's a fresh kill. But a cold dead body floating in the ocean? Fuck no. Sure, a shark might take a nibble, but when he realizes it's not a tasty seal, he'll abandon it and leave it floating in the ocean to inevitably wash up on shore.

I consider walking away, not particularly interested in spending my night watching the brothers make their kill, but despite my boredom, I stay, finding myself curious about their hunting style. I've never been one to work with others. I don't like coordination, and I sure as hell don't like sharing my plans. As a general rule, I don't play well with others, but their dynamic intrigues me, and when it comes to the time for me to take their lives, I want to know exactly what I'm in for.

The second Sharkbait fully steps out of the store, he turns to his right and walks directly toward the brothers. Fucking idiot. Does he not sense them there? Get chills down his spine when he realizes he's in imminent danger? Where are his basic survival instincts?

He starts unwrapping a burger and takes a hasty bite as though he hasn't eaten in days before crossing the road right in front of the bus shelter. Though to his credit, The Boneyard Slayer is still so buried in his phone that he doesn't even realize his target is right in front of him. The Texan Reaper on the other hand is watching it all with a keen eye while glaring at his brother to get his shit together.

Sharkbait steps up onto the walkway, just past the bus shelter, and continues on his way, his every brain cell fully focused on the burger in his hand. I realize this guy thinks he's going to sail right through to the end by simply hiding out. He hasn't got a damn clue that he's a weak player, and that right there is one hell of a fatal mistake.

Fuck. These games are really starting to bore me. Why include so many incompetent players? I thought I was coming here to play with the best of the best. Shadow and Siren are obviously excluded from that. So far, they're the only two who have been able to show just a shred of promise, and the only two I'm going to struggle to end, while everyone else is nothing but fodder to be played with.

With their target beginning to put distance between them, The Texan Reaper pushes off the wall and stalks Sharkbait down the street, and I follow them along the roof, simply stepping from one rooftop to the next. It's not long before The Boneyard Slayer finally glances up to realize he missed his shot and hastily shoves his phone in his pocket and begins rushing to catch up. Only the sound of his rushed feet on the pavement has Sharkbait stiffening.

I roll my eyes. It's about time the fucker realized he was in trouble.

His burger is lowered from his mouth, and he glances over his shoulder to see The Boneyard Slayer hurrying after him, and to be honest, it's not a pretty sight. The Boneyard Slayer looks like an overweight ex-football player who's trying to play with his kids, but the fitness just isn't there anymore, and even from my vantage point on the roof, I can hear his heavy panting.

Sharkbait's eyes widen in horror, and it's clear he had no idea how easy he was to track. He pauses for just a second, and as he frantically looks around to make a game plan, he finally notices The Texan Reaper across the road.

My brow arches, waiting to see what will happen, but more importantly, needing to learn their style. Sharkbait all but shits his pants, and as The Texan Reaper steps off the sidewalk with the intent to cross the road, Sharkbait takes off, sprinting down a back alley.

I skip across to the next roof, giving myself a better viewpoint, and as Sharkbait bolts down the alley, the brothers follow closely. I shake my head. I should have known Sharkbait would be foolish. He doesn't strike me as the type to have basic survival instincts.

The alley he chose is a dead end, and all he's managed to do is back himself into a corner. Knowing your surroundings is the first rule of the business. You always need an escape plan. Every time you step out of the house, you need to know where you are at all times and how to disappear—especially in a town where the cops are aware of War Games. Hell, over the past week, Blue Springs managed to bring in some cops from the next city over and a few FBI agents as backup, not that it'll be an issue for me or any of the other top killers in these games. While the FBI certainly are good at what they do, we're better.

As for Sharkbait, he seems like the type to make colossal mistakes and have his ass hauled away in cuffs. Though considering tonight's latest mistake, he won't ever see the light of day again.

The brothers slow their advance, allowing Sharkbait more than enough time to work himself into a cold sweat, and though it's a little late, it looks like those basic survival instincts have finally kicked in.

The brothers stalk him like prey, creeping deeper into the alley, and as I watch them, my earlier thoughts are confirmed once again. The Texan Reaper is the one calling the shots. His brother follows his lead and waits to be told what to do. I can't help but wonder why. Is The Boneyard Slayer not capable of calling the shots? Does he not have the brains to pull off a kill by himself? Though one thing is for sure, despite this being a team effort, something tells me that The Texan Reaper is the one who's going to walk away with Sharkbait's identity tonight.

Sharkbait makes a move, realizing he still holds his burger in his hand, and in a split-second decision, launches it at The Texan Reaper's face. Both of the brothers are caught off guard and Sharkbait uses the distraction to make his move, sprinting as fast as he can between them.

The Texan Reaper roars in frustration as the burger lingers on his face, and as Sharkbait tries to make a run for it, The Boneyard Slayer's hand whips out, clutching Sharkbait by the back of his man bun.

He hauls him back and throws him hard against the brick wall of the alley. I can practically hear his skull crack with the force of the throw, but he barely gets a chance to cry out as the brothers launch their brutal attack on him, letting out every bit of their anger.

It's disgusting. I don't like brutal kills like this.

Taking a life is supposed to be poetic. There's supposed to be an art to it, but this is just messy. It's anger and revulsion, brute strength against a man who had no hope of defending himself. I don't like it; there's no honor or compassion here, but it's not my problem to deal with right now. I'll make it right when I end their lives.

With disgust pulsing heavily through my veins, I don't bother to watch the end of their brutal kill, but as I turn to go, something in the darkness catches my attention.

Shadow.

Only she's not watching the brothers make their kill, she's watching me.

"HEY!" I call out, and in a split second, she's gone.

Fuck.

I take off at a sprint, hurrying after her and tracking her into the darkness. My chest heaves as I try to catch my breath, running down the street and bypassing the alley where the brothers are violently taking a life. I search the darkened street, trying to listen to my senses, but just like the first time I went after Shadow, she vanishes like a ghost.

What the fuck?

How has this kid evaded me twice now?

"I just want to talk," I say into the darkness, my gut telling me she's around here somewhere. "I don't want to hurt you."

I stand in the middle of the road, my hands outstretched as if to show my intentions, but I suspect this kid has done more than her fair share of research on me. She knows exactly what I'm capable of, and just how quickly I can make it happen, so it's up to her to decide if she's capable of trusting my intentions.

I don't move an inch for well over five minutes, sensing her around me somewhere, and just when I'm about to give up and walk away, Shadow emerges from the darkness, striding right into the center of the deserted street, staring at me just as I stare at her.

She doesn't speak, simply waits to figure out what the hell I've waited here for, and honestly, I haven't got a clue what I should be asking her.

"How?" I ask, that simple word covering just about everything I need to know.

"How what?" she throws back, making sure to keep a distance.

"How are you capable of evading me?"

Shadow holds my stare and shrugs her shoulders as though it's no big deal. "Same way you're capable of evading everyone else, I guess. I was trained that way."

"I've trained myself over the past fifteen years, perfecting my skills and pushing myself to be the best. I have been tortured, been through excruciating training, been shot at, and pushed myself until I bled. I have died and come back more times than I can count. Nobody at this level is capable of achieving what I have achieved without years of brutal training and significant trauma. You are a child, nothing more than a twelve-year-old girl. You shouldn't be capable of evading me, yet here we are."

"First off, I'm thirteen. And yes, it is entirely possible for me to evade you if you consider that perhaps you are not the best in your field. I am."

"You are?"

"Yes."

"And how did you possibly become that way? People like us don't just get to be the best without going through hell first."

Shadow scoffs. "What? Like taking a stroll through hell is hard? I call that a normal Tuesday."

My brow arches, and I take a slight step toward her, watching as her sharp stare tracks me. She backs up, her hands preparing to grab a weapon.

"Don't do it," I warn her. "Like I said, I don't want to hurt you, but if you make a move, I'll have no choice but to retaliate, and I don't think that right here in the middle of some deserted street is really where you want to test whose reflexes are faster."

The slightest flash of unease appears in her blue eyes, and it's enough to have her backing up again, her steps filled with hesitation. She's uncomfortable, unsure of what she should do or what move to make, and while she might possibly be the best, she's also still just a kid.

Her gaze shifts, checking our surroundings, and when I inch toward her again, she looks ready to bolt. "Do you have somewhere safe to stay? Food? Water? A bed?"

Shadow scowls at me. "I know how to look after myself. I'm not a child."

"Answer the question."

She clenches her jaw, and I can't help but wonder if she's being snappy with me because I'm questioning her ability to care for herself or if this is standard thirteen-year-old-girl behavior. I'm going to guess option number two.

"Why do you keep stalking that Siren girl like some kind of creeper? You've gotten close more than enough times to take her out, but you never do. Why?"

I arch my brow. "Have you been watching me that much?"

"I watch everybody."

I stare back at her, and the silence begins to grow heavy when I finally respond, figuring if I were to show a little vulnerability, then she'll be willing to be honest in return. "First of all, Siren is not a girl. She's a woman. And as for why I haven't eliminated her yet, that's complicated."

"You like her or something?"

"Or something," I agree. "Now, don't act as though your little change of topic didn't go unnoticed. Do you have somewhere safe to stay and are you capable of feeding yourself?"

She clenches her jaw again, and this time, I don't wait for her to change the topic or throw teenage bullshit my way. I dig into my pocket and pull out my wallet before fishing out a couple hundred dollars. "Hotels are expensive and you'll burn through this in days," I tell her, placing the cash on the ground in front of me, knowing damn well she's not going to try and get any closer. "There's a lot of holiday homes down near the lake. Try and find one of them instead—an empty one, preferably with no security system. Once you've secured a home, take yourself grocery shopping. Bread, milk, cereal. All the necessities."

"I . . . I don't know how to cook."

I nod. "You should be able to find frozen, ready-made meals in the grocery store. You just put them in the microwave. If you try to eat takeout each night, you'll run out of cash."

She nods again, only this time, she drops her gaze, and instead of seeing a cunning young killer, I see nothing but a lost little girl. "Shadow," I say, demanding her attention again. She lifts her gaze back to me, and if I thought there was any way she'd let me help her further, I would offer everything I have. "If you're in trouble, you come to me. Do you understand?"

"I can handle myself," she argues.

"You can barely feed yourself," I remind her. "There will come a time in the coming weeks when these games start running out of contenders, and you'll find yourself with a target on your back. You're just a kid, Shadow. I don't want to see your name listed among those who've been eliminated."

"You won't."

"See to it that I don't."

And with that, I back up a few steps, leaving the cash in the middle of the street before finally turning and walking away. Then, just before I reach the alley where the brothers just brutally killed Sharkbait, I turn back and stare up the street, relieved when I see no sign of Shadow or the cash on the asphalt.

11

SIREN

We're ten days into War Games, and I'm itching to get a few more kills under my belt, but now that so many of us have been eliminated, the game is getting harder. The weak ones have been sniffed out, leaving us with only ten, including me. We're officially halfway through, but something tells me that each day, the stakes are going to rise. It's been nothing more than a vacation so far, but the contenders are starting to get antsy now that the FBI found some DNA evidence that links Sharkbait's death to The Boneyard Slayer. Things are going to move fast and be messy from here out.

Sharkbait's body was found dismembered in an alleyway a few nights ago, and since then, everybody has been laying low, but not anymore. I'm sick of sitting by and waiting for something to happen. It seems that everybody is waiting for others to make a move, and so far, nobody is doing shit. They've gotten too comfortable, wanting to bide their time until the final few days in the hopes that someone else will do all the dirty work and they can swoop in at the last minute and take the win. But I'm not about to let that happen.

Tonight, I'm rocking the boat.

Giddiness pulses through me as I follow Eagle through the streets of Blue Springs. It's clear why she hasn't been taken out already. She's good, more than just a strong contender in the games, and taking her out now is nothing more than a power move. By this point in the competition, everybody should have more than enough information on the other contenders to know who and what they stand for. They should know about their kills, what their style is, and how they even landed their ass in a game like this. They know who their biggest competition is and who they need to watch their backs around.

Eagle is the underdog. There's nothing mysterious about her or how she made a name for herself in the industry. As far as her reputation suggests, she's a sure shot. She never misses a target. She makes clean, precise kills. She's someone to watch, and maybe given another few years, she might have even managed to steal my crown. The only thing she lacks is experience.

Taking her life tonight will rattle the other contenders. I'm making a move they won't expect, eliminating a player who'd otherwise be here until the very end. When someone steps outside their comfort zone and doesn't act as expected, it leaves them unsteady. I don't like predictability; that's when people end up dead, and I won't be just another number forgotten about after War Games.

Eagle reminds me of myself, and while I expect her to put up the kind of fight that will engage my mind in ways that others like The Boston Maneater or 343 could never even begin to understand, actually taking the final blow to end her life will be bittersweet. I don't know what's gotten into me today, but for whatever reason, I feel heavy about this one. Maybe it's because Eagle and I could have been amazing friends in another life. If things were different, or if we'd met outside of this bullshit, I just know we would have hit it off and swapped war stories while annihilating a bottle of tequila.

Shit.

I need to focus.

I caught wind of Eagle a few nights ago after she made an attempt on Gasoline. However, in true Gasoline style, the building went up in flames and she slipped away. Eagle didn't get out of that one unscathed, and having no other choice, she broke into the local veterinary hospital to steal all the first aid she could get her hands on. It was a colossal mistake, but after I almost scalped myself earlier in the games, I no longer feel it's my duty to judge people for their fuck ups. We're all desperate, and none of us are thinking straight.

There are two separate bandages wrapped around her left arm, and I can only imagine how much that must hurt. I haven't had to deal with burns before, but I know women like Eagle, and they only succumb to first aid when the pain is almost too much to bear. This will make things interesting, but I pride myself on being fair. If I need to subdue her, it'll be done without targeting her injuries.

From the way she leads me through the streets, she's more than clocked me behind her and is attempting to lead me to a location she's already checked out. It doesn't matter though. She can lead me wherever the hell she wants. I've done my research on this town, and I know it better than the back of my hand. There's nowhere she can lead me where I won't have the upper hand.

Eagle takes a left, and her plan becomes clear. The local butcher.

Fucking disgusting.

A meat locker isn't exactly somewhere I wish to spend any of my time, but I applaud her creativity. I just hope this isn't where she's been crashing at night. However, I'm grateful that this is purely the butcher store and not actually the local abattoir. I can handle a lot of things, but a slaughterhouse is not one of them.

Just as I suspected, Eagle slips in through the back of the butcher store, and my stomach begins to cramp at just the thought of walking in there after her, but I do what I have to do and take the plunge.

As I follow her inside, I look left and right before walking through the door, expecting her to jump out at me at any chance. Instead, I find her standing dead center of the butcher's large human-sized refrigerator.

"You're following me," she states, her sharp stare locked on me as the smell of fresh meat assaults my senses and makes my cramping stomach begin to turn.

"Yes."

"You're not very good," she says. "I clocked you over thirty minutes ago."

I smile. "You were supposed to. You think I was following that closely out of sheer stupidity? I wanted a fair fight, and that wasn't going to happen if I got the drop on you. Besides, I was curious. I wanted to know where you'd bring me, and to be honest, I'm surprised. This isn't exactly a location I'd pick."

Eagle shrugs her shoulders. "Butchers have a way of making some people feel . . . queasy, and judging by the way your face has drained of color, I'd say you're one of those people."

I shake my head, swallowing over the bile rising in my throat. "Nope. Not me."

"Right," she says, casually striding toward me. "You know, my daddy was a butcher for thirty years before—"

"You killed him?"

"What?" she gasps in horror. "No. I loved my father. He was a great man. He died after an incident with the cartel."

"Well, shit," I say with an awkward cringe. "Sorry, it's just that most of us killers turned out the way we did because we have daddy issues."

She watches me through a narrowed stare. "What's your trauma?"

"Oh, you know. The usual."

"What's the usual? He raped you all through your childhood and the second you could, you gutted him like a fish."

Horror blasts through my chest. She couldn't be further from the truth, but I understand why she went there. Reality is, it happens a lot more than anyone thinks it should. "Shit. I don't know you nearly well enough to trauma dump on you, but what I will say is that for me, my life wouldn't be the way it is now if it weren't for my piece of shit father, and if I were so lucky to get the chance to take his life, I'd make a fucking holiday out of it."

Eagle nods. "So, you said you wanted a fair fight?"

I nod in return. "That's right."

"How fair?"

I arch a brow and slowly reach for the gun holstered around my thigh. I hold it up and release the magazine, letting it fall to the ground before tossing the gun aside. I kick the magazine, letting it slide toward the empty gun that just happens to be positioned right under a big piece of meat that's hanging by a giant hook in the ceiling.

"Okay," Eagle says, taking her own gun and doing the same. "Knives?"

Reaching for the knives hidden all over my body, I start tossing them aside, while being extra careful with the two blades of Reaper's. "You don't strike me as the type who requires weapons to get the job done."

"I'm not," she agrees before disarming herself.

I feel naked without my weapons, and I can only assume that she feels the same. The only difference is that on top of feeling naked, I also feel like I'm going to hurl at any point. While Eagle here looks as fresh as a daisy, probably reminiscing about all the good times she had with her father.

After tossing my last knife aside, I rotate my cat-ear ring, hiding the sharp points on the inside of my palm. She comes for me, her fists already balled into weapons of their own. Excitement cracks like lightning in my chest, and I immediately spring on the defense, evading her with ease.

We trade punches, fists flying with skilled precision as knees and high kicks are brought into the mix. It's a mesmerizing dance, and honestly, this is the type of shit I love.

I've gotta give it to her, she's good. Better than good. She's got strong punches with fast reflexes, and if this were nothing more than training, I'd keep her around simply to keep me on my toes, but she's not better than me.

"You're good," I say, getting through her defense and landing a shot right at her ribs.

She grunts in pain, but it doesn't slow her down as she hurls a punch toward my face. "Thanks, that means a lot coming from you," she says in a chipper tone, switching things up and grabbing my wrists as I throw another punch. She yanks me forward and uses my momentum against me, letting me stumble right into the cold meat hanging from the ceiling, my face smacking right against it.

I whip around, not allowing her another chance to get the drop on me as I desperately hold back a gag. "Low blow."

"I know, but you're faster than me. I did what I had to do," she says unapologetically as I ram my knee into her thigh with the power of a freight train. "Holy fucking shit."

Eagle stumbles back, and I go with her, relentless in my attack, throwing a few more punches and knocking her off balance. I was more than happy to drag this out to allow us both to enjoy this fight before inevitably ending it, but I'm not a forgiving person, and after yanking me into a meat carcass, it was over for her.

Her ass hits the ground, and as I come for her again, I deliver the blow to her temple that has her tapping out. "Fuck. Shit. Stop, please," she begs, knowing I could end her life in a matter of seconds.

I hold back and watch as she crumbles with exhaustion, tears filling her eyes. "I can't . . ." she says. "I can't die like this. This isn't what I want. I . . . I . . . "

I let out a sigh, glancing around the massive refrigerator before finding a chair, and as Eagle curls up on the floor, completely defeated, I grab the chair and drag it to the center of the room.

"Here," I say, reaching for her and helping her to her feet before wrapping my arm around her waist. I walk her over to the chair, and as she hobbles, I take the majority of her weight. Reaching the chair, I lower her into it, and she lets out a heavy breath, in more pain than I had originally thought. "You okay?"

"Think you broke a rib."

"Shit. Sorry."

With Eagle barely able to move, I fetch all of my weapons, putting them right back into place as I keep an eye on her. Once everything is secured, I find heavy chains and drag them over to Eagle before wrapping them around her ankles and wrists. "Sorry," I say, still feeling so heavy about all of this.

"I get it," she says. "I'd be doing the exact same thing if roles were reversed."

"Do you need water or something?"

She gives me a small smile. "So I can piss myself when I die? No thanks," she scoffs. "Can I just ask one thing? No—wait. Two. Can I ask two things?"

"Like what?"

"My little sister," she says. "Is there any way you'd be willing to check in on her every now and then? She doesn't know what I do for work, and she's going to be crushed when she realizes I'm gone. I just . . . I need to know she's going to be alright. Both our parents are gone, and it's just been the two of us for so long. She's not going to have anybody."

I cringe, not really sure about this. "I don't know. I'm not a babysitter."

"She doesn't need babysitting. She's not a child. She's twenty-two. She just needs someone to check in on her every few months to make sure she's not making any terrible life decisions, which she will. She does it all the time, and they mostly have something to do with stupid boys who only want one thing from her."

"Okay, okay," I say. "I can check in on your sister."

Eagle lets out a heavy sigh of relief. "Thank you," she says.

"Dare I ask what the other thing is?"

Her gaze darkens as she lifts her head, staring me right in the eye. "Gasoline. I want you to end that bitch's life as though she'd personally wronged you. She deserves the worst kind of death."

"What happened with her?"

Eagle clenches her jaw and glances away, clearly not wanting to talk about it, but there's no disguising the flash of fear that darkens her stare. Something terrible went down, and while I might never know what that is, that doesn't mean I can't get sweet revenge for Eagle. "Consider it done," I tell her.

"Thank you, and Siren?" she murmurs, a heaviness entering her tone, realizing this is it. "Watch your back with that one. She's not only clever, she's vindictive and angry at the world. She'll do what she can to make it as brutal as possible. And that includes burning you alive."

My brows furrow as my heart starts to race. "Is that what she did to you?"

Eagle purses her lips. "Just watch yourself when it comes to her. I have high hopes for you. I think Reaper and Shadow might be an issue, but I like you. If anybody should come out of this alive, I want it to be you."

A shiver sails down my spine just moments before a deep tone fills the room, the sound making my heart race. "Why are you dragging this out, Little Siren?"

Ahh fuck.

Eagle sucks in a gasp, her sharp gaze flicking around the room until Reaper makes a point to step out of the shadows, and all I can do is let out a heavy sigh. "You again? Really? Are you stalking me?" I ask, unable to keep from noticing the way his tight black shirt fits his body or the way his tattoos peek out from the neckline of that very shirt, leaving me desperate to see what's underneath.

His gaze locks on me, barely noticing Eagle who can do nothing more than gawk. "Yes," Reaper states flatly, not a hint of deception in his voice—a voice that just so happens to have me needing to relieve the ache between my thighs. "Why wouldn't I? A beautiful woman who thinks she has the ability to take me down. What can I say? You've piqued my interest."

That was more than clear when he had his body pressed up against mine in that back alley, but all that memory has done for me is send me spiraling every time I close my eyes. "Oh, lucky me," I throw back at him, doing the bare minimum to act as though his very presence doesn't have an effect on me, but this is Reaper we're talking about. He can see right through my bullshit.

"Uhhh . . . What the fuck is going on here?" Eagle asks, looking between the two of us, unsure if she needs to be confused or terrified.

Glancing back at her, I risk taking my eyes off Reaper, but something tells me that he means me no harm. After all, he just admitted to stalking me, which means he's been more than close over these past few days. If he wanted to kill me, he could have at any point, and yet, for whatever reason, I'm still here.

Holding Eagle's stare, I give it to her straight. "Someone—not naming any names—clearly wants to fuck me," I tell her. "He saw me make one kill and now the arrogant prick is obsessed."

"Fuck, girl. I know you're incredible at what you do, but you realize who the fuck it is you're taunting, right? That's Reaper. *The* fucking Reaper. You're gonna get yourself killed."

I shake my head. "The man's been following me for days, camping outside my villa, searching through my trash, sniffing my underwear. If he wanted to kill me, I'd already be long gone," I explain. "Which only leaves one option—the asshole wants to fuck me." Reaper simply stares back at me, not denying it, but he doesn't need to. After what went down in that back alley, we both know it's true. "It's flattering," I tell him. "But I didn't take you as the stalker type."

His eyes seem to light up, making something clench deep in my stomach. "I see that smart mouth of yours wasn't just a once-off. It's more of a core personality trait."

I can't help but grin. "And?"

"You're right. I would very much like to fuck it out of your system." Well damn.

"Holy fucking shit," Eagle breathes beside me, gaping at Reaper as though she can't believe what she's seeing. "The fuck are you waiting for, girl? Get on your knees and let him fuck it out of your system. Give a dying woman her last wish."

I can't help but laugh, as I pull one of his knives free from the sheath in my top, just to let him know I have it. "Now, why on earth would I go and do that?" I taunt, spinning the tip of the blade on my fingers, desperately wishing I was already on my knees, giving him exactly what we both want. "He can go and fuck his hand for all I care. Though, after our last meeting, I suspect he's already been doing a lot of that."

A stupid grin stretches across my face, and I let out a sigh as though Reaper's very presence in this butcher's shop means absolutely nothing. "I'm here to win War Games and get back to my normal life," I add, knowing damn well it's a lie because I have no intention of harming Shadow.

Eagle scoffs, gaping at me as though I've lost my mind. "Hell, if you're not going to suck this man's cock, at least give me a crack at it."

I roll my eyes, unsure why I suddenly feel so possessive of this terrifying man across the room. "Oh please," I say to Eagle. "With those broken ribs, you'd be lucky to even get on your knees and open your mouth, let alone come close to satisfying him."

Reaper lets out a sigh, and it's clear by his tone that he's had enough. "Come on, Siren. I have better things to do with my night. Make your kill so we can leave."

"Shit."

My gaze slowly turns back to Eagle and a wave of guilt washes over me as she meets my stare. We really could have been good friends outside of this world. "Make it quick," she whimpers as a single tear rolls down her cheek.

I nod. And with that, the blade in my hand flies through the air in the blink of an eye and sinks deep into her throat, severing her spine and instantly taking Eagle out of the game.

12

SIREN

Sitting across from Reaper in a hotel restaurant, I can't help but feel as though this is some fucked-up version of a date. I don't even know how we got here. After I ended Eagle's life and took her ID to add to my collection, the heaviness was weighing on me, and before I knew it, Reaper's hand was at the small of my back, leading me out of the massive refrigerator and into the cool night.

I was set to start the long, lonely walk back to my car, but Reaper stayed right at my side, and as we strolled past the luxury tourist hotel, he steered me through the door in silence. One second I was questioning what the fuck he was doing, and then next, I was sitting opposite him in a small, intimate booth.

Is this a date? I hope like fuck it's not because I make a point not to date. In fact, apart from Jeremy Musgrove in eighth grade, I've never been on an actual date. I make a point not to allow myself to get too close to men. Sure, I more than use them to satisfy my needs, but I don't exactly have a career that allows me to have a life. I have Mila, and that's all I'll ever need.

"Why'd you show her so much compassion?" Reaper asks me, sitting back in the booth, his big knees invading my personal space beneath the table. "You could have spared yourself all the guilt and put a bullet between her eyes without getting to know her first. You dragged it out."

"Are you asking a genuine question or trying to reprimand me?" I ask, my brow arching. I'm not exactly fond of how everything went down with Eagle, but if I had the chance to go back, I don't believe I'd change a thing.

"Both," Reaper admits. "I'm struggling to understand you, and I don't approve of putting yourself at risk. At any moment, that woman could have taken your life. She's a trained assassin, and while she wasn't as good as you, that doesn't mean she couldn't have taken your life. You allowed her too many opportunities to end you."

I shake my head. "I am aware of what I did, but we had an understanding. We fought fair without any weapons, and I won. It was understood that I was going to kill her, and she accepted that, whether it was going to take one second or all night. And as for having compassion, is that a bad thing? It makes me human."

"We can't afford to think like humans in this line of work, not if you want to survive."

"I'll be fine. Thanks for the advice, but there's no need to worry about me."

Reaper just stares at me as though I'm a misbehaved child, and the longer he does, the harder it becomes to ignore, and then just as he knew I would, I break. "Okay, fine. There was something about her. I could see myself in her, and if we had met under any other circumstances, Eagle and I, I think we could have really hit it off. I don't allow people into my life. I have one friend and that's it, but Eagle . . . I feel like we could have had a really amazing friendship. Plus, I wasn't just going to put a bullet between her eyes when I needed information out of her."

A waiter chooses that very moment to appear at our table with a menu, and there's no way he didn't hear what just came flying out of my mouth. He gapes at me in horror, his gaze flicking between mine and Reaper's. "Uhhhhh . . ."

I laugh it off, acting as though it was a misunderstanding. "Oh my goodness. Your timing is impeccable. How funny. I'm a true crime author. Just trying to work out a scene."

"Oh," the guy says, letting out a heavy breath, the relief evident in his eyes. "Thank God. For a minute I thought—"

"What? That I'd killed someone?" I laugh. "Oh my god. How funny!"

The waiter takes a minute to calm himself before finally pulling out a notepad and pen. "Now that we've confirmed you're not out here shooting people, do you know what you'd like to order?"

"Uhhhhh . . . can you give us a minute?" I say, dropping my gaze to the menu, having absolutely no idea what this place serves.

Reaper rolls his eyes and takes the menu out of my hands before passing it straight back to the waiter. "Why are you pretending as though you don't know what you want? Every single night for the past ten days, you have eaten the same shit on repeat. Pasta, chicken, or burgers. You eat what you know and don't venture outside of that."

My jaw drops. I knew he was watching me, but I didn't realize he was watching quite that closely. "Your point?" I question, feeling slightly embarrassed. I like food, and of course I venture outside of just that . . . sometimes. But the truth is, he's hit a sore point. I eat the meals my mom used to make for me when I was a little girl. They're my comfort foods, especially when I'm away for work.

Reaper lets out another sigh and turns his attention to the waiter. "Give her a chicken parmigiana with fries and a side salad," he says, hitting the nail right on top of the head and making my stomach growl with hunger. How did he know that's exactly what I was craving?

"Sorry. We don't do pub food," he says, turning his nose up at my order. "This is a luxury restaurant. Fine dining at its best. If you wish to eat like children, perhaps you could visit McDonald's or Wendy's."

Reaper slowly turns his gaze, locking onto the waiter's stare, and I see the very moment the waiter realizes just how spectacularly he fucked up. Reaper stands and the waiter begins to shake before a word has even been said. "The lady would like a chicken parmigiana," he rumbles. "Are you telling me you are incapable of giving her what she wants?"

"I . . . I . . . No, sir," he says, visibly swallowing as he begins to stammer over his words, clearly realizing what kind of man he's currently dealing with. "Is there any . . . anything else I . . . I can get for you? Perhaps some wine? The dessert menu to browse. Not that . . . Not that you need the menu. You can have anything you'd like."

"The chicken parmigiana will be fine," Reaper says. "Steak and vegetables for me."

The waiter scurries away, and Reaper casually takes his seat opposite me, his knees brushing against mine under the table. "What the fuck was that?" I demand.

"What was what?"

I shake my head. Is he serious right now? "You can't just go around intimidating everyone who tells you no. That's not how the world works."

"I don't mold myself to fit in with how the world works, Little Siren. The world molds to me," he tells me. "Now, back to Eagle."

I let out a heavy breath, feeling that I've already said what needed to be said. "Maybe I'm getting soft," I admit. "Losing my edge."

He shakes his head. "I don't believe so," he says. "I don't think it's a bad thing to crave friendships with those you can relate to or those who simply have an understanding of why you do what you do."

I bite my lip, my emotions all over the place. I don't know what's going on, why I'm here, or what he wants with me, and to be honest, I'd prefer to be back at my villa on the phone with Mila while finishing off a bottle of tequila.

Tonight hasn't been my night, and right now, I'm on the edge.

"What are you doing, Reaper? Why are we here, and why are you trying to give me all this grand life advice? I had a bad night. I'm off my game and letting my emotions get in the way. I just need the night, and I'll be fine tomorrow."

"Okay. You want to know why I'm here? You intrigue me."

"I figured that out the second you pushed me up against the brick wall, and I could feel your cock grinding against my stomach."

"You know damn well I didn't grind my cock up against you in that alley. If I had, there's no way you would have been able to walk away. I would have fucked you right there. But you're lying, that's not when you first realized."

"You're right. I knew it that first night after the initial meeting when I was on the roof and you were just . . . staring at me. I wasn't sure. I thought you were either intrigued or you just wanted me to know how easily you could have ended my life."

"Both things can be true."

A smirk pulls at the corner of my lips. "And now? Do you still want to show me just how easily you could end my life?"

"Make no mistake, Siren. I still plan on killing you when the time comes, but until then, I don't see why I can't see how deep you can take me or how fucking tight your sweet cunt is," he tells me in that deep, rich tone that sends adrenaline coursing through my body, lighting me up in ways I never imagined. "I wish to taste you, to bend you over and see how effortlessly you come apart for me."

I suck in a breath, my thighs clenching beneath the table as my heart rate rises.

"I want to break you, Siren. I want to fuck the attitude out of you, and don't even try to pretend like you don't want this too," Reaper continues. "I can smell how hungry you are, know just how tight you're having to clench those pretty thighs just to relieve the ache I put there. You're desperate for me, Siren."

Well fuck. How am I supposed to respond to that?

"You don't know what you're getting yourself into," I tell him. "I'm not the girl who's going to simply roll over and allow you to have your way with me. If you bite, I bite back. And I'm sure as hell not about to just give it up for you."

Reaper scoffs, and it's clear he thinks I'm all talk, but as I watch him, I can't help but wonder if there's more to this. "What do you really want?" I ask. "If all you wanted was to fuck me, you could have easily pulled me into a side alley or a bathroom. You saw how quickly my body reacted to yours the other night. You know just how easily you could have gotten what you wanted, but you didn't. Instead, you brought me here. There's an ulterior motive."

"There's no ulterior motive."

"Oh sure. I'll just believe the word of the world's most wanted contract killer."

The waiter returns right at the wrong time, two plates in his hand, and I watch as his brain comprehends exactly what was just said. His eyes widen in horror, and the plates in his hand start to shake.

"Fuck me," Reaper mutters under his breath, having to take the plates from the terrified waiter before fixing him with a haunting stare. "You heard nothing, and if I get wind that you've opened your big mouth, you'll have me to deal with. Is that understood?"

He nods so fast that I fear his head will pop right off his body, and not a moment later, he stumbles away, leaving me to deal with Reaper.

"You really must scan your surroundings before you open your mouth."

"Why would I possibly need to do that when I'm sitting with none other than the infamous Reaper? Haven't you heard? He's taken a career change. He's no longer in the business of ending lives. He's taken up stalking instead."

Reaper just stares. "Are you done?"

I shrug my shoulders. "I could go on. I had more about you being a sex-crazed psychopath, but I can stop. Talk of sex clearly makes you very uncomfortable," I say, raising my foot under the table and pressing right between his legs, taunting him. "If you can't handle it, I could always stop."

Reaper sucks in a breath, not knowing me well enough to know if I'm just bluffing or if I'm about to crush his crown jewels. "You don't know who you're fucking with," he says as his hand shifts beneath the table and casually rests on my ankle, more than ready to disable me if it comes down to it, but all I can do is grin.

"Tell me, Reaper," I say, pressing my foot into him a little harder. "What's your ulterior motive?"

He narrows his gaze. "You tell me what you think it is."

I think for a moment before finally deciding it doesn't matter if I were to be honest. "I think you want to work with me. I think I've surprised you, and while I might have made some questionable choices that you don't necessarily agree with, I think you see the value in having me as an asset. I'm already ahead in the game by miles."

"Did you forget who you're talking to?" Reaper questions, making me realize he actually doesn't give a shit if I try to castrate him with my foot or not; his reflexes are too fast. "I don't mean to insult you, and while I do agree that you are certainly an asset, I'm a solo act, always have been. Plus, five nights ago, I watched you accidentally hang yourself at the scene by your hair. You are valuable, just not to me."

"Well, shit," I laugh, releasing the pressure under my foot, only he doesn't release my ankle, just happily allows me to leave my foot wedged between his legs. "Way to kick a girl when she's down."

"That was certainly not my intention."

"I can handle it. I'm a big girl," I tell him, removing my foot anyway, not sure I'm comfortable enough to be that bold with him. "But for the record, I wouldn't want to work with you either. You strike me as the *my way or the highway* type, and I'm sure from your senseless stalking, you've realized that I don't mesh well with that bullshit." He arches a brow, and for whatever reason, I feel I need to go on. "I don't play well with others."

"I don't believe that to be true."

"No?"

"You had compassion for Eagle. Had a fair fight and agreed to watch over her younger sister, and when 343 was bleeding out on the ground, you made awkward small talk despite almost being scalped. You're a kind person despite your tough exterior."

"Is this supposed to be some kind of gotcha moment?"

"No, just an observation."

"And what other observations have you made?"

"That The Texan Reaper and The Boneyard Slayer are going to be issues."

"The brothers?" I say. "I figured they were working together."

"You knew they were brothers?"

I nod. "I have a photographic memory, plus I am diligent in my research. I tracked their prior kills and narrowed down the location. They were all within a thirty-mile radius, and once I found one of the brothers, finding the other was a piece of cake. They've been working as a team since they murdered their parents as teens. They're brutes. It wasn't hard to find information on them. There's a bunch of it, starting from their younger years. They're reckless and violent, and while they don't come with brains, it doesn't make them any less dangerous."

Reaper watches me through a narrowed gaze. "You were able to find out all of that."

"Like I said, I'm diligent in my research. I have a thick file on every contender in these games locked securely inside my brain. I know just about everything there is to know about everyone . . . Well, except you and Shadow. You two seem to be a mystery."

"Perhaps you're more of an asset than I gave you credit for."

I scoff and stand from the table. "If you wanna get between these legs and into my head, you're going to have to try a shitload harder than that," I tell him. "Unless you have information on Shadow you're willing to share?"

"Not likely."

"That's what I thought," I say, before turning my back and walking away, more than happy to leave him with the bill, though considering how terrified the waiter was of Reaper, I can assume there will be no bill. He'd just be happy to see us walk out of here.

I make my way out of the restaurant, feeling more than proud of myself while also knowing that the rest of my night is going to consist of me madly trying to get myself off to relieve the intense ache between my legs.

Heading down the sidewalk in the direction of my car, a large body steps in behind me, and warm hands clutch my waist. "What was it that you said when you walked away from me last time?" Reaper questions, his deep tone rumbling through his chest. "That the next time I get you all worked up and wet like this, I better have the balls to follow through."

His hand circles my waist, and as I suck in a breath, it travels down. Anticipation burns through me, and if he's not careful, I'll end up screwing him right here in front of the hotel restaurant.

Reaper's hand doesn't stop until it's cupped between my legs and when the heel of his palm grinds against my core, a deep groan slips from between my lips. "Tell me, Little Siren, just how wet are you?"

I relax my body weight back into his, knowing I'm about to be both metaphorically and literally screwed. I tip my head back as his palm works me through my jeans, and just as I go to respond and tell him just how easily he's got me trapped, something flashes through the darkness.

My back stiffens and sensing something's wrong, Reaper instantly goes on alert, his hand snapping away from me like lightning. "What is it?" Reaper questions, his sharp gaze searching the darkness.

"There's someone there."

He inches away from me, giving us both space to prepare ourselves in case this turns into a fight. I see the flash again, but it's not so much of a flash but a shadow moving through the darkness, and without question, I know exactly who it is.

"It's Shadow," I call out, already breaking into a sprint.

"Fuck," Reaper grunts, heavy on my tail. "You hurt her, and I'll have no fucking choice but to take you out."

"Who the fuck do you think I am?" I call back at him while keeping my sharp gaze locked on the shadow moving through the darkness. "She's a kid. As if I would ever hurt her."

"Alright. Let's get this little ghost."

I push myself faster, not taking my eyes off her for one second, and when she darts down behind the back of the hotel, I follow right behind her with Reaper taking off in the opposite direction.

Determination pushes me faster. I've been so concerned about this kid, desperate to know who she is and where she came from. Fuck, I just need to know if she has food and water and somewhere safe to sleep at night, but tracking her has been impossible. She's a literal ghost. She doesn't exist anywhere, which leaves me with a million questions.

Following her around the back of the hotel, I'm only a few steps behind when Reaper steps out in front of her, blocking her only escape and bringing her to an immediate stop.

She panics, her terrified gaze flicking between me and Reaper. She's got nowhere to go, nowhere to run, and as she mainly focuses her attention on me, I realize that I'm the one she's scared of, not Reaper.

"She's not going to hurt you, kid. She just wants to make sure you're doing alright."

Shadow visibly swallows, her terrified gaze morphing into nothing more than uncertainty as she stares back at me. There's nothing but silence around us, and I wait, not moving an inch as I allow Shadow to come to the decision on her own if she's willing to trust me.

Then, in the blink of an eye, her body relaxes, and she glances back toward Reaper. "I'm hungry," she murmurs, her tone so soft that it throws me off. I had expected her to have an edge, a type of disdain in her tone that warns people to keep away. But there's nothing like that. She's just a girl, out here in the big, wide world, terrified of this mess she's been thrown into.

Reaper nods and steps toward her before ushering her closer to me. "Alright then," he says. "Let's get you fed."

13

REAPER

Walking back into the hotel restaurant with Shadow in front and Siren at my side, a strange sense of contentment comes over me. It's something I've never felt before and something I can't even begin to understand, but before I get the chance to question it, the waiter who so painstakingly took our orders earlier steps out of the kitchen.

"No," he gasps in terror, the sound so subtle, and yet somehow it's capable of drawing the attention of the whole room.

I resist the urge to smile. A man like this would never survive in my world. He'd be the first to go on principle alone. When Siren and I left barely ten minutes ago, he was thrilled. I could see the relief in his eyes as we walked out the door. It's as though he held his breath the whole time we were here, and now that we're back, he looks about ready to shit his pants.

We continue striding through the restaurant, and as we approach him, I pause, placing a hand on Shadow's shoulder, bringing her up short. "Let me make this clear," I tell the waiter. "My friends and I are going to go and sit down at a private booth, and in exactly three minutes, you are going to come to our table with a glass of wine for the lady, and a burger for the kid. Is that understood?"

The bottom half of his jaw begins to chatter, and I have no doubt that he's remembering exactly what was overheard before. It's no secret to the locals of Blue Springs that something has been going down in their town. The multiple deaths, the unusual police presence, and the sense of unease they get when they step foot outside their doors. Their town isn't safe, and he knows it.

"Y—yes," he stumbles out, his gaze dropping to Shadow. "A burger, Miss?"

Shadow glances at me for a second before turning her gaze back to the waiter. "Can I have a soda as well?"

"Of course," he says, trying his hardest to look cheerful. "Coming right up."

The waiter scurries off, and we continue through the restaurant, weaving through the busy tables. "Seriously?" Siren says beside me, her words barely audible. "The guy is already terrified of us. Was that really necessary?"

I turn my gaze, meeting her stern stare. "How do you mean? The child is hungry. I was simply putting in her order. Would you have preferred I waited until after the waiter had finished shitting his pants?"

Siren rolls her eyes, knowing damn well that I see right through my own bullshit. I enjoyed that, and she knows it. What can I say? There are certainly perks of being part of the one percent. People give me a wide berth and when I want something, it tends to fall right into my lap. I don't ever have to try, to plead, to beg. It comes to me naturally . . . and by naturally, I mean through others' fears.

People don't want to cross me or risk upsetting me. They may not know who or what I am, but they feel it in their chest. They know I'm not someone they want to fuck with, and because of that, they go out of their way to please me.

"You don't scare me, Reaper," she murmurs.

I hold her stare, pausing right in the middle of the restaurant, preparing to call her bluff, and as I take a step toward her, I wait for the inevitable flash of her eyes, warning me to back off, but it never comes.

Unease rocks through me, and I realize that she's not lying. She's genuinely not scared of me anymore, and I don't know how to feel about that. My whole brand is based on the sole fact that people are terrified of me. Yet, all I see in Siren's eyes is need.

"You're treading on shaky ground," I warn her. "Be careful what you wish for."

Siren steps even closer, her body pressing against mine and making my skin burn from her touch. "Here's the thing," she whispers, her soft breath brushing across my collar. "I don't think I'm the one making wishes they have no business making."

With that, she steps back and continues on her way to a table, leaving me standing motionless in the middle of the restaurant, unable to do a damn thing but stare after her.

What the fuck is happening here? Why has this woman so completely fucked with my head?

As I watch Siren and Shadow make themselves comfortable at a private table in the corner, I get my shit together and keep walking toward them, that strange feeling of contentment returning.

Ease weaves its way through my veins as I walk toward the two women who have, in one way or another, left me completely stumped. Yet being here with them both at this moment just feels right.

Joining them at the table, I can't help but notice the way that Siren and Shadow watch each other. They're both unsure, don't know what's about to come from this unexpected meeting, or if they can risk trusting one another, and when I take my place at the table, it's almost impossible not to notice the way the two of them seem to relax.

Siren watches me, her gaze suggesting that I've got a shitload of explaining to do, but she'll get nothing from me until I know she can be trusted. For now, it's Shadow we need to focus on.

Turning my attention on the terrified kid, I fix her with a heavy stare. "You were following me again."

She shakes her head and flicks her gaze toward Siren for the briefest moment before returning to me. "I was following her actually," she admits before returning her stare back to Siren. "You know this guy is stalking you, right?"

Siren lets out a heavy sigh. "It has come to my attention on a few occasions."

Shadow nods, probably not knowing what to do with that information. She might understand that Siren intrigues me, that I'm attracted to this woman, but it's clear in the way she watches Siren that she doesn't understand why she hasn't attempted to deal with me yet. And to be honest, I'm relieved. She's very clearly a smart kid, and from what I gather, her innocence hasn't been corrupted. She knows I like Siren, but doesn't know what I want to do with her, and for that, I'm grateful.

"You realize at some point, he's going to try and kill you?" Shadow questions as though Siren's completely forgotten why she's here in this godforsaken town.

Siren laughs. "I'm more than aware," she tells the kid. "But here's the thing. He's had more than enough chances to take my life. He could have killed me whenever he wanted, but I'm still here, sitting right across the table from you. I may not be able to trust a single soul in these games, but I can trust that men are simple creatures. And more than that, I can trust my gut, and right now, my gut tells me that he has no intention of killing me yet . . . if at all."

I scoff, my gaze whipping to her. "That gut of yours is going to get you in trouble," I warn her. "Don't think for a second that I won't kill you when the time comes."

Siren winks, and something inside me crumbles. "Not if I get to you first."

"Fuck me," Shadow mutters under her breath. "The two of you just need to do it already."

My gaze whips around to Shadow, gaping at her as I mentally go over the words that just came out of her mouth, making sure I heard her correctly. But fuck, there's no mistaking that, and judging by the way Siren is gaping at her too, it's clear that I was wrong. Perhaps this kid does know exactly what I want with Siren.

"I . . . ummm . . . what?" Siren says, her face flushing just as the waiter arrives at the table with her wine and Shadow's soda. Siren takes the wine from him, and before it even hits the table, she lifts it right to her lips and downs every last drop. She immediately hands the glass back to the guy. "I'm gonna need more, and keep 'em coming."

The waiter scurries off like a good little boy, and the second he's gone, Shadow launches her inquest. "So like . . . are you two a thing? Working together?"

I scoff. "I work alone."

A smirk stretches across Siren's lips, and as she glances at me, a strange fluttering occurs deep in my stomach. "Ahh, so you don't need me then," she states, her voice lowered. "You're content with jerking off alone in a cold shower."

My gaze narrows on her. Maybe she has a point. Perhaps I don't always prefer working alone.

"Watch yourself, Little Siren."

Shadow watches us from across the table, scrunching her lips into a disgusted cringe. "You two are gross."

Siren simply smiles, more than proud of herself as she settles her stare back on the kid. "Why were you watching me anyway? Do you do that often?" she asks, right as the waiter returns with a burger bigger than the kid's head.

Shadow can hardly answer the question because she's staring at the burger as though she can't possibly think about anything else. "Ummm . . . What?" Shadow grunts, her hands already scooping up the burger.

"You were following me," Siren repeats. "Why?"

Shadow takes a bite, and her eyes roll in her head. "Ohmygod," she groans around the food, her words smooshed together. "Thisissogood."

"Shadow," Siren pushes.

"I follow everyone."

"Everyone?"

"That's what I said."

"You're able to track everyone? Just like that?"

She takes another bite, barely having finished off the first one, and before she even chews her food, she shoves the straw of her soda into her mouth as well. The fuck is up with this kid? She's acting as though she hasn't eaten in months, but that couldn't be right because I only just gave her money to make sure she had everything she needed.

Shadow simply shrugs. "You gotta be the best to beat the best," she says, and as she eats her burger, I watch as she relaxes, getting chatty as she eats. "And you two? You're the best. Right after me, of course. But you know who's not the best? Those brothers."

"You knew they were brothers?" Siren asks, her brow arching, clearly impressed.

"Doesn't take a genius to figure that one out," Shadow continues, and I do what I can to not take offense. I didn't realize that immediately, and it wasn't until Siren's confirmation that I believed it to be true.

"Don't you go searching out trouble with them," I warn Shadow. "They're not like me or Siren. If they catch you in a back alley, they won't offer to feed you. They'll beat you to death."

"I know," she says, a wariness in her eyes. "I've already had a run-in with them tonight, but after I saw how they killed Sharkbait the other night, I knew to get out of there. I'm not looking to be a victim."

Siren clenches her jaw, her eyes flashing with anger. "They targeted you?"

Shadow shrugs her shoulders and keeps her gaze focused on her burger. "Yeah, sure. They targeted me. Or maybe I might have targeted them."

"Are you insane?" Siren demands. "You're a kid. You can't be putting yourself in unnecessary danger like that."

"Just because I'm a kid doesn't mean I can't handle myself," Shadow throws back at her. "I know what I'm doing."

"I'm sure you do, but these aren't the kind of people who are going to take it easy on you because you're a kid. They're going to kill you, and it'll be brutal. They don't give a shit. You can't go out looking for trouble. Sure, track them all you want. Do all the recon you need, but choose your targets wisely."

"Like you do?" Shadow demands around a mouthful of food. "I saw your kill tonight. That was nothing. You should have just let Eagle walk. That kill doesn't count."

"So you're saying that I should have allowed her to go and given her the opportunity to potentially kill me later or kill . . . I don't know . . . you, maybe? Maybe I should have let her live with her broken ribs and burned arm and let the brothers or Gasoline come back to finish the job in a much nastier way. She was lucky that I was the one who came after her tonight, and she knew it. Having compassion doesn't make me weak. It makes me human."

Shadow presses her lips into a tight line and dips her chin before slowly nodding. "I'm sorry. You're right."

Siren watches her through a narrowed stare, and after what feels like a lifetime, her body finally relaxes and she moves the conversation along. "What's your plan, Shadow? How are you going to get through these next twenty days?"

She takes another bite, and I stare at her burger, shocked by how quickly she's putting it away. "I'm a watcher," Shadow explains. "I don't like getting involved in all the bullshit. I've been trained to learn everybody's weaknesses, and at the very last moment, swoop in and end the game."

"And how's that going for you?" I ask.

"So far, I don't know. Apart from you two, there are six other contenders who need to be taken out. The brothers, Gasoline, Raven, Silver, and The Executioner. I've been able to figure out every single one of them and can already see how they'll meet their end during these games. The only two I can't seem to figure out are you two."

"What do you mean?" Siren asks.

"Neither of you are playing by your usual MO."

I nod, approving of this child more with every word that comes out of her mouth. "You're clever."

Shadow shakes her head. "Considering I'm sitting at a table across from the very two I can't seem to figure out, perhaps that means I'm anything but clever," she says. "How do I know you're not working together and plan to shank me out by the dumpsters after you finish feeding me?"

"You don't," Siren tells her. "But like I said, it's about trusting your gut. You can either choose to trust that Reaper and I mean you no harm, or you can choose not to. That's your prerogative. I can't force you to believe something, and I can't force you to believe someone's intentions based on nothing more than their words. This game is a fight to the end, and while I would be honored to earn your trust, the truth is, you shouldn't trust a damn soul in these games."

"She's right," I add. "The single most effective way to survive is to trust only yourself."

Shadow holds my stare. "You're saying you don't want me to trust you?"

"Not at all. I'm saying to be wary. At the end of these games, there's going to be a decision that needs to be made. Only one of us will be able to walk free at the end of the month. I know who I'd like that to be, and I assume Siren is on the same page. I trust her to make the right decision, just as she's trusting me to do the same. It's now up to you if you can live with that."

"It sounds like you're asking us to work as a team," Shadow questions.

Siren narrows her gaze, her heavy stare locked on mine. "Hmmmm. Peculiar."

"I work alone," I remind them.

Shadow laughs to herself before finishing off the rest of her burger and scooping up her soda instead. "Something tells me this is going to be fun."

Siren rolls her eyes and fixes her stare back on the kid. "Where have you been staying?"

Shadow's carefree attitude quickly disappears, her shackles rising back into place. "Why?"

"You have bags under your eyes. You're not sleeping, and judging by the way you just annihilated that burger, you're not eating either. Do you know how to care for yourself? Have clean clothes, toiletries?"

"I . . ."

She glances away, not wanting to answer, and I press her to continue. "Answer the question, Shadow. I gave you money to buy yourself groceries. What happened to that?"

Siren's brow arches, and she whips her gaze back to me. "You did what? When?"

Ignoring her inquisition, I keep my stare focused on Shadow, not allowing her the chance to slip past this conversation. "What good is having groceries if you can't do anything with them?" she questions, her voice low and ashamed. "Apart from the fact I already told you I don't cook. It's not as though I have a way to transport them. Shall I pile up the back of someone's Honda and steal their car—a car which I don't know how to drive—or should I just carry them on my back?"

I let out a heavy breath. I fucked up.

That was a huge oversight on my part. I gave her the resources I thought she needed to look after herself, but in reality, I did nothing but make myself feel like I'm some kind of hero. I didn't help her at all.

"Okay, here's the deal," Siren says, clearly seeing I'm at a loss. "I'm assuming you know where my villa is?"

Shadow simply smirks and Siren rolls her eyes. "Of course you do," she says. "I like to cook. I cook myself something every single night, and while I might not have a wide variety of dishes that I'm willing to experiment with, they're still delicious."

Siren grabs the napkin off the table and pulls a pen from somewhere inside her cropped tank before writing down a six-digit code. "Here, this is the code to my villa, not that you'll actually need it to break into my home. Every night, at precisely seven o'clock, there will be a freshly cooked meal on my kitchen table for you. Eat it or don't. It doesn't matter to me, but it will be there all the same," she tells her. "If it's not eaten by seven thirty, it will be waiting for you in the fridge. There is also a blanket on the sofa, which folds out to a bed if you so happen to feel the urge to stay for a while. Just . . . Please don't stab me in my sleep."

Shadow gawks at her, just as lost for words as I am, and honestly, I don't know if I should applaud her for going out of her way and showing so much kindness to this child or if I should berate her for being so fucking stupid. After all, Shadow will eventually have to kill her because, let's face it, despite the tough game I talk, I'd prefer to fuck her than kill her, and welcoming her right into her home like that is asking for trouble.

Shadow visibly swallows. "You'd really do that for me?"

"I'm not about to let you starve. While you might be some kind of creepy child spy turned assassin, you're still just a child. You shouldn't be here, despite how good you might be."

Her gaze drops to her hands, and it's as though she's never had anyone care for her before. "Thank you," she murmurs, the words sounding hard to say.

"My pleasure."

"Speaking of being a child spy turned assassin," I say. "How did you become this way? Who trained you?"

Her gaze snaps up, and suddenly that childlike innocence and gratefulness vanishes, leaving nothing but the terrified child I saw in the back of the alley. Her gaze flashes between me and Siren, and as we both start to raise our hands to calm her down, she rushes to her feet and makes a break for it, vanishing out of the restaurant like the ghost that she is.

"Fuck," Siren says, an accusation clear in her tone. "Now look what you've done. She was only just starting to come around."

I shake my head. "That kid's got a long way to go before she starts coming around," I tell her. "But one thing is for sure, it's not us she's terrified of, it's her home."

"That makes her a threat," Siren murmurs, devastation thick in her tone. "She'll be desperate to win that prize money and free herself. She won't be reasoned with and will keep going after the others. We need to keep an eye on her."

"If you haven't noticed, keeping an eye on her is fucking impossible. She's the only person who has ever evaded me."

Siren's gaze widens in shock. "She did?"

I nod, almost ashamed to admit it. "Twice, and if it weren't for you seeing her outside the restaurant earlier, it would have been three times."

"Shit."

"Mmhmm," I say. "All I know is that this game won't be ending because there's no way in hell I'm going to let her get the drop on me, but I won't allow you or anyone else to end her life either. She's too young for this shit."

"I agree," Siren says, picking up the wine glass she didn't even see the waiter refill. She throws her head back and drains the glass before getting to her feet. "We have to protect her."

I stand with her, placing my hand on her lower back after tossing a hundred-dollar bill on the table. "The question is, how the fuck are we supposed to protect a ghost when we have no fucking idea what she truly needs protection from?"

14

SIREN

Sleep doesn't come easy after the night I just had with Eagle, Reaper, and then Shadow. It was more than just eventful, and now my brain is struggling to turn off. I'm exhausted. All I want is to drown in my sorrows and fall into a deep sleep, perhaps even ignore my alarm and stay in bed until someone drags me out of it.

It's after two in the morning, and at this point, I think my eyeballs are literally falling out of my head, but for whatever reason, the sweet peace of sleep just won't come. Maybe it's because I foolishly gave Shadow the code to get into my home, though I don't anticipate her actually using it. She could easily break in if she wanted to. Same goes for Reaper actually, and judging from tonight's conversation, I wouldn't be surprised if he were hiding out somewhere in the bushes outside.

Yet the thought of him being close by no longer terrifies me.

I think I like it. The idea of Reaper stalking me is kind of a turn-on. He's incredible, the absolute best in the business. He spent years perfecting his skills, and for whatever reason, I'm the person who intrigues him. If he just wanted to get his dick wet, he could walk into any bar and take his pick, but he likes me.

Okay, maybe *like* is a strong word for it, but he's certainly intrigued, and that excites me in a way I could have never imagined. I like his eyes on me, like the way his knee brushed mine under the table, but when we stood outside that restaurant before seeing Shadow and he slid his hand down my body and cupped my pussy . . . fuck! I was ruined.

The thought of it has me squirming beneath the blankets, and the next thing I know, my eyes are closed as my hand skims under the sheets and down between my thighs. I push my fingers inside the waistband of my sleep shorts, diving down to the apex of my thighs as my back arches off the mattress.

Fuck. Reaper has ruined me.

My fingers brush over my needy clit, and just as I begin to visualize the way that Reaper would so easily destroy me between the sheets, a subtle creak sounds deeper within my villa.

My hand rips out of my pajama shorts and within the blink of an eye, I'm on my feet, a blade in one hand and my phone in the other, bringing up my surveillance feed. A quick check of the outdoor area comes up empty but as I check the inside feed, my heart starts to race for a whole new reason.

Reaper stands right in the center of my kitchen, leaning against the counter as though he hasn't got a care in the world. One foot is kicked over the other, his arms crossed over his wide chest as he stares directly into the camera.

Shit.

I don't bother dressing, but I don't release my hold on the blade either before trudging out into the hallway in nothing but my sleep shorts, a black cami, and a deep unfulfilled need throbbing in my core.

Making my way out to the kitchen and living area, I prop my shoulder against the wall and glare at Reaper, seeing him perfectly despite the darkness, and I can't help but be grateful for the fact he's chosen the brightest area in the villa to stand. He wasn't trying to scare me, hence why he took up space right in front of my kitchen camera. He simply wanted to draw me out.

He's just as huge and imposing as he's always been, but now when I look at him, I don't feel that same fear I got that very first time. He doesn't scare me anymore, and that's on me. I should fear him. I should be running in the opposite direction. Instead, all I want is to tear every article of clothing off him and have my wicked way with him.

God, what I wouldn't give to strip him bare and lick him from head to toe, to taste every inch of him, to please and satisfy him.

Instead of attacking him with my tongue, I lift a brow and feign indifference. "Is there a reason your big ass body is currently invading my kitchen?"

Reaper stares at me, and those usually lethal eyes somehow seem a little . . . softer now. Goosebumps spread across my body, and when he pushes off the edge of the counter and moves toward me, my heart races in a way I've never experienced before. "We never finished our conversation," he rumbles in that deep tone, sending my world into a complete tailspin.

A stupid smirk rests on my lips, and with every slow step he takes toward me, the excitement grows. "And what conversation would that be?"

There's a teasing hint in my tone, and judging by the way his dark eyes flash with hunger, he knows that I'm fully aware of what he's talking about. He needs his chance to prove that he's man enough to make me beg, but I'm not just going to hand it to him; I'm going to make him work for it.

Reaper steps right in front of me, his dark eyes capturing me and locking me into his vortex. He lifts his hand, and for just a moment, my heart stops racing, maybe stops beating altogether, as I wait to see what he's going to do. Then, when those very fingers find my collar and begin trailing down past the curve of my breast and skimming down to my waist, my heart lurches back into action.

His hands leave a pebbled trail across my skin, and electricity pulses through my veins. This is what I've been desperate for, what I've been craving since that very first encounter with him.

I don't take my eyes off him, watching his every movement, more than aware of just how quickly he could end my life. Mila would be so angry with me. I can just imagine what she'd have to say about this, but if I'm going to go out, then I might as well go out screaming in pleasure.

Reaper dips his head, his lips barely a breath away from my ear.

"You know exactly what conversation I'm talking about," he rumbles, then in a flash, his strong hands are at my waist, lifting me off the ground. He whips us around, and in a flash, my ass hits the edge of the kitchen counter and my knees spread on either side of his hips.

He presses into me, his rock-hard cock firm against my throbbing core, and when he rocks his hips, it's just about all I can handle before I melt right off the damn counter. I can feel the full outline of his cock and there's no denying just how big he is.

He's not just ready for me, he's starved.

"Tell me this isn't what you want," Reaper murmurs, rocking his hips again and grinding that thick cock against my aching clit, making me desperately wish my sleep shorts would disintegrate into a million pieces and let me have him. "Tell me you haven't been riding your fingers all fucking night, wishing it was me inside you. Tell me you haven't been wet every second of the day, thinking about the way I'd spread these pretty thighs and fuck you bare, taking you inch by inch."

I swallow hard, the desperation eating me alive. "I'm not going to deny it," I murmur, lifting my chin so that my lips brush straight past his, teasing him with the promise of everything they can do. "The thought of what you could do to me has kept me up for nights on end, knowing just how deep you'd take me, how you'd slam into me with powerful thrusts and make my pussy shatter around you. But do you really think I'm going to let you walk in here and just take whatever you want? That I'm going to sit here and beg you to take me? Beg you to drop to your knees and fuck me with your tongue?"

Reaper pulls back just an inch, meeting my stare, and the challenge he finds there has his dark gaze narrowing. He doesn't respond, clearly aware that I have a plan of my own, and as his interest grows, he waits to see what I have in store for him.

All I can do is smile as I reach back for the bag behind me on the counter, my fingers curling around the cool metal before shoving him back. Reaper inches away, allowing me space, and after sliding off the edge of the counter, I step back into him, forcing him further back.

Placing my hand against his chest, I take another step until his big body has eaten up all the available space in the kitchen and his back is forced up against my refrigerator. "Here's the thing," I murmur as my hand lowers on his body, skimming down past his waist to the massive bulge in his pants. I palm him through his pants, watching as his eyes flutter with satisfaction, and as I press up to my tippy toes, I lean closer to whisper in his ear. "I don't play fair, Reaper. I play to win, and only one of us is going to win tonight."

Reaper groans, and the sound rips through me like liquid ecstasy.

"You like that?" I question, continuing to palm his impressive cock.

He clenches his jaw, refusing to answer because both of us know that I have him right where I want him. I'm the one in control, and the only way he gets what he wants right now is if I decide to give it to him. But like I said, it's never that easy.

I offer him a sugary sweet smile, batting my lashes as though I'm the innocent one here. "Here's the deal," I whisper, my body pressing against his big one just as I reach around him, slip the metal handcuff over his wrist, and lock him to my refrigerator. "I'm yours to have any way you want, but there's just one caveat."

His eyes darken with excitement and I don't pretend that he isn't fully aware of the cuff around his wrist despite not having reacted to it. "And what's that?"

"You've gotta catch me first."

His eyes blaze with the challenge, and as my heart bursts with a strange mix of fear and excitement, I take off like lightning, knowing those handcuffs won't keep him down for long.

I bolt through the front door, sprinting faster than I have in my life, swallowing the laughter that threatens to burst out of me. I've never been so desperate and hungry for someone, only to run at the very last second. I could play this game a million times in my life, but there's only one man on this planet capable of actually catching me, and that man is Reaper.

He's the hunter, and I'm the prey. And this just became the most exciting game I've ever played.

My feet are silent against the ground despite my frantic sprint through the holiday resort. I bypass the pool and the tennis courts while keeping off the main roads, knowing that my hunter would already be out on the streets, tracking my every step.

My heart races as the adrenaline pulses heavily through my veins, and despite knowing that the world's deadliest man is hot on my heels, I can't seem to wipe the grin off my face.

The way this man is going to fuck me tonight . . . shit.

I need to focus on trying to evade him first, though, if I were a smart woman, I wouldn't put too much effort into it. After all, my ultimate goal is to get caught and punished for being such a brat, but I can't hand him the win. That's too easy. He's already told me once that he likes to work for his kills, and I don't suppose that this would be any different. He likes the challenge, and that's exactly what I plan to give him.

Reaching the boundary line of the holiday resort I make quick work of the fence, launching myself right over it before landing in a ridiculous crouched pose to gain my balance. Then, without a moment to waste, I sprint back into action.

I dart through the streets, not daring to look back. I don't doubt he's already close, but for now, my only focus is to put distance between us. I stick to the shadows, the darkness my only ally tonight. The streets are deserted, and despite how desperately I need him to catch me and have his wicked way with me, I'm not about to have him fuck me in a dirty alley behind a grocery store. I want this to be perfect, and with that in mind, I take a sharp right, heading toward the biggest tourist location Blue Springs offers—the lake.

Moving closer toward the lake, my heart races for a million different reasons, but the way chills begin creeping over my skin, I realize he's closing in on me. The hunter has found his prey, but is he fast enough to capture her, or will she evade him?

"You can't run from me, Little Siren," that deep, alluring voice calls from behind me, sending shivers shooting down my spine and making me realize he's a lot closer than I realized.

Unable to help myself, I glance back over my shoulder and see Reaper casually strolling behind me as though he hasn't even broken a sweat, but that's not possible. I feel as though I've run a marathon, and I realize that I didn't even stand a chance, but the smirk on his lips suggests he enjoyed it all the same.

I turn around and start walking backward with a shit-eating grin across my face, noticing the handcuff still dangling from his wrist. "From where I'm standing," I call back. "It looks like I can."

Reaper's gaze narrows, and when he breaks into a run, a squeal tears from deep in my chest. I stumble over my feet as I frantically turn my ass around and bolt toward the lake. A laugh bubbles from my throat, and I do what I can to keep pushing myself faster, but let's be honest, I'm more than ready for this man to catch me.

I've never been more excited in my life and just as my feet finally reach the water, a strong arm locks around my waist, lifting me off my feet. "You really think you could evade me, Little Siren?"

A stupid laugh tears out of me, and before I know it, I'm flipped around, my chest pressed against his and my legs wrapped securely around his waist, more than capable of feeling the whole outline of his cock pressed firmly against my core. "No," I admit, slowly reaching for my black cami and pulling it over my head. "But it proved just how far you're willing to go to have me."

Reaper growls, his gaze roaming over my bare tits. "You've got no fucking idea." And not a second later, we crash down into the water.

My knees hit the damp shore as Reaper settles himself behind me. "I hope you're fucking ready for me, Siren," he says, one hand scooping around my body and cupping my tits as his other hand drops down between my thighs, feeling just how wet I am through my sleep shorts.

"I've been ready since the second you touched me in that goddamn alley."

"Good."

His thumb and forefinger roll over my pebbled nipple, pinching, and the pleasure rocks right through me, sending an electrical current shooting right to my core, and as I press back against him, desperate for relief, Reaper slips his hand inside my shorts, instantly finding my entrance.

He slides two thick fingers inside me, and I don't hesitate to ride them. "Is this what you've been needing, Little Siren? You need me to fuck you with my fingers?"

I shake my head, my hips jolting when he stretches his thumb to my clit and begins rolling tight circles. "I want you to fuck me with your mouth, and only after I've come on your tongue can you fuck me with that thick cock of yours."

"Is that so?"

"Mmmmm," is all I can manage to say.

Then in a flash, his fingers tighten on my nipple, pinching hard before he shoves me forward, bending me over until my face is against the damp sand of the shore, my ass high in the air. His fingers are free of my cunt, and I cry out in frustration, but then his thumbs dig into the waistband of my sleep shorts.

He drags them over my ass, exposing every vulnerable piece of me, and I've never felt sexier. "You'll get my mouth, Little Siren, but you'll be patient," he rumbles just as I feel his fingers back at my cunt, pushing deep into me from behind.

His fingers circle within me, massaging my walls, and as my eyes roll, all I can do is scream out in pure ecstasy. "Yes," I pant. "Just like that."

Reaper fucks me with his fingers, and I can't help but slip my hand between my thighs and roll my fingers over my needy clit, showing him just how much I like it. "Let me be clear," he rumbles, his voice thick with desire as he pushes his fingers deeper. "This is mine. Your pleasure is mine. *You are mine.*"

Well, shit.

"Yours," I groan as those fingers work their magic.

I feel myself right on the edge when he slowly releases his fingers from my cunt, and just when I go to cry out in devastation, his warm tongue dances through my center. "Oh fuck," I groan, pressing back against his face and lowering my fingers from my clit as he takes over.

His tongue is like liquid ecstasy as it works over my needy clit. He sucks and nips, and when his fingers return to my cunt, pushing deep inside of me and massaging my walls, I know I'll never feel anything as good as this again.

I push my knees wider, arching my back to offer him as much of myself as I possibly can as the cool water of the lake dances over my skin. "More," I groan, and without hesitation, he gives me exactly what I'm asking for. "Holy fucking shit."

He works me in a way the battery-operated boyfriends in my bedside drawer could only dream about, and when I feel that familiar sensation building deep inside me, I know it won't be long until I see stars.

Reaper's tongue is perfect, but his fingers are the star of this show, and as they curl inside me and find my G-spot, my world detonates. "Oh, GOD!" I cry out as I come hard, deep pleasure rocking through me as my orgasm claims every single inch of my body.

My walls spasm around Reaper's fingers, wildly convulsing, and as he continues working me, massaging his fingers over my G-spot again and again, the intensity only increases. My whole body shakes as my fingers curl into my palms, creating tight fists, but he doesn't relent. He's intent to not only meet my expectations but to blow them right out of the water.

I cry out, the intensity becoming too much, and as if already knowing where my limits are, he finally begins to ease up on my body. I reach my peak, and the moment I start to come down, I gasp for air, my whole body violently shaking.

The pleasure is too much, too good, and my whole world is completely knocked on its ass. I didn't even know I could come like that. I didn't know anything could be that intense or good.

When I finally come down, struggling to catch a full breath, Reaper finally pulls back, freeing his fingers from my trembling cunt. "Fuck, Little Siren. Do you have any idea how sweet you taste?"

A shiver sails down my spine, and I can't help but grin, but when I hear the familiar sound of a zipper, I realize I have all but three seconds to recover before he takes me again, only this time, it's going to be the sweetest kind of brutal.

"I'm going to fuck this sweet little cunt, Siren," Reaper growls, freeing that thick cock. "And I don't plan on being gentle. You have no idea how just the thought of slamming inside of you has tormented me."

"Then what are you waiting for?" I whisper. "Take me, Reaper. Fuck me."

I feel the heavy tip of his cock against my entrance, mixing with my wetness and as the anticipation builds and the thought of how he will stretch me begins to plague my mind, I push back against him, fucking drenched for him.

"Reaper," I groan, needing him to take me now.

His tip dances through my wetness, teasing me with everything he's about to do, and as his strong hand grips my hip to hold me still, I almost come apart before he's truly had me. Then as I push back against him again, he finally inches into me.

He gives me just the tip, and I already feel my walls needing to stretch. His fingers tighten on my hip, and I have no doubt that come morning I'll have the perfect imprint of his fingers left on my body. He gives me another inch and my eyelids flutter, but it has nothing on the soft grunt that sounds behind me.

"Fuck, Siren."

"Take me deeper," I beg.

He pushes further, and my walls keep stretching to accommodate his sheer size. He's only got to be halfway, but it's already driving me wild. I don't know how I'm going to take all of him, but I'm no quitter. My walls quake as my hips jolt, the undeniable pleasure already too much, but he doesn't dare stop, taking me until he's fully seated inside.

"Oh fuck," I groan, my pussy never having felt so full.

Reaper doesn't move, both of us needing a minute, but when my walls clench around him and his fingers tighten, I realize that despite talking a big game, I'm still the one in control. I have the power to bring him to his knees and I've never felt so alive.

"Fuck me, Reaper," I demand. "Give me what I need. Otherwise, I'm taking this into my own hands, and we both know you'll crumble like a little bitch."

His hand comes down over my ass with a sharp smack as a deep growl rumbles through his chest. "You don't know what the fuck you're asking for." And with that, Reaper draws back and finally starts to fuck me.

He sends fast, powerful thrusts my way, rocking that thick cock in and out as my walls clench around him. He holds me still, and my body immediately folds to his every will, undeniably becoming his.

Reaper's hips roll as he draws back, and with every new thrust, he sends me further into oblivion, taking me at every possible angle. The water splashes around us as the moonlight dances across the massive lake, but all that matters is the way he fucks me, the way he brings me back to life.

My walls tremble around his primal thrusts as my body quickly grows weak, his pure animalistic desperation feeding the intense need within me. It's everything I thought it was going to be and so much more.

"Touch yourself," he demands through a clenched jaw. "Show me how you like it."

I groan as my hand slips between my thighs, my fingers brushing over my needy clit, and as I roll tight little circles, matching the rhythm of his powerful thrusts, my whole world becomes his.

"Fuck, Reaper," I pant, feeling that familiar build inside of me and knowing it won't be long until he throws me right over the edge.

"Just like that, Little Siren. Take it for me."

I clench my eyes, trying to hold on to it as that deep voice does something wicked to me. I've never felt so alive, so powerful, and beautiful. I need to bring him to his knees and feel the way he comes undone.

I push back against him, taking him impossibly deeper as my fingers frantically roll over my clit. "Oh, God," I groan, my pussy clenching tighter around his thick, veiny cock. "I can't . . . I—"

"Shit, Siren," he grunts, his fingers digging into my skin, the desperation in his tone sending me spiraling. "Come for me, baby. Show me how fucking tight you can squeeze me."

My eyes roll to the back of my head, and not a second later, I let go, my body crumbling to his will as I shatter like glass, my orgasm exploding from within as stars dance in my vision. My walls wildly spasm as hot bursts of pure electricity pulse through my veins.

"Fuck, Reaper!"

He thrusts into me again and again, and as I completely come apart, Reaper struggles to hold back. The intensity shooting through me is too much, and I can hardly catch my breath as my hands ball into tight fists.

Then just as I reach the highest peak of my orgasm, Reaper

succumbs to the intense pleasure, joining me as he finally unravels, shooting hot spurts of cum deep inside my cunt with a loud, desperate roar.

15

REAPER

Siren paces through the shore of the lake, dragging her feet through the cool water in nothing but my shirt as I sit on the damp sand, watching her move from left to right. Her little cami and sleep shorts were nowhere to be found, but the second they were removed from her body, I couldn't care less about them.

Siren is one of those women who should be in a constant state of nakedness. Her body is flawless, absolutely perfect, and I'm going to make it my personal mission to devour as much of it as I possibly can before these twenty days are over.

"Okay, tell me this," she says, pausing ankle deep in the water and looking back at me. She's been asking me questions for the last twenty minutes, trying to get to the bottom of all the intel she was able to dig up on me, trying to decipher what's real and what was fabricated by local enforcement. "What's your real name?"

Fuck me. I'd be more comfortable asking her to perform a rectal exam on me than giving up that kind of information. I've held my name close for a long time, not having to use it in close to fifteen years. The few people who are closest to me don't even know it, and yet, for whatever reason, I haven't told her to fuck right off with her line of questioning. Perhaps it's the post-nut clarity that's making me play nice in the hopes she'll allow me to have her again, because fuck, after that first taste, I'm addicted.

"Oh, come on," Siren says, walking over to me and dropping down in my lap, her knees on either side of my thighs as I feel the warmth of her sweet cunt through the front of my pants. I have to work hard not to remind myself that she's not wearing any underwear. "You figured out my name, and not only that, you used it against me. It's only fair that I know yours."

I let out a heavy breath. "I don't use my real name."

Siren nods, and sadness begins to consume her. "I understand that more than you could possibly know."

"Do you want to talk about it?"

She offers me a sad smile, trying to push through the pain of whatever trauma is plaguing her mind. "No, but thanks."

I nod, not wanting to push her on something that so clearly affects her so much. Instead, all I want is to make her happy, to see just a fraction of a smile pull across her lips, and to bask in the way her eyes light up. "My name," I say, feeling more vulnerable than I ever have in my life. "Is Nikolai Volkov."

Her eyes widen in surprise, the sadness in her eyes quickly fading away. "You're Russian?"

I shrug my shoulders. "I suppose. I never knew my parents or where I came from. I was left at the door of an orphanage in Jersey at six months old with nothing more than a birth certificate and a blanket. I've lived in the US all my life."

"Shit, I'm sorry," she says. "Did you ever try to track your parents down?"

"Once," I admit. "My mother died a few years after I was born from a drug overdose, and my father . . . He was a piece of shit. Turns out that my mother was trafficked at sixteen years old and sold to my father. I guess he raped her until he knocked her up, and after she'd given birth, he either tossed her aside or she made a break for it. I never really got a chance to get all the details before I snapped his neck."

"Fuck."

"Yeah. That was my first kill."

Siren holds my stare, nodding before dropping her gaze to my chest, a heaviness flashing in her eyes. "Mine was a friend of my foster father's when I was fourteen," she tells me. "I apparently needed to be taught a lesson, and he thought he was the one to do that."

"Shit," I say, fucking hating when that shit happens to kids. Don't get me wrong, it's terrible no matter the age, but when the innocence of youth is involved, it grinds on my nerves. Especially when it comes from someone who's supposed to protect them.

Siren places her hand on my chest and my body instantly relaxes. "Don't worry, he was castrated before he could use it on me."

Thank fuck for that.

She leans back onto my legs, simply staring at me. "I'm curious about you," she tells me. "What makes you tick?"

"What makes me tick?" I question, unsure how to even answer that. Fuck, I don't even think I know what that means.

Siren grins. "Yep. What makes you tick? What gets under your skin?"

"Are you trying to figure out ways to best me? Because it's not going to work. Nothing gets under my skin."

"I don't need to figure out how to best you," she tells me. "The second I cuffed you to my refrigerator, I realized I already had. If anyone is going to bring you down during these games, it's going to be me. Besides, look at you, Reaper. I got you pinned on the ground. I could kill you before you even knew what was happening."

Laughter threatens to burst out of me, and if I wasn't such a quiet, broody guy, I might have even let it. "There are two things wrong with that statement."

"Dare I ask what they are?" she throws back at me.

I grin. "Number one. You haven't got me close to being pinned, and the only reason I've allowed you to use me as a bench is because the way you're leaning back, gives me the perfect view of your sweet little cunt."

Siren sucks in a breath, grabbing the front of her shirt and pulling it down just enough to cover herself. "And number two?" she prompts.

"Number two," I say, grabbing her around the throat and gently pulling her into me, her lips barely a breath away from mine. "You couldn't kill me even if my hands were bound and my cock was buried deep inside you."

Siren laughs, her eyes shimmering with excitement. "Careful now, you might be giving me ideas."

Her grin is addictive, and I release my hold on her throat, but as she sits up closer, she drops her gaze to my chest, following the lines of the reaper tattoo that covers most of my body. "This is insane," she murmurs, her fingers brushing across the design, following it up to the ink that runs up the side of my neck. "I've been wanting to find out what this was since the second I saw you."

"And?"

"It's terrifying."

"I don't wish to scare you, Siren."

"I know," she whispers. "But that doesn't mean that the idea of who you are and what you're capable of shouldn't haunt me. You're going to kill me no matter what happens between us in the next twenty days. I'm right to be wary of you, just as I should be wary of everyone else, Shadow included."

I nod, agreeing with her completely, and yet the idea of having to end her life suddenly isn't sitting so well with me. Before tonight, I could have done it. I would have made it quick, made sure she didn't feel any pain, but now . . . I don't know. Something has shifted within me.

Lifting my hand, I brush my fingers across the soft skin of her jaw, watching as she folds into my touch. "I don't want to kill you," I tell her. "But I will have to in order to protect Shadow."

She simply holds my stare. "I came into these games so confident that I was going to win. I didn't expect you to be here, and I sure as hell didn't expect to find Shadow. I was such an idiot. The second I got the invitation, I could barely contain myself. No part of me thought there was a chance I wouldn't be going home at the end of it, and now that I'm realizing how wrong I was, I'm not ready to die. I've barely had a life outside of work. Never gotten to love someone or be loved in return, never gotten to have a real home or start a family."

I pull back, meeting her stare straight on. "You want to start a family?"

"Well, no," she admits. "I don't particularly care for having kids or anything like that, and to be honest, I'd be a terrible mom, but I want to be able to have the option to start a family if I wanted. Maybe a dog family. I've always wanted a golden retriever."

Understanding fills me. I've been where she is a million times before, but in our line of work, a normal life isn't always something we can have. We aren't able to put down roots and make plans for a future because we never know where we're going to be, who we'll meet, or what job will come next. Not to mention the risk of starting a family only to have your past creep up on you. It's too dangerous, and that's when hearts start getting hurt. It's better this way. Easier. Cleaner.

"I tried the whole girlfriend thing once," I admit.

Siren arches her brows. "Bullshit. You?"

I nod. "Seriously. Her name was Becca, a cute little brunette with big ole titties."

"There's no way," she laughs. "How did you possibly swing that? Did she know what you do for a living?"

I grin. "No. I told her I was an investment banker, but the night I came home after failing to outrun a grenade, she put it together that perhaps I wasn't exactly who she thought I was. It didn't last long after that."

Siren gapes at me in shock, slowly shaking her head. "I just can't wrap my head around the fact that you thought you could possibly pull off being an investment banker. Have you looked in a mirror lately? But also, you can't outrun a grenade? Are you kidding me?"

"Says the woman who accidentally hung herself by her hair."

She rolls her eyes. "Okay, whatever," she says. "So we all make stupid little mistakes sometimes. It happens to the best of us."

I shake my head. "We can't make mistakes like that in these games."

"Some would argue that this right here was a mistake."

"No, Siren. This right here is a lot of things, but a mistake is not one of them."

She holds my stare, her gaze locked so firmly on mine. "You're surprising me, Reaper," she murmurs, keeping her voice low as though she doesn't trust her tone to come out right. "You're not what I expected."

My heart rate kicks up a gear as I lean back onto my palms and watch her. "And what's that?"

"I thought you would have left afterward, or at the very least killed me now that you got what you wanted, and while that would have sucked, I would have been okay with it because that's what I was expecting, but sitting with me . . . It's messing with my head. I'm not supposed to like you."

"Here's the thing, Siren," I say. "Just because you let me chase you down to the lake and fuck you, doesn't mean I've had nearly my fill of you. We have twenty more days, and I intend to spend every minute we have left buried in your sweet little cunt. And as for liking me? You're treading in dangerous waters. You shouldn't like me. You shouldn't even *want* to like me."

She shakes her head, leaning back into me and hooking her hand around the back of my neck. "Just because you do the things you do and have seen all the things you've seen, doesn't make you any less human. You're deserving of love and affection just as much as I am."

I let out a heavy breath, appreciating that more than she could know, but I have many demons, and this right here is one of my biggest ones. "How can people like us, people who've callously slain multiple men and women be deserving of love?"

"For me, I know that I'm still a good person. I have good intentions and a good heart. I don't just walk out of my home and murder the first person I see like The Texan Reaper would. I kill those who are deserving of death. I do my homework, and at the end of the day, I can walk away from a kill with my dignity intact," she tells me. "And while I know I don't know you very well, and I don't know what motivates you to do what you do, I can tell from the way you've protected Shadow and how you're sitting here with me now that you have a good heart. You're a good man, and you shouldn't deny yourself love just because you've taken lives."

I don't know how to respond. I've spent my whole adult life content with my decision that I wasn't worthy of spending my life with someone, yet in the space of three seconds, this woman has me reconsidering my whole belief system.

"I can't lie, Siren. You're surprising me too," I tell her.

"In a good way or a bad way?" she asks.

"An unexpected way."

She laughs. "Who knows, maybe this is all an act, and I'm playing you just to get close."

I shake my head. "Like I said, I'm too fucking good, baby. You can try and kill me all you like, play me until your fucking fingers bleed, but you won't kill me, and it's not because you're not capable. I've been watching you, Siren. You're good. Too fucking good. The way you work is like a dance. It's intriguing and yet devastatingly beautiful. To be killed by you would be nothing but an honor, but unfortunately, no matter how good you are, I'm better."

Siren grins and leans into me. "You know what I like about you underestimating me?" she questions, pushing up off me and starting to walk away.

"What's that?" I call after her.

She glances back over her shoulder, a seductive grin on her lips. "You'll never see me coming." And with that, she slips away into the darkness, leaving me gasping for air.

I follow her home from a distance, tracking her every step before watching as she makes her way back inside her villa and takes herself to bed. Then as I sit outside her villa, watching over her for the night and making sure none of the other six contenders decide to make her a target, I realize that I'm not just intrigued by this girl, I'm obsessed.

16

SIREN

Ahhhh fuck. Mila is going to kill me, but I can't bring myself to regret what happened with Reaper last night. He was everything. Rough when I needed him to throw me around, and a gentleman when I needed him to show me he was more than just this mystical monster living in my mind.

But the sex.

Holy fucking shit.

A man like Reaper needs to be cloned a million times, and then all those clones need to host workshops about how to satisfy your woman. Because damn. I have never been so intensely satisfied in my life, but the only issue with being dicked down so well is that it leaves a woman desperate for more. Don't get me wrong, it was the first time in ten days I've been able to sleep without a desperate need clawing from within, but by the time I woke up again this morning, that need was even worse.

I need Death's dick, and I need it now!

"What are you doing?" A voice suddenly sounds in my ear.

I cringe. Mila is the one person I can't live without, and I absolutely adore her, but she's also the only person who's going to be able to see right through my bullshit.

"Uhhhh . . . Just out for a walk," I say, making my way down the main street of Blue Springs and doing what I can to keep my gaze locked on Raven across the street.

"Bullshit. In the eight years I've known you, you've never once gone out for a voluntary walk. You're on the hunt."

"Am not!"

"Lie to me again and I'll reach through this phone and punch you right in the tit."

Shit.

"Okay, fine," I say with a heavy sigh, crossing the road as Raven rounds a corner. "I'm tracking Raven and figured I'd go for it. This is the first time since day one that she's fucked up enough to be able to be tracked. Who knows when she'll emerge from her hiding spot again."

"Siren," Mila whines. "I thought you were going to lay low for a while. You're the only one putting in any work around there. Let the others risk their lives instead."

I groan. "I can't just walk away now. I'm too close. Besides, I'll make it quick and then head straight back to the villa."

"Walk away," she says. "You've walked away a million times before. If circumstances aren't right, you always walk away, and right now, circumstances aren't right. You've been doing too much, plus don't act like I don't know that you went out for a late-night run last night. I saw the surveillance feed. Reaper came for you, and considering you're still alive, he didn't just come for you, he *came* for you, which begs the question, WHY THE FUCK HAVEN'T YOU SAID ANYTHING ABOUT IT YET?"

Ahhh shit. I should have known she'd have the notifications on for the villa surveillance cameras. She would have seen Reaper appear in my kitchen in the middle of the night and watched as he stared down the camera, waiting for me to emerge. She would have seen the way he put me on the counter and then how I handcuffed him to my fridge before making a break for it.

Considering all of that, I'm surprised she's waited so long to bitch me out about it.

"Ooop, Raven's walking into a bad cell service area. You're breaking up."

"Don't bullshit me, Siren. I checked this shit before you even got to Blue Springs. The cell service is perfect. There are no dead spots. Now quit stalling and tell me all about your night with Reaper. What happened? Did he get you on your knees?"

A stupid grin stretches across my face as I follow Raven off the main street and through a park. "Oh, he got me on my knees alright," I laugh. "It was incredible, Mills. When I cuffed him to the refrigerator, I told him if he could catch me, he could have me any way he wanted me, and shit. When that man is determined, he doesn't disappoint."

"Holy shit. I can imagine. A man like that . . . fuck. He was rough, wasn't he? He doesn't strike me as the kind who wants to take it slow and gentle."

"You're damn right about that," I murmur, remembering the night so well that everything below the belt clenches with need, desperate to do it all over again.

Mila laughs. "Shit, Siren. I'm going to need a complete run down. Start right from the beginning, and then you're going to have to tell me how the hell you managed to even breathe around a man like that. He's terrifying, and yet, he's the most delicious man to ever walk the earth. Oh, what about those tattoos? They're everywhere, aren't they? Holy shit. Why haven't you started talking yet? How am I supposed to live vicariously through you if you won't open your damn mouth?"

A stupid grin stretches across my face. "Have I told you about my awkward dinner with Shadow and Reaper last night?"

"I swear to all that's holy, Siren. TELL ME ABOUT THE FUCKFEST WITH REAPER!"

Putting my best friend out of her misery, I launch into my story, giving her every last detail, starting from the moment he barged in on my kill with Eagle, right down to the way he followed me back to the villa. I tell her about the way his fingers dug into my skin and the way his body rolled with every powerful thrust.

I give it to her straight, not daring to skip a single detail as I follow Raven through the park and down under the bridge that arches over the massive lake. My gaze shifts toward the water's edge, looking at the very spot Reaper and I had spent almost two hours at last night, and just as I start to brag about the way he made me come on my knees, Raven appears right in front of me, her brow arched and a blade clutched tightly in her right hand.

"Ahh shit," I mutter to Mila, making yet another mistake in these games and allowing myself to get distracted while on a hunt. "I'm gonna have to call you back."

"Good luck," Mila says just before the line goes quiet, and with that, I'm left to face down Raven and finally put this bullshit between us to bed.

Raven and I have competed for the same contracts for years. The issue is that she hates being second best and is a cold-hearted bitch. She tried to pin four of her kills on me back in Seattle. I guess she hoped the FBI would lock me up and throw away the key. I have no respect for someone who wants the cops to do their dirty work.

"If I wanted to spend my afternoon listening to you rave about fucking Reaper, I would have just asked."

I feign a laugh as I take a quick look around our surrounding area, making sure we're alone under the bridge, then I unsheathe one of Reaper's blades from my favorite corset. Raven isn't stupid. She's been doing this almost as long as I have. She wouldn't be foolish enough to make a move on me in front of an audience, especially in broad daylight. She's picked her scene well. Only problem is, this is going to be my scene, not hers. After all, I don't make a habit of losing.

Reaper and Shadow though, they're going to be a problem, one I haven't even begun to figure out. Shadow is a no-go zone. I can't even stomach the thought of touching her, and as for Reaper, how am I supposed to kill him now? Not that I actually think I could when it came down to it. He didn't get as far as he's gotten by allowing his emotions to rule his survival. He's too good, and as it stands, I only have nineteen days to figure out how the hell I'm going to best him.

"Are you even listening to me?" Raven demands, gaping at me as though I've completely lost my mind. "Is your ego seriously that big?"

Ahh fuck. Now I've gone and gotten distracted again, and now this raging bitch is offended, probably assuming I think I don't even need to pay attention to end her life. Just fucking great. There's nothing worse than trying to kill someone who's been freshly pissed off.

"I . . . uhhh. No. My ego is perfectly proportional, but that's got nothing to do with you. I've had a bit of a weird night."

"I don't give a shit about your weird night," Raven tells me. "Let's just get this over and done with so I can be on my way."

Oh wow. She actually thinks she's going to beat me. That's kinda sweet. I love when someone comes jam packed with that positive delusional optimism. It's a wonderful trait, something I unfortunately haven't had the luxury of having. I prefer to go into these things with my head screwed on properly, otherwise, you end up dead, and that's not something I feel that I need in my life right now.

"Alright," I tell her, adopting a fighting stance as it occurs to me that Reaper is probably here somewhere, watching from afar. And if Reaper is here, there's also a good chance that Shadow is here too, and I wouldn't want to disappoint them by not putting on a killer performance. "Just remember, you asked for this."

Raven scoffs, and without a hint of hesitation, she comes for me, racing ahead with her blade clutched tightly. I simply wait, calling on every ounce of my patience as I watch her with a sharp eye, and as she takes her final step toward me and lunges with her blade, I simply step aside.

Her momentum sends her flying right past me, and I bring my blade down, slicing straight through her thigh as she goes. Raven cries out, and as I whip around to face her again, she stumbles, struggling to right herself after the blow.

"You fucking bitch!"

"I'm the bitch?" I scoff. "Were you not here just now? Did you not see the way you came at me? Have a little class. I thought we were going to do this like ladies."

Raven clenches her jaw, anger flashing brightly in her eyes, and while I've made plenty of mistakes so far, she's just made the biggest one of all. You never fight angry. It may make you dangerous and unpredictable, but it also makes you sloppy. She should know better.

She lets out a battle cry and rushes me again, only this time, I meet her with the same force she brings, throwing my arm up and blocking her lunge as my fist slams into her ribs. We trade punches, and it quickly turns into a lethal dance.

There's no denying it, she's good. But she's not as good as me. She has skill, speed, and precision, but so do I, and unfortunately for her, nobody trains like I do.

Raven keeps coming at me, and when she rears back, preparing for another devastating blow, she leaves herself open. I take my shot, slamming my boot right into her chest. Her body flies back against the brickwork of the pillars holding up the massive bridge above us.

She sputters a cough, the blow winding her, but before she can pull herself together, I whip around, sending my foot up in a beautiful spinning kick that meets her temple.

Her head rocks on her shoulders, and as she struggles to find her feet, she drops the blade in her hand, letting it clatter to the ground.

I take a breath, having the perfect opportunity to make my kill, but I don't go for it, not feeling comfortable ending someone's life while they're already down. Instead, I wait, knowing my moment is coming. "God, I fucking hate you," she spits, leaning heavily against the bridge. "Can't you ever just let me have one fucking win?"

Raven takes a second to regain her balance, and I take this opportunity to switch blades, reaching for Reaper's other one. After all, they both deserve to have their moment in the spotlight. "The fact that I haven't ended your life despite the six times you've left yourself open should be more than enough of a win for you," I tell her, taking a step toward her and watching the way her eyes follow me. "But I'm bored now. I've allowed you plenty chances to try and pull your shit together and make this somewhat of a fair fight, but your arrogance is getting in the way. It's time to end this, Raven. You've been fun competition over the last few years, but it's over now."

"It's not."

"It was over for you the second you accepted your invitation to War Games," I tell her. "Now hurry up and make your move. I don't want to kill you while you're stumbling against a wall, and I doubt after everything you've achieved during your career that this is how you want to go out. Now, come at me so I can give you a respectable death."

Raven holds my stare, her eyes narrowing to slits, and just as she reaches for a new blade from the holder on her thigh, she lets out a roaring battle cry, storming toward me with everything she's got. Her long, thin blade is angled right for my eye, and in the split second it takes for her to lunge toward me, it becomes obvious that she has no game plan at all. Critical thinking has gone out the window, and all that's left is undiluted rage and desperation.

Her blade hurtles toward my face, but at the very last second, I break to the left, clutch her arm, and slam her own blade straight through her stomach. Raven cries out in agony, her eyes widening in horror as she gapes at me, understanding quickly dawning. "I . . . I'm not going to win," she breathes.

"No," I tell her. "You're not."

Her brows furrow, and when tears fill her eyes, a new determination comes over her. She knows she's going out, and just like I offered, she wants to go out fighting.

Then in a flash, she grabs a smaller dagger from her belt, and despite the long blade still protruding from her stomach, she lunges at me again. Only I don't have the heart to stand here and watch her suffer, so when her small dagger narrowly skims past my face, I whip out with my own blade, sending it soaring across the front of her throat.

Raven goes down, dropping to her knees as blood gushes from

her open wound, splattering across the sidewalk and quickly pooling beneath her. She clutches her throat as she looks up at me. "Tell . . . tell my—"

She crumbles, falling forward onto the long, thin blade, plunging it so deep into her that its sharp tip lurches out of her back, piercing right through her spinal cord, and all I can hope is that she doesn't suffer long.

No other words come from her, and I can only guess what she was trying to say. *Tell my family that I love them. Tell my husband, wife, boyfriend, or girlfriend that I'm sorry. Tell my brother that I always thought he was a self-righteous asshole.* It's always the same. In those final moments before death, people find clarity and realize what truly matters in the world.

Letting out a sigh, I make a mental note of the people I need to visit following the games, assuming I actually make it out of here alive. After double-checking that Raven is actually gone, I pull her body to the edge of the bridge pillars and hide her in the bushes. Someone will find her eventually.

With storms due to roll in this afternoon, I don't bother washing Raven's blood off the sidewalk. Instead, I look through her pockets until my fingers curl around her identification.

"Thank you," I tell her, adding it to my little collection while confidence rumbles through my chest, knowing damn well that I'm in the lead. No one else in these games has even come close.

I believe Reaper has three—Graves, Crimson Rain, and Slasher. Texan Reaper has one—Sharkbait. And this one right here brings my grand total to eight—Stone, Grim, Blade, Boston Maneater, 343,

Midnight Killer, Eagle, and now Raven.

There's no denying it, I'm on fire. Though to be fair, I still consider 343 to belong to Reaper, seeing as though he was the one to make the kill, and at some point, he's going to return for that. But the math is still on my side, and even if Reaper were to take my life and claim possession of all these kills, I think it's only fair that I be awarded some kind of participation trophy. After all, I've put a lot of effort into these games. Nobody has made quite as many kills as I have.

Content that I've done everything that needs to be done here, I get on my merry way, sheathing the blades back into position as I put one foot in front of the other. Then after clearing the bridge, I pull out my phone and bring up Mila's number.

"Where was I?" I ask as she accepts the call.

"You were just about to tell me how thick his cock was."

Well, shit. Yes, I was.

17

REAPER

My fist pulses manically, working up and down my cock as I clench my jaw, desperate for a release. This shit is getting ridiculous. Every time I watch Siren make a kill, it's as though I lose control of my fucking dick and nothing can bring me relief except for actually sinking into her sweet little cunt.

It's barely been twenty-four hours since I had her at the lake, and it's all I've been able to think about. I'm supposed to have more control than this. I'm supposed to be better, but one taste fucking destroyed me. If I had walked into her kitchen and fucked her right there without a damn word, I would have been fine, but she just had to go and cuff me to that damn fridge and make a game out of it. And fuck, it was the best game I've ever played.

Siren is refreshing.

I've never been able to sit down with someone and discuss my work, never been able to be shamelessly myself without being judged, ridiculed, or called a fucking monster, and I suspect she's in the same boat. The lives we live aren't compatible with the picket-fence lifestyle, only with Siren . . . it might be.

I wouldn't have to hide with her, wouldn't have to pretend to be something I'm not, and . . . fuck. Why am I even thinking about this? Come the end of the month, I'm going to have no choice but to end her life, and while I'll do what I can to make it as quick and pain free as possible, it'll fucking gut me, but I won't have to suffer for long because the moment I end her life, I'll drop to my knees in front of Shadow and have her take mine.

It's a real fucking Romeo and Juliet tragedy.

Just my fucking luck. The second I find a woman that I might actually be compatible with, and I have to fucking kill her. But then, what if I don't? What if there was a way for the three of us to escape this unscathed? Shadow could claim the win, and Siren and I could . . . no. I can't even go there. We'll be hunted for the rest of our lives, and that's not a life worth living. Besides, Siren and I prefer to hunt. A life on the run simply wouldn't do.

Bracing my hand against the cool tiles of the shower, I drop my head into the spray of water while desperately trying to work her out of my system. These games really aren't playing out how I thought they would. I expected a lot to come from this, but I never saw Siren coming. She completely blindsided me, and I'm so far out of my comfort zone that I have no fucking idea how to proceed. All I can do is continue to stalk her through the night and hope like fuck she'll invite me in. Not that I usually care to wait for an invitation.

My fist pumps up and down the length of my cock, grasping firmly as I clench my jaw, desperately trying to get myself there. Before taking her last night, I could have easily jerked off and finished with nothing more than the image of her in those black jeans and corset tops, but now, that release isn't so easy to come by. My hand doesn't even come close in comparison to what it's like to be buried deep inside of her.

Frustration burns through me and I have no choice but to give up, leaving me with the worst case of blue balls known to man. Turning off the water, I step out of the shower and grab my towel before quickly drying off and walking into my bedroom.

I get busy dressing, finding a pair of black pants and stepping into them, more than ready to get my ass over to the holiday resort and work Siren out of my system once and for all. I pull my pants up and start working the fly when the slightest movement catches in my peripheral vision, and I duck down just in time to evade the blade flying toward my face.

I whip around, finding none other than The Texan Reaper standing in the doorway of my bedroom. It becomes abundantly clear that the fucker thought he could get the drop on me, and honestly, it almost fucking worked.

I was caught off guard—a position I've never found myself in— and it has everything to do with Siren and her sweet little cunt fogging my brain. But whether I've made a mistake or not, this asshole has made a bigger one by trying to make me a target, and judging by the momentary flash of regret and fear in his eyes, he fucking knows it.

His plan was clear—take me out in one fell swoop. He didn't account for what might happen if he missed. He was too fucking egotistical to think missing was even an option, and now that he has, he better fucking run.

I spring into action, launching after him as he spins on his heel and takes off like a fucking bat out of hell. I have to give it to him, the fucker is fast, but so am I.

Instead of wasting precious seconds weaving through my home to find the exit, he aims right for the living room window, running at full speed before launching himself into a ball. With his arms braced in front of his face, he smashes through the thin glass and drops into a roll on the other side.

I follow right after him, grabbing a blade off the hallway table as I dart past it, then in seconds, my bare feet hit the grass as I sprint after him. The Texan Reaper runs through the center of the road, not having the brains to stick to the shadows, and despite how obvious he's being, I keep myself to the shadows anyway. At some point, the moron is going to glance back over his shoulder, and when he doesn't see me right behind him, a false sense of security will be his demise.

He darts through the streets of Blue Springs, and the further he runs, the more my pent-up frustration over my serious case of blue balls begins to catch up to me, and the fact that he was even able to enter my home without me noticing starts to really piss me off.

I follow him right through the main street of Blue Springs, and just as I suspected, when he takes a brief moment to look over his shoulder and finds the coast clear, he begins to slow his pace. He walks right past the alley where he and his moron brother shamelessly beat the life out of Sharkbait, and by the time he slows to a walk, it's clear the fucker thinks he's just gotten away with his life.

He pauses for a moment, bracing his hand against the pole of the street sign and hanging his head, trying to catch his breath. As he stands in the deserted street, he starts to laugh.

"Fuck me," he says to himself before finally pushing off the pole and starting down the street again, clearly having allowed himself just enough time to catch his breath and recover after what he probably assumes was the closest call of his life.

Cutting through the stores, he turns down a back alley, and I shake my head, having done more than enough research on this town to know that alley offers nothing but a dead end. This guy really is a fucking moron, but if he really wants to send himself to an early grave, then who the hell am I to deny him?

Stepping out of the shadows, I cut across the street and slip into the back alley behind him. I follow him a few steps and watch as his back begins to stiffen. His senses tell him that something isn't right, and I bet right about now, there's a chill sailing down his spine.

"You just made the biggest mistake of your life," I say, my voice sailing right down the alley.

The Texan Reaper pauses before whipping around with wide eyes.

"You don't seem so brave now," I taunt.

He clenches his jaw, and I see the exact moment he realizes that his only way out of this alley alive is to fight his way out of it. "I ain't losing."

I scoff. "You lost the second you tied your name to mine."

His eyes widen again, and I have to hold back a laugh.

"Oh, you didn't think I knew what you were up to?"

Embarrassment flashes in his eyes as he reaches for a blade. He wants to be the one at the top of the food chain, but unfortunately for him, he lacks the skill and creativity it takes, which is why he's taken it upon himself to tie himself to me. Instead of working harder, he developed the warped *fake it 'til ya make it* mentality. But like I said, I work alone, and I sure as fuck don't have time for assholes like this.

I open myself up, allowing him the chance to make the first move, and he doesn't let me down. Similar to the way Raven went after Siren today, he recklessly charges forward without a game plan.

His fist hurtles toward my face, and I evade it with ease before sending a punch of my own straight into his ribs. The sweet sound of his bones snapping under the force only spurs me on. He grunts, but a little broken rib isn't enough to take him out of the game. He pushes back, attempting to trade blows, but the only one actually landing any is me.

He gets his ass handed to him, blood spurting from his split lip and brow, and when I land a solid kick to his chest and he slams against the brick wall of the alley, he crumbles. His eye is already swollen shut, and while I haven't quite broken his leg, I've done more than enough damage to ensure he won't be walking home tonight—not that he'll be walking anywhere when I'm through with him.

The Texan Reaper spits a mouthful of blood at my bare feet, and my lips twist in disgust. This one was personal. I could have just ended his life, gotten it over and done with, but after years of this asshole riding my coattails, a little revenge felt necessary. Besides, all that pent-up frustration from my blue balls had to go somewhere, right?

Pulling my blade out of my pocket, I step toward The Texan Reaper, more than ready to get this over and done with. "What do you say?" I taunt, twisting the blade between my fingers. "Make it quick with a shot straight through the eye into the brain, or perhaps I should just gut you like a fish?"

"Go to hell," he spits.

"I'm already well on my way," I tell him. "I suppose I'll see you there."

Then just as I go to make my kill, a feminine gasp sounds from the opening of the alley, followed by a guy's voice. "Hey. What the fuck do you think you're doing?"

Fuck.

My head snaps up, taking in the group of teenagers standing at the top of the alley. There are at least seven of them. Three girls and four boys, each of them looking barely eighteen, probably out looking for trouble on this beautiful Saturday night.

My hand tightens on the blade as I consider my options. I could finish the kill and get this asshole out of my way while scarring these kids for the rest of their lives, or I can slink away and come back to finish him off another time. I've never walked away from a kill, but now that the kids are starting to pull out their phones to record, I doubt I have any fucking choice.

"Shit," I mutter before smirking at The Texan Reaper. "Consider yourself lucky. I'll be back for you, and when I do, I'll make it fucking count," and with that, I disappear, kicking in the back door of one of the stores in the alley and cutting through the building, doing everything in my power to evade having my face uploaded on social media. I've gone to such extreme lengths to keep myself invisible, and The Texan Reaper won't be the reason for my downfall, not tonight, not fucking ever.

Slipping out an office window of the store, I'm able to jump over a back fence and finally escape out into the next street, and just as I hear the familiar sound of sirens breaking through the night, I slip away into the shadows like the perfect fucking ghost.

That was too fucking close, and I don't like it. Not only did I have to leave a mark still breathing, but my home was compromised, and my identity was almost caught on camera. This is not how I play. I don't almost get caught, and I sure as fuck don't leave targets alive.

I'm slipping, and it has everything to do with Siren.

Making my way back to my home, I have no choice but to race through another shower, rinsing the blood off my skin before finally getting my ass dressed properly.

I can't do this anymore. Allowing myself to get close to Siren isn't only fucking with my head, it's compromising everything. It's too dangerous. My head isn't screwed on properly, and because of that, I've allowed fucking amateurs like The Texan Reaper to almost get the drop on me. This isn't okay. I'm supposed to be the best, and right now, I'm a fucking joke.

If I can't seem to fuck her out of my system, then there's only one other option left for me to salvage these games and ensure not only my survival, but Shadow's as well—tonight Siren must die.

18

SIREN

A weight dips beside me on my bed, and my eyes spring open into the darkness of my bedroom to find Reaper hovering before me, a knife in the palm of his hand and that lethal stare locked right on me.

Fear rushes through my veins, and before he gets a chance to officially take me out of the competition, I snap into action.

His arm starts to arc toward me, and as I suck in a breath, I use every ounce of strength I have and bring my knee up, slamming it hard into his crown jewels before frantically rolling. Reaper drops hard, groaning in agony as his blade plunges deep into my pillow, right where my head used to be.

My heart races faster than it ever has before as I scramble off my bed and make a break for it. My feet pound against the floorboards, not daring to waste a second looking over my shoulder. He's down and out. There's no way he could just simply recover from a blow like that to his balls, but this is Reaper we're talking about, and he's a different breed.

I fly out of my bedroom with such force, I knock into the hallway wall and use it to brace myself as I rush through the darkness.

I'm such a fucking idiot. After what happened between us at the lake, I stupidly convinced myself that he wouldn't hurt me. At least, not yet. I thought we were good, but I was clearly wrong. All I know is that over this last week and a half, I have more than imagined what it would be like to wake up to find Reaper in my bed, but that sure as fuck wasn't what I had in mind.

"You're gonna fucking pay for that!" I hear Reaper holler after me, his deep, rumbling tone sending the most fearful chill down my spine and making me realize he's recovered a lot quicker than I anticipated. But how? Are his balls made of steel? No man should have ever been able to recover from that. His balls should be somewhere up in his stomach right about now.

"Drop dead, asshole," I yell back, finally breaking free of the hallway and scrambling around the corner before barging through the kitchen.

My panic is too much, and I can't help but glance back to find Reaper right on my six, and as a terrified squeal tears from the back of my throat, he reaches out and locks his fist around the long rope-like plait of my hair, pulling me to a violent halt before slamming me against the kitchen counter.

I cry out in pain, and in a flash, his body is hard against mine, keeping me pinned as he presses his blade against the base of my throat. He's breathing heavily in my ear, and despite how easily he subdued me, it's clear that I've managed to inflict some sort of pain on this mystical creature behind me.

My whole life flashes before my eyes, and as my heart races faster than the sound of light, I realize it's all over. Unwanted tears fill my eyes, but I refuse to let them fall, knowing I'll never get to see Mila's face again, never get to experience love, or enjoy the beautiful things in life.

He takes his time, and the longer he takes, the harder it becomes to hold back the tears. "Do it," I growl, my voice thick with desperation. "Just fucking do it."

Reaper hesitates, and I feel the very moment his hand begins to shake. I grab his wrist, preparing to shove him away if I get even the slightest chance.

He takes a breath, and a moment later, the blade shifts away. "I can't," he says, that deep, terrifying tone now filled with an unsettling agony. Then, before he has a chance to find sanity, I shove his hand down against the counter, and as one of the knuckles in his hand breaks, I disarm him and curl my fingers around the hilt of the blade.

Whipping around, I shove the blade against his throat, backing him up against the very fridge I cuffed him to barely twenty-four hours ago. My chest heaves with desperation and anger as my tears fall. I can't do it either.

Reaper simply stares back at me, the two of us locked in each other's orbit.

"I can't," I whisper, never having felt so out of my comfort zone in my life.

"I know," he tells me, swallowing hard enough that the blade cuts into his skin. I pull back just a fraction, not wanting to truly hurt him, and in a flash, he shoves my hand away. The blade clatters to the ground, and he reaches out and grips the back of my neck, pulling me in hard against his magnificent body.

His lips crush down on mine, kissing me deeply, and I instantly melt into him, throwing my arms around his neck as he holds me tighter than any human ever has the right to do. His hands are on my body as his tongue swipes into my mouth, warring for dominance. My knees go weak, but his strong arms hold me up and give me exactly what I've been needing.

It's hungry and desperate, and I can't seem to get enough, and when his hands roam lower to grab a handful of my ass, all I can do is press into him, silently asking for more.

He grinds against me, and our frantic kisses become something more. Before I know what's happening, both our hands are reaching for our clothes, manically tearing them off, and the longer he's not buried deep inside of me, the more desperate I become.

"Fuck, Reaper," I gasp, absolutely starved. I need this man more than I need my next breath.

"I know, Little Siren. I've got you," he vows just as he tears my thong clean from my body. The second it's gone, I scramble back, all but climbing the counter and pulling him in. I release his thick, veiny cock from his pants, barely having a chance to pump my fist up and down before he's slamming inside my needy cunt.

"Fuuuuck," he groans, just as desperate for this as I've been for him.

I groan, throwing my head back as I lean against my palms, inching my ass right to the very edge of the counter as Reaper fucks me like a god. He's so fucking beautiful with that magnificently sculpted body and that grim reaper tattoo that covers his warm skin. He's fucking perfect, but the way his body rolls with every powerful thrust . . . fuck. I can't tear my eyes off him.

"God," I moan, my legs already shaking.

"Fuck, Siren. I've been dreaming about this sweet . . . little . . . cunt." He says each word between his commanding thrusts, his jaw clenched with hunger as his fingers dig into my thigh.

"Destroy me," I beg him.

He pounds into me, that thick cock stretching my walls and taking me deeper than I ever thought possible. I've never been so full, and just like when he fucked me by the lake, I know I'll never experience anything as good as this for as long as I live. I'm addicted, and despite begging him to destroy me, we both know he already has.

His muscles bulge as he grabs hold of me, and just as I feel that familiar build deep inside of me, a loud BANG sounds through the villa just as a bullet whizzes past both of our faces.

"What the ever-loving fuck?" I squeal as Reaper grabs me and hauls me off the counter and onto the floor, not daring to pull out of me.

More bullets rip through the villa right where we were both just standing.

BANG! BANG! BANG!

Reaper grips my ass, holding me up off the ground as my back presses against the edge of the kitchen island counter, still slamming that thick, delicious cock deep inside of me. He grits his teeth, not letting a damn thing get in the way of this.

Glancing up toward the top of the counter, I see the handle of my bag, so I reach for it before pulling it down and letting it fall heavily to the kitchen floor, groaning as that build continues growing rapidly inside of me.

I scramble through the bag until my hands curl around my loaded gun, and as Reaper fucks me, I shoot back toward the kitchen window, hoping like fuck I manage to hit this asshole.

"Who the fuck is it?" I ask, not liking shooting blind.

There's a pause as whoever it is reloads, and Reaper takes his chance to peek out the window. "Fuck," he grunts as a hint of regret flashes in his lethal stare. "It's The Boneyard Slayer."

"What?" I groan, clutching onto his shoulder as that thick cock rams so deep inside of me I feel him in my throat. "What the hell is he doing here? I've been careful, and a moron like that doesn't find me unless an even bigger moron has led him here."

Reaper cringes. "My bad," he says, thrusting again. "But to be completely clear, I came here with the intention to kill you, so compromising your location wasn't exactly supposed to be an issue."

"Fucking hell," I grunt, ducking again as a fresh round of bullets rain down around us. *BANG! BANG! BANG!* "Shit. If he's here, then surely his brother is around here somewhere too. I doubt the asshole would have the balls to come at both of us on his own."

"Yeah . . ." Reaper says slowly. "About that . . ."

I let out a heavy sigh.

Having a better vantage point, Reaper takes the gun from me and shoots back, and while I'm sure he's probably one of the best sharpshooters in the country, those bullets are going anywhere but his target while he's focused more on fucking me than eliminating the threat. And to be honest, I'm not even mad about it.

"What the fuck did you do?" I demand over the sound of the raining bullets.

"It was nothing, really."

"REAPER!"

"Okay, fine," he grunts, pausing for just a second to send a few more bullets flying back at The Boneyard Slayer as I reach for a new magazine from my bag. "His brother tried to get the drop on me, so I had no choice but to retaliate. Only, I was interrupted before I could finish the job."

"What?" I screech. "You left witnesses?"

"No. I left him. They were just teenagers. I couldn't fucking slit his throat in front of them, plus they were breaking out their phones. I had to bail."

"Shit."

Frustration burns through me. This isn't just a little fuck up, this is a colossal one. Not only did he walk away from a target without a confirmed kill, but he had witnesses who were minors and almost had video evidence. Not to mention, in our line of work, we can't afford to make this personal, and having some asshole's brother come for revenge . . . that sounds fucking personal to me.

"I figured I'd come back and finish the job later. It's not as though he's going to be capable of coming for me for another week or so."

"Yeah, well, the job's brother is currently trying to get revenge," I mutter, pushing off the edge of the island counter and shoving Reaper back against the fridge, taking control and riding him just as I've been dreaming about for the past eleven days.

My hips rock, and in this position, he's seated so deeply inside of me that my walls immediately start to convulse. "Holy fucking shit," I grunt as my nails dig into his massive shoulder, but when he reaches down between us and presses his thumb to my clit, sending a hot wave of electricity pulsing through my body, all I can do is throw my head back and cry out with the sweetest pleasure.

"You fucking like that, baby."

"I ain't your baby," I tell him. "You led this asshole to my door. What the fuck is wrong with you?"

"You're what's fucking wrong with me, Siren," he says, gripping my ass and digging his fingers into my skin as I ride him like he's never been ridden before. "You've been in my head since the second I saw you. I'm not thinking clearly. I'm making fucking mistakes, Siren, and I don't make mistakes."

"That's why you came here tonight," I say. "If you took me out of the picture, you could get over it and focus on the game."

He nods, and honestly, it's the most romantic thing anyone has ever said to me. "As for this guy," he continues, making a point of shooting back at him again. "He'll be dead soon enough and you won't have to worry about it. But I get it. You have every right to be pissed at me. I'm just as pissed with myself as you are. I don't fuck up. Ever. It was a first for me, and I don't fucking like it. It makes me feel weak, and it has everything to do with the way this sweet little cunt owns me."

Having this kind of power over such an impressive man gives me goosebumps, and in response, I clench my walls around him, watching the way his eyelids flutter with the deepest need. His fingers tighten on my ass, and despite the bullets still turning my villa into nothing more than rubble, he tosses the gun down and grabs me.

Reaper lifts me off him and shoves me down against the floor on my knees, bending me over so my face is against the ground and my ass is up in the air. He positions himself behind me, and just like at the lake, he slams into me from behind, his thumb at my ass as his other hand clutches my hip, holding me still.

BANG! BANG! BANG!

He fucks me like a goddamn beast, his thrusts more powerful than the bullets blasting through my villa. My body instantly becomes his as he shows me exactly how my cunt owns him. He wraps my hair around his fist before pulling my head back, and just like at the lake, I reach between my thighs and rub tight circles over my needy clit.

"See this," he grunts through a clenched jaw, his thrusts so powerful and addictive as he pushes his thumb inside my ass. "Now that we've determined that I can't fucking live without this, you're mine. This sweet little cunt—all fucking mine. I am your pleasure, Siren. You belong to me."

My pussy begins to shatter, my walls wildly spasming around his thick cock, and as my orgasm blasts through me, I cry out with heavy, panted breaths. "Yours. I'm yours."

"Fuck," he breathes, the relief in his tone sounding as though he'd feared how I would respond to him, but after he claimed me at the lake, I figured that was just how he liked to talk while he fucked. Only this time it was different, there was a profound demand in his tone, and I realize he means every last word. I belong to him, but what he fails to understand is that he now belongs to me too.

I come hard, my orgasm completely destroying me, and as Reaper comes with me, our whole fucking souls merge as one. I don't know what this is or what it means, especially during War Games, but there's no turning my back on it now.

I'm his and he is mine, right to the fucking end.

I come down from my high when more bullets blast through the window, only they come from the living room and I adjust my gaze, able to see our shooter clearly now, which also means he's more than capable of seeing us too.

Reaper sighs as if realizing the same thing. We have to move—unless we feel like being shot—and right now, all I want to do is fuck this beast of a man all over again.

BANG! BANG! BANG!

"Fucking hell," I mutter, reaching for the discarded gun and inserting a fresh magazine. More bullets fly toward us, and despite the threat they pose, I get to my feet. Standing right in the middle of the war zone, I raise my gun, take aim at the asshole outside my living room window, and take one final shot.

The bullet pierces right through his shoulder, and I curse, knowing my post-orgasm shaky knees are completely responsible for missing the imaginary target I put right between his eyes. And honestly, missing in front of a man like Reaper is nothing short of embarrassing, but considering his gaze is locked on my ass, I think it's safe to say he didn't even notice.

The Boneyard Slayer falls back, the force of my bullet sending him sprawling to his ass, and as if finally remembering who the fuck I am and the damage I can cause, he scrambles to his feet and takes off like a bat out of hell.

"Fuck," I grunt, itching to go after him as I look around for my clothes.

"Don't even think about it," Reaper says, that deep tone sending electrical currents right to my core.

"Why the hell not?" I ask, turning to face him only to find him on his feet behind me, that glorious body completely on display and teasing me with everything else it's capable of offering.

His hand takes my waist, pulling me in before letting that very hand drop to my ass. "The brothers will still be there tomorrow. Let them lick their wounds for now."

"And why should I do that?"

"Because I'm not nearly finished with you, and when I tie your wrists to your fucking ankles, I need your mind focused solely on me, not some other man."

"Oh really?" I say, a grin pulling at my lips as I press my hand to his chest and feel the steady rhythm of his heart beneath. "And if I tell you no?"

Reaper growls, and I feel his cock harden between us. "I don't know if you're ready for that kind of trouble."

"Speak for yourself, Reaper. I can handle anything you've got. It's you I'm worried about," I say, turning on my heel and stalking back to my bedroom. "Hurry along, Reaper. I'm in charge now, and don't forget that gun. I've got the perfect spot for it."

19

SIREN

Placing the hot bowl of spaghetti bolognese down on my new kitchen counter, I stand back and smile, knowing Shadow would appreciate this. After meeting with her a few nights ago in the luxury hotel restaurant that was too fancy for a standard chicken parmigiana, I've been sticking to my word and doing everything I can to make sure the kid eats a healthy meal every day.

Even after my small villa was shot up and turned into a house-sized strainer, I still took the risk and welcomed her into my new place. It only took her a few hours to figure out where I'm staying now, and honestly, it couldn't have been that hard.

I'm still at the holiday resort but in a whole new villa. Though, this one is more like a fancy suite, and while it's a little more risky staying here, I couldn't resist. There's something about this little holiday resort that's really started to grow on me. Perhaps it's the pool and the short walk to the lake that gets me. Either way, I'm content here for a little while.

I place a spoon and a fork down beside the bowl of spaghetti before adding a soda and a to-go bag filled with a fresh sandwich, a piece of fruit, and a bottle of water, knowing damn well the kid can't survive on her own. I haven't yet figured out where she's sleeping every night, but I hope she's safe. Either way, I've left blankets on the sofa every night, hoping she'll take me up on my offer, but so far, she hasn't allowed herself to trust me enough to let her guard that far down. I swear, she's probably the type to sleep with one eye open. I wonder if she even knows what it's actually like to be a regular child. Has she ever experienced jumping over the waves at the beach or building sandcastles? Did she ever learn how to ride a bike, or did she even have a baby doll to play with as a little girl?

My heart breaks for her, but knowing there's nothing more I can do until she's comfortable trusting me, I go for a walk, leaving her to be at peace in my new little suite.

I make my way down to the lake, strolling along the shore and holding my shoes as I drag my feet through the cool water. It truly is beautiful down here, and if this town wasn't tainted by the aftermath of War Games, this would probably be somewhere I'd like to settle down one day. You know, way in the future after I've retired. Assuming I somehow make it out of here alive. Not that I have high hopes with Shadow as a contender, but if I have to lose, I'm glad it's for her.

On the other hand, Reaper would carve his own heart out and offer it to her on a silver platter if it meant that she would live.

It's only been a few days since he showed up in my villa and tried to take my life, and since then, we've spent more time together than I could have anticipated. To be fair, most of that time is spent naked with our bodies grinding together, but when we're not, he happily sits beside me on the couch, both of us with our laptops open, working on tracking the remaining five contenders.

So much for not wanting to work together. He's doing it without even realizing, but having someone to bounce ideas off has come so naturally to him. To be honest, I don't even know if he realizes that we've been working as a team, but when that moment comes, I'm sure it'll be the equivalent of being punched right in the vag.

Pulling my phone out of my back pocket, I bring up Mila's number and chat with her for over an hour as I make the full walk around the lake while ignoring the security notifications rolling in, letting me know Shadow arrived at my suite and is happily annihilating her dinner.

As I make my way under the bridge, I tell Mila every little detail of the time I've spent with Reaper over the last few days, but I stop and cringe when I see the familiar dark stain on the concrete leading to the bushes. I assume Raven's body is still hidden deep within the garden because she hasn't made the headlines yet. And knowing I shouldn't be anywhere near this crime scene, I decide it's probably time to head back.

Shadow isn't exactly comfortable with company, especially company she doesn't fully trust, but I was hoping to catch her before she left, maybe try to get to know her a little better. After all, she's been dropping by for dinner for the past few nights without fail, and maybe that's enough for her to realize that I'm the kind of woman who sticks to her word.

After making my way back into the resort, I stride to my door, making my presence obvious as I walk up onto the front deck and enter the access code. I dangle my bag a little and fake a cough just to give her the extra warning in case she's not ready and wants to slip out the back, then I turn the handle and step into my little suite.

The suite is quiet as I walk in, no familiar sound of a fork scraping the bottom of a bowl or a chair shuffling across the floor. My brows furrow, and I walk deeper into the suite, desperate to figure out where she is or if she's even still here at all.

I creep toward the kitchen with my hands out, trying to show her that I mean her no harm, and just as I turn the corner to peer into the kitchen, a hand shoots out of nowhere pressing a drenched cloth over my nose and mouth.

Panic blasts through me. I only have mere seconds to save myself before the chloroform knocks me unconscious, and I become a puppet for the master to manipulate. I try to fight this person off, having no idea who stands at my back, but as the chloroform begins to take effect, I quickly grow weaker.

My heart races as I claw at the hands blocking my airway, and when my lungs begin to scream for sweet oxygen, I'm left with no choice but to take a deep, gasping breath, sucking in nothing but pure chloroform.

Darkness dances behind my eyes, and just as my body begins to give in to the rich, lethal chemical, a flash of bright red hair cuts across my vision. My mind tries to make sense of it, tries to figure out exactly what I'm seeing, but the dizziness rushes over me, and not a second later, everything goes dark.

A laugh breaks through my unconsciousness, and I force my eyes open despite the fogginess clouding my mind. My head pounds, and there's no telling just how long I've been out cold. A flash of red cuts through my grogginess, and I try to focus on the room around me, but the splashing sounds make it hard to concentrate.

What the fuck is going on?

I come in and out of consciousness, my body determined to give in to the dizziness, but I'm not having it. Whatever the fuck is going on here, I'm not about to succumb to it. I'm not dying today, nor am I about to die barely halfway through the games. I'm no runner-up, and I'm sure as fuck not the type to get participation awards. I win. I've always won, and today isn't going to be any different.

Focusing on the red blob until it finally begins to take form, I see a woman with blazing red hair, and it doesn't take a genius to figure out this is Gasoline—the woman Eagle warned me about. This is exactly what she did to her, and while Eagle was lucky enough to escape with her life, she was left with deep scars. Despite everything I did to Eagle, it was Gasoline who terrified her, and that speaks volumes.

I watch the older woman for a moment, trying to make sense of everything around me. I'm still in my little suite at the holiday resort, sitting in one of the chairs by the dining table, and as she goes around the small suite, the smell of gasoline assaults my senses.

My brows furrow, and I blink through the fogginess, realizing that she's dousing the suite and preparing for one hell of a blaze.

Panic soars through my chest, and the reality of my situation sobers me. She's going to burn me alive, just as she tried to do to Eagle. Only this time, she's already had a failed attempt, so I can guarantee she learned from her mistakes. She doesn't intend to fail twice.

I'm fucked.

Shit. Shit. Shit. Shit.

I have to get out of here.

As the woman circles the suite, murmuring to herself, I pull against my heavy limbs, quickly realizing just how dire my situation is. I'm not only chained to a chair, but the chair has also been chained to the heavy table, leaving me no hope of escape.

I pull at my bound wrists and ankles, my heart booming loudly in my ears. The headache is intense, and the fogginess threatens to knock me out again, but I do everything in my power to keep myself from failing. My wrists quickly turn bloody from the way I pull at my binds, and after trying for much longer than I should, I realize just how hopeless this is.

I'm not going anywhere. I'm going to die right here in this chair, burned alive. If I'm lucky, the smoke inhalation will kill me first, and if I'm not . . . I guess I'm about to discover how it feels to have your flesh burn right off your body.

"Ahhh, well look who decided to join the party," Gasoline chimes as she glances up from dousing the couch in gas. "I was worried you were never going to come to, and that just doesn't seem like any fun. What's the point of burning someone alive if they're not even conscious enough to hear their screams?"

Holy fucking shit. This woman is batshit crazy.

She moves on from the living room, leaving a thick trail of gas as she struts through the small kitchen, making sure she doesn't miss even an inch of the suite. "You know, it was appallingly easy to track you down," she tells me. "At first, I thought you were going to be a threat. Your name has this whole stigma about it, and I foolishly believed it to be true. Yet here you are, taken down without even the hint of a fight. Kinda disappointing actually."

I clench my jaw, not willing to give her the satisfaction of seeing my fear, but my lack of response doesn't seem to bother her. Hell, she doesn't even look at me as she continues with her little taunts.

"I've been tracking you for days, and if it weren't for that dumbass Boneyard Slayer shooting up that other place, I probably wouldn't have found you at all, so you have him to thank for your untimely death," she explains. "Though I have to admit, you let me down."

I can't help the scoff that tears out of my mouth. "Oh please. Tell me how exactly I managed to do that."

"Ahhhh, Princess Barbie finally joins the conversation." The redhead claps her hands before turning her wicked stare on me, only after dealing with the lethal one of Reaper's, hers is nothing but child's play. "I wanted to see how the elite live, steal your tricks of the trade, and gather what information you'd been able to find on the other contenders, but it's become more than clear that you have nothing, and instead of spending your time doing recon, you've been too busy getting your rocks off with Reaper. You're pathetic, not even a hint of a trace on the other contenders, just some whore bitch, waiting around like a sitting duck, just begging to be picked off. You're so fucking pathetic, you didn't even see me coming."

I roll my eyes and instantly regret it as the subtle movement does nothing but make my headache that much worse. "That's where you're wrong," I tell her. "But it's not my fault you just have no idea where to look. I know every detail about every last contender. I know where they're staying, where they go for lunch, and when they took their last shit. I know everything about you, bitch. I know how you killed your whole family, burned them alive, and then went fucking crazy. You've spent more time in mental hospitals than out of them."

Gasoline roars in anger, and it's clear she doesn't appreciate being insulted, but honestly, I couldn't give a shit. It's not as though sweet-talking her and being her best friend is somehow going to get me out of here.

"Shut your fucking mouth," she snaps, throwing the gas at me, drenching me from head to toe. She steps right into me, holds the gas can above my head, and begins to pour it over my hair, letting it cover my face in some bullshit attempt at trying to waterboard me. "Say what you want, but it won't fucking matter when I'm through with you."

I sputter over the gas pouring down my face, and I'm grateful when the can runs empty. She huffs and throws it aside, but one thing is for sure, I'm not just screwed, I'm completely fucked.

"Don't mind me," she says, patting down my pockets and grinning to herself as she finds exactly what she's looking for. She digs into my pocket and pulls out the stack of eight IDs I've been collecting over the past two weeks. "Oh my, you really have been busy. Perhaps I underestimated you after all. Guess that really doesn't matter now."

She slides the stack into her back pocket before continuing to pat me down until she finds mine. I've kept it separate this whole time. "Ahh, here we go," she chimes as she holds up the little identification card. "Kienna James. Hmm, I took you as a Jessa or a Katie, something a little streamline for a streamlined bitch like you."

The sound of my legal name on her tongue is worse than the thought of being burned alive. I have to clench my jaw to not take the bait, despite how it has my stomach clenching in agony.

"You know, this is the one mistake I made with Eagle," she tells me. "I was going to go back for her ID after she was dead, but the bitch got loose and escaped. Even if she had escaped, she would have been as good as dead without her ID. Just like you are now."

"You're a fucking joke," I tell her. "Your mistake wasn't just not taking her ID, it was assuming it would still be there after her body burned. What kind of dumbass are you?"

She clenches her jaw. "Call me a dumbass all you want, but you're the one doused in gasoline and chained to a fucking chair," she tells me before turning her back and making her way to the door. "See you in hell, bitch."

And with that, she pulls out a packet of matches from her pocket, lights one, and as she stares at the small flame at the end of the match, she grins, truly getting off on this shit.

The moment seems to drag out forever and as she tosses the lit match back into the small suite, I watch with horror as it falls to the ground and quickly takes effect. I hear the door slam, but my attention is focused solely on the flames quickly licking through the suite.

"Fuck. FUCK. FUCK. FUCK!"

I tear at my binds, my bloody wrists screaming in protest as the flames create a thick smoke that immediately fills my lungs.

The panic is like nothing I've ever experienced in my life, and all I can do is sit back and watch as thick, raging flames spread through the suite. At least this way, Reaper doesn't have to worry about killing me himself because at the rate these flames are turning into a full blaze, there's no saving me now.

The couch catches light, sending the flames soaring so much closer toward me as the locked suite quickly becomes overwhelmed with thick, billowing smoke, leaving nowhere for it to escape.

The heat is like nothing I've ever known, and as my skin starts to sting from the heat of the flaming couch, I cry out in agony, knowing it's only going to get a million times worse. Fear grips me in a chokehold as tears stream down my face. I'm not ready to die, but tonight I'll meet my maker.

I start to cough, my lungs desperate for sweet oxygen, but all I inhale is the thick smoke clouding the air. It's too much, and as the flames lick closer and closer, the heat becomes unbearable. I cry out, screaming for help. There must be someone in this resort who can help, but who the fuck is going to run into a fire like this? They'll be better off running as far as their legs can take them.

My lungs scream in agony, and as I take shallow, desperate breaths, I realize this is it, and I pray to whoever exists above that the smoke claims me before the flames do.

My vision blurs, and I will myself to succumb quickly as I cough and sputter over the thick smoke, choking on it as it bears down on me, suffocating me with its intense force. The coughing claims me, and just as my head lolls and the unconsciousness creeps back in, a shadow cuts through the smoke, pulling at my bound wrists, but it's too late.

There's no saving me now.

20

REAPER

Tracking The Boneyard Slayer back to the home he shares with his brother, I watch as they do what they can to recover from their injuries. The two of them clearly have no idea what they're doing when it comes to first aid.

To be honest, after the shot Siren took on The Boneyard Slayer the other night, he's lucky to be alive. The bullet pierced his shoulder, and from what I can tell, it's still lodged deep in there, but had it been just an inch to the left, it would have gone right through him, and the fucker probably would have bled out.

As for The Texan Reaper, it seems the asshole is recovering just fine. His eye is still swollen shut, and there will be plenty of bruising staring back at him in the mirror for the next few weeks, but from what

I can tell, he has no issue getting around. They'll both be back on their feet in no time, and when they are, I'm going in for the kill.

I sit back and prepare for a long night of recon when my phone buzzes in my pocket, and my brows furrow. Nobody knows this number. It's not available to the public or even listed on any telemarketer lists. The only people capable of finding it are those who are specifically searching for me in the form of one hell of an incredible hacker.

I glance at the screen for a moment. I don't like taking calls for the slight risk of being traced, but something compels me to hit accept and lift the phone to my ear. Without saying a word, I simply listen to whatever needs to be said.

"You need to get to Siren now," a panicked woman screeches, the fear in her tone feeling like a hand just physically reached inside my chest and squeezed the living shit out of my heart. Quickly going through the shortlist of people this could possibly be, I come to the conclusion that this is Siren's best friend, Mila, who professionally prefers to go by the Tech Girl. Siren has done nothing but tell me how much she loves this girl, and for her to intervene in War Games and seek me out, this is as serious as it gets.

Siren is in trouble.

"What?" I rush out, already on my feet.

"Gasoline got to her. If you don't get to her now, she'll . . . she'll."

Fuck. Anyone but her. "Where?"

"The resort. Please. Don't let her die, she's all I've got," Mila says as I race to my car, leaving the brothers behind. "If she dies . . . fuck. I swear, I will come for you."

I end the call, not having time to deal with her wild, whiplashing emotions on top of trying to get to Siren, and within seconds, I'm in my car, fishtailing it around and hitting the fucking gas.

I push the car to its limits, weaving in and out of what little traffic is on the roads, and as I drive, I can't help but notice the billowing smoke polluting the air, and despite not having any fucking clue what kind of situation Siren is in, I just know that's her.

I'm not far from the resort, but every second that passes feels like a lifetime. I cut through the main street of Blue Springs before flying right out the other end. When I pull into the resort, I don't bother stopping for the boom gate. I simply speed straight through it before racing toward the thick, billowing smoke.

My stomach sinks the closer I get to the blazing property, and as I screech around the final corner and skid to a halt, the onlookers diving away from my car, I realize there's no fucking hope here. Nobody could have survived a fire like this. I can't even get inside to check.

Despair tears through my chest as I bail out of my car and drop to my knees, and the sound of the ceiling collapsing breaks me. I've never felt agony like this.

Emptiness fills me, and I catch myself on my palms, struggling to breathe, but it has nothing to do with the thick smoke. I've failed her. Since the night I stood in her kitchen and realized I couldn't take her life, I knew that I would do anything to protect her, to keep her until my dying days, and the one time she needed me, I let her down.

The pain is like nothing I've ever known, but even over the roar of flames, a soft grunting sound coming from the back of the property catches my attention.

I get to my feet and run, racing around the corner of the burning building to the back where I find Shadow dragging Siren's body from the building, both of them covered in soot, their skin angry from burns. Shadow is barely keeping on her feet while Siren is . . . fuck. I don't even want to think about it.

Hearing me coming, Shadow looks back at me, tears in her blue eyes. "I don't," she starts, violently coughing as she sways on her feet. "I don't know what to . . . do."

Her eyes flutter, and just before she has a chance to collapse, I crash into her, scooping Siren's lifeless body into my arms and gripping Shadow's wrist. I pull them away from the raging flames, but Shadow can barely manage to stay on her feet. I'll drag her if I have to. I'm determined that neither of them are going to die on me tonight.

We get just a few feet away, far enough that the flames don't threaten to sear my skin while still behind the property and out of view of the nosey onlookers with their video phones. I crumble to the ground, laying Siren in the grass before slamming my hands over her chest and performing CPR, breathing much-needed oxygen into her lungs. There's no telling how long she's been out, and as I frantically try to save her life, Shadow succumbs to exhaustion and collapses behind me.

"FUCK!"

I don't dare stop the compressions on Siren's chest, but I have no choice but to release just one of my hands so I can reach behind me and make sure Shadow still has a pulse. Relief floods me, finding that she's just passed out, and I go back to giving Siren my full attention as I pump her heart for her and breathe into her lungs.

"COME ON," I roar, clenching my jaw as the desperation to save her eats me alive. "I'm not losing you like this, Siren. FUCKING BREATHE!"

I keep working on her, not daring to give up, and as I duck down to breathe for her again, she begins to sputter, violently coughing as she tries to take a much-needed breath. "Holy fucking shit," I say, sitting back on my heels as I stop the compressions.

Siren's eyes open, and I've never seen anyone look so fucking exhausted. Her skin is clammy and burnt, and every breath she takes is shaky, wheezy, and shallow. She must be in so much pain, but for now, she's alive, and that's all that matters.

"I . . . I—"

"Shhhh," I say, taking her hand as she struggles to get the words out. "You're okay. Rest now, beautiful Siren. I've got you."

Her eyes flutter, and not a moment later, she passes out, only this time her heart is beating, and I take a moment to collect myself, running my hands down my face and trying to catch my breath.

I've never been so fucking scared in my life. The thought of losing her before we've even had a chance to begin? Fuck. Reality is, I might still lose her in the coming weeks, but it won't be by my hand. War Games is unpredictable, and no matter how hard I can try to save someone, there'll be another asshole right around the corner, ready to take her out. All I know is that I'm not ready to let her go. Not even close. When that time does come—in a few weeks or years down the track—it's going to destroy me, and the only hope I have is that Shadow's capable of ending my life before the agony of losing Siren truly hits me.

I hear the sirens in the distance, and just as I go to get up and lift Siren into my arms, Shadow comes to, blinking awake, and I pause, glancing down at her as she tries to figure out where she is and what the fuck just happened. She looks up at me, pushing up onto her palm as I crouch down and hold her bright blue stare.

"Take it slow," I tell her before indicating toward Siren. "You saved her."

Her eyes widen, seeing Siren motionless beside us, and I pick up Siren's hand again, gently squeezing it. "She's just passed out," I tell Shadow. "You got her out just in the nick of time. You saved her life, but now's not the time to try and process everything that just went down. The fire department is on its way, and I don't doubt the cops are right on their tail. We've gotta get out of here before it's too late."

Shadow visibly swallows and nods before slowly getting to her feet, and I do the same, lifting Siren into my arms before making my way back around to the front of the little suite. Shadow walks with me, but as I go to open the car door, Shadow keeps walking, intent on getting out of here.

"Don't even think about it," I say. "Get your ass in the car."

I don't know what it is, but something pulls her up short. She stops and turns back, holding my stare for just a moment. I expect a fight. I expect her to try and make a break for it, but for whatever reason, she simply nods and moves around to the passenger side of my car and climbs in.

Satisfied that she's not about to make a break for it or take off with my car, I lay Siren across the backseat, and as the sirens get louder, I climb into the driver's seat and hit the gas, determined to get these girls out of here.

Pulling up to the property I've called home for the past two weeks, I lift Siren out of the car, and Shadow hurries around to open the front door for me. I carry the passed-out killer in my arms, holding her tighter than I've ever held anyone in my life, and as I lay her down in my bed, I can't look away from her face, needing to double-check her pulse and make sure she's still breathing.

Then, being content that Siren is going to be alright, I make my way back to the living room where Shadow stands awkwardly, not knowing where to go or what to do. "Okay, here's the deal," I tell her, holding her bright stare. "I'm not doing this shit where you get to run around and have all the fucking freedom in the world. I worry about you, and I know for a fact that Siren does too. I know we're not your parents, probably the furthest people from it, and I'm sure learning to trust us is going to take time, but I am a man of my word. So when I tell you that neither myself nor Siren wish to cause you any harm, you can have faith that I mean that to my core."

Shadow goes to open her mouth and interrupt, but I hold up a finger and continue. "This is what's going to happen. I'm not letting Siren out of my sight. She'll stay here with me, and just as she was doing before, I'll make sure there's a home-cooked meal on the table for you every night. Only, you won't be leaving. You come home every night, you eat your dinner, and then you go to sleep. There are three other bedrooms in this house, take your pick."

"But what about the competition?"

"I don't give a shit what you do during the day. Go and track every asshole and their best friend for all I care, but at night, you come home so that Siren and I can sleep easy knowing that you're safe and being fed properly. There is no competition between us. Is that understood?"

Her gaze shifts around the room, unsure of what to do or say, but for whatever reason, she nods. "Okay," she finally says, lifting her chin. "I'll stay here with you."

"Thank you," I say, having expected that to go a million other ways, except for like that. "I know Siren would appreciate that."

She nods again, which is when it gets awkward, and I realize that I actually have no idea how to talk to a thirteen-year-old girl, let alone one who's a trained killer and probably boasts more kills than Siren and I combined. "Well, make yourself at home. There's food and water in the fridge, and all the bedrooms are made up. Pick which one you like best and make it your own," I tell her. "I'm going to go and sit with Siren if you need me."

I give her a tight smile, and as I turn to walk away, Shadow calls after me. "She's going to be upset."

I pause and glance back. "Sorry?"

"Siren," she confirms. "I've been watching her, and she loves those two blades she stole from you. She's going to be upset that she lost them in the fire."

I nod in understanding. I did notice that she coveted those blades, and because of how much she loves them, I didn't bother to try to get them back. To be honest, I figured at the start that after she was killed, I would take them back, along with all the identities she'd collected, but now, I want her to keep them. They suit her, and as for those blades, there's plenty more where they came from.

"I'll handle it," I tell her, appreciating this kid more with every conversation we have. I go to walk away again before turning back one last time. "Listen, kid," I say, holding her attention. "You did good today. You were brave. Not many would have run into that fire to save someone they barely knew. You should be proud of yourself."

Shadow nods. "She showed me kindness when she didn't need to. Not many people would go out of their way to help someone like that. I like her. I don't have people in my life who actually . . . care enough to look out for me. I didn't want to lose that."

"You're a good kid, Shadow," I tell her. "You'll always have a place here with us."

She offers me a small, unsure smile, and with that, I turn and make my way down the hall, determined to spend every last second I can at Siren's side. Then, as I step over the threshold into my bedroom and lay down beside Siren, I vow to myself that no matter what, someone will pay for what happened tonight, and when they do, they're going to curse the day they ever laid eyes on my girl.

21

SIREN

As I wake in the warmth of two strong arms, I try to push past the blanket of grogginess that makes my body feel heavy. I instantly melt into Reaper's hold as I peel my eyes open to a new day. My head aches, my lungs ache, and my chest . . . holy fuck. But nothing matters more than the fact that I'm alive and in his arms.

The memories of my night assault my mind, and despite the distraction of being in Reaper's orbit, I can't make them fade away.

In my line of work, I've had more than enough close calls. I can't even count on one hand how many times I've been shot. My body is practically a road map full of scars telling the story of the hell I've endured over the past ten years, but last night was different. I've never felt fear like that, never felt my lungs burning from the inside out. The heat inside that suite was like nothing I've ever known, and while I could empathize with Eagle's trauma, now I understand it.

"You good, baby?"

I clear my throat, cringing at the immediate burn. "I thought I told you that I'm not your baby."

Reaper scoffs, and in the one sound, it's clear as day that he has no intention to stop using that goddamn word. "How're you feeling?" he asks, sitting up and reaching for a glass of water and painkillers.

A smile pulls at my lips, loving that he was thoughtful enough to have that prepared for me, and as he holds them out toward me, I do what I can to sit up. "Thanks," I say. " I feel like I've been hit by a truck."

"Nothing quite like being burned alive."

I swallow the little painkillers, cringing as the pills work their way down my hoarse throat. "You know me," I mutter. "I'm all about experiencing everything life has to offer, but this particular experience . . . I don't know. I don't recommend it. Zero out of five."

A forced smile pulls at Reaper's lips, and it's clear he's trying to make me feel better about my situation, but there's no sugarcoating this shit. It is what it is, and the only way past it is to give it time . . . and to slit Gasoline's throat. I'm sure that will have a wonderful healing effect on my soul.

Reaper lays back down, stretching his arm out behind my head and offering me a place to lay, which I take without hesitation. "I don't know what I would have done if you weren't there to pull me out," I tell him, getting comfortable against his chest, owing him my whole damn life.

"It wasn't me," he murmurs as his fingers brush across my skin. "Shadow was the one who pulled you out. Nearly fucking killed her too, but she wasn't giving up."

"What?" I breathe, pushing up against his wide chest and meeting his haunted stare. "Shadow?"

Reaper nods. "She beat me there and didn't hesitate racing in after you. I don't know how it went or what happened in there, but when I arrived, she was dragging your lifeless body out the back. She didn't give up until I got there, and the minute I had you, she collapsed in the grass."

"Fuck," I say, my heart starting to race as a million different emotions overwhelm me, remembering the moment a shadow cut through the thick smoke. I was delirious and couldn't breathe or even scream anymore, but I remember hands pulling at me. I assumed they belonged to Reaper, but it wasn't him. Shadow risked her life to save me, and I don't know how to feel about that. Of course I'm so grateful for her sacrifice, but she's just a child and should never be put in a position where she has to make the decision to risk her own life for someone else's. "We need to find her. She could be hurt."

"She's here," he tells me. "She's sleeping in one of the bedrooms and has no immediate plans to leave. She's good. Just a few small burns, nothing that can't be fixed with a cool compress and a first aid kit."

"But—" I let out a heavy breath, never having been so conflicted in my life. "Why would she do that?"

"For the same reason you cook her a meal every night. She cares and wants you to be okay."

I swallow over the lump forming in my throat and lower myself back against Reaper's chest, only now just realizing how dirty I am. I'm covered in soot and ash with grass stains across my lower half, probably from where Shadow dragged me. My skin is burned, but from what I can tell, it's nothing too substantial, and as for my wrists, they're going to need a bit more attention.

I can't stop thinking about Shadow fast asleep somewhere deep inside this home or the fact that my suite no longer exists. I can't help but glance up at Reaper, meeting his hooded stare. "I suppose you're keeping me hostage here for the foreseeable future."

He scoffs, not even needing to answer, and I roll my eyes, realizing he has absolutely no intention of letting me leave. "We're like some kind of dysfunctional family," I tell him, the words sending a wave of warmth soaring through my chest, making me realize that I wouldn't have it any other way. Finding a family wasn't exactly on my bingo card during War Games, but now that we somewhat resemble it, I can't fathom the idea of losing it.

A soft laugh rumbles through Reaper's chest, and the sound is the best type of medicine. "I suppose we are," he agrees.

A stupid smile pulls at my lips, and as I settle back into the sheets, I start thinking a little more logically. All the stuff I brought here is gone, burned to a crisp. My custom tops and weapons, even my laptop, disintegrated into nothing but ash. "What am I supposed to do? All my stuff is just . . . gone," I say, trying to figure out what the rest of War

Games is going to look like for me.

Reaper shakes his head. "Don't be worrying about all of that. Clothes and weapons can be replaced. You can't. You're alive, and that's all that matters."

I scoff. Clearly this man's priorities don't quite line up with mine because not having a weapon within arm's reach isn't exactly a way I'm comfortable living. Though, considering this is Reaper, I don't doubt there are weapons hidden all over this home. All I'll need to do is go hunting and my stock will be replenished. But it's not the same. Most of those weapons had sentimental value. The first custom blade I bought. The two I stole from Reaper the night he saved my ass. The dagger I'd used to kill the man who put his hands on me at fourteen. Every weapon I had meant something to me, and those memories are going to be hard to say goodbye to.

"Stop overthinking it," Reaper tells me, squeezing my thigh.

I let out a breath, and feeling frustrated with my situation, I sit up before slowly getting to my feet. Reaper hovers over me like a prison warden. "Take it easy," he warns. "You fucking died on me. I left bruises on your chest from giving you CPR, and I'm not about to let it happen again."

"Then, by all means, come with me."

His brows furrow, and I slowly begin to cross the bedroom and make my way into the bathroom. "I need to shower," I tell him, knowing he's more than noticed the current state I'm in, not to mention the gasoline that's festering in my hair. "I need to wash my hair and just . . . be clean, then after that, we're going to figure out the most brutal way to end Gasoline's life."

"I told you," he says, a strange note in his tone. "I work alone."

I scoff. We've been working as a team these past few days, he just doesn't realize it yet, but he's more than just a simple team player. "Not anymore, *baby*," I say, mimicking the tone he uses every time he calls me that filthy word. I'd prefer if he called me his little slut or a filthy whore, but baby? Ugh. It makes my skin crawl. "She stole all the IDs I'd collected over the past two weeks, stole my identification, and then tried to burn me alive. She's not getting off with a simple bullet between the eyes."

"Okay," he finally says. "Together."

I nod and turn my back on him as I peel my clothes off my scarred body, and when my arms start to give out and my muscles begin to hurt, Reaper takes over, stripping me down. He leans into the shower and turns on the water, and with his hands on my hips to keep me steady, he leads me into the shower.

The water rushes over me, washing the black soot from my skin, but I'm going to need a little more than flowing water to clean this shit off my body. Reaper stands behind me, fully clothed, and as I place a hand against the cool tiles, keeping myself balanced, he takes my hair and gently starts unplaiting the long rope-like strands.

"I failed," I murmur, feeling the weight of everything that happened last night resting on my chest, or perhaps that's just the bruises Reaper left from the compressions he gave me to keep my heart pumping.

"You didn't fail, Siren. You got comfortable. You let your guard down, and you didn't check your cameras before entering the premises.

You made mistakes, but it makes you human. Just be grateful that you're alive and you have a chance to even the score."

"She has my ID. She used my real name."

"And?" he prompts. "That doesn't suddenly give her an edge. It's a name. Whether you use it or not. She's not better than you. She had no hope of beating you in a fair fight. She had to get you while your guard was down, otherwise, she wouldn't stand a chance. But the way I see it, you're now in a position of power."

My brows furrow, and I glance back over my shoulder, meeting his eyes as I try to figure out how the hell he came to that conclusion. "Come again?"

"With any luck, your name will appear on the death toll. The whole suite was burned to the ground. They have no idea that you weren't in there, which means you're a ghost. Nobody is watching you now."

I shrug my shoulders. "Not if Gasoline stayed and watched the show. If she did, she now knows there's an alliance between you, me, and Shadow. We'll be an even bigger target."

"Perhaps," he agrees. "But that's the risk you take when you play War Games."

I let out a heavy sigh, closing my eyes and trying to relax as he works shampoo into my long hair. A soft groan rumbles through my chest, and honestly, I don't think I've ever had someone care for me in this way, not even as a child. It's well out of my comfort zone, but I can't find it in me to ask him to stop.

My heart races, and I don't exactly understand why, but what I do know is that waking up in his bed after he spent the night trying to save me means something. This is more than just the games now. If he didn't care, he would have let me die. It would have sucked, but he would have moved past it in a couple of days, and that right there scares the shit out of me because had the roles been reversed, I would have done the very same thing.

Fuck. I think I'm falling for this man.

He rinses the shampoo out of my hair, and before I know it, his hands are lathered with soap, gently moving across my aching skin. The soot washes off my skin, and as his hands roam over my body, I relax into him, letting him take me away into a world of blissful pleasure.

"Reaper," I moan.

"I got you," he promises as his hand skims down my body and slips between my thighs, brushing past my clit and making my hips jolt.

I suck in a gasp, and as he circles back and does it again, my knees begin to shake. My body is too sensitive, and I don't have the ability to hold back. His hands continue moving, not wanting to linger anywhere too long and risk hurting me further, and when it's time to rinse the soap off, Reaper reaches for the shower head above us.

He brings it down over me, washing the bubbles off my body inch by inch. His arm locks around my waist, holding me against him, and as I close my eyes, his lips come down on my neck, gently kissing as his lips move along my sensitive skin.

I grip his arm around my waist, needing it for support, and as the shower head trails down low over my stomach, I suck in a breath. He doesn't stop, and as I tilt my head, allowing him more access to my neck, he trails the water down over my hip.

Anticipation builds deep within me, sensing where he's going with this, and I don't dare ask him to stop, needing it more than I need my next breath. Then finally, he reaches the promised land, and the water gently shoots right against my core.

My knees weaken, and my body instantly wakes up, having to grip his arm tighter to keep myself up. "Holy shit," I breathe, tilting my head back to his shoulder as his arm around my waist shifts up, giving him space to grasp my breast and roll my nipple between his skilled fingers.

Reaper adjusts the shower head, changing the setting from the normal flow to the massager, and I gasp as the water pressure shoots directly against my clit. He circles it around, not keeping it in the same spot and risking overstimulating me, and the pressure is just right.

"Fuck," I pant, my eyes rolling in the back of my head.

"Just let it go," he says, enticing me with that deep tone, but I'm not there yet.

I need more. *I need him.*

Reaching behind me, I feel for Reaper, finding the front of his drenched pants, and for just a moment, I expect him to pull away, to tell me no, or to say this is all about me, but he allows me free rein as I undo his fly and free his massive cock from the confines of his pants. "Please," I groan, wrapping my fingers around him and madly pulsing up and down his thick shaft, feeling the ridges of his angry veins.

"Are you sure? I don't want to push you too far."

"I need you inside of me," I tell him.

Reaper doesn't hesitate, shifting my hips back and taking my thigh to open me wide. I have no choice but to release my hold on him and grasp for balance against the wall. Then as the water thrums against my needy clit, Reaper slowly pushes inside of me, gently rocking back and forth as my walls stretch around him, accommodating his impressive size.

"Oh God," I groan.

It's everything I need, and I'm completely at his mercy, but I wouldn't have it any other way. It's as if he knows exactly what I need as I need it.

His soft grunts surround me, and knowing my body has the ability to make him feel this way has me desperate to please him. I want to give him everything. I want to make him feel as good as he's making me feel right now, and the second my skin doesn't feel as though it's melting off my body, that's exactly what I'm going to do.

The water pressure against my clit has me in a chokehold, and as Reaper slowly rocks in and out of my needy cunt, it becomes too much for me to resist. The intensity builds inside of me like a coil tightening, ready to spring, and as the water shoots against my core, I have no choice but to let go as the coil explodes within me.

My orgasm shoots through my veins and sends a wave of ecstasy crashing over me as my knees begin to shake. I grip Reaper, holding on to him with everything I have as he continues thrusting into me, rolling his body with such perfect, precise movements.

My eyelids flutter as my orgasm continues to build, and when Reaper comes with me, the softest grunt fills the cramped shower.

"You're so goddamn beautiful when you come," he tells me in a deep, gravelly tone. "When your sweet little cunt squeezes me like that . . . fuck."

A lazy smile settles across my lips, and I lean back into him, my energy quickly dwindling as I come down from my high. He releases my thigh before locking his arm around my waist once again, holding me up and shifting the shower head away from my over-sensitive clit.

He adjusts the setting back to the normal flow before fixing it back into its position above our heads, then he turns me in his arms and simply holds me. "I thought I was going to die," I tell him.

"Not on my watch, Siren," he rumbles. "I still have fifteen days to devour you, and I'm not about to let either of us lose a single one of those seconds."

I shift my stance before lifting my chin and meeting his heavy stare. "Why?" I whisper. "Why does it matter to you so much?"

He shakes his head, his dark gaze mirroring the unease that I feel deep in my chest, and I can't help but wonder if he's having the same realization that I am—that there's something more here, something profound between us. "I wish I knew."

His words sit with me, and after letting out a breath, I reach behind me and shut off the water. Reaper wraps a towel around me, patting me down to avoid rubbing my wet, aching skin. Then, as I finish drying off, Reaper peels off his wet clothes, and I grab one of his clean shirts.

He helps me pull it over my head, and I can't help but notice the way it smells just like him. Then as he starts to dress himself, pulling a shirt over that incredible grim reaper tattoo and hiding it away, I find myself wandering out of the main bedroom and searching for the girl who saved my life.

My heart races, unsure what to say to Shadow or how to even be around her. The last time I checked, she wasn't sure about me, always inching away and watching me as though she wasn't sure if she could trust me, but surely things are different now.

Making my way down the hall, I let my fingers drag along the drywall, the exhaustion still gripping me in a chokehold. There's no telling when the last of my energy will fade away and leave me scrambling on the ground.

I pass two bedrooms, finding them both empty, before setting my sights on the final one at the opposite end of the hallway. It makes sense for Shadow to want to put as much distance between her and us as possible, and if I were smart, I should be putting distance between us too. Yet no matter how hard I try, I keep finding my way back to him. Either that or he's the one finding his way to me. Honestly, I don't really know anymore. But what I do know is not being the object of his desires is somewhere I never want to find myself.

Creeping toward the final bedroom, I approach the closed door and gently rap my knuckles against the hardwood. I don't announce myself or wait for her to welcome me in. If she's as good as I suspect her to be, she would have heard my footsteps down the hall and known they were too light to be Reaper's. Then when I didn't stop and turn toward the kitchen and living room, she would have known exactly where I was going.

Taking the handle, I slowly open the door, taking my time so as not to startle her. I don't want her to fear me, and despite her knowing that I'm already here, barging in like a raging bull isn't going to give her confidence that she can trust me.

Peeking my head inside the room, I find Shadow standing beside the bed. It's made perfectly, not a single bump in the blankets, and I can't help but wonder if this is normal practice for her. Has she been standing there beside it all night, or did she allow herself a few hours of vulnerability to sleep before making the bed to military perfection the moment she woke? And in which case, why hasn't she moved since then?

"May I come in?" I murmur, meeting her bright blue stare.

She shrugs her shoulders. "I suppose."

I offer her a tight smile, feeling so far out of my league that I don't know where to go from here, but I suppose, being the adult in the room, I have no choice but to try and wing it.

I swallow over the lump in my throat and immediately regret it. The burn in my raspy throat is already proving to be a bigger pain in my ass than Reaper. Then, reminding myself that I'm not a wuss and that this beautiful, selfless child did something so incredibly brave, I step into the room and walk right into her, throwing my arms around her petite body.

She stiffens in my hold, and her awkwardness suggests that she's never been hugged for even a second in her short life. "Thank you," I tell her, holding her tighter and refusing to let go. "You saved my life, Shadow. You were so incredibly brave, and while it was reckless and dangerous to risk your own life for mine, I will always be grateful."

"I . . . uhhh. I was just doing what anyone else would have done in my situation," she says, slowly beginning to relax as she lifts her arms and awkwardly wraps them around me.

"No, Shadow. Nobody would have done what you did in there," I tell her. "They would have stood back in fear and listened until my screaming stopped. You ran in and risked your own life just for the chance of saving mine. There's no way I could ever thank you enough."

Shadow holds me just a little bit tighter, and when she buries her face into my shoulder, I realize just how deprived this child has been of affection. "Nobody has ever cooked me dinner before," she says, her words muffled by my shoulder. "You and Reaper . . . You're both nice to me for no reason other than because you want to be, and I . . . I've never had anybody care about me like that."

My hand shifts from her back to her hair, and I hold her there for just a moment longer, not daring to move until she's the one to pull away. And when she does, it doesn't go unnoticed just how close she remains to me. "Look," I start, placing my hand on her shoulder and holding her blue stare as I realize that Reaper's hovering in the open doorway behind me. "I can't pretend to know how the next two weeks are going to play out. I can't promise that someone isn't going to get the drop on me or that I'm going to be here right until the very end, but what I can guarantee is that I'm not going to walk away until someone physically takes me out. I need you to survive, Shadow, even if it means ending both mine and Reaper's lives. I can't fathom the idea of one of these assholes hurting you, of someone like Gasoline doing to you what she did to me, and while I have so many questions about how you came to be here in the first place, just know that all I want is to protect you."

Shadows nods and lets her gaze fall toward Reaper behind me. "But I don't want to kill you . . . either of you."

"I'm sorry," Reaper says, stepping into the bedroom that somehow seems so much smaller with him inside of it. "But that's the nature of the game. The three of us can have each other's backs and eliminate the other contenders. We can face this as a team if we must, but there will come a time when you will have to take our lives. There's no other way out of this."

"And if I don't?"

I offer her a sad smile. "Then Reaper and I are going to have no other choice but to pull some of that fucked up Romeo and Juliet bullshit and take ourselves out. You not walking out of this alive is not an option."

"Why can't we all walk out of here alive? How would they ever know?"

"They'll know," Reaper says, his gaze shifting to mine, a question I can't quite decipher lingering within his lethal gaze. "And when they figure out that they've been played, the bounty on our heads would be astronomical. We wouldn't be able to shake it."

Shadow lets out a heavy sigh before nodding her head again. "Okay, so that's the game plan," she says. "We take out the final five contenders, and when the time comes . . ."

Reaper steps into my side, his fingers brushing against mine. "We lay our lives down and allow you the chance at having a real childhood, only ten million dollars richer."

22

REAPER

I'm not going to lie, these past few days, the heaviness weighing on me has become almost insufferable. I've never spent days at a time with people, especially people I care about, and with every passing minute, it becomes abundantly clear that I can't stomach the idea of losing them.

Siren is . . . I don't even understand what she is to me, but when she's in my bed, wrapped in my arms, my heart races so fast that I fear it could explode. It's more than just a fierce type of lust. I've lusted over women more than I care to admit, and it never lasts long, and it sure as fuck doesn't get stronger after I've already had what I wanted from her.

This is more, and it's scaring the fuck out of me because I know that when the time comes to end her life, I'm not going to have the strength to do it. Nor is Shadow, for that matter. The two of them have become closer over these past few days. They're inseparable, and I can't help but feel that Siren has taken on a motherly role with her.

The two of them went shopping on my dime to replenish the things Siren lost during the fire, and it was almost comical to watch them both fawn over all the bullshit they bought. They're like two peas in a pod, and they don't even realize it. They bought a bunch of clothes and makeup, and while Siren wasn't able to find her usual style of clothing in the limited stores on offer in Blue Springs, it'll do. But what really thawed my cold heart was watching the two of them loot all the weapons of the contenders who didn't make it. It was like two kids on Halloween returning home with all their candy.

True to her word, Shadow has stayed with us. She stays with Siren during the day, and after helping Siren with dinner, she ventures out in the early evening to do whatever the fuck she feels needs to be done. But she's always back by ten or eleven and takes her ass to bed. We truly are some kind of dysfunctional family, and I'm finding that I wouldn't have it any other way. Just like Siren and Shadow, none of us have ever experienced what family life is like, and I find myself clinging to it. But truth be told, I'm terrified of losing it.

Siren is still shaken after the fire, but she hasn't let it bring her down. If anything, it lit a spark under her ass to get back out there and show these fuckers that she can't be messed with. After the fire, we were hoping that War Games would announce her death, which would have given Siren one hell of an edge in these games, but when her name didn't appear in the update, we came to the realization that the higher powers of War Games are more connected than we really knew.

She spent the last few days tracking the remaining five contenders, but the majority of her attention has been focused on Gasoline. After watching the psychotic redhead closely, it became abundantly clear that she's somehow created an alliance with the brothers. It's not ideal, and it makes them an even bigger threat, but in reality, when three morons get together to plan shit, it doesn't necessarily mean what they come up with is going to be particularly effective. Either way, we need to keep vigilant, and now that the three of us are living under one roof, it makes us a bigger target—one I hope the others are too intimidated by to even attempt to take us down.

Today's focus—The Executioner.

The guy is an ex-cop, and he moves like one too. I'm surprised he hasn't been targeted at this point in the competition yet. He seems to be . . . lacking. Everything about him is obvious, and even as he makes his way toward the massive lake, he seems to walk with his chest puffed out and a stick up his ass. The fucker has no idea how to be discreet or blend in and become invisible.

I've been tracking him for the better part of the morning, getting a feel for who he is and what his day looks like, and to be painfully honest, the guy is fucking boring. There's not a remarkable thing about him. Just another ex-cop who wanted to experience the thrill of being the bad guy.

From the research I did, his kills are all executioner style, and as for his victims, there's not a damn connection between them. He has a god complex and targets men and women who he believes need to be taught a lesson, but today, his bullshit is coming to an end. I don't particularly like making kills in broad daylight, but Blue Springs has been particularly quiet today.

Perhaps it's the statement the FBI put out last night, warning the residents about the killers on the loose. Everybody is staying in, keeping themselves safe, but truth be told, they're the safest ones here. None of us care to make a problem with the residents, that's not our purpose, and honestly, making sure they're locked in their homes is nothing but a benefit for the rest of us.

From what I can tell, the FBI is still focusing on the dismemberment of Sharkbait and has since stumbled upon Raven's body under the bridge. They finally ruled out the fire at Siren's suite as no accident. Not to mention the other bodies that have been called in.

Their resources are spread thin, so despite having the FBI here in Blue Springs, they're too busy to see anything that's going on around them. But it's fine, I'm more than happy to hunt down these killers for them, and if they need The Executioner delivered to them on a silver platter, then I'm more than happy to oblige. Though, I can guarantee that when I'm through with him, he won't be in a state to answer questions.

I follow him to the lake, and it's clear from the way his gaze shifts from left to right that he thinks he's tracking someone. As he turns to make his way to the water's edge, his body stiffens, and my theory is confirmed.

His hand hovers over the gun at his hip and the move makes me want to take him out on principle. It's a cop move, but more than that, it's an easy way out. Don't get me wrong, I love a good gun, but using a gun in a game like this is almost considered cheating. Either way, he's found himself a target, and I can't help but feel like today just got a little more interesting.

Adjusting my stance from behind him, I peer up ahead, trying to figure out which of these fuckers he's going after, and as I see the back of a woman with her hair up in a high pony and the long strands plaited down to her ass, my stomach sinks.

Siren.

What the fuck does she think she's doing? I thought she was spending the day doing recon on the brothers, but here she is, striding down to the water's edge, dragging her feet through the water, and doing nothing but making a fucking target out of herself.

The Executioner picks up his pace, hurrying after her while doing what he can to be discreet, but truth be told, he's as discreet as being turkey slapped by a fucking elephant's cock. He thumps his way down to the lake, and I don't even have to try and conceal myself to stay hidden behind him.

He's focused solely on Siren's ass and has no consideration for anything around him.

He begins to lower his hand over his weapon, grasping the handle, and I release one of my knives from the belt around my hips, clutching the handle in my palm. The blade feels like an extension of myself, and as I watch him closely, waiting for him to make his move, I prepare to end this.

Siren continues on her way, completely unaware of the two lethal men behind her, and as The Executioner raises his gun, preparing to take his shot, a twig snaps under his foot.

Siren pauses and whips around, her eyes wide as a blade releases from her hand and sails perfectly through the air, whipping straight past The Executioner, but not before amputating his whole fucking ear. The blade spins toward me, and I simply tilt my head to the left, letting it sail right by me as The Executioner grips the side of his head and roars in agony. "FUCK!"

"What the hell are you doing here?" Siren demands, her gaze locked on me as she ignores the wailing man between us as he drops to his knees in agony.

"Me? What about you?" I throw back at her. "Do you even realize how close you just came to losing these fucking games? This asshole almost put a bullet through your head while you were too busy taking a nice afternoon stroll in the sun."

Siren rolls her eyes and props her hands on her hips, clearly irritated with me as I double back a few steps and collect her blade. "It was a trap, you moron. I've been leaving breadcrumbs for him for three days, and he finally took the bait. I lured him here, and now my whole fucking plan has gone to shit."

Well, shit. That might have been a slight oversight on my part, but at hearing her words—with his non-amputated ear, of course—The Executioner stiffens, his gaze snapping up just long enough to realize just how fucked he is. Then, before Siren gets a chance to berate me further, The Executioner scrambles to his feet and takes off at a sprint, leaving a trail of blood behind him.

Siren simply stares at me as he gets away. "Seriously? Now I'm going to have to chase him to make my kill. Do you have any idea how inconvenient that is?"

The Executioner gets further away, and as I stare back at the woman I may or may not be falling in love with, all I can do is smirk. "Not if I get there first."

Her beautiful face falls, her eyes widening, realizing just how serious I am, and without a second of hesitation, she turns on her heel and flies after him, intent to make her kill and take claim of his identification.

"Over my dead fucking body," Siren calls over her shoulder as she makes a break for the reeds, her bare feet digging into the sandy shore as she goes.

I can't help but laugh as I start after them. This may not be the most exciting game I've ever played. That position is solely reserved for the night Siren cuffed me to the fridge and let me fuck her after I caught her, but this is coming in a close second. There's something about being in competition with this woman that excites me, and I can't get enough.

I've got to give credit to The Executioner. For a retired cop, the fucker moves fast, but he's not faster than me or Siren. He makes it all the way to the entrance of the massive cave system to the right of the lake. The caves are dark and offer protection, but I'm a hunter by nature, so there's nowhere inside those caves he could possibly hide from me.

The Executioner disappears into the caves, followed shortly by Siren, and despite how dark it is, I know she can sense exactly where he is. It only takes me a second to catch up to her, and I silently move in by her side. "Don't even think about taking this kill," she mutters, trying to keep her voice low, though I don't know why she bothers. I have no doubt that The Executioner knows exactly where we are.

"Wouldn't dream of it," I lie, a smirk pulling at my lips.

Siren scoffs. "You're so full of shit."

A laugh rumbles through my chest, and as the sound bounces off the cavernous walls, Siren takes off at a run. My laugh rumbles louder, and when the cave forks, splitting into two, I start heading the opposite direction. "You're going the wrong way," I taunt.

"Am not."

"You sure about that?" I call as the darkness eats me up.

A moment passes, and silence falls around me as the sound of Siren's footsteps comes to a halt. A second passes and then another before the sweetest sound fills the cave. "Fuck!"

The grin that tears across my lips is almost psychotic, and hearing as she backtracks before following after me down the right side of the cave, I pick up my pace simply to taunt her.

"Fucking asshole," Siren mutters as she comes up behind me. "I put too much effort into trapping this loser. I'm not about to hand him to you right at the finish line."

"You want him, baby, then take him from me."

Siren skips ahead of me, spinning around and walking backward as she meets my stare. "Call me baby one more time, and I'll have no choice but to rip your vocal cords out of your throat and strangle you with them."

Fuck. This woman knows a thing or two about foreplay. "I'd like to see you try."

Siren scoffs and turns back around before pausing in the middle of the cave. I move in right behind her, unable to keep from putting my hands on her waist and circling one down over the front of her hip.

She smacks my hand away before I get any lower and distracts us both from the real reason we're here. "You can have me after I take out this dirty pig," she murmurs, lifting her chin as if to sniff out the very animal we're hunting. "Assuming you can control yourself enough not to come in your pants while I put on a show."

My hand trails up her body before circling her throat, and as I gently squeeze, she melts against me. "I told you, *baby*. You're not beating me to this kill, but I'll still claim your sweet cunt either way."

Siren groans, and with a sharp push of her hips, she slams her ass back against my cock, almost bringing me to my knees as she sprints deeper into the cave, more than locked on her target now. "You're gonna have to try harder than that, Reaper," she calls over her shoulder as she disappears into the cave.

I kneel down, my fist pressed against the hard ground as I take a second for my balls to settle back into place, and despite the damage this woman insists on doing to my balls, I think I was right—I'm falling in love with her.

Fuck that. Who am I kidding? I'm already there. But despite how I might feel about her, that doesn't mean I'm about to hand her the win on this one. If she wants it, she's going to have to pry it from my cold, dead hands.

I take off after her, this time being as silent as the ghost the other contenders fear me to be, and as I creep into a wider opening of the cave, I find Siren well and truly on the hunt. Her blade is clutched in her hand, her target locked and loaded.

The Executioner cowers behind a boulder, and I make my way toward him as his gaze remains locked on Siren. He's so unaware that he doesn't even realize I'm here. Though I doubt that Siren suffers from the same inadequacy. She knows I'm here, she can sense it in the way a chill sails down her spine every time I walk into a room. Though I hope by now she's learned to trust that chill and know that without a doubt, I will never hurt her. Even fifteen days from now when I'm supposed to end her life.

I can't do it, and despite the rules of this bullshit game, I *won't* do it.

I'm in love with this woman, and I won't be the reason for her death. There's got to be another way because I refuse to believe that the very moment I find someone worthy of spending my life with, she'll be torn away. I don't care what I have to do; this game ends with me, Shadow, and Siren still breathing.

"Little pig, little pig," Siren begins to coo. "Come out, come out wherever you are."

The moron whimpers, and I roll my eyes. How fucking stupid can one man be?

I watch as he reaches for his gun again, gripping it tighter than

Siren's sweet little cunt grips my cock each night, and as he takes a few shaky breaths, I realize he's preparing to make his move, stupidly thinking he could still get out of here alive.

He should have known better. Siren is too good. There's no beating her. Well, except for when I try, but I look forward to the day she gets the drop on me.

As if sensing that something's about to happen, Siren adjusts her grip on her blade, and instead of preparing myself, I just keep strolling toward The Executioner, trusting Siren to have it under control. Then the second The Executioner makes his move and springs out from behind the boulder with his gun aimed toward Siren's beautiful face, she launches her blade toward him with every ounce of strength she has.

The blade spins, whipping toward him, and I watch with pure elation as it slices straight through his wrist, amputating his whole fucking hand. He roars in agony as the bloodied heap drops heavily to the ground, gun and all, and all I can do is watch with pride.

That's my fucking girl. It's a shame I'm going to take this kill right out of her capable hands.

The Executioner falls to his knees, gripping his newfound stump as blood pours over his fingers. There are tears in his eyes as he howls in agony, and the way his cries echo off the walls of the cave is simply magical.

His ferocious stare is locked on Siren, and as she slowly strides toward him, it's clear he's forgotten who the real threat is here. Then, to make sure the fucker isn't missing out on all the fun, I step out of the shadows and move in right behind him. I reach out and gently tap his shoulder, and when his head whips around with wide, terror-filled eyes, the deepest excitement fills me.

He instantly begins to scramble away, using his feet and elbow as he struggles to hold on to his new stump. "Oh, right . . . ummm," I say, feeling giddy. "BOO!"

He squeals like a little bitch, and just as I go to lunge toward him, Siren breaks into a sprint. "Oh, fuck no," she yells, swan diving toward me and The Executioner with a new blade in her hand. I catch her midair and avert her body weight, dropping her into a forward roll that sends her flying right past me and The Executioner.

A laugh rumbles through me, and she quickly gets back to her feet as I focus on my kill. "Bastard," Siren roars behind me, then just as I take a step toward The Executioner, Siren launches herself onto my back. Her legs lock around my waist as her arm twines around my neck, pulling tight. "Don't make me drop you again."

I try to peel her off me, but as her blade swings toward my thigh, I have no choice but to fight back, and within seconds, we're rumbling on the dirty ground like two horny teenagers, each of us still trying to inch toward the target as he does everything in his power to crawl away.

Siren gets ahead, springing free from my hold and swiping toward The Executioner with her blade, and I catch her by the back of her jeans, yanking her fine ass back. "Oh, no you don't, baby girl," I say, just moments before trying the exact same thing, only her foot to my throat more than slows me down.

Siren laughs and flashes me the most perfect smile. "Oops."

Fuck me. This woman will be the death of me. Literally.

"Little Siren, I promise, you will pay for that."

She grins back at me, tossing the blade in her hand and catching it perfectly in her palm, preparing to take another swing. "I'd like to see you try."

Then, with every bit of strength she possesses in her perfect body, she lunges toward The Executioner again, her blade aiming right for his throat. I fly after her, my arm locking around her slim waist, and as our bodies propel forward, I disarm her, taking the blade right out of her grasp before plunging it straight through The Executioner's eye.

23

SIREN

My chest heaves as Reaper and I crash to the dirty ground, his strong arms bracing around my body and protecting me from the impact. I have no fucking idea what happened, but somehow The Executioner is dead with my blade protruding from his right eyeball, but I wasn't the one who put it there. Only, I could have sworn that blade was in my hand when I lunged for him.

How the fucking hell did that happen?

I suppose this is what I get for baiting a man like Reaper. Though he was technically the one to bait me, and I loved it.

Perhaps I've gotten too comfortable with him and forgotten exactly what he was capable of. After all, there was a reason I was so petrified of him when we first met, and it'll be wise to remember that.

Only, I don't think he's ever going to hurt me. He's somehow gone from being my greatest threat to my fiercest protector. Even if he's an asshole who makes me work for my kills . . . or lack thereof. But there's no denying that from the second he dared to go after my target, I've never had so much fun.

Having said that, I still can't figure out how the hell he managed to disarm me and claim my kill all within the blink of an eye. Though one thing is for sure, there's no questioning his skill. He's better than the best. He's in a league of his own.

I shove him off me and sit up, leaning against my palms as I attempt to catch my breath. "What the fuck was that?"

Reaper simply grins at me as though he didn't even break a sweat during the most chaotic fight 'til the end I've ever been involved in. "I told you, Little Siren, that kill was mine, and I don't care if you sat on my face and ground that sweet little cunt against my tongue to distract me, I was still making that kill."

I scoff, getting to my feet as I stride over to The Executioner's body and rummage through his pockets for his ID. "Just because you were the one who made the kill, doesn't mean that it doesn't belong to me. I was robbed. I had it in the bag, and you know it."

"Say what you want," he murmurs, slowly getting to his feet and watching me carefully. "But I made that kill, and you know it."

Finding his wallet, I pull out his driver's license and look over it before holding it up. "Then I suppose you're going to want this?" I ask, holding it out toward Reaper. His gaze narrows, and as he reaches to take the little plastic card out of my hand, I yank it back, grinning maniacally. "You want it. Come get it."

Then, without skipping a beat, I take off at a sprint, deeper into the cave.

"Fuck me," I hear Reaper mutter behind me before jumping into action. He chases after me, and the stupidest squeal tears out of me as he does, but I forge ahead through the darkness, heading deeper into the cave.

I run around bends and take turns I wouldn't have expected to be here, and when I hear the sound of rushing water, I head toward it. Reaper follows behind me, and despite not running very fast, he makes a point to not catch me, allowing me the chance to lead him astray. If this were any other time, and I was any other target, he never would have allowed me to get this far.

The rushing water gets louder, and I continue around one last bend before coming to a startling halt, my eyes widen in wonder as I take in the breathtaking view before me. A natural pool sits in the middle of the cave, and the ceiling has been washed away by the force of the waterfall streaming into it. The darkness is gone, replaced by the beauty of the vast sunlight streaming through the top of the cave.

It's the most magnificent thing I've ever seen.

The water is crystal clear, and the sun shines through the hole in the top, reflecting against the spray of water as it rushes in, it looks like a million sparkling diamonds dancing in the sky.

"Woah," Reaper says, moving in behind me, his hands falling to my waist. "That's—"

"Everything," I whisper.

Reaper gently turns me, his dark gaze resting against mine as his fingers find my chin and lift. "No, Siren. *You're* everything."

My heart races as the sweetest rush begins pulsing through my veins, filling me with an emotion I don't know if I've ever felt before. Butterflies appear in the pit of my stomach, and as he closes the gap between us and lowers his warm lips to mine, I finally understand it.

I'm in love with him.

I kiss him back, The Executioner's ID falling from my fingers as I lace my arms around his neck. His hands tighten on my waist, holding me to him as he deepens our kiss, and the hunger intensifies within me.

His lips drop to my neck, and I suck in a gasp, tilting my head to the side and offering him more as my eyelids flutter, pure ecstasy tearing through me. "Reaper," I moan, my fingers digging into his skin, silently begging for more.

"I've got you," he murmurs against my neck.

My chest heaves for air, and I can't resist him a moment longer. I reach for his shirt, pulling it over his head and tossing it aside before dropping my hands to his strong body. My fingers roam over his wide shoulders and down to his chest before sailing lower to the sharp ridges of his abs. His body is carved from stone, pure perfection, and I love every inch of it.

He doesn't hold back, reaching for my tank top and peeling it off me as I become desperate to feel him inside of me. It becomes a frenzy of reaching for one another, tearing off clothes as our lips frantically seek the other's, and before I know it, his hands are at my ass, lifting me into his warm arms.

I lock my legs around his waist, and as his lips return to mine, he walks us toward the water of the natural pool. He inches in, and the further he gets, the colder it seems to become, but with the heat radiating off our bodies, I barely notice the freezing temperature.

His body against mine is everything I've ever needed, and when he presses me up against the side of the natural pool and arches my back over the curved wall, I suck in a gasp, feeling as his fingers trail over my body.

He's waist-deep in the water, with my hips barely skimming across the top of it, and as I lean back over the cave's natural curve, his lips work their way down my body. A soft moan slips from between my lips and as his fingers softly move across my skin, leaving a trail of goosebumps, he leans down and closes his mouth over my needy clit.

A loud groan tears from deep in my chest, and as I listen to the sound of the powerful waterfall raining down around us, Reaper claims me in the way only he knows how.

His tongue works over my clit, flicking and rolling as he reaches down and finds my entrance, slowly pushing two thick fingers deep inside of me, tormenting me with the sweetest pleasure. "Oh God," I groan as my hips jolt, and his skilled tongue makes my eyes roll.

I feel his grin against me, and as I reach down between my thighs and knot my hand into his hair, he curls his fingers inside of me and massages my walls. "Fuck," I groan, my hips having a mind of their own as I tighten my hold in his hair.

Reaper is relentless, and as his fingers work over my G-spot again and again, I'm completely at his mercy.

It's too much, and as I feel that familiar tightening deep inside my core, building by the second, I know it's only a matter of time before he completely rocks my world.

The spray from the waterfall rains over me, dancing across my sensitive skin as Reaper's tongue continues its sweet torture. I can't take it a second longer, then as his fingers dive back inside of me, massaging my walls, I explode, unable to hold back.

My orgasm tears through me, and I cry out, my voice echoing off the walls of this incredible cave. "Holy fucking shit," I say with a heavy pant, tipping my head back as ecstasy pulses through my veins. Reaper doesn't relent, and as he grins against my core, my orgasm intensifies.

His fingers curl and spread, massaging as my walls crumble around him, shattering like glass as they wildly convulse. My whole body spasms, and by the time I start coming down from my high, I can barely catch my breath.

"God, Reaper," I groan, loosening my hold in his hair as he finally pulls back and allows me the chance to relax.

"Don't get too comfortable, Little Siren," he says, reaching for me and pulling me back into his arms, my legs locking around his hips once again. "I'm not nearly finished with you."

I can't help the grin that pulls at my lips, feeling his hardness against my overly sensitive core. "Oh, really?" I ask, hooking my arm around his neck and holding on as my other dives down beneath the water and circles his thick cock. "And dare I ask what it is you think you're going to do to me?"

Reaper turns and makes his way toward the rushing downpour of water. "Don't play coy with me," he warns, that deep tone like a potent drug to me. "You know exactly what I'm going to do to you. Now be a good girl and let me fuck this sweet cunt before I fucking explode."

Well damn. Who the hell am I to deny a request like that?

My hand pumps up and down his cock, and as his gaze locks onto mine, I can't help but grin back at him. "I'm more than happy to let you fuck me, Reaper, but what I won't do is be your good little girl."

"Is that so?" he questions, bringing us closer to the edge of the waterfall as he adjusts his hold on me, fisting his cock and guiding it to my entrance. "Then I suppose you leave me no choice but to teach you a fucking lesson." And with that, he slams that delicious cock deep inside my needy cunt.

I cry out, throwing my head back in ecstasy as my walls shamelessly adjust to his impressive size, stretching around him and offering no mercy. Then, just as he ruthlessly begins to fuck me, he takes one final step, sending us directly under the force of the massive waterfall.

"Holy fuck," I call out as the water rains down over us.

My pussy clenches around him, and just when I think this is as far as he's going to take it, his big hand closes around my throat and pushes my head back, tipping it until the water is raining down over my face.

I take a gasping breath, and as he fucks me within an inch of my life, I quickly realize that attempting to breathe is going to result in either a sexual drowning or a really pleasurable waterboarding session. And honestly, I don't hate it.

"If you wish to breathe, sweet Siren, then be a *good girl* and come for me," he tells me as that thick cock thrusts in and out, slamming deep inside of me and raining havoc all over my body. "Once you give me what I want, I'll give you what you need. It's that simple."

His voice is barely audible over the sound of the massive waterfall, and honestly, I don't know what kind of strength he must possess to be able to hold us here without being washed away, let alone continue to fuck me with such vigorous passion.

He pushes me back further so that my spine is almost flat against the water's surface, and as the waterfall rains down over us, the water drums against my body, and more specifically, my sensitive nipples and clit, creating an overflow of electricity pulsing straight through my body and directly to my core.

My eyes roll behind my closed lids, and as my lungs begin to scream, desperate for sweet oxygen, I have no choice but to try and take a breath. Water quickly invades my mouth, and I sputter against it, gasping for air, but my body is too worked up, and as the water hammers against the rest of my body, stimulating both my nipples and clit, I become more worked up.

I squirm under his touch, but I'm not ready to tap out of this one just yet. All I know is that this is too good to call it quits, but if I have any intention of being able to walk away from this, I'm going to have to come soon, and judging by how worked up he's got me, it's going to be a good one.

My lungs are almost at a breaking point, and as Reaper rolls his skilled hips back and thrusts deep inside of me again, I'm launched right over the edge, coming in an explosive fit. My orgasm tears through me with rage, and as my whole body begins to spasm, Reaper pulls me out of the water, allowing me the chance to gasp for sweet oxygen.

With my chest pressed against his, I clutch onto him as I struggle to catch my breath. It has no effect on the raw intensity rocking through my body, nor do I think it has anything to do with not being able to take a breath. No, this has everything to do with the sheer intensity of the epic orgasm currently ripping through my body. My pussy convulses around his thick cock, and as I completely come undone, Reaper comes with me, shooting his hot load deep into my throbbing cunt.

"Breathe, baby," he murmurs, leading us away from the raging waters as his hand moves up and down my back, making sure he didn't push me too far. "Slow, deep breaths."

"I'm okay," I promise him, overwhelmed by the concern lingering in his deep tone, and despite how close I came to drowning in that waterfall, I know he wouldn't have let that happen. He's the fiercest killer across the globe, and yet I trust him implicitly. He'd sooner lay his own life down before letting mine falter. But that doesn't mean he's not willing to push boundaries. And fuck, these are boundaries I didn't realize I wanted to cross.

Reaper walks us right over to the edge of the pool, and I unwind my body from his before draping myself over the edge and turning back to take in the sheer beauty of the natural pool and the roaring waterfall that just violated me in such a glorious way.

I've been across the world, taking out targets in every corner of this magnificent planet, and despite everything I've seen, there's no doubt that this right here is one of the most breathtaking places on earth.

I can't tear my eyes away from it as Reaper hovers at my side, reaching out of the pool to the bundle of clothes that's dangerously close to falling into the pool with us.

We chill out for a while, and when Reaper steps back into me and drops his lips to my neck, I instantly melt into him, more than ready for round two. Only this time, I fully intend to be in control. Just because I might have enjoyed being waterboarded by a waterfall deep inside a cave doesn't mean that I'm about to let that bullshit fly.

"Fuck, you're so beautiful," Reaper murmurs, his lips so soft against my skin.

"Mmmm," I groan, pressing my ass back against him.

"Remember when you cuffed me to the fridge?" he asks just moments before I hear the soft click of metal filling the wondrous cave. He laughs in my ear and takes my hand, lifting it out of the water, only to find a metal cuff locked around it with the other end attached to the natural cut out of the pool wall.

"What the ever-loving fuck, Reaper?" I demand, pulling against the cuff. "Unlock me."

All I can do is gawk at him as he climbs out of the pool with water gushing off his perfect body, making my mouth water. He strides across to the bundle of clothes and grabs his pants before pulling them on. He doesn't bother doing up the button before finding The Executioner's driver's license on the ground and scooping it up.

"You won't be needing this," he tells me before shoving the ID deep into his pocket and winking at me with a stupid smirk across his delicious lips. He turns to make his way out of the cave, and I curse myself for not taking a better mental map of the course I ran before stumbling upon the pool. "Good luck finding your way home, my sweet Siren."

"Reaper," I warn.

He moves to the path that leads out of here before pausing and glancing back at me. "I'll be waiting for you," he says.

"Don't you dare leave me here, you giant dildo."

Reaper laughs, and with that, he disappears, leaving me with nothing but to figure out how the hell I'm supposed to escape this. I can't help but laugh. I love this infuriating man, but there's no doubt about it; Reaper is one hell of an asshole.

24

SIREN

Waking up to a lonely bed, I pull the sheets back before rubbing at my tired eyes. It was a long night. I was out of the handcuffs within seconds, but the problem came when trying to navigate my way out of the caves. I got lost at least twenty times and had to start leaving markers to know if I was walking a path that had already been walked.

I wasn't impressed, and just to be a stubborn, petty asshole about it, I stayed out the rest of the day and then made a point of sleeping in one of the spare bedrooms, doing everything in my power to ignore the beast-like man who has thrown my world into the sweetest chaos. The only issue is, I know for a fact that I went to bed in the spare room, yet somehow, I'm waking up in the main bed, and I have no idea how that happened. Some top super killer I am.

Letting out a heavy sigh, I grab my phone and make my way into the bathroom, quickly handling business and getting myself ready for the day. As I shower and change, I chat away to Mila, checking in to let her know I'm still alive and telling her all about the insanity that was yesterday.

We chat for almost an hour, and by the time I venture out of the main room and down the hall toward the kitchen, Mila and I have covered just about everything from the color of Reaper's man nips right down to the way my thong is wedged right up my ass.

She's right in the middle of telling me all about some new tech software that's supposed to be released this month, and as she raves all about it, I walk into the kitchen and come to a startling halt. A big pink gift-wrapped box sits right in the middle of the kitchen counter with my name scrawled in messy boy handwriting, and a stupid smile pulls across my lips.

"What is it?" Mila asks.

"Huh?"

"You gasped," she tells me.

"I gasped?"

"Yes."

"Well shit," I laugh, not having even realized. "There's a box," I tell her as I stride toward it, sparing a smile for Shadow, who sits next to the box, not caring in the slightest about its sudden appearance in our kitchen.

"What kind of box?" Mila questions, sounding suspicious.

"A gift-wrapped one with my name on it."

"Oooooh," she says excitedly before switching the flip. "Wait. It could be a trap. Does it say who it's from?"

Pulling the phone away, I switch the call over to FaceTime before turning it around and showing Mila the large box. "I don't know," I tell her just as Shadow cuts in, not bothering to turn her gaze away from the bowl of cereal before her. "It's not a bomb, if that's what you're thinking. It's from Reaper."

"Oooooh. It's gotta be an apology for leaving you stranded in that cave yesterday," Mila cuts in as giddiness flourishes through me. "That's kinda romantic."

I don't have a lot of people in my life and wasn't one to ever receive birthday presents growing up, and to have someone care enough for me to get me something means more than Reaper could ever know. All I ever wanted as a kid was to have what the other kids had, and unfortunately, that wasn't a reality for me. I had to work for everything I got, and when Mila came into the picture, the two of us pushed ourselves to the brink of exhaustion until we were capable of having the life we wanted for ourselves. Any gift we bought each other was slaved over, and to receive this gift now . . . It could be a moldy banana, and I'd still be grateful for the thought.

Moving closer to the table, I inspect the pretty box, trying to decipher what could possibly be inside, and judging by Shadow's lack of interest, I can only assume that she already knows what hides within.

I reach for the big pink bow right on top, and as I start to pull it apart, Mila giggles with excitement. "Holy fucking shit," she rushes out. "Hurry up and open it."

A stupid smile stretches across my face, and I tug the bow harder, releasing the pretty ribbon before lifting the lid off the box and setting it aside. I glance down into the box and suck in a breath as the decapitated head of The Executioner stares back at me, the blade still protruding from his eye. But on top of that, the very ID Reaper had plucked off the dirty cave ground and taken off with rests peacefully on top of The Executioner's forehead.

"Wait," Mila grunts, certainly having a very different idea of what constitutes romance. "Is that—"

"The Executioner's head served to me literally on a silver platter?" I say, finishing her sentence as Shadow decides she's suddenly interested enough to peer up from her cereal and glance inside the box. "It sure is."

"That's disturbing."

"No," I say with a soft sigh, my heart filling with the sweetest joy. "It's the most romantic thing anyone has ever done for me."

Reaper chooses that exact moment to walk through the front door, his glorious tattoos on display as his shirt dangles from his shoulder. His body is coated in a sheer layer of sweat, and judging by the way every single one of his strong muscles bulge from his sculpted body, it's clear he's just put himself through one hell of a workout.

His gaze comes to mine the second the door closes behind him, and as he holds my stare, my heart races faster than it's ever raced before. "You got me a head in a box," I whisper as he watches me from across the room, waiting to see what he's about to walk into.

"I fucked you under a waterfall and then abandoned you in a cave," he tells me as though I hadn't experienced it all myself. "You refused to sleep in my bed, so I figured I owed you an apology."

I go to respond when Shadow gets to her feet, her face scrunched up in disgust. "Gross," she mutters before reaching into the box and grabbing the handle of the blade. She yanks it out, and The Executioner's eyeball goes right along with it, and with her prize in hand, she struts down the hall and takes herself to her room.

Reaper scoffs as he makes his way toward me. "She finds the idea of me fucking you gross but has no issue carrying around a dead man's eyeball."

A stupid smile cuts across my face, and I can't help but laugh. "She's thirteen. I don't think we're supposed to understand her."

Reaper steps right into me, wrapping his arms around my body and grabbing my ass before lifting me up and settling me on the edge of the kitchen counter, right next to the one-eyed head. He moves right between my legs, his hands resting on my thighs as his gaze locks heavily onto mine. "Did I fuck up?" he asks just as the familiar sound of a call ending comes from my phone, reminding me that I was in the middle of a FaceTime call with Mila. Well, not anymore. I'll have to remember to call her back.

I shake my head as my arms wind around his neck. "No."

"But you slept in a different bed," he tells me. "I didn't fucking like it. My time with you is limited, and I don't want to waste it like that."

"I'm sorry," I whisper, leaning in and brushing my lips over his. "I was being petty and stubborn. I've never been good at accepting when someone gets the better of me, and yesterday . . . You kicked my ass. I was embarrassed that I couldn't even figure my way out of that stupid cave. I should have known better."

"Don't—" he starts.

"No," I say. "It's okay. I've made so many mistakes during these games, and I hate myself for it. I'm better than this."

"What does it matter?" he asks. "We're both fucking dying in eleven days. So what if we fuck up and make mistakes? To be honest, I don't even give a shit about the games anymore. All that matters to me is spending what little time we have left making you happy."

"Speaking of what little time we have left," I murmur, lowering my voice so that Shadow doesn't hear me from down the hall. "I've been thinking about that a lot, and what if we didn't kill each other? This thing between us . . . this is more real than anything I've ever had, and I'm not ready to let it go because of some bullshit games. I don't want this to end."

"I'd be lying if I said I hadn't been thinking about the same thing," he tells me. "But we'd be opening ourselves up for a life on the run. We'd be hunted every fucking day. Is that the life you really want? You would never be able to go home, never be able to see Mila again. It'd just be me and you with a fucking bounty on our heads."

"And Shadow." His brow arches, and I continue. "As if I'm about to leave her to go back to whatever bullshit life she came from. She's better off with us."

"Siren—"

"Don't pretend like you don't agree with me. You know I'm right."

Reaper lets out a heavy sigh before lifting me off the counter, walking us through to the living room, and dropping down onto the couch. I straddle his lap and sit up against his strong thighs, my fingers brushing against the sharp ridges of his abs.

"You are right," he tells me. "I'm not ready to let you go, but I don't see how we could possibly get out of Blue Springs without submitting ourselves to a life of hell. I'm a hunter, Siren. I'm not prey. And the only way we're getting out of here is in body bags."

Leaning into him, I wrap my arms around the back of his neck as I snuggle into his chest. "I just . . . I can't do it," I tell him, feeling completely helpless about our situation. "I can't kill you, and I won't stand back to allow anybody else to do it either. Not even Shadow. I can't . . . fuck. I can't lose you yet. I'm not ready. I want a life with you, Reaper. I want everything. I want to love you."

His body stiffens, and he glances down at me, that dark, lethal stare locking onto mine. "Are you in love with me, Siren?"

I swallow over the lump in my throat, unsure what to say. A man like Reaper doesn't strike me as the type who's capable of handling declarations of love, but I'm not willing to lie to him, not if we only have eleven days left. "I think so," I tell him truthfully. "I've never felt this way about anybody before. I don't know if this is what love feels like, but if it is, then yes. I've never been so in love in my life."

His arm locks around my back, and he pulls me in tighter, our bodies pressed together as one. "It's okay, my sweet Siren. I won't let anything happen to you. Nobody is taking you away from me."

My brows furrow. A minute ago he was telling me the only way we're getting out of Blue Springs is if we were carted out in body bags, and now suddenly, nobody is going to take me away from him? Why would he . . . unless . . .

I lift my gaze, meeting his hollow stare again, and I see it clear as day. The same overwhelming emotions that cause havoc inside my chest lie right there in his eyes. "You're in love with me too," I state, knowing it without a single doubt.

"Yes, Siren."

I drop my gaze and rest back into his chest as his strong arms hold me in a way I've never been held before. "Shit," I murmur, not knowing where to go from here.

"My thoughts exactly."

We sit in comfortable silence for almost an hour, both of us deep in our own thoughts, when his hand brushes down my arm. "Tell me why the sound of your own name pains you so much?" he asks, his voice so welcoming that it takes me a moment to understand what he's actually asking. After repeating the question in my head, my heart lurches, fear raining down over me, but I quickly realize that he's not asking to gloat. He's not looking for information to use as a weapon against me; he simply wants to understand who I am and what made me the way that I am.

I let out a heavy breath, my gaze dropping to his chest. "I was only six when my mother was murdered," I tell him. "We weren't exactly well off, and from what brief memories I have, it wasn't exactly a happy home, but my mom . . . She only ever wanted the world for me. She was my best friend, and I remember that, no matter the circumstances, she would make everything better. My father, on the other hand—"

"Shit, Siren. It's okay. You don't need to share this if it's too much."

"It's okay," I tell him. "It's not what you're thinking." I take a shaky breath before figuring out how to explain the evil, vile man that was my father. "My memories of my father are . . . jaded. I don't remember him in the same way. I only remember the constant yelling and how my mother would hide me behind her leg every time he would start ranting at her about dinner not being ready or the house being a mess. He made her sad, and because of that, he made me sad too. I think he struggled with mental health, but I was too young to know what that was or to even realize that he needed help."

"You were six, Siren. It wasn't your responsibility to care for the health of the adults in your life."

"I know that," I tell him. "But I can't help but wonder if I had, maybe things would have been different."

His fingers skim across my waist and return to my arm, holding me tight against his warm chest. "What happened?"

"My memories of that night have always been fuzzy, but from what Mila and I were able to find from the police records, my father had been sacked from his job, and he came home drunk with a gun. The neighbors had mentioned they heard yelling and called for help, only they were too late. He shot and killed my mom in our living room, tried to kill me, then turned the gun on himself."

My eyes fill with unshed tears, and I do what I can to blink them back as I reach down between us and find the hem of my tank, pulling it up just enough so that he can see the scarring on my ribs. "He shot me through the chest and punctured a lung, and as I screamed for my dead mother, I was forced to watch as he held the gun to his head and pulled the trigger." I lower my shirt back down just as he goes to reach for it, and now that he knows, I'm not sure I can handle him touching me there. "That vision has stuck with me for eighteen years. Every time I close my eyes."

Reaper's hands fall to my thighs, gently squeezing. "I'm sorry, Siren. I had no idea."

I shrug my shoulders. "Nobody does. I asked Mila to scrub it from existence. I didn't want anyone finding out and being able to use it as a weapon against me or have access to the crime scene photos that went along with it."

He nods in understanding. "Shit, baby. I'm sorry I brought it up, but I'm struggling to see how it pertains to the use of your real name."

A sad smile pulls at the corners of my lips, and despite how agonizing that story is to share, it's what happened after that has caused me the most grief over the years. "I was in the hospital for months following the shooting. Day after day, I was alone. All I had were the nurses and doctors who cared for me, and the day I was finally released, I had a caseworker buckle me up into her car, drive me halfway across the state, and drop me off at a home with a family I'd never met. I had nothing left of my old life, no memories of my mother to take with me, only the name she'd given me."

"Kienna James," he murmurs, and as the words come out of his mouth, I realize they don't hurt as much as they once did.

I nod. "My life became intertwined with my new foster family, and they weren't good people. They never hurt me or tried to touch me, but they resented me for whatever reason, and as that got worse, they used my name as a taunt, and I realized that I had to hold on to it with everything that I had. It was all I had, and I wasn't going to let these people destroy it. I spiraled from there. I was only with them for a few months before bouncing to my next family, but from day one with that new family, my name was mine and mine alone."

"I know you may not be ready, but one day, I'd like to call you by your name," he tells me. "I want to know you for you. Siren is just one portion of the woman you are, but I want to know the woman you are inside. I want to know the woman you've hidden away for all of these years."

I swallow hard, resting my hand on his chest again as I nod. "I think I might be okay with that," I tell him. "I don't know how or when it happened, but I trust you. You're not going to hurt me. I feel safe with you, and while I might need some time to be okay with hearing my name again, I can work on that for you."

"Then I suppose I can do the same for you," he says. "When the time comes, I'd like to reintroduce you to who I really am, not as Reaper or the ghost you feared at the start of these games, but as Nikolai Volkov."

"I'd like that."

He nods. "To be honest, I'm not even sure I fully understand who he really is, but if you'd like, we can work it out together."

"Together?" I gasp, teasing him. "You're not suggesting we work as a team, are you?"

Reaper groans and rolls his eyes, and I can't help but laugh.

"You've got yourself a deal," I tell him as my heart swells deep inside my chest. "Though I've gotta admit, I don't think I have any fucking idea who Kienna James is either. Last time I talked to her, she was only six years old with more trauma than any kid should have to hold. I don't know what kind of person we're going to uncover."

"Then it's a good thing we're both trained in expecting the unexpected," Reaper says. "Whatever you want to throw at me, baby, I can handle."

"Oh yeah?" I say, adjusting myself on his lap and leaning in, my lips hovering over his. "Well, I've got something else a little unexpected, and I'm dying to see just how well you handle it."

Then, without another word, I close the gap and drop my lips to his, and as if on cue, he picks me up off the couch and walks past the one-eyed dead head and straight to our bedroom, kicking the door closed behind him.

25

SIREN

Tonight Gasoline dies, and I've never felt so giddy about making a kill in my life.

Reaper practically sent me on my way with a kiss and a packed lunch, telling me to have a great day. But truth be told, I think he was jealous. Ever since the fire, he's wanted revenge on this vile woman just as much as I have, but he knows I need this more. Besides, he thinks the brothers are planning something, and until he figures out what that is, he'll be tailing them.

Mila has been working on tracking Gasoline for the past few days, and this morning, we finally got a hit. She's been staying in one of the old warehouses in the industrial area where this whole bullshit started. Personally, I find staying in a warehouse unimaginative. The

Boston Maneater did it too, and I can't figure out why they would want to spend their last days on earth in a rundown building with no heat or access to working amenities. I get that living it up in a holiday home like Reaper, Shadow, and I have been doing certainly has its disadvantages, but I wouldn't trade a working bathroom and a proper bed for anything.

With my car becoming a casualty of the suite fire, I had no choice but to walk my ass out to the industrial park, and after already knocking out many of the big contenders of War Games, I really don't mind the stroll. Hell, I even let my guard down and try to enjoy the fresh air. Though despite doing what I can to enjoy my night, I keep to the shadows. My typical assassin-style outfit, complete with the black lips and long rope-like hairstyle is more than enough to draw the wrong kind of attention, and after the FBI have been sniffing around Blue Springs, the last thing I need is to get my ass caught.

There are only a few contenders left in the competition. The brothers, Gasoline, and a woman named Silver. For the most part, she's managed to fly under the radar, and I haven't paid much attention to her. I assumed she would be taken out by someone else earlier in the game. Yet as I approach Gasoline's warehouse, I can't help but notice the silver-haired woman creeping around, and judging by the way she's carrying herself, this is definitely not a planned visit.

Hmmmm. Interesting.

My brow arches, and as I stick to the shadows, Silver attempts to be discreet. She glances around, missing every possible sign that someone is watching her, and despite not knowing much about her skill level, it's clear who will be the one walking out of this one tonight.

I shake my head. There's nothing I loathe more than an unfair fight, and someone like this has no business going after a woman like Gasoline. However, I can understand why. During that very first meeting in the warehouse just down the road from here, when these two women introduced themselves to the circle, it was clear that there's a history there, and I bet Silver has been waiting for her chance to get the drop on Gasoline. The only issue is that tonight isn't the night, nor is any other night.

Gasoline is a snake. She doesn't fight fair, and her idea of beating someone is by stabbing them in the back. There's no honor in the way she kills, but I wouldn't expect anything less from a serial killer. Silver might have the chance to surprise her, but Gasoline won't allow her to have the upper hand for long.

When Silver disappears into the rundown building, I launch myself over the back fence and slip in through the side entrance, immediately getting smacked in the face by the putrid stench of gas, telling me I'm more than in the right place. The main overhead lights are out, but there's a few spotlights that create just enough glow to catch Silver as she creeps through the building with a blade in each hand.

She looks left and right as if trying to sniff out Gasoline, but with the foul smell in the air, I don't know what she's expecting to find. There are gas cans everywhere, and my stomach starts to sink. I'm getting a bad feeling about this.

I can't be burned alive again. That shit wasn't fun the first time, and if that's her backup plan, then I need out. I won't risk that again.

There's too much accelerant littering the warehouse, and it would only take one simple spark to send this place up in a blaze. The fire at the resort will look like a campfire compared to what happens here.

Silver creeps right into the center of the warehouse when I notice something in the rafters, and I lift my gaze, only to find Shadow watching over me. My jaw drops, and as she cringes, it's clear she knows she's been caught. I hold my hands out in the universal sign for *what the ever-loving fuck do you think you're doing?* And when she simply shrugs her shoulders in apology, all I can do is shake my head.

Now is not the time to discipline my delinquent child . . . or whatever she's supposed to be to me.

I narrow my gaze at her, letting her know that we're going to have words about this when we get home, and just as a cocky smirk tears across her gorgeous face, a flash of red hair catches my attention.

Gasoline.

She stands in a narrow doorway, her gaze locked heavily on Silver, and I realize that we've all been caught in her trap. We were lured here, and now she's the one with the upper hand.

I signal to Shadow to watch Gasoline, and just as Shadow nods in understanding, my phone buzzes in my pocket. I ignore it, realizing it must be Mila checking in, but when a second text comes through, I reach for my phone. Mila knows I'm out, but she also never messages twice. It's got to be Reaper.

Swiping my thumb across the screen, I unlock my phone and check the message.

Reaper - Get out of there. It's a trap.

Reaper - Fucking answer me, Siren.

Shit.

My gaze snaps back to Shadow, trying to figure out how the hell I'm supposed to get her out of here before this shit turns sideways. But it leaves me wondering how the fuck Reaper knew that.

Siren - Can't. Shadow's here. I'm not leaving without her.

Reaper - Fuck.

I clench my jaw, trying to figure out a game plan when a figure slips in through the back entrance, quickly followed by another at the main entrance.

The brothers.

Reaper was right. They're working together.

"Fuck," I mutter under my breath before double-checking that Shadow has seen what I've seen. But I shouldn't doubt her. She argued once that despite her young age, she knows what she's doing, and yet I can't help the need to look out for her.

With her backup in place, Gasoline finally finds her backbone and steps out of the darkened doorway, announcing herself to the room with a cocky attitude that has me desperate to kick her right in the vagina with a studded boot.

"Where is she?" Reaper's deep tone suddenly says from right behind me.

I jump, my heart launching right out of my fucking chest before scolding myself for not realizing he was here. He was spending the night tailing the brothers, and the second they made their way inside the warehouse, Reaper would have followed them straight in.

"Rafters," I say, indicating toward the ceiling.

Reaper's sharp gaze sails to the ceiling, and he spots her immediately, but when she gives him the same guilty smirk she offered me, I can't help but laugh under my breath.

"Shit," he mutters.

"My thoughts exactly."

His gaze sweeps the warehouse with confidence, and in a matter of seconds, his face shifts. I know he's figured something out.

"Certainly took your time," Gasoline says, her chilling voice sending shivers spiking across my skin and throwing me right back into that resort suite with my wrists and ankles bound to the table. Her gaze flicks toward the corners of the room, and as if on cue, The Texan Reaper and The Boneyard Slayer step out of the shadows, leaving Silver defenseless.

The Texan Reaper drags a heavy chain behind him, the sound of it against the concrete enough to turn my blood cold. "Had to lose a tail first," he says, clearly having known that Reaper was following them, but he's too fucking daft to realize he followed them right into the warehouse.

Silver panics, her gaze flicking around the run-down building, frantically searching for a way out, but she won't find one. Every last exit is covered.

"They don't know we're here," I tell Reaper, pointing out that this trap was solely for Silver, and while I waltzed straight into it, I'm not a target tonight. If they were as clever as they thought they were, they could take out all four of us and win this shit. Only, they don't possess the skill nor the brains to pull it off.

The three of them begin to creep toward Silver, and she whips around with her blades, trying to find a way out of this. In pure panic, she makes a break for it, lunging for the main entrance. She throws her knife at The Boneyard Slayer as she passes him, barely grazing his thigh, and before she can get another step, he darts out toward her, grabbing her by her upper arm and throwing her back into the center of the warehouse.

Silver stumbles and falls, and by the time she can even attempt to get back on her feet, the brothers and Gasoline are already on her. They tie her up with the industrial-sized chain, and with her small frame, she doesn't stand a chance.

"You really thought you could get the drop on me?" Gasoline taunts, pulling out that same packet of matches and pulling one free. My stomach sinks. "Look around you, Silver. You're nothing but an old fool."

Silver spits at her, and Gasoline instantly hurries into her, slamming a booted foot into Silver's ribs. "You fucking bitch," Gasoline grunts. "You're gonna suffer for that, mark my fucking words."

Silver laughs despite being at a complete loss. "Mark your words?" she questions. "You couldn't do shit if you didn't have brainless one and two doing all your dirty work for you. You know they're going to slaughter you the first chance they get, right? You don't mean shit to them."

"Let's just get this done," The Texan Reaper demands, clearly done with their bullshit.

Silver just scoffs, looking back at The Texan Reaper. "You better watch your back too," she says. "I've known this bitch for twenty years, and the second she gets a chance to cross you, you'll be chained in a warehouse just like this."

The Boneyard Slayer rolls his eyes and goes to take a step when his attention sails up to the rafters, making my stomach tighten with knots. "Fuck," he roars, tossing the end of the chain he's holding to the ground as he breaks into a sprint. "IT'S THAT FUCKING KID."

Chaos erupts, and both Reaper and I dart out of the darkness. My one and only goal is to get to Shadow, and I'm trusting that Reaper will handle the rest, but it all happens too fast. "SHADOW, RUN!" I scream at the top of my lungs.

Shadow rushes to her feet, making a break along the rafters, and The Boneyard Slayer rushes after her while his brother launches into action, noticing me and Reaper immediately. Deciding Reaper is his biggest threat, he darts toward him as Gasoline freezes, her sharp gaze quickly assessing the chaos.

She knows she doesn't stand a chance in this warehouse, and without a fucking care, she tosses the lit match toward the gas tanks as horror pounds through my chest. She takes off at a sprint toward the back exit as my feet slam against the ground, only having a few seconds to save myself.

The Texan Reaper roars something to his brother, but the deafening boom of my pulse beating in my ears makes it impossible to hear a damn thing except for the sound of my own fear. I don't take my eyes off Shadow as she races across the rafters, and then just as a strong arm locks around my waist and yanks me aside, Shadow throws herself right out of the second-story window, glass shattering around her.

My body is violently yanked, and the next thing I know, I'm flying through the main entrance and crashing to the hard ground as the piercing scream of a terrified woman fills the warehouse behind me. A body slams down over mine just moments before an almighty *BOOM* blasts through the warehouse.

"FUCK," Reaper roars over me as the searing heat of an explosion hits our backs, shooting plumes of fire up into the dark sky. His body crowds mine, his arms bracing around my head as he buries his face into my back. "SIREN? BABY, ARE YOU GOOD?"

"Fuck," I groan, unable to tell if I'm hurt from the explosion or from Reaper's impressive weight crashing down over me, but none of it matters as I try to shove him off me. "SHADOW!"

Reaper is off me in seconds, grabs my arm, and drags me to my feet as we race through the night, desperate to get Shadow.

We find her face down in the overgrown bush by the side of the warehouse, the wall of the rundown building having mostly protected her from the blast, but that doesn't mean she got off scot-free.

"Shadow," I gasp, crashing down to my knees beside her and grabbing her arm as I quickly roll her over, but before I even get a chance to assess her, Reaper is there, scooping her into his strong arms.

"We have to get out of here."

Shadow fights his hold, and relief soars through my chest. "I'm okay. I'm okay," she rushes out, pulling herself free. "I can walk."

Not wanting to overstep her boundaries, Reaper releases her and allows her to balance on her own two feet, and despite her protests, he keeps his hand on her upper arm as we hurry away from the massive blaze.

"What the fuck just happened?" I demand as we slip into a back alley that offers us privacy from the road and the sirens that are quickly coming this way.

I lean against the wall of a building, closing my eyes as I try to catch my breath, but feeling Reaper's gaze on my body, I open them again and find him assessing me for injuries. "You okay?" he asks, his voice deeper than I've ever heard it.

I nod and immediately start doing the same, noticing burns all over his back and arms—burns that would have been mine had he not thrown himself on top of me. "You?"

"Fine."

He's the furthest thing from fine, and seeing that I've noticed the burns across his bronze skin, he simply pulls me into him and locks his arms around me, pressing a kiss to my forehead. "I'm fine," he repeats, his tone demanding compliance.

"Gasoline and the brothers?" I ask, shifting my gaze to Shadow and checking her from head to toe for the millionth time in the last few seconds.

"From what I could tell, they got out," he tells me before pulling back and indicating further down the alley, silently telling us it's time to get our asses out of here before the FBI scours every inch of the industrial park.

"Fuck. I was hoping that would have wiped them all out so this shit could have been over," I murmur. "But if anything, us showing up and robbing them of a satisfying kill is only going to piss them off, especially with Silver out of the competition. It's going to be us three against them, and the only way they're going to be able to break us down is to pick us off one at a time."

Shadow walks up ahead of us, and as she reaches the end of the alley, she begins climbing up an old dumpster, preparing to launch herself over the back wall. "Is this my fault?" she asks, pausing as she looks back at us. "If I wasn't there, they would have made their kill and then taken off for the next week. They wouldn't be focusing on us just yet."

Reaper shakes his head. "Whether you were there or not, they've run out of options. If they want to win this thing, they have no choice but to lure us out, but we're not going to let that happen. It's important now more than ever that we stick together. We can't be going off on our own. I can't risk losing either of you."

Shadows nods and reaches for the edge of the wall, preparing to pull herself over. "So what do we do?"

Reaper lets out a heavy sigh as Shadow pulls herself up on top of the wall and glances back down at us. "We figure out one hell of a game plan, but before we do that, we eat."

"Now that's a plan I can get down with," Shadow says before dropping down on the other side of the wall, her feet not making even the slightest sound as she lands.

I follow suit, and before I know it, Reaper is dropping down beside me, and the three of us start the long trek back home.

We take every backstreet we know, doing whatever we can to keep off the main roads as they become flooded by emergency services trying to figure out how an old warehouse that hasn't seen the light of day in years suddenly blew up.

Almost an hour passes when we reach the city center of Blue Springs, and despite how silent Shadow is, there's no denying the sound of her rumbling stomach. "You wanna stop at a diner?" I ask her as we stride down the street in silence.

"Oh god, yes," she says with a sigh of relief. "I'm starving."

I roll my eyes. No matter how much we feed this kid, she is always hungry, and honestly, I don't know where she's putting it. She's practically skin and bone.

We stop at the next diner, picking a private booth close to the back exit, and before the waitress has a chance to hand us the menus, Reaper rattles off a quick order, getting us each a burger and fries, and demanding she make it quick.

"Okay, Shadow," Reaper says as the waitress scurries off to grab us some drinks. "You're killing me here. I can't sit by and not ask anymore. How the fuck did you end up here?"

My eyes widen, shooting toward Reaper. We've made a point not to ask her about her life, hoping that she would open up when she was ready, but time is quickly running out, and despite how comfortable she's become with us, she hasn't dared to even whisper about her life or how she managed to become one of the best contract killers at only thirteen. I won't lie, curiosity has been killing me too, but I've managed to bite my tongue so far. Reaper apparently doesn't possess the same self-control.

Shadow freezes, her gaze shifting to me, and seeing that same curiosity in my eyes that she sees in Reaper's, she lets out a breath, and I prepare myself for whatever's about to come out of her mouth.

"I, umm . . ." she pauses, grabbing hold of the napkin on the table and quickly tearing it to pieces. "I was raised in an organization that trains children to become super spies and assassins. We're stolen from the hospital right after birth. We're never even held by our birth mothers. They were told their babies were stillborn, and from there, the babies were shipped off to their underground training camp, which is where I stayed until I was enrolled in these games. There's no love there. Toddlers learn how to handle weapons before they learn to walk, and the second they are capable of holding their own, they are taught to fight."

Tears fill my eyes as I look at this sweet child. "Tell me this is a sick joke," I beg her.

Shadow shakes her head, glancing away as though the emotion in my eyes is too much for her to bear. "We're not raised to have the same values and morals as normal children. We don't ride bicycles or indulge in arts and crafts. Up until you hugged me in my room the other day, I'd never experienced that in my life. We're raised to be fearless robots, yes-men to our captors, and we're taught that our lives are expendable. We're nothing more than a number, and when our number is called, it's an honor to do our part, even if it means sacrificing yourself for the mission."

Holy fucking shit.

My heart breaks for her, and all I can do is reach across the table and take her hand, knowing without a doubt that Reaper and I have to do something about this. We can't let her take the win only to end up right back there after we're gone.

"What do you mean number?" Reaper asks, his usual mask of indifference beginning to slip.

"The organization . . . They don't believe in names. It weakens us. It's seen as an unnecessary luxury that conforms to typical family values. Offering somebody a name is to give them value, and once they've been given that, they will learn to depend on it, and soon enough, they are a slave to their emotions. Allowing yourself to be ruled by simple human emotions . . . It's weak. And weakness has no place in our organization. I am known as thirty-eight."

I squeeze Shadow's hand, drawing her dark gaze back to mine. "To have love doesn't mean to be weak, Shadow," I tell her. "To allow yourself to open up to another and learn to trust shows incredible strength. To have vulnerability and make mistakes . . . it makes us human, and that's perfectly okay. Surely you can see that."

She nods, her bottom lip beginning to quiver. "I am starting to learn that," she tells me before shifting her gaze back to Reaper. "I don't ever want to go back to that place."

"You won't," he vows to her. "I promise you, Shadow. I don't know how this is going to play out or what's going to happen, but these games end the second the brothers and Gasoline are dead. I'm not sacrificing either of you, and the second we can, the three of us are getting out of here together."

"You really mean that?" she asks, sitting up straighter.

"Yes, Shadow. You, me, and Siren; we're a family now. I have your back, just as I expect you to have both mine and Siren's. From here on out, we stick together."

Shadow nods just as a burger and fries are placed down in front of her. "Okay," she finally says, as a smile pulls at her lips. "I've never had a family before."

"Neither have we," I tell her, my heart breaking for everything this girl has been through in her short thirteen years. "It's a learning curve for us all, but we're going to figure it out along the way."

"Okay," she says again. "I just have one question."

"What's that?" I ask.

"Are families supposed to share everything? Because Reaper's got these really cool custom blades that I've been dying to get my hands on, and if I'm being honest, I already stole three of them."

Reaper scoffs. "I fucking knew some of those blades were missing."

I can't help but laugh as I meet Shadow's gaze. "I'll make you a deal," I tell her. "If the three of us get out of Blue Springs unscathed, I'll order you all the custom blades your little heart desires."

"You've got yourself a deal," she tells me with a wide grin before finally scooping up the burger that somehow seems bigger than her whole head and taking a massive bite, ultimately shutting her up for the next forty-five minutes.

26

SIREN

Rolling over in bed, I stare up at the ceiling as an uneasy feeling settles in the pit of my stomach. I can't put my finger on it, but something doesn't feel right. "What's wrong?" Reaper murmurs beside me, locking his strong arm around me and pulling me in tighter against his body.

"Not sure," I say, pulling out of his hold and sitting up. "Something just . . . doesn't feel right."

He sits up with me, watching me through a cautious stare. "Something's really not right, huh?"

I shake my head, unable to figure it out. There's physically nothing wrong, and there's no reason for me to have woken up in the middle of the night, but I can't seem to shake it. It's been five days since the explosion at the warehouse, bringing us to day twenty-eight, and while Gasoline and the brothers haven't been able to draw us out, they're quickly running out of time.

I've been on the edge ever since.

They've had more than enough time to regroup following the explosion, and while Reaper and I have been dying to head out and hunt these bastards, with Shadow to worry about, we're not willing to risk putting her in the line of danger.

We've been watching them like hawks, waiting for them to make a move, and from what we've been able to gather, they haven't been able to locate us. Instead, they've attempted to draw us out, laying traps and breadcrumbs in hopes that we'll let our guard down and come to them, but this ain't our first rodeo, and we're not reckless serial killers like they are. We're hunters, and we're ready to eat.

We've had their location pinned for the past four days, watching their every move, and the longer we wait, the more frustrated they become. They're getting desperate, knowing there's only a handful of days left in the competition, and if they don't take us out by the end of day thirty, the sorry bastard who created this fucked up game will take us all out, which isn't exactly a position any of us want to find ourselves in.

Don't get me wrong, Reaper, Shadow, and I will be fine. We can handle a simple threat with ease, but the moment he realizes he can't get to us himself, he'll put a bounty on our heads so big that not even we can escape it.

Needing to settle this uneasiness in the pit of my stomach, I reach through the darkness and feel around for my phone, and when I don't find it on my bedside table, I haul my ass over to the edge, making sure it didn't fall off. "Fuck. My phone's gone," I say, following the cable of my charger and seeing the phone missing from the end.

"Shit."

We both spring out of bed, and I'm halfway down the hall within the blink of an eye. "Shadow?" I call out, racing toward her room as Reaper follows behind me, his phone in his hand.

I don't bother to knock. Instead, I just barge right through the door only to find her bed empty and her boots and weapons gone. "Fuck. She's gone after them," I say as we both whip around and head straight back to our room, getting ourselves dressed and ready within seconds.

"They're on the move," Reaper murmurs, checking the pinned location we had for the brothers and Gasoline as we load ourselves with weapons.

"Where?" I rush out just as the familiar sound of my phone ringing comes from the kitchen. My brows furrow, and I dart out of the bedroom, hurrying to catch the call with Reaper hot on my tail, both of us scanning the house as though a threat could pop out at any moment.

My phone is in the middle of the counter, and I scoop it up, finding Mila's name across the screen. I swipe my thumb across it and lift it to my ear, then, before I can even say a word, Mila's voice comes rushing through the phone. "Oh, thank fuck. You're alive," she breathes. "Did you get them all? Is it over?"

"What?" I demand, still shoving weapons into every crevice my outfit offers.

"What do you mean *what?*" she questions. "I sent you their location over an hour ago. You confirmed and said you were making your move."

"What the fuck are you talking about? I've been asleep the past few hours."

"I . . . I don't know what to tell you," she says as I pull my phone away from my ear and put the call on speakerphone before going through my recent messages, and just as Mila suggested, she sent me a text over an hour ago letting me know they were on the move, and just as she said, there's a confirmation text from me saying that we were on it.

"FUCK!" I grunt, grabbing Reaper's keys and tossing them to him as I step into my boots. "That was Shadow. She took off without us."

"Shit."

"Where are they?" I rush out, already hearing the sound of Mila's fingers rushing across her keyboard as we barge out the door and into Reaper's car, not bothering to lock up behind us. What's the point? By the time we return here, it'll be over, and the last of the threats against our lives will be neutralized.

"I've got them in the old abandoned amusement park," Mila says as Reaper peels out of the driveway, white-knuckling the steering wheel.

"Got it," Reaper says.

He pulls to the left out of the driveway, the wheels squealing against the asphalt. It's at least a ten-minute drive to the old amusement park, but right now, every fucking minute counts. If they've got her, they won't hesitate to take her out. One wrong move, and it's over for Shadow, and I'm not about to let that happen.

"Let me know how it goes," Mila says, a hint of fear in her soft tone.

"I will," I say, swallowing over the growing lump in my throat, and with that, Mila ends the call, knowing we're in for the fight of our lives. We need to concentrate now more than ever.

"What the fuck was she thinking?" Reaper demands. "We told her they will try something like this. They drew her out, and she fell right into their fucking trap."

"She was probably thinking that she wants this shit to be over," I throw back at him, ready to defend that girl right to the end of the world. "She's just a kid who's been taught that sacrificing themselves for a mission is honorable. Let's just focus on getting her out of there, and after that, we can rip into her about going into this bullshit alone. Until then, she's our only focus."

"What if it's already too late?"

"It's not," I say, clenching my jaw. "I'd know."

"You had that feeling in bed. What if—"

"Don't say it," I beg him. "This isn't over yet. She's going to be fine. She can handle herself just as well as we can, even when backed into a corner. We're going to get her back, and the moment we do, we set our focus on them, not giving them a chance to get away again. We end this tonight no matter the cost."

Reaper nods, his fingers tightening on the steering wheel, and the closer we get to the amusement park, the more he begins to resemble that terrifying beast I saw in the warehouse during that very first night. His eyes are as dark as night, completely hollow and void of life. He's lethal, and that's exactly the vibe I try to replicate.

Nothing is stopping me from getting to our girl.

"The amusement park is huge," he tells me. "We have no choice but to split up."

"I know," I tell him, mentally going over the park map that I'd become accustomed to before I'd even arrived in Blue Springs. There are too many variables and too much space that needs to be covered. We need a whole fucking team for this, but it's just us, and lucky for Shadow, we're the best she's ever going to get. "This is exactly what they wanted."

Reaper nods in agreement. "Keep your wits about you. Stick to the shadows, and if you have a shot to take them out, don't hesitate. Until this is over, you don't stop. Watch your back and don't falter."

"I won't," I tell him, feeling that same energy pulsing through my veins just as Reaper pulls into the massive parking lot, his screeching tires alerting anyone in the vicinity that we're here. "I'm ready."

The car comes to a halt right by the front entrance, and Reaper reaches across, taking my hand. "Don't fucking die," he tells me, and all I can do is hold his stare and nod, speaking the same exact words right back to him in silence.

Don't fucking die.

He blows out a heavy breath, and with one last squeeze of my hand, we make a break for it, both of us pouring out of the car and instantly becoming nothing more than lethal hunters moving through the entrance of the old amusement park.

Reaper goes to the left as I turn to the right, and as my feet pound against the pavement, my gaze sweeps for any sign of Shadow. My heart races in a way it never has before. I've been overcome by adrenaline in fight-to-the-death situations more times than I can possibly count, but this one feels different.

I've never felt such overwhelming fear like this before. The knot in my stomach grows, and the deeper I get into the amusement park, the tighter that knot becomes. I should have found her by now, should have found some kind of hint.

Terror grips me, and just as I loop back around an old merry-go-round for the second time, a piercing scream cuts through the night, and before the sound has even finished tearing through the sky, I'm running with one of Reaper's custom blades in my hand.

I follow the sound, and just as I break out past a crumbling Ferris wheel, a fiery blaze cuts through the sky.

My heart sinks, and for a moment, I don't know if that scream cutting through the night is coming from me. I keep running toward the blaze, and as my vision adjusts, I realize the firefly blaze is a cart on the rollercoaster tracks, and the scream is coming from inside it.

"Fuck."

My gaze darts from left to right as I run faster than I've ever run in my life, frantically searching for Gasoline. Because where there is fire, there's usually a redheaded bitch trying to make her escape. But not tonight. She's not getting away with this.

My gaze darts to the rollercoaster track before sailing back to the ground. She's gotta be close by, somewhere near the entrance of the massive ride, and just as I approach the ride, my lungs heaving for sweet oxygen, I see the flash of red I've been looking for.

Desperation cuts through me as she makes her getaway, and I dart to the left, lining myself up perfectly with her as I rear my arm back. "Hey, bitch," I roar.

Gasoline glances back over her shoulder, her eyes widening in fear, realizing that she hasn't gotten away with this, and before she has a chance to put one foot in front of the other, I fling my arm forward, letting my blade sail through the air.

It plunges right through the center of her throat with so much force, a portion of the handle becomes lodged in her airway, and I don't bother to check just how quickly the bitch dies as I continue toward the track.

I would have loved to take her out in any other way, to make her truly pay for the hell she put Eagle through and the brutal way she attempted to do the same to me, but with Shadow on that burning cart, I have no choice but to be okay with this.

I don't stop for the blade or even bother to collect the stack of IDs she stole off me. It doesn't matter to me anymore. Instead, I sail on past her limp body and through the entrance of the massive rollercoaster.

The track is huge, and judging by the look of it, these rides haven't been in use for ten or twenty years. There's no telling what's going to happen to that burning cart on these tracks, and with Shadow inside of it, I'm not willing to find out.

I skip over the bars that block people from stepping out onto the tracks and forge ahead. The cart is already halfway around the track, so I head in the opposite direction, ready to catch it as it passes through.

The smell of gasoline is thick in the air, and as I race along the tracks, I keep my eye on the prize, desperate to get to her.

Shadow's squeals cut through the night, and I know without a doubt that it's not the fear of the fiery cart that has her screaming, it's the agonizing burn of the fire against her delicate skin.

The track bends toward the sky, and the further I run, the higher up I go, but nothing can stop me now, and as I begin to reach the very peak of the track, standing high over the amusement park, I have no choice but to try and time this just right.

The fiery cart is blazing around the tracks, traveling at a speed no human could possibly keep up with as it whips around the tracks and flies around the sharp bends. My feet don't stop moving, and just as the cart speeds toward me on a parallel track, a bullet whizzes through the sky, grazing my upper arm.

"FUCK!" I screech, ducking down just in time to miss another.

The cart is barreling closer, and I don't even get a chance to look back to see who's shooting before I have to jump, launching myself off the track and through the air. My body crashes down into the fiery cart, slamming into Shadow's chest as three more bullets sail past us.

"Shit," I say as Shadow lets out a loud cry at the impact of my body slamming into her chest.

I adjust myself in the small space, narrowly avoiding the flames creeping up the sides of the cart every time we begin to lose momentum. I'm frantically trying to figure out how to get her out of here while being all too aware of the deep dive the cart is about to take down the track. There are cable ties locked around her wrists and ankles, but I keep searching, knowing these cable ties aren't an issue for Shadow. That's when I notice the heavy rope wrapped around her chest, bracing her to the cart.

Another bullet whizzes by, and I curse under my breath. "Who the fuck is shooting at me?"

"The Boneyard Slayer," Shadow yells over the noise of the roaring wind whipping past us.

"Fuck," I grunt, trying to focus on the issue at hand.

My blades will easily get through the rope, but there's so much of it that neither of us are about to get out of this cart without injury, and having said that, I get straight to work slicing through the cable ties at her wrists and ankles.

"What the fuck did you think you were doing coming here alone?" I demand, starting on the thick ropes as I keep my head down, hidden away from the constant bullets, but I'm not worried. If it were anyone else, the bullets might actually have a chance of taking me out, but The Boneyard Slayer is a lousy shot.

I tear through the bottom rope, giving Shadow enough space to start moving her arms and the second she can, she grabs a knife from my thigh holster and gets right to work, frantically trying to help me free her.

"You said we were a family," Shadow grunts as the wind whips violently through my hair. "This is what family does for each other. I couldn't stand the thought of you two going out and trying to save me when I could have saved us all."

"This is your idea of saving us?" I say, noticing the fresh tears in her eyes. "Shit, Shadow. Do you have any idea—fuck. We can fight about it later, for now, we just need to get you out of here."

"What about you?" she demands as more bullets sail over our heads, one of them getting way too close to Shadow.

"Don't worry about me. I'll be fine," I say, slicing through another rope as the flames blister my skin.

We cut through enough rope that Shadow is finally able to shimmy out of the destroyed bindings, and just as she's free enough and goes to pull herself away from the blaze at her back, she looks up ahead on the track. "Shit," she grunts.

I look back over my shoulder, seeing the way the track takes a steep dive before sailing straight into a twisting loop, and with neither of us locked into this damn cart, there's no way we could both hold on. Then grabbing a gun out of my holster, I shove it at her chest. "RUN!"

"But you—"

"FUCKING RUN, SHADOW."

She clenches her jaw, and after closing her hand around the gun, she climbs up onto the small seat of the burning cart and launches herself onto the track. She doesn't skip a beat, breaking into a sprint through the barrage of bullets, and just as I see Shadow's head disappear behind the raging flames, I have just enough time to clutch onto the burning handlebar of the cart as it falls down the massive dip of the track.

My body flies, jolting around inside the cart, and when it whips around the loops, I'm thrown out of the cart, barely having enough strength to hold on. I do everything in my power to swing my legs up into the upside-down cart, and just as I do, we hit another loop, throwing me out again.

The track quickly levels out, swooping low to the ground, but not being the end of the ride, I have only a second to get off the rollercoaster from hell. Just as the burning cart hits the lowest point of the track, I jump, throwing myself into a forward roll on the hard asphalt.

My back grazes the ground, my skin tearing to shreds, but I spring back to my feet because this fucking ride is not even close to over. With Shadow free, I take off after The Boneyard Slayer.

He sees me coming from a mile away, and as I dodge and weave past every bullet he's got, he realizes the game is up. There's not a damn thing he can do to get away from me now, and I'm not even a little bit surprised when fear flashes in his eyes and he turns to run, knowing he doesn't stand a goddamn chance against me.

27

REAPER

The sound of gunshots echoes from a distance, and considering it's coming from the right side of the park, I have no choice but to trust that Siren has it under control. We made our deal, and nobody wins if I change the plan this late in the game.

I've searched this half of the park for almost thirty minutes, and just as I'm about to convince myself that it's clear and head over to assist Siren, I finally find him. The Texan Reaper.

A sinister grin tears across my face. I've been waiting too fucking long for this. I was content with giving him an easy death, making it quick, but after the bullshit he's caused, the callous way he murders, and now after luring Shadow out of the safety of our home and using her as bait, I'm going to be sure to enjoy this.

The Texan Reaper slinks through the park, having no fucking idea that he has an audience, and as I follow him past the poor excuse of a bumper car arena, I listen for Siren. The gunshots are still firing through the darkness, and as we creep closer to the center of the park, I hear the distinct sound of a rollercoaster.

My heart races, desperate to go to Siren, to see what fresh hell Gasoline has planned because, let's face it, The Boneyard Slayer doesn't have the brains to pull off anything worthy of a mention. He's a yes-man through and through.

As for his brother, he's a different breed.

The Texan Reaper takes a look around, double-checking the coast is clear before slipping through the entrance of the funhouse, and I roll my eyes. Could he have been any more cliché? But as they say, play stupid games, win stupid prizes.

I follow the bastard into the funhouse, pausing by the door as I listen to the sounds. I have to have my wits about me. His whole game plan during the past month has been to lure contenders out and trap them. It's what they did to Silver only a few nights ago and again to Shadow. I can't go into this assuming this isn't another trap. I have to watch myself, otherwise, it won't be me going home to Siren tonight, it'll be this asshole, and when he does, it's not going to be to tell her how fucking beautiful she is and then fuck her up against the refrigerator. He'll do everything in his power to brutally murder her, and I'm not about to let that happen. As Siren said, we end this tonight.

Neither of us is leaving this amusement park until all three of the final contenders are dead.

Making my way deeper into the funhouse, I step into a dimmed room of mirrors, and my senses are instantly off, seeing nothing but myself. Multiple reflections stare back at me, and I realize I was right. This is a fucking trap. There's no hiding in here. If The Texan Reaper didn't know I was following him before, he sure as fuck knows now.

As I creep deeper into the room of mirrors, I grasp the blade at my hip. I don't like it. It makes me uneasy, but it's not exactly the worst situation I've ever been in. But facts are facts, and I'm only human, so if this room of mirrors makes me uneasy, it sure as fuck makes The Texan Reaper uneasy too.

"Come on, asshole," I murmur, inching deeper into the room, only to be trapped by the mirrors and have to change direction. "You lured me in here. You got what you wanted, now stop being such a little bitch and come out to play."

A low laugh rumbles through the funhouse, and my gaze flicks back and forth, scanning over every reflection staring back at me when a figure appears behind me.

The Texan Reaper shows his face with a blade in his hand and a cocky grin, then without warning, he rears back and releases the blade, launching it toward my face. Only I don't flinch. I don't even blink when the blade hurtles toward my face and comes up short as it slams into one of the many mirrors, cracking it right through the center.

"Shit. That's seven years of bad luck," I say, a grin pulling at my lips.

His face falls, realizing his fuck up, and in a flash, he whips around and darts away, just as disoriented by the mirrors as I am. Only difference is now that he cracked a mirror, I have a marker that tells me exactly where I am, which allows me to follow him.

I watch his million reflections, and with every step I take in his direction, his panic increases, getting deeper into the room of mirrors and even more disoriented. "Give it up," I say, refusing to say his bullshit name out loud. "You have no chance here. Surrender, and I'll make it quick."

The Texan Reaper scoffs. He knows I'm lying. I have no intention of making this quick. It will be just as brutal as his murder of Sharkbait, and just as unforgiving as what he and his brother did to Silver.

I continue creeping closer, keeping my gaze locked on his reflection as he barrels through the mirrors, frantically trying to find a path. Each time his face slams into a wall, he has to backtrack, wasting precious seconds. It's fucking perfect but also pathetic. Had he been able to pull this shit off, perhaps I would have had just an ounce of respect for him, but considering he couldn't do enough homework to properly map out this mirror maze before leading me in here, he's only proving how much of a fraud he truly is.

Getting close enough to be able to smell his fear, I adjust my blade in my hand, more than ready to prove how I received my alias. When the sound of heavy boots slamming against the ground booms through the funhouse, my back stiffens, and I pause just a moment before The Boneyard Slayer barrels through the room.

I see his reflection in the mirrors, but within seconds, the asshole gets lost. His gaze flicks from left to right, holding his hand up to keep from slamming into the mirrored walls.

"Brenton?" The Texan Reaper calls.

"That fucking bitch is after me," he rushes out.

"I told you to deal with her."

"I fucking tried."

"What about the kid?"

"She got away."

A grin pulls at my lips. Both Shadow and Siren are okay, and as The Boneyard Slayer makes his way deeper into the maze, Siren appears in the mirrors. "Fuck," she murmurs, moving into the mirrors, taking only a moment to get her bearings and notice the smashed mirror, using it as a marker just as I had.

There's a blade in her hand, and while I can see the way she's second-guessing herself with every turn she takes, I know she can handle this. She makes her way deeper into the mirror maze, taking every turn to bring her closer to me, while the brothers take every wrong turn, finding themselves at dead ends and having to backtrack.

At this point, they'll walk right into us, and we will barely have to lift a finger.

I stand dead center in the funhouse, watching the reflections of the brothers while watching Siren's back, and the further she gets into the maze, the clearer the marks on her body become. She's injured, and they're not just marks from taking a beating, they're burns. She's had a run-in with Gasoline, and I can only assume that because she's here, that means Gasoline has been dealt with.

It takes Siren only a minute to find the center of the maze, and as she does, I step into her, catching her around the waist. "You good?"

I ask, my gaze sweeping over her body for only a second before returning to the brothers as they fumble around, trying to find one another—something we can't allow.

"I will be as soon as we end this and get out of here. These mirrors are trippy. I don't like it."

"Shadow?" I ask as Siren instinctively moves beside me, taking up a fighter's stance, ready for anything that comes our way.

"They tied her to a cart on the rollercoaster and lit it up before sending it along the tracks. She had no choice but to sit in the flames while it went around the track."

"Fuck. Is she okay?"

"Superficial burns, but she'll be alright. She's pissed though. She didn't say it, but I think she's upset with herself that she walked into a trap."

I nod. "We'll deal with it as soon as we get out of here. For now, we need to keep focused. We can't let these assholes slip away."

Siren doesn't respond, but the determination in her eyes is more than enough confirmation that she's with me, so with The Boneyard Slayer closer to our left, we move toward him.

Creeping through the maze of mirrors, we move in a way that backs The Boneyard Slayer into a corner, only he's too fucking stupid to realize it. I watch as the bastard starts to believe he actually has the upper hand. The mirrors clearly fuck with his head, and when he gets a lock on Siren, he begins to stalk her. I shake my head, watching his performance. He's not even discreet, and as Siren leads him further into a corner, I keep my eye on his brother.

The Boneyard Slayer watches every move she makes, and as he creeps closer toward her, I do the same. Then, just as he thinks he's got the drop on her, he takes his blade and lunges toward her with everything he's got, only he slams face first into a solid mirror, the glass splintering under the force.

I laugh, and as he whips around, his eyes wide with fear, I lunge just as he had, my blade slicing through his lower abdomen as I gut him like a fucking fish. He gapes at me as if not understanding what the fuck just happened, and as if on cue, his organs slide out of him, his intestines like a rope of bloodied sausages falling to the ground with a wet plop.

The Boneyard Slayer lets out one single breath, and with that, he falls to his knees, crushing his organs under the weight of his meaty body.

"Goodnight, motherfucker," I mutter just as Siren steps out, looking at the mess covering the ground, her brow arched in approval.

She goes to say something when a loud roar tears through the maze. "YOU'RE BOTH FUCKING DEAD," The Texan Reaper bellows, rage in his eyes, clearly having watched the show through the mirrors. Only there's something off in his stare. He's not pissed that we took his brother out, he's pissed that we took out his one last advantage to the top. After all, if he were going to win, he would have had to slaughter his brother at some point.

The Texan Reaper takes off at a run, a blade clutched tightly in his hand as he uses the wall of mirrors as a guide, but he's too disoriented to make a single correct turn, and as he attempts to get to us, we make it easy, heading right for him.

"HEY!" A piercing scream is heard at the opening of the mirror maze. My stomach sinks, and both Siren and I come to a screeching halt, my gaze whipping toward the entrance to see Shadow staring directly at The Texan Reaper. "You want them, asshole. You're going to have to get through me first."

"Fuck," Siren breathes beside me. "What the hell is she doing?"

The Texan Reaper pauses, weighing up his options, and seeing a clear path out of the mirror maze that gives him a direct line to Shadow, he takes it, sprinting after her.

"NO!" Siren screams as we both break into a sprint, racing to get out of here. We stumble past each other, both of us too overwhelmed by fear that we allow the maze to fuck with our heads, taking longer than it should to get out of this fucking hellhole.

Siren is a step behind me, and as I find the path out, I grab her hand and pull her with me as we break out into the cool night air. We race ahead, seeing Shadow in the distance, and for the first time since meeting her, she runs right through the center, keeping out of the shadows, perfectly visible to anyone who'd want to use her as a target.

"She wants to be caught," Siren rushes out, seeing the very thing I'm seeing. "Foolish child. She's trying to save us."

I grit my teeth, hating the thought of this kid trying to sacrifice herself for us, and more than that, I hate that she was raised to believe this is her only option. Self-sacrifice isn't the honor she thinks it is because if she were to get hurt, neither myself or Siren would be able to live with ourselves following this. And because of that, when the three of us get out of this fucking godforsaken town—which we fucking will—dealing with that organization and the underground training camp will be one of my top priorities.

The Texan Reaper begins to gain on Shadow, and my heart races with fear. "FUCKING RUN, SHADOW," I call behind her, knowing she could run laps around this asshole without breaking a fucking sweat.

"No, no, no," Siren frets, unsheathing a blade from her thigh holster, then just as The Texan Reaper gets close enough to reach out for Shadow, Siren launches the blade with everything she's got.

The blade sinks heavily into the back of his shoulder, and he roars in agony, but it's not enough to take him out. His hand closes around Shadow's forearm, and he violently yanks her back, whipping her around so that her small back is pressed against his massive chest. He whirls them both around, looks us dead in the eyes, and rears his arm back, his blade glistening in the moonlight.

Siren lets out a bloodcurdling scream just as The Texan Reaper whips his hand forward, aiming right for Shadow's throat, but she throws herself down and twists, her arm shooting up like lightning and squeezing the trigger of Siren's favorite gun.

BANG! BANG!

The bullets plunge right through the bottom of The Texan Reaper's chin and through the back of his skull, and I watch with wide eyes as his heavy body instantly crumbles to the ground.

The final contender of the games has been eliminated.

28

SIREN

The sun is only just kissing the horizon as the three of us drive in silence back to the place we've called home for the past two weeks. The lake is calm with the soft glow of the early morning fog resting on top, and the air in Blue Springs somehow seems sweeter.

I haven't been able to get my thoughts in line since the moment Shadow appeared in the doorway of that funhouse. Sacrificing herself for us . . . It was a feeling I never want to experience again in my life.

I've never been so scared or felt so helpless, and when she pulled that gun and took the final shot, finishing these games for good, the relief was bittersweet. We made it through together, and yet the whiplash of emotions has left me feeling rattled, and I don't think

I'm going to be okay with it for a while. I need time. I need space to breathe, to simply look at Shadow and see that she's in one piece, and more than that, I need to figure out a way to erase the memories of Shadow on that burning cart and being pulled into The Texan Reaper's chest.

Reaper pulls into the familiar driveway, and as the three of us clamber out of the car and make our way inside, Reaper waits for me, dropping his hand to the small of my back. The touch is everything, and as we walk through the door together, it's just a little easier to breathe, but I know this moment of peace will be short-lived.

It's the morning of day twenty-nine, and we have until the stroke before midnight tomorrow night to figure out how the hell we're going to get out of here in one piece.

There's no winning for us.

Option one is to give our lives and allow Shadow the chance to get out of here without a target on her back. Give her a chance to live a proper life away from the assholes who raised her. A chance to have some kind of childhood. She could go find Mila, and the two of them would be unstoppable together. Or, option two, the three of us could break out of here together and live a short life on the run with a bounty on our heads that we couldn't possibly escape.

I don't exactly love our options.

Making our way inside, I start pulling weapons off me, needing to lighten the load, and honestly, I wouldn't be surprised if I ended up naked right here in the living room, simply needing a break from all the death that seems to be resting right on my shoulders.

Reaper continues to the kitchen when Shadow turns and heads for her bedroom. "Hold up," Reaper says. "You're not going anywhere. We need to talk about this."

Shadow pauses in the entrance of the hallway, slowly turning on her heel and arching her brow as she stares back at Reaper. "What's there to talk about? We all survived, and now we can figure out what comes next."

Reaper shakes his head and points to the stool under the kitchen counter. "Sit."

"Shit," she mutters under her breath before sparing me a quick glance. I can't offer her anything except a slight shrug of my shoulders, having no idea where this is about to go, but what I do know is that I have more than a few things that need to be said. Realizing I'm backing Reaper in this, Shadow slowly begins making her way over to the kitchen stool, doing everything in her power to take her time, dragging her feet and refusing to meet Reaper's harrowing stare.

He begins pacing through the kitchen and realizing he has no idea how to handle this, I simply sit on the arm of the couch and watch as he tries to figure it out. After all, he's running this show. What kind of girlfriend—if that's what I am—would I be if I didn't let him spread his wings and figure it out for himself?

Shadow slides her ass onto the stool and braces her elbows on the counter before fixing Reaper with a puppy dog stare, trying to break him before he's even begun, but she should know better than that. Reaper doesn't break for anyone . . . Well, maybe except for me.

Reaper finally stops pacing before turning his stare on Shadow.

"You fucked up, kid."

"What?" she demands, her eyes widening so fast I fear they're going to pop right out of her skull. "I saved your asses."

Woah. Okay. She took that one too far. Reaper and I could have more than taken care of The Texan Reaper without breaking a sweat, but she just had to go and make herself a martyr. It was unnecessary. When I told her to run, she should have done that, and I should have been able to trust that.

Reaper scoffs. "Respectfully, Shadow. You didn't," he tells her, not bothering to sugarcoat it for her. "You threw yourself headfirst into a dangerous situation, risking your own fucking life, for something we more than had under control. I get it, Shadow. You're just a kid and you want to prove yourself, and don't get me wrong, I'm so fucking grateful that your plan to take him out worked, but it was unnecessary. You could have gotten yourself killed for nothing."

"It wasn't for nothing," she argues back. "You said we're family. You both said we're family and this is what families do. We save each other's asses even if it means sacrificing yourself."

Reaper shakes his head before letting out a heavy breath. "No Shadow, being family isn't about sacrificing yourself," he tells her. "It's about having each other's backs and working as a team, but there's no teamwork when there's no trust, and tonight for us to be able to take out those brothers, we needed to trust that you were as far away from that amusement park as possible, and you weren't. You broke our trust when you decided to leave in the middle of the night, thinking you could handle the three of them yourself, and you broke our trust again when you didn't get the fuck out of there."

Shadow clenches her jaw, dropping her gaze to her hands on the counter. "I'm sorry," she murmurs. "I just . . . I wanted everyone to be okay. You, me, and Siren . . . I've never had anyone care about me the way you two do, and the idea of losing you both scared me. I thought I could handle it."

My heart breaks, and I pull myself off the armrest before flying across the living room to the kitchen and pulling her into my arms, holding this sweet girl to my chest. "It's okay," I tell her before second-guessing myself. "Well, no actually. It's not okay. What happened tonight was the furthest thing from okay. But I'm just happy you're alive. Seeing The Texan Reaper grabbing you like that and not being able to do anything about it . . . Shadow, that was the single most terrifying moment of my life. I'd take a million nights burning in a fiery suite over having to witness that again."

She nods her head against my shoulder, and I hear as she lets out a shaky breath before deflecting her emotions. "Exaggerating much? Nobody is stupid enough to want to experience that fire again, let alone a million more times," she murmurs.

I can't help but laugh as I release her and as she winces, I realize just how tight I was holding her burned skin, and yet she didn't say a word about it. "Come on," I say, patting the stool she was just on. "Let's get you fixed up and then we can figure out where the hell we're supposed to go from here."

Reaper fetches the first aid kit and sets it up on the counter. "Are you still mad at me?" she asks Reaper, watching as he grabs things out of the kit.

"I'm furious with you, Shadow," he tells her. "I'm going to be furious about it for a very long time, but if you're asking if we're okay, then yes. We're okay."

She nods before letting out a shaky breath. "I can deal with that," she tells him as I start working on Shadow's burns and Reaper begins working on mine.

We fall into a comfortable silence, each of us lost in our own thoughts, when Shadow's head raises, her gaze lifting to mine. "So, what happens now?" she asks. "Am I taking you both out or what? And if so, how do you wanna go?"

I gape at the kid and pull away from her, double-checking there are no weapons in her immediate vicinity. "Ahh, what?"

"I'm going to have to kill you both, right? I'm not saying I want to, but if I have to, I'd prefer to do it in a way you're comfortable with. Unless," she continues, glancing between me and Reaper, "you'd prefer to take each other out."

Reaper and I spare a glance at each other, both of us lost for words and unsure what to say when Shadow begins to laugh. "Oh my god. I'm screwing with you. You should see your faces," she laughs. "As if I'd want that after everything we've just been through. And in case either of you haven't quite figured it out, I'm not going to survive out in the big wide world on my own. I need you both there."

"Holy fucking shit," I mutter under my breath, needing to grip the edge of the counter as my heart races at the thought of having to end Reaper's life and not getting to love him every day of forever.

Reaper shakes his head. "In case you hadn't already figured it out, you're on dishes duty for the rest of your life."

"Sir, yes Sir," Shadow says, saluting him as she gets to her feet, deciding that she's had more than enough first aid despite me only getting through half of her back. "Can we pick this up tomorrow? I need to crash, and from the looks of it, you two have a lot to figure out."

"Like what?" Reaper questions.

"You know, like how the hell we're going to get out of Blue Springs unscathed, and what this means for your awkward relationship."

My brows furrow. "Huh?"

Shadow grins. "You really haven't thought about it?" she questions, trying not to laugh. "If we somehow get out of here, then I assume we're going to live together somewhere, and that means the two of you are skipping right over the whole dating thing and basically becoming my parents. I mean, are you dating? Going steady? Or are you practically married? Should I call you Mr. and Mrs. Reaper, or are you going with something a little more modern? Mr. and Mrs. Siren, perhaps?"

Reaper glances toward me, neither of us knowing what the hell we're supposed to say. "Uhhhhhh . . ."

"That's what I thought," Shadow says in a teasing tone, practically skipping down the hallway, more than proud of how easily she just threw our whole relationship into chaos. "Why don't you two figure that out while I go sleep like a baby?"

Brat.

Shadow laughs the whole way down the hall. The next thing we hear is her bedroom door slamming behind her, and I'm left gaping at Reaper. "I, ummm . . . I don't need to be called Mrs. Reaper," I tell him, not wanting him to think that I expect anything more from him than what we already have. Besides, something tells me if we suddenly filed for a marriage license, it might raise a few alarm bells with the FBI, and that right there could be a fatal mistake.

Reaper grins and takes my waist, lifting me up onto the kitchen counter and stepping between my thighs. "I don't need to marry you to know that you're mine, Kienna," he says, making me suck in a gasp at the sound of my name on his lips. "But when we do get out of Blue Springs, I fully intend on taking you with me and starting a life together. I haven't gone through this past month with you, just to lose you at the finish line."

I swallow over the lump in my throat. "Are you sure?" I question, my heart racing a million miles an hour.

"Never been so sure in my life," he tells me. "You, me, and Shadow, we're a dysfunctional family, and I wouldn't have it any other way."

I wrap my arms around him and pull him in, his words healing the deep abandonment issues I've had since the moment my mother was so brutally taken from me when I was only six years old. "I love you, Reaper," I whisper. "I want nothing more than to start a life with you, I just don't see how we're supposed to get out of here to make that happen."

"I know," he murmurs, pulling back and gently brushing his lips across mine. "We have a little less than forty-eight hours to pull it off, and so far, all I've been able to come up with is to fake our deaths. Let

Shadow hand over the IDs we were able to find, take the prize money, and once we've officially been declared dead, we start fresh."

I nod, agreeing with him until I truly start thinking about what being declared dead would mean for both of our careers. "Wait. If we're dead, we can kiss our careers goodbye. We can't accept contracts without someone piecing together that we're alive, which is only going to set off alarm bells for the asshole behind War Games, which puts us right back at square one."

"Then we don't work," he tells me. "We've both been contract killers for years. Don't pretend like you're not sitting on millions of dollars. Between us, we have more than enough cash to last ten lifetimes."

"I know," I say. "It's not about the money. I just feel like I worked hard to get where I am today, and I don't want to wave goodbye to any of that. Not working is not an option for me."

"Okay," he says with a nod, his hands squeezing my thighs. "Then we'll factor that in. We'll still work, maybe even continue with Shadow's training if that's what she wants."

Holding his stare, I try to figure out how the hell we're supposed to make that happen, and judging by the slight crease between his brows, he's just as lost as I am. It's one thing to have these grand plans for a future together, but if we can't get out of Blue Springs without getting a bounty on our heads, then what's the point in any of this?

"How?" I whisper, my heart falling out onto my sleeve.

"It all comes down to the asshole who organized this," he says, having read my mind. "We fake our deaths, and if we can get to him before he realizes that he was played and puts the bounty out, then we're free. We'll have it all. The three of us together. A real chance at having a family."

"Fuck, that sounds good, but Mila and I have tried to find him a million times before. He's more of a ghost than you and Shadow are," I say, suddenly wishing we hadn't taken 343 out of the competition quite so early. Maybe with both him and Mila working together, they might have been able to trace the untraceable. "I don't think we can pull it off."

"I don't know," he says, scooping me off the kitchen counter and into his arms as I lock my legs around his waist. "All I know is that we need to try. But first, we sleep. We're not going to get anywhere trying to plan some grand escape plan after the night we just had. My brain is fried, and don't even try to tell me yours isn't. We rest, and then after Shadow wakes up, we figure this shit out together."

"I couldn't agree more," I tell him. "Only, I need to shower, and don't think for one second that you're not coming with me."

29

SIREN

The water rains down over me as Reaper slams my back against the cold tiles, and despite the burns on my back that we only just finished first aid for, I can't help but lean into the coldness, finding the sweetest relief.

His lips come down on mine as I reach between us, curling my hand around the base of his thick cock and slowly pumping my hand. My thumb roams over his tip and makes him shudder against me.

"Fuuuuck," he groans, his lips moving against mine before lowering to the sensitive skin below my ear. I can't help but tilt my head to the side, allowing him more space to roam, and as he does just that, his fingers find my entrance while holding my thigh up with his other hand.

Two thick fingers dive deep inside of me, curling just the way I like it, and massaging my needy walls. I grind against the heel of his palm, and without skipping a beat, he stretches his thumb up to my clit, rolling tight, fast circles that drive me wild with need.

"Oh god," I groan, tipping my head back in elation as the sweetest pleasure pulses through my body.

Reaper lifts his head from my neck, holding my stare. "No, baby. I'm your fucking god now, and you worship me on your fucking knees."

"Oh yeah?" I question, my lips quirking into a wild grin.

His only response is to hold my stare and before he gets a chance to drop his lips back to my neck, I fall to my knees and worship him the only way I know how. Opening my mouth wide, I take his thick cock right to the back of my throat as his glorious body protects me from the flow of water raining down over us.

My tongue works up and down his impressive length, rolling over the tip of his salty cock before hungrily diving back in. I keep my hand around the base of his cock, slowly working him up and down, matching the rhythm of my mouth, and as he braces his hand against the shower tiles, I know I've got him right where I want him.

"Spread your pretty thighs, Kienna," he demands, watching me from above, and fuck, the way he says my name in that deep, gravelly voice almost has me coming undone. "Show me how you work your sweet clit while you take my cock."

Not having the heart to deny this exceptional man, I oblige before the words have even finished leaving his mouth, spreading my thighs as far as they'll go before showing him exactly how much I like it. My fingers roll over my clit, and while it's certainly not the way he works me with his fingers deep inside of me, it'll still get the job done.

I take him right to the back of my throat, moaning as I work my clit, and when he reaches down with his free hand and curls it into the back of my hair, I tease him with my tongue. I give him everything I've got as I grind against my fingers, and feeling that familiar build deep inside of me, I push myself further, taking him even deeper and listening to the sound of his desperate grunts.

He's on the edge, and nothing has ever made me feel so fucking feminine in my life. I need him to come, need to taste his warm seed hitting the back of my throat.

I push him further, taking him right to the edge, enjoying this more than any woman has the right to, and as I take and take, I throw us both over the edge. My orgasm comes shooting through me, but I don't stop fucking him with my mouth as the pleasure explodes within me, coursing through my veins and making my toes curl.

Reaper comes with me, his hold tightening in my hair as he curses under his breath, but it's his hot, salty seed that hits the back of my throat that has me giddy with excitement, knowing just how quickly I can bring this man to his knees. I swallow down every drop on offer, and only when we both come down from our highs do I release him, simply staring up at him with a smile as he watches me in wonder.

"Holy fucking shit," he mutters, his chest heaving with heavy breaths. "Why the fuck haven't we done that before now?"

A laugh rumbles through my chest, and before I can come up

with some bullshit response, his hands are on me, pulling me back to my feet and slamming me against the cool tiles again. He kisses me with a fierce hunger, and I melt into him as he lifts me off the ground and wraps my legs around his waist, keeping me pinned with his hips.

I feel him harden between us, and I realize that after my performance on my knees, he's ready to settle the score, and I won't lie, I love that level of enthusiasm in a man.

His pelvis grinds against my core, and as a desperate groan tears from within my chest, he drops his lips to my neck. I'm already so worked up, and the idea of waiting even a second longer sends me into a near panic. "Please," I beg. "I need you inside of me."

"Fuck, baby," he groans. "I can't resist when you say please."

Good to know. I file that little piece of information away for later, and when he shifts his hips back and lines that perfect, thick cock up with my entrance, a giddiness rumbles through me. He inches forward, and as his tip pushes inside, my hips begin to jolt, the desperation taking control.

"Reaper," I beg.

He pushes further, and my walls begin to stretch around him, adjusting to his sweet intrusion, and when it becomes too much for both of us, he slams the rest of the way inside me. "Fuck," he grunts through a clenched jaw as he pauses, both of us needing a minute before he starts to move.

My walls contract around him, frantically trying to adjust to his sheer size as I knot my fingers into the back of his hair and hold on for dear life. "Fuck me, Reaper."

He groans and despite not being quite ready, he draws his hips back, and when he finally slams into me again, we both groan. "Oh God," I grunt, grasping his massive shoulder with my other hand, my nails digging into his warm skin as he holds me against the wall.

His hips pull back again, and I can't tear my eyes off him, watching as his whole body rolls with his powerful thrusts. It's everything, and as he fucks me, I completely come apart.

My eyelids flutter as my eyes roll with pleasure, and as my walls squeeze around his thick cock, he grunts, barely able to hold on. "Fuck, Siren."

"Kienna," I demand. "Call me Kienna."

He groans deeply and leans back, thrusting his cock deep inside of me. He gives me exactly what I want in the form of that deep, gravelly tone that always drives me wild. "Take it, *Kienna*. Let me feel your tight little cunt come on my cock."

"Oh God."

His words are too much, and without warning, I explode around him, my walls violently convulsing as my whole body spasms, my hips frantically jolting with wild pleasure. It storms through my body like a tsunami crashing over me, pulsing heavily through my veins and sending the most potent ecstasy through my body.

I throw my head back, not able to handle the raw intensity, but with my body pinned against the wall, I have no choice but to take everything he gives me. "Fuuuck," he groans as my world is thoroughly rocked, and as my cunt squeezes around him, he comes with me, shooting hot spurts of cum deep inside of me.

He doesn't stop moving, and with every thrust, his pelvis grinds against my sensitive clit, sending shivers sailing through my body and increasing the intensity.

My nails are deep in his skin, and I only notice when a trail of blood mixes with the water and falls over his massive shoulder, and judging by the pure elation on his face, he didn't notice either.

I release my hold on him, and as we both start coming down, he braces his arm against the wall above my head, leaning into me as we each try to catch our breath. "Fuck, baby," he says, adjusting his hold on me as I try to lower myself to my feet and stand on shaking legs.

Needing the protection of his big body to keep me upright, I place my hand against his chest and feel just how fast his heart is racing as he clutches my waist. His forehead drops to mine, our chests moving as one. "If I ever lost you, Kienna . . ."

He doesn't finish his sentence, but I nod, knowing exactly what he's trying to say as I feel it just as strongly within my own heart. "I'd sooner give up my own life than ever have to face one without you," I tell him. "You, me, and Shadow."

"Family," he says.

I nod, and we stay just like that until the water begins to run cold, and we're forced out of the shower. He wraps me in a towel before grabbing another for himself, and by the time we're finally dressed and climbing into bed, a heaviness washes over me.

Reaper pulls me into his arms, his fingers dancing across my skin as I lay against his chest in one of his many black shirts. "Sleep, Kienna. You need to rest, then when we wake, we'll figure out how the hell we're supposed to pull this off in the next—" Reaper pauses, checking the time on his phone. "Forty-two hours."

The idea of our time running out makes me feel sick, and all I can do is nod against his chest, but the exhaustion is creeping up on me fast, and I know just how right he is. We both have to sleep if we're going to have any chance of coming up with a plan that could possibly get all three of us out of this godforsaken town alive.

"Forty-two hours," I repeat, the heaviness clear in my tone.

"We'll figure something out," he promises. "We didn't come this far just to lose it all at the finish line."

Trusting him with my life, I nod, and just as I go to close my eyes, the door barges open, and in a flash, Shadow is standing at the foot of our bed, my gun resting so casually in her hand.

We both sit up, my eyes wide as I take her in. "I'm sorry," she tells us, her eyes filled with a strange mix of fear and betrayal. Then, before I have a chance to even move, she pulls the trigger, sending a bullet straight through the center of Reaper's chest.

I scream, my heart racing in fear as Reaper's heavy body slams back down against the mattress, blood immediately pouring from the wound in his chest. "NO," I scream, slamming my hands against his chest before looking back at Shadow in horror, unable to recognize the girl looking back at me.

"It's the only way," she says as his blood pours over my fingers.

I shake my head, fear pounding through my chest as I do everything to save Reaper, only I see the intention in her eyes and I know I'm next. "No, Shadow," I panic, knowing if I go down, there's nobody left to save Reaper. "Don't do this. Don't—"

BANG!

30

MILA

ONE MONTH LATER

Tears stream down my cheeks as I drop down on the bench that overlooks the whole of the Seattle cityscape. It's beautiful during the day, but at night, it always took Siren's breath away. I've always been a landscape girl. Give me a beach or a mountainside any day, but Siren always had a thing for the big city.

She used to drag me up here nearly every weekend, spouting bullshit about how the walk was good for us, but no matter how allergic I was to exercise, she always managed to get me up here. Truth be told, I actually enjoyed the walk. I just enjoyed giving her a hard time more.

She was my best friend, and any time I spent with her was my favorite part of the day. And now as I stare at the little plaque that overlooks Seattle, I can't help but feel broken. It's been almost a month since the end of War Games, and the moment I saw the death toll with both Siren's and Reaper's names on it, I couldn't believe my eyes.

My heart shattered into a million pieces, and I haven't been able to put it back together. She was my only family, my only friend, and while I knew this was a very real possibility, I always saw her as greater than life. She never messed up, never faltered, and despite knowing the chances of her coming home after the games, I believed with every fiber of my soul that she would beat the odds and stride back through my door.

I reviewed the surveillance footage from that house a million times over, watching as Reaper and Siren laid down to go to bed, watching as she fell even more in love with him before Shadow came in and brutally betrayed them.

They wanted to love her as their own, wanted to give her the kind of life that was stolen from her the moment she was born, but her instincts took over. I've been so angry, and honestly, I don't know if I can even blame her. She was raised in a damn training camp. There's no telling what kind of values they drum into those children, but I think it's safe to assume it's nothing good.

She was sent to War Games with one motive: to win. And that's exactly what she did. I suppose I should give her a round of applause. She won. She outsmarted them all.

Shadow aligned herself with the strongest players in the game, and just when she had gained their trust and manipulated them into loving her, she betrayed them in the worst way.

None of us saw it coming, and that much is clear by the image of Siren's face when Shadow pulled the trigger. Her expression will be burned into my mind for the rest of my life.

I watched that footage so many times that I could replay the whole thing on a loop inside my head, watching over and over again as my best friend screamed for the man she loved, desperately trying to save him before being shot herself. I can clearly picture the way her body rebounded off the mattress as she fell, the way Shadow dropped to her knees and cried afterward, and the way Reaper bled out onto the white duvet.

It's not fair. It shouldn't have ended like that.

I sit and stare out at the cityscape until the night air begins to chill, then just as I go to get up, somebody sits down beside me, a tissue in their outstretched hand.

I suck in a breath, my gaze lifting from the manicured hand to the familiar face staring back at me.

"What?" I breathe, staring at the face I never thought I'd see again, certain I'm seeing a ghost.

"I'm sorry it took me so long to come see you," Siren murmurs, offering me a small smile.

"I . . ." I throw myself into her, crushing her as I wrap my arms around her slender body. Heavy tears stream down my face as my heart breaks a million times over.

Siren holds me, letting me get my tears out as they quickly morph into deep sobs. "It's okay, Mills. Get it all out," she says, her hand rubbing up and down my back, and for just a moment, I wonder if I'm going crazy. If my grief is forcing me to imagine the whole thing, but she's really here. She's alive, but that's not possible because I saw her die on the footage. I saw the moment she took her final breath.

"You were dead," I say into her shoulder.

"Yes," she agrees.

My brows furrow, and I pull back, taking the tissues from her hand as I shamelessly try to wipe the tears from my face, only the second they're gone, they're replaced by new ones. "I don't understand," I say. "I watched you die. I saw your name appear on the death toll right under Reaper's."

"I know. I did die, right there next to Reaper. It was as real as it gets," she tells me, pulling the neckline of her shirt aside and showing me the angry scarring on her chest. "Shadow shot us, but she also saved us."

I shake my head. "No. No, that's not what happened."

"She put the footage on a loop after she left the room. It was the only way. We were being watched so closely. With Graves, Reaper killed him in the hotel, and within six minutes, his name was already on the death toll. We had to move fast, and yes, I have to admit that Shadow surprised us, but she had one hell of a good plan. It needed to look real."

"I'm not understanding."

"After she shot us, she called for an ambulance, and as we laid in bed, slowly bleeding out, she looped all the feeds within the house. To you and to anyone watching, it looked as though we bled out on that bed. It looked as though we died. When in reality, the paramedics were already working on us."

My brows furrow, and I shake my head, understanding what she's saying but not believing a word of it because I saw her die. I saw every second of it and felt the grief tear through my chest.

"I'm right here, Mills," she says, taking my hand and squeezing it. "We all are."

Siren waves to a spot behind me, and I glance back over my shoulder seeing both Shadow and Reaper leaning against the hood of a black SUV. Reaper gives me a small smile and a chill sails down my spine. I watched this man fall in love with my best friend for a month, and despite seeing every part of him on those surveillance cameras, nothing could possibly prepare me for seeing him in the flesh. He's simply terrifying.

As for Shadow, she looks guilty as shit.

"Wait. There's so much I don't get," I say, looking back at Siren. "You said you died."

"I did. Technically," she tells me. "In the ambulance and again in the hospital. My heart gave out a few times, but I was revived. Same with Reaper."

"Shit. But how though? The number one rule is to avoid hospitals and cops, and that would have brought both. Your identities—"

"It's complicated," she says, "and had it been my own plan, I probably would have done it differently, but our backs were against the wall, and we did whatever we had to do to get out of there. But we posed as the real homeowners of that house, claimed a murder/ suicide gone bad, just like my parents, and while the cops were left with more questions than answers, it was enough for them to go on and not watch us so closely. Besides, the cops and FBI agents in Blue Springs were already so busy with the aftermath of War Games and all the bodies that came along with it, that our *incident* easily slipped through the cracks."

"Shit, Siren."

"You're telling me," she mutters under her breath. "We slipped out of the hospital the second we were up for it and have had Shadow taking care of us this whole time."

"Wow."

"She's incredible," Siren says, glancing over my shoulder and smiling at the girl who I thought ripped my heart right out of my chest. "It had to be timed so well, and she pulled it off incredibly. I think she must have been planning it for a while."

I let out a heavy breath and lean back against the bench, holding onto her hand in a death grip, terrified that she might just disappear and I'll never get her back. "So what now?"

Siren fixes me with a heavy stare. "I want to come home, Mills. Seattle is where I belong. I want to go back to my apartment and start a life with Reaper and Shadow. I want to go back to work. I want to be here with you, but I can't."

I shake my head, not seeing the bigger picture. "Why?"

"The second our identities are flagged, we'll have a bounty out on us that we can't escape. The prize money Shadow won would look like child's play, and we'll be hunted by the kind of people who make Reaper look like a fairytale. I can't risk it, and the only way to avoid that is to take out the asshole behind War Games."

I suck in a breath, my heart hammering in my chest, knowing exactly what she's asking me. "I . . . I've tried, Siren. A million times. I've searched every corner of the web. He's invisible."

"Mills—"

"I'm sorry," I say, tears filling my eyes. "You have no idea how desperately I wish I could help you, and you know I'm going to start searching the second I get home, but I'm not good enough. I can't find him, no matter how hard I try, it's not possible."

"I believe in you, Mila," she tells me, clutching my hand again. "If anybody can find this guy, it's you."

I let out a shaky breath, haunted by the idea of letting her down and being the reason she doesn't get to come home. But more than that, being the reason she might end up with a bounty that not even the likes of Reaper could shake. "I'll try," I promise her, vowing to myself that I will do anything it takes and cross any boundary I have to finally find this guy. I won't let her down.

My mind begins to swirl with a million different options I could try when a deep voice sails through the night. "Kienna. It's time."

My back stiffens, and I gape at my best friend. "Did he just call you—"

"Yeah," she says with a dorky smile, swooning over the guy and making me realize just how much his love for her has healed her from the inside out. "It's kind of a thing now. I'll tell you all about it when I see you next, but I have to get going. We can't stay in one place for too long. It's too risky."

"Okay," I say, my heart slowly piecing itself back together as she leans in and pulls me into a tight hug. "I'll get you what you need so you can come home."

"I know you will," she tells me. "I love you."

"I love you, too."

Siren pulls back and gets to her feet, and I can't help but notice the way she glances down at the plaque I had made in her honor. "Well, that's kinda morbid," she laughs before giving me a small smile. "Thank you."

I nod and with that, Siren walks away, and I watch as she joins Reaper and Shadow before falling straight into Reaper's waiting arms. He presses a kiss to her forehead then opens the door like a perfect gentleman.

The three of them get into the car, but Siren pauses a moment, glancing back over her shoulder and offering me a beautiful smile. "I'll be seeing you, Mila," she says, and not a moment later, she gets into the car, and the three of them drive away. Then as I watch the car go, I promise myself that even if it kills me, I won't stop until I bring them home.

EPILOGUE

REAPER

SIX MONTHS LATER

"Jesus Christ," I mutter, looking over the impenetrable compound that Harriet Wicker has built herself while Shadow and Kienna get into position. It's been a long time coming, but if anyone is going to do this, it's going to be us.

I'm sure another version of War Games will pop up in the coming years, and at some point, someone will put together the pieces and realize that Kienna and I aren't exactly as dead as we're supposed to be. But as long as Harriet Wicker goes down, there's no one else with enough motivation or skin in the game to put up the money for a bounty.

Once she's eliminated like the hundreds of deaths she's been responsible for over the years, we'll be as free as birds. Well, sort of.

In our line of work, there's only a certain amount of free a person can truly be. Our identities need to be kept under wraps, considering Shadow had no choice but to hand over our IDs at the end of the game. The FBI believes us to be dead, and we need to keep it that way, but if they happen to catch onto us, we have new identities ready to go with multiple exit strategies, something I've never really had to think about, but now that I've found my family, I won't allow a damn soul to take it away from me.

"Ready?" Mila questions in my ear.

"Ready," I confirm. "Shadow?"

"Ready."

"Kienna?" I ask.

Kienna's familiar groan sounds through my earpiece, and my back stiffens for just a moment before her whispered voice comes through. "Fuck, I really need to pee."

Fucking hell. This is why I've never been a fan of working in a team. When I'm out on my own, it's only me I have to cater to. But these three women . . . fuck. They drive me crazy, but it's the kind of crazy I wouldn't give up for the world. They don't need to know that though.

Either way, we can't afford to fuck this up. Our lives are literally riding on this. We have one shot to get it right, and if we're even a second too late, it could be detrimental to our survival.

Mila spent four and a half months searching for this bitch, and the moment she found her, we started working out a plan—You know, after getting over the fact that this wasn't some loser with back acne, jerking off in his mother's basement to snuff films.

"I told you not to drink that whole fucking soda in the car," I scold, shaking my head. "Can you figure yourself out, because it's go time in less than twenty seconds? Either hold it or piss in your pants, but we're not waiting for you to find a bathroom. We're in the middle of the fucking desert."

"Damn it," Kienna groans. "I can hold it, but if you even think about coming near me with that attitude, I'll have no choice but to pin you down and give you the worst kind of golden shower."

I roll my eyes as Shadow's voice sounds in my ear. "What's a golden shower?"

Fuck me.

"It's a—"

"It's nothing," I say, cutting off Kienna's explanation. "We need to focus."

"Power out in seven seconds," Mila says, thankfully forcing Shadow and Kienna to cut the bullshit and get in the zone. "Five . . . Three. Two. One."

The compound falls into complete darkness, and without another word, I throw myself over the high gates, dropping down to the ground as I hear Kienna and Shadow doing the same. We have twenty seconds before the backup generators come on, and even less time to take out the four armed guards patrolling the compound and get inside the main building before reaching Harriet's den undetected.

The moment I hit the ground, I switch my lenses over to night mode, getting the perfect view of the compound, and without hesitation, I make a break for it. My feet slam against the ground, pushing me toward the entrance of the main building as I spot one of the armed guards with his back to me as he talks into his earpiece, frantically trying to work out the reason for the blackout.

"Night Hawk One, are we under attack? I repeat, are we under—"

My blade slices across the front of his throat, and he goes down without me skipping a beat. As I glance at my watch, I realize we still have thirteen seconds. I hear Shadow, both in the distance and through my earpiece, as she takes out a guard, and not a second later, I hear the same from Kienna.

"Three down. One to go," I murmur.

"Go," Kienna grunts. "I've got the fourth."

Trusting her to handle it, I race to the entrance of the building, getting there at the same time as Shadow. "Time?" I question, punching my gloved knuckles straight into the security panel for the massive sliding door.

"Eight seconds," Mila says in my earpiece just as a pained grunt comes from Kienna.

"Baby?"

"Not your *baby*," she mutters before I hear the familiar sound of a blade plunging deep inside a body. "The fucker got me with a knee to the vag. Almost pissed my pants."

I roll my eyes as I grab all the electrical cords and tear them out, completely disabling the security door before getting my fingers around the edge of the door and pulling it back with everything I've got.

"Five seconds," Mila says.

I get the door open just enough, and before I can even glance back to search for Kienna, she tears past me, breaking through the threshold into Harriet's den as Shadow dives in after her.

"Four."

I follow suit, picking up speed, ready to have Kienna's back as my gaze locks onto Harriet at her desk. There are screens and monitors surrounding her, and she is madly pressing the keys, desperate for them to power up again, but as long as we have Mila on our side, she won't be getting back online . . . at least not in the next four seconds.

"Three."

Hearing the sound of Kienna's feet pounding against the linoleum, Harriet whips around, and taking all of a heartbeat to realize who the fuck we are, her eyes widen in horror, but it's too late for her. She was dead the second we got through that door.

"Two."

Coming in with raging speed, Kienna launches herself off the ground, and as Harriet rears back in her seat, preparing to whip around and do whatever the fuck she thinks she can do on a dead computer, Kienna crashes into her, her boot slamming against her temple and sending her sprawling across the ground.

The chair goes with her, the wheels catching and dropping the frame right on top of Harriet before bouncing and slamming into the wall of monitors behind her.

"One."

The backup generator kicks in and the room is lit with clinical light. The screens flicker back to life as Kienna gets to her feet.

"Woah. Fuck," Mila says, getting a bird's eye view into Harriet's den. "Bring me back all of that shit."

"All of it?" I grunt, all too aware of just how far away we parked and how many monitors and screens are here. I'm going to be hauling this shit back and forth for hours, but considering the four armed guards are dead, I suppose it doesn't matter if I were to drive the SUV right up inside this very room. It's not as though there's a working security door to keep us out anymore.

"All of it," Mila confirms.

Shit.

Harriet begins to get up, and I watch as her gaze flicks between me, Shadow, and Kienna. Then when Kienna moves around the back of the computer screens, stealing the coffee cup off Harriet's desk, she makes her move, darting toward her computer.

My heart lurches, knowing she could ruin our whole fucking world with a single push of a button, and without hesitation, my hand sweeps down past my hip, collecting my blade and launching it toward her in one fluid motion.

Harriet gets one foot to the ground before my blade sinks through the back of her neck, severing her spine. She gurgles, and in the same motion, falls heavily to the ground as blood quickly pools around her.

"Yeah, not today bitch," I mutter, walking toward her and making sure she's well and truly dead. Only as my gaze sails over her limp body, I realize that my blade isn't the only one protruding from her neck. There's an identical one directly beside it and considering the angle Shadow is standing at, it came from her.

Lifting my gaze, I arch a brow, more than impressed, only the little brat smirks back at me. "For the record," she says in a tone that suggests I'm not going to like what's about to come out of her mouth. "I beat you to it. You might have severed her spinal cord, but I made the kill."

"Bullshit," I say, glancing over Harriet's throat again.

"You got playback, Mila?" Shadow questions.

"Sure do," she says. "Hold please. Just need to slow it down."

I clench my jaw and narrow my gaze at Shadow, certain she's talking shit when Mila's voice comes through the earpiece again. "You know I'm actually terrified of you, Reaper, so the thought of giving you bad news is actually making me break out in hives right now, but the kid is right. She beat you to the drop."

Kienna chuckles to herself across the room, and I glance up to find my woman with her pants down around her ankles and an empty coffee cup wedged between her thighs, desperately relieving herself. "The fuck do you think you're doing?"

Kienna's head whips up. "I told you I was desperate," she argues back, not an ounce of shame in her tone. "Now if you wish to keep the romance alive in this little relationship of ours, then I highly suggest you stop being a creepy swamp turd and look away. Let a girl pee in peace."

"Fucking hell," I mutter, making a point of turning around despite having seen this woman do a shitload worse than that.

I shake my head as the only noise filling the room is the sound of the monitors whirring mixed with the sound of Kienna's piss hitting the bottom of the coffee cup, and honestly, how is she still going? Does she have the bladder of a fucking elephant? "Babe, you're going to need a second coffee cup at this rate."

"COVER YOUR EARS!" she roars at me, and in order to save myself from being drenched in the contents of that very coffee cup, I do exactly as she asks and make a point of covering my ears. Only, I can still hear everything through my earpiece.

Kienna quickly wraps it up, and with Harriet out of the way and no sign of any bounties on our heads, we're officially free to fall back into our normal lives. Only, instead of settling back in the Big Apple, I'll be making Seattle my new home with my girls, and I can't fucking wait.

"So, what now?" Shadow asks an hour later after we finished retrieving the car and start making a move loading every piece of top-grade equipment into the back of the SUV.

"Well," I start, quickly glancing at Kienna and only continuing after she nods, confirming my thoughts. "We were going to let you make that call."

Shadow pauses and glances up at me, her brows furrowed. "What's that supposed to mean?"

Kienna moves to my side, meeting Shadow's confused stare. "It means that we want to go after the organization that raised you," she explains. "I can't bear the thought of babies being stolen from their mothers and forced into this life. Then spending their childhood in training camps. It's not a life I would ever want for my own child, and because of that, I think it's time we step in and officially put an end to it. However, it's your call. Despite my feelings about this organization, it was still your home, and the monsters who raised you were somewhat your parents. If you're not comfortable with it, we'll put the idea on the back burner for a while, but if you are, then I say we go for it."

"You want to take them out?" she questions.

I shake my head. "I don't just want to take them out, Shadow. I want to destroy them and tear their training camp to pieces until there isn't even a shred of it left. I want to return those babies back to their families and offer them the childhood that you should have had, and as for the older kids . . . I don't know. I suppose they should be given a choice of what they want. Either way, I want these assholes to pay for what they've done, and if you're on board, I want you to be the one who calls the shots."

Tears well in her eyes and panic soars through my chest, thinking that maybe Kienna and I were out of line to even bring this up. A soft smile pulls at the corners of her lips, and she races into us, throwing her arms around us at the same time.

"Thank you," she breathes before wiping snot across my chest. "I'm in."

"Thank fuck," Kienna breathes, wrapping her arm around Shadow's back. "Then the second we get home and settled in Seattle, we'll start working out a plan. It's not going to happen overnight. Might even take us years before we have all the information we need to track down every last bastard involved in this organization, but I promise you, Shadow. We're going to get every last one of them."

"Yeah, we are," she agrees before pulling away and scooping up another monitor to load in the back of the SUV, and I can't help but notice the skip in her step or the massive smile resting on her lips.

Feeling my heart swell in my chest, I go to get back to work when Kienna pulls me back, throwing her arms around my neck and pushing up onto her tippy toes to kiss me. "We're free, Nick," she says. "We're the family we were always meant to be. We can have a home. We can go back to work, do all the things we love, and check in on Eagle's sister like I promised. We can even get one of those stupid picket-fence houses and a golden retriever puppy and call her Tinkerbell. We can have it all. Just you, me, and Shadow."

A throat clears in our ears and Kienna rolls her eyes. "You, too, Mila."

"Thank you. A little recognition every now and then would go a long way," she murmurs as I lock my arms tighter around Kienna, unable to look away from those gorgeous green eyes as the idea of the life we're about to have truly sinks in. I could marry her. It'd have to be under a false name, but I could give her that if she wanted. I could give her a baby, or seven, but for now, I'll stick with simply giving her my everything just as she's given me.

"Do you mind?" Kienna says to her best friend. "I'm trying to have a romantic moment with my man."

"Ugh. Gross," Shadow mutters from behind us.

"Yeah, I'm with Shadow," Mila says. "You two are gross. But I can take the hint. I'm logging out before I catch whatever disease came and turned you both into the romantic type. See your asses back in Seattle."

There's a soft beep in the earpiece, letting me know it's offline, and I pull it out of my ear before slipping the tiny piece of tech into my pocket and getting back to my girl. "Where were we?" I murmur, a grin playing on my lips.

"You were about to start making out like horny teenagers like you always do," Shadow mutters.

"Damn straight we were," Kienna says as a wide smile cuts across her face, and not a second later, I scoop her up into my arms and bring my lips down on hers.

THANKS FOR READING!

If you enjoyed reading War Games as much as I've enjoyed writing it, please consider leaving a review!

https://www.amazon.com/dp/B0DSV95MC7

OTHER BOOKS BY SHERIDAN ANNE

www.amazon.com/Sheridan-Anne/e/B079TLXN6K

DARK ROMANCE STANDALONES

Pretty Monster | Haunted Love | Darkest Sin
Midnight Stage | War Games | The Thorns We Wear

DARK CONTEMP ROMANCE SERIES - M/F

Broken Hill High | Haven Falls | Broken Hill Boys
Aston Creek High | Rejects Paradise | Bradford Bastard

DARK CONTEMP ROMANCE - RH

Boys of Winter | Depraved Sinners | Empire

NEW ADULT SPORTS ROMANCE

Kings of Denver | Denver Royalty | Rebels Advocate

CONTEMP ROMANCE

Play With Fire | Until Autumn | Remember Us This Way

HOLIDAY ROMANCE

The Naughty List | Santa's Dark Secret